Ash

A NOVEL

Holly Thompson

Stone Bridge Press • *Berkeley, California*

Published by
Stone Bridge Press, P. O. Box 8208, Berkeley, CA 94707
tel 510-524-8732 • sbp@stonebridge.com • www.stonebridge.com

For a reading group guide plus background information about Japan and
the world of *Ash*, visit www.stonebridge.com/ash/WorldOfAsh.html.

Passage on page 81 from *A First Zen Reader* by Trevor Leggett (Boston
and Tokyo: Charles E. Tuttle Co., Inc.); used by permission. Passage on
page 121 from *A History of Haiku*, vol. 1, by R. H. Blyth (Tokyo:
Hokuseido Press); used by permission.

10   9   8   7   6   5   4   3   2   1   2005 2004 2003 2002 2001

ISBN 1-880656-65-5

for Bob

Acknowledgments

I WOULD LIKE to express my deepest gratitude to the extended Konishi family of Shibushi, particularly Katsumi and Kuniko, and Fumio and Eiko, who introduced me to southern Kyushu, ensured that I would fall in love with Kagoshima, and patiently answered my questions year after year as this tale grew. Also invaluable to the writing of this book were the guidance and Satsuma warmth of Kohei and Noriko Imamori of Aira-cho, Kagoshima. I am indebted to Professor Takayoshi Ogawa of Yokohama City University, Professor Yo Takeuchi of Kyoto University, Masayoshi and Tomoko Sakai, and Atsushi Aoki for their assistance. Mount Holyoke College awarded me a Class of 1905 Fellowship that enabled me to conduct initial research in Kagoshima and Kyoto, and librarians at the Japan Meteorological Agency, the Japan Information Center of the University of Pittsburgh, Yokohama City University, Tsurumi University, and Columbia University's Starr East Asian Library were particularly helpful in locating crucial resources. Finally, I would like to thank my publisher Peter Goodman for his wisdom in the shaping of *Ash*.

HOLLY THOMPSON

July 14, 1970

YELLOW. THEY'RE both wearing yellow. Caitlin a gingham smock with rickrack along the hem, and Mie a citrine party dress with a bow on each puffed sleeve.

Caitlin likes when they wear the same colors, and she wishes her hair were crow black to match Mie's. At least their last names are close—Oide and Ober. Someday they will marry brothers, they've told their parents. Someday they will live in the same house. On the way to school in the mornings, they pretend they're twins with their red leather rucksacks—strutting along, copying one another with hands on hips, mimicking each other's accents. And when their mothers take them to department stores downtown, they like to gaze on themselves, side by side, in long mirrors. Once Mie told the greengrocer they were sisters, and when the woman, hefting a crate of daikon, asked, mocking, how it was that Mie spoke Japanese and Caitlin English, Mie turned to Caitlin and said matter-of-factly, *"She doesn't speak English, do you?"* and they hooked arms and left the store chattering noisily in Kyoto dialect.

Today they're holding hands along the Uji riverbank. Plastic insect cages hang from long ribbons around their necks and thump against their stomachs as they walk. The ribbons are yellow too. They can't get enough yellow. Caitlin grows dizzy with yellow. She doesn't see how she could have ever liked blue.

Ahead their fathers talk, stopping now and then to look back at them. They enjoy being out with just their fathers—no younger sisters to slow them down, no mothers to tell them how to stand or sit or speak. And Mie's mother is so pregnant now, that Caitlin can't look at her without grimacing. She's too big, and Caitlin wants her to be small again and is glad her mother isn't huge and waddling.

Sometimes Caitlin and Mie wave to their fathers, and every so often they race up the bank toward them. But mostly they ignore the two men to swing their nets at dragonflies, to test a rock shaped like a seat, or to watch a fat stick twirl crazily through the foaming white water.

In the cages, jostled about, cling the hoppers and cicadas they found at the temple. The priest's wife helped them hunt while their fathers sat on the veranda talking with the priest. They're disappointed not to have found any beetles, but the priest's wife has promised she'll save in a terrarium whatever unusual insects she finds in the garden for them to claim the next time Caitlin's father comes to visit her husband.

As they walk along the riverbank, they scan the grasses and rocks and agree that if they catch something neither of them already has in her collection at home, they'll share it. Caitlin can keep it at her house for a night, then Mie at hers. They often take turns this way with their finds—piggyback hoppers, gold bugs, coins from the gutter, pottery shards, a spark plug. Once they even traded their pillows, and Caitlin liked falling asleep on cotton full of the scent of Mie.

But there are hardly any insects to be found in Uji's heavy mid-July heat, so they stop eyeing the short grasses beside the path, and instead swing their arms back and forth as they walk. They know they'll at least see cicadas in the cherry trees up along the road that follows the river. So they sing: songs they've learned at school, Four Leaves hits, and songs of their own to which they've coordinated hand motions. Mie bats at dragonflies that zoom near, then as a joke puts her insect net over her head. Caitlin does the same, and they walk upriver examining the bank, the bridge to the island, and the backs of their fathers through the tiny diamond holes in the mesh.

But when they spot the flicker of blue tail at the tip of Mie's shoe, they yank the nets off. Caitlin isn't sure what they've seen—she can't imagine an insect so long and blue and shiny—only dragonflies, but they don't slither. Mie cries, *"Tokage!"* and Caitlin furrows her brow. Lizard? She's never seen one blue.

They scramble and stalk over the damp and mossy rocks, nets

poised, swatting at grasses and lifting concealing stones to follow the lizard's wriggling path, until suddenly the water is there, taunting with spray, too loud, too close, too white. The lizard darts beneath a rock, Caitlin points, then straightens, and a hand brushes the length of her calf like a feather.

A S H

1985

One

ON A TUESDAY in early July, the weathermen of southern Kyushu predicted a fair day for drying wash, a poor day for studying, and pronounced the rainy season officially over. Cicadas began to drone as if on cue, and mildewed shoes were brought from closets to sun on verandas and landings throughout the prefecture, but in the city of Kagoshima the skies remained thick and gray, and passengers debarking from a bus in the late afternoon popped open umbrellas as they stepped to the road. When the bus labored on, they covered their faces with handkerchiefs as a dark churning cloud swirled about them. Students dragged book bags across the street toward the beach, and women stooped with groceries continued up the side-walk as Caitlin, the sole foreigner, paused on the curb to lift the damp strands of hair from her neck and fish a baseball cap out of her day pack.

Twisting her hair and tucking it up under her cap, Caitlin frowned at the patina of ash that dulled every surface—leaf, rock, concrete, and chrome—even in this northern corner of the city. She headed for the entrance of what she'd hoped would be verdant gar-dens, yet seeing the gray blanketing the green, she wondered just how many weeks must have passed since she'd ventured anywhere besides her schools, the pool, and the local markets. But she was pleased at least to be alone and unfollowed, away from schoolgirls who clustered about her like gnats, humming the same insipid phrases over and over—could they touch her hair, did it hurt when she'd had her ears pierced, did she have a boyfriend, could she eat with chopsticks. She needed the full quiet of a weekday afternoon among passive plantings, ash-coated or not.

She entered the Iso Gardens following the path by the patches of hot pepper plants, the *janbo* mochi shop, and the preserved and roped-off villa. She'd hardly been out at all during the drizzle and wet of the last five weeks and had half-expected her malaise to dissipate now that summer was officially on and the ash a fine dust again, not sludge. But everything appeared flat and dull, the shrubs too pruned, the stone lantern contrived, and the copper rainspouts that draped like beaded necklaces from the corners of the villa no longer ingenious. The summer before, she'd been elated to be back in Japan after fifteen years, even in July, and even in remote Kagoshima—the volcano had seemed romantic then, the ash intriguing. Yet when she pictured the city now and tried to describe it in letters to friends or family back home, she saw only the eerie noon darkness that reminded her of old industrial Pittsburgh photographs, and in the face of that dense gloom she saw an irrational drive for control—hosed sidewalks, dusted fruit and vegetables, chamois-glossed cars, courteous queues, pressed uniforms and white gloves. She'd renewed her teaching contract for a second year—for lack of other options and because she still felt the need to be in Japan—yet she wondered how long she'd last, with this year's ash fallout already nearly thrice that of the annual record set some seven years back and with unnerving air shocks now commonplace. Alarmed to see the extent to which the formerly lush gardens were suffering, the extent to which photosynthesis had been thwarted in this city, she kicked at a strip of grass by the walkway. A sooty cloud blew up around her ankles.

She looped around the falls and the bamboo groves nestled against the steep mountain slopes, then paused on a path near some women with baskets picking leaves and debris from moss; they were the first people she'd come across all day who hadn't irked her. She lingered, observing them with envy, until one of the women looked up and nodded. Caitlin ducked to avoid conversation and continued along the path, eventually circling the carp pond.

She stopped to give one of the rocks along the edge a quick dusting and sat down—knees drawn up, skirt pulled down to her ankles. Mottled fish lurked just beneath the surface of the filmy water before her, and she set her pack down behind her, tossed a few pebbles, and watched as the carp tumbled over one another to gulp at the fanning ripples. With a corner of her full skirt she wiped the gritty sweat from her forehead then sat still, eyes closed, listening for that unnerving ticking she was certain she could hear—of the particles settling like flour onto her hot skin.

When she opened her eyes, she noticed a girl in a middle-school uniform sitting in spotty shade across the pond, her back slightly turned and her chin raised as though she were sunbathing. Determined to avoid schoolgirls, Caitlin rose and hurried away with her face down. From a safe distance, she glanced back. The girl was crouched over a sheet of paper in the middle of the path. Curious, Caitlin watched her wipe a finger down the paper's length, examine her fingertip, rub it clean on her skirt, then sit down pondside, shake the paper, and with a pen, begin writing.

Caitlin was struck by the image and tried to envision the sight without ash—this girl by a carp pond writing what must be, judging from her upward glances, poetry. Caitlin assumed it to be haiku and counted off syllables with her fingers, then laughed to herself; she couldn't envision Basho using his fingers.

But as if she'd heard the laugh, the girl glanced up from her writing. Caitlin turned away and tried to feign sudden interest in the large lobed leaves of a nearby shrub, but the girl rose, waving, so Caitlin rushed off in the opposite direction. Walking at a fast clip, then jogging, she finally landed in the open oppressive sun at the base of the ropeway. She was about to pay for a ticket at a small booth when an arrow pointing to a path made her decide on impulse to hike to the summit. She'd come for solitude, she reminded herself. Why not hike?

The path was steep—she had to tie a knot in her skirt to keep from stepping on it, and her blouse was soon drenched—but with the foliage overhead so thick, she found relief from the ash and sun. She paced herself to avoid slipping on the still rain-slicked earth underfoot and to ration her energy in the heat. When she paused to catch her breath in the close tropical air, the whine of cicadas merged with the pulsing rush of blood in her temples.

At the summit, she untied her skirt in a deserted open park and sank down on a bench, dripping and flapping her blouse, before proceeding to the ropeway station. By the observation platform, a few people stood about waiting for the next gondola down, and she slipped past them to put a coin into a drink machine for a can of oolong tea. She downed it quickly, turned toward the platform, and started; the poetry girl stood leaning on a railing watching her. She must have used the ropeway, Caitlin thought.

Without acknowledging the girl's nod, Caitlin claimed a place against the railing overlooking the bay and the great shadow that loomed on its quivering surface. Ash streamed up from the south peak of the almost-island Sakurajima and blew westward in a frothy cloud over the bay toward the city and volcanic beach and the train rails that wound north to the foot of the hill on which they stood. Caitlin leaned forward eyeing the volcano, that minacious presence, determined not to look away from the billows twisting and rolling toward Kagoshima although it stressed her to watch all that ash continue to pour forth. How many times had she wished for the disappearance of that jagged peak; how many times had she wished for its replacement with a passive, solid mountain, something still, calm, long tamped down and covered with cedars and firs? She couldn't understand how people went on living in this city, let alone on that island, decade after decade, time and again surveying the damage after lapilli showers, and ever sweeping, ever dusting, under that immense shadow.

She'd nearly forgotten the girl standing just to her right, when out of the corner of her eye, she saw her reach a hand under the flap of her bag and extract a piece of paper. Caitlin kept her eyes forward, still on the bay and volcano, but in the blurred periphery of her vision she could see the girl reading with what seemed to be intent and exaggerated concentration. When Caitlin finally glanced over, the girl met her eyes at once, grateful. "Would you mind doing me a favor?"

Caitlin could barely hide her surprise. "I hadn't expected to hear English."

"My father's American," the girl said, and Caitlin now saw that the Japanese features were indeed diluted; the short hair had a natural brown sheen and framed an angular face with a prominent, freckled nose. The girl handed over the paper, and Caitlin smiled in spite of herself, pleased on this sultry day in this dreary city to be shown someone's fresh poetry. She read the title aloud though and balked; "'The Last Will and Testament of Naomi Yamashita Johnson.'"

The girl leaned toward her and whispered, "I need you to sign my will."

Caitlin stared, searching for the joke in her eyes, but the girl remained intent and somber, lips drawn taut in concentration. Caitlin read on in silence:

> Please enact this will in the event that I, Naomi Yamashita Johnson, do perish before my 20th birthday.
>
> To my mother I leave my lacquer box of tickets and post-cards and my bicycle since hers is rusted. To my father I leave my diaries and notebooks because they are in English. To my cousins Izumi and Hideaki I leave my collection of magazines and *manga*. To Grandma and Grandpa Johnson I leave my photo albums since they didn't get to see me or my life very much except summers. And to Yamashita Oji-ichan I leave my *shodo* portfolio and my brushes, *bunchin,* paper, and inkstones. I leave my savings account to my mother and father.

Below she had drawn two lines; under the one with her signature she had printed her full name, and under the other the word "Witness."

Caitlin felt queasy. She took off her baseball cap and combed her fingers through her hair, damp and greasy from the humid air and the climb. "This is ridiculous," she said. "I can't sign a—what are you, thirteen?" The girl shook her head. "Fourteen?"—the girl nodded—"a fourteen year old's will." Caitlin watched her face cloud and added, softer, "You need two witnesses anyway."

The girl looked out across the bay and up into the ash, and Caitlin followed her gaze to the deep folds and wispy fringes.

"I'll add another witness," she said. "Please."

Caitlin laughed. "No, that's not the point." She gazed down below the railing at the tops of the bamboo trees, their long fronds waving like giant ferns, but talk of wills above such a drop made her calves twinge. So she looked away, to the water, then crept with her eyes over the bay, over the scattered windsurfers below—where her boyfriend, Hiroshi, would be if it were Saturday and where she wished she were at this very moment—then across the water to the base of the massive volcano.

"Naomi—that's your name I take it—whatever do you need a will for?" Caitlin held the paper out over the rail and had the urge to let it drop, to see it flutter down and nest somewhere in the swaying grove. Her hand was trembling.

Naomi averted her gaze. Caitlin eyed her uniform. "What school do you go to?" When Naomi didn't answer, she added, "Well, there's not much sense in my asking. I don't know many junior highs—I teach in high schools all around the prefecture. Maybe you'll be in one of my classes someday." Then Caitlin shook her head. "What am I saying—you wouldn't be taking English."

"I might," Naomi said, petulant. "The teachers make me sit through all their lessons now without even changing the assignments. They're embarrassed my English is better than theirs." She flicked her hair back and glanced sideways at Caitlin. Then she looked out over the bay again and added, "But I probably won't go to a public high school. My parents want me to go to an international school, to learn more creatively they say. But it's really so I can meet others like me. Other half-wits."

Caitlin ignored the comment and turned back to the will before her. "What's so important about your twentieth birthday?"

Naomi shrugged.

"You're not ill are you?"

Naomi shook her head, opened her mouth, then clamped it shut again and thrust out her hand. "Just give it back. You don't need to sign it."

Caitlin hesitated, handed her the will, and watched her stuff it back inside the bag. Then she stood beside Naomi, staring out over Kinko Bay and the ash-veiled city, unsure exactly of what to do next and feeling a shot of guilt for not being able to sign her name to what was probably a silly romantic gesture—TV dramas always included characters on the brink of suicide.

An announcement blared that a gondola was ready for boarding. Caitlin was hot and anxious to head back into town, but she looked from the steep grade that fell away before her to the young girl on her left and winced at the thought of that body careening down the slope and crashing through the trees. "Come on," she said, "let's catch that gondola," and when Naomi hesitated, gripping the rail with both hands, she added, "I'll buy you one of those ices down at the bottom. It's too damned hot up here."

She could see Naomi's mouth working and was tempted to grab her by her knobby wrists and haul her back from her precarious stance on the cliff edge, but she didn't want to startle her. Tentative, she gave her elbow a light tug, yet instead of the resistance she'd expected and braced herself for, she was met with compliance; Naomi turned, head down, to follow. Caitlin stepped aside for Naomi to enter the station first but kept her hands in front, tensed and ready to reach out if the girl made a dash.

When the door of the gondola was finally latched shut and they were seated firmly on a narrow wooden bench, Caitlin had to cough to disguise a gusting sigh of relief. She leaned her head back against the window and felt the car swing forward and drop as sweat trickled down her sides. To her left, Naomi turned, pressed her face to the glass, and, through stains of ash droplets, watched the slate bay and the base of the volcano disappear as they plummeted down.

▲ ▲ ▲

At the foot of the hill near the souvenir shop, Naomi ordered shaved ice with aqua syrup. Caitlin opted for kelly green, the least offensive of the too bright options, and they carried their melting mounds to a bench near the parking lot. Naomi had hardly spoken since they'd left the overlook platform, and Caitlin waited while the ice slipped down their throats and cooled them slowly from the inside out. When the satisfaction of sitting and eating had stretched a solid calm between them, she asked, "Do you live near here?"

Naomi spoke into her bowl. "Below the Nanshu Shrine. You know, where those graves are—Saigo Takamori and all. You speak Japanese?"

"Yeah, but you must be completely bilingual," Caitlin said. Naomi nodded. "I'm envious."

"Don't be. It doesn't do me any good."

Caitlin raised her eyebrows.

"It doesn't make me any more Japanese."

"Why should you want to be more Japanese? You've got it great, two cultures, two languages."

"I swear," Naomi said, "you must know my parents. Do you live near here?"

"No, down by the river, near Hirata-bashi."

"Oh, you're lucky. We sometimes get bypassed—depending on the wind. You have more accumulation down there." Naomi tilted her bowl up over her head, dribbling the last of the thin blue syrup into her mouth.

"You talk as though you like it."

"I do. So many years just a dusting, then suddenly, poof, ash like snow every day. It's an honor, don't you think?"

Caitlin shook her head, amused, then asked Naomi if she had any brothers or sisters.

"Nope, just me and my mother and father. My cousins live next door, but they hate the ash too. Everyone does. Except me. Volcanoes deserve respect. Sakurajima is one of the most active volcanoes on earth." Naomi gloated and turned to Caitlin with her hand outstretched. "You done?" Caitlin gave her the empty bowl, and as Naomi walked off to find a trash can, she spit discreetly on her sticky hands and wiped them on her skirt.

When Naomi sat back down Caitlin leaned forward with her forearms on her knees. Her watch said nearly six, and she was hungry and thirsty for something more substantial than sweet water. "Look," she said, "I'm heading into town. Why don't we take a taxi—you're sort of on the way, and I don't feel like getting back on a bus."

Naomi crossed her arms and cast a glance at the main road. "I'll take the bus, thanks."

"Why? I'm going your direction anyway. I'll pay."

With a sullen tilt of her head, Naomi said, "You want to tell my parents."

Caitlin was taken aback by the sheer accuracy of this statement when she hadn't quite realized her intentions herself. She raised her voice. "Well no, I'm just heading back into town, and you're not that far out of the way."

"Right," Naomi said sarcastically.

"Look." Caitlin was beginning to lose sight of her original concern for the girl. "I won't say anything, I promise. But if your parents or your cousins see me, they'll wonder why some foreign woman is dropping you off, right?"

Naomi thought for a moment. "I'll say I was sick."

"Fine," Caitlin said exasperated. "We'll say you weren't feeling well and that I offered to bring you home. I won't mention the will at all. Deal?"

"Deal."

They approached a taxi at the entrance of the parking lot and scooted in when the back door popped open. After they'd turned off the main road, Naomi guided the driver through a series of lefts and rights, and Caitlin was soon lost. The sun sat low and fat just above the hills, tinting the neighborhood sepia through the July haze, and the driver alternately crawled and raced through the narrow backstreets.

"I don't lie so well," Naomi suddenly said. "When we get there I'll go in and get my father, so you can tell him how sick I was. Okay?"

Caitlin rolled her eyes. "Whatever you say."

At Naomi's instruction, the taxi slowed to a stop in front of a small, wooden two-story house in a cluster of similar structures, vying like weeds for their own patch of space and light. She jumped out, hollering over her shoulder for the driver to wait, threw open the gate, and ran up the walk to disappear inside the doorway. Caitlin stepped out of the cab. Over the hum of the idling taxi, she could hear Naomi shouting for her parents. In a moment, the front door swung open again and a man with graying disheveled hair appeared beside Naomi in the entryway shoving his feet into a pair of shoes as he looked out at the car. Gesturing toward Caitlin, Naomi led her father down the walk.

"Dad, this is Caitlin . . . Over?"

"Ober." Both she and the father bowed as they shook hands.

"Carl Johnson. Glad to meet you. Won't you come in for a bit? I can offer you a beer at least—you do drink beer, don't you?"

She thanked him but explained that she was headed home—she'd simply dropped off Naomi on her way since she'd looked rather pale at the gardens. Caitlin watched him feel Naomi's forehead with the inside of his wrist, struck by the fact that such a Japanese-looking girl could actually have genes in common with this tall, gawky man. The only features they seemed to share were the long face and bony, ridged nose.

"No fever it seems," he said to Naomi, then he turned back to Caitlin. "Well, I'd like to thank you somehow. Rain check? Naomi tells me you're an English teacher—like most of us expat fools. You have any vacation coming up?"

"Not until August," Caitlin said, itching to be on her way, back in her apartment eating instant ramen or better yet, she suddenly thought, in the sports club pool, timing her laps. She had no desire to become further entangled in Naomi's lies or to be at all connected with a suicidal adolescent. She knew it was not the sort of friendship she needed.

But Carl was saying, "How about Friday after work? I'm sure you could use a brew or two then," and Caitlin smiled in spite of herself, though she doubted that at the end of a long week of teaching, when she was so tired it was all she could do to be civil with Hiroshi, she'd feel like socializing with people she barely knew. Yet Carl was beginning to win her over; there were so few Americans in this town, so few native English speakers, that Caitlin found herself softening with the craving to speak more of this deliciously fast, idiomatic English. Finally she said, almost against her will, "Well, my work load does lighten next week." And before she could change her mind, she'd agreed to dinner on Friday.

"We'll get a headstart celebrating summer," Carl was saying. "About five or so?" He turned to Naomi who was standing defiantly, hands on hips, elbows jutting. "Your mother's home by six on Fridays, isn't she?"

Naomi nodded but gave him an exasperated look. "*Dad,* the taxi's waiting."

"Right, well, come around five, and we'll have a beer to warm up."

Caitlin thanked him, and Naomi's father gave an exaggerated stage bow and said loudly, "Say no more. Naomi did you thank the kind lady?"

"Of course I did." She bowed deeply, mocking her father, who hardly noticed as he ushered Caitlin into the car. Caitlin rolled down the window, and as the cab pulled away she waved and shouted to Naomi, "You take care of yourself. And stay away from heights." She watched the girl smile and stifle a giggle at their mutual joke, bringing a hand up to cover her laugh. But before Naomi's hand clapped fully over her mouth, the smile had transformed into a frown, and an angry look flashed from her eyes as she caught Caitlin's near betrayal.

Two

BY NOW CAITLIN was nearly salivating with the need to swim. She instructed the driver to hurry to the sports club, but on the way, he began to probe with the usual benign questions about where she was from and what she was doing way down in this part of Japan. With every question posed, she could feel his foot lift off the accelerator and the car slow, so she turned away from his friendly glances in the rearview mirror and abbreviated her answers, becoming steadily more short and irritable.

When the cab finally pulled over and the door popped open, she stuffed the fare into his hand and ran up the steps of the club. In the locker room she tore off her clothes, pulled on the bathing suit, cap, and goggles she'd taken from her bag—she never went anywhere without them—showered, hurried poolside, shook her legs and arms impatiently, and dove in. She rode the dive, began her kick, then pulled her first stroke—nothing was ever so satisfying as that first strong pull.

She was alone in her lane, and she picked up speed, then adjusted her pace after the turn until her breathing grew short and even. Back in her element, Caitlin forgot about Naomi, Friday's dinner to which she already regretted consenting, and her mindless, unrewarding day leading conversation activities at a high school in the hills west of the city. She was so weary of being a novelty, so tired of smiling—in the water she could finally let the muscles of her face slacken.

The pool was a tonic, for Caitlin felt truly at ease only when moving through water, beating it, with that warm flush to her body. She always dove straight into a lane and swam at race speed, freestyle, for ten laps until her face and limbs were heated and feverish, and only then would she switch to the back- or breaststroke. The crawl always reigned superior in her mind; no other stroke could generate that smooth, cutting sensation. Sometimes with the exhale of bubbles she hummed bars of tunes, anything that caught in her ear, the songs spurting along in a forced two-four beat with each draw of an arm.

She was swimming daily now at this sports club she'd joined just after moving to Kagoshima the summer before. But during the past spring, she'd nearly abandoned her membership, preferring to swim off Iso Beach with Hiroshi on his sailboard. He'd play with her endurance, tease her along, and far out in the bay when he knew she was ready for a rest or a tow into shore, he'd tack and force her upwind into the waves or against an outgoing tide. Caitlin loved it, struggling after him until her shoulders screamed. Then she'd roll onto her back, spread her arms wide, the lava fields and spewing south peak of Sakurajima on one side and the lush slopes of Mure-gaoka plunging into the bay on the other, the city piers to the south, and the dark sand beach that she'd swum from a mere fingernail along an unforgiving shoreline. Sometimes she'd close her eyes, waiting and listening, out in the open, for Hiroshi to pull up alongside her.

When the June rains arrived, she'd returned with reluctance to the pool and the neat confinement of the lanes, but then, even on rare days of hazy sun, she found she couldn't resume the beach routine. Hiroshi would plead, but Caitlin couldn't face the sand, the swarm of bodies, bright sails. She knew her repulsion had little to do with the beach and even less to do with Hiroshi; it was just that time of year. Caitlin had tried to explain her sudden beach aversion to Hiroshi by telling him she'd never managed to sustain a relationship through the summer, but Hiroshi hadn't understood her cryptic sentences, and the more he'd showed his consternation, the more she'd tripped over her verbs. He seemed to believe the summer months reminded her of a former love, left back in the States, and Caitlin let it go at that.

So instead of the beach, Hiroshi began pushing pubs in the evening, and Caitlin would often join him. But away from the space of the bay, confined to seats at a table or bar in low light, just the two of them, they found they had less to say. Caitlin tried to keep the talk energized and centered on Hiroshi's life, their mutual friends, and their jobs, but there were gaping silences. It wasn't that she didn't want to share other parts of her life, she just knew that if she started in on some subjects she couldn't be sure of what she'd say.

When conversation lagged, Hiroshi would sometimes say, *"Let's go to your place, just to talk,"* but Caitlin had yet to agree—not out of prudishness or deference to the prudishness of her neighbors, but out of a need to cordon off some sacred, private space. They'd established a routine of biking from pub to pub to meet up with Misawa and other friends, for if they were moving, or in a group, they were fine. But as the rainy season dragged on, and the days grew more sultry, rarely did they wander off with excuses, as they often had after spring beach days in the early months of their relationship, for a couple secluded hours in one of the city's "love" hotels.

By the time July had rolled around, Caitlin had reestablished a strict pool routine, swimming before school in an attempt to shake her moodiness. The workout enlivened her, imbuing her with enough energy and false enthusiasm to sustain her through morning classes, but she grew drowsy after lunch. She bought a jar of instant coffee to keep in her desk at her base school, and the teachers stationed at desks on either side of her, noting the switch from tea, chided her about being homesick for the States, about parties and boyfriends. *"No, no, it's this weather,"* Caitlin said, *"and the ash."*

Then this past weekend, determined to throw off the malaise, she'd added afternoon swims, increased the number of laps, and begun timing herself. This meant she would see even less of Hiroshi, since she was so physically drained after she'd bussed, trained, and biked home from outlying schools and the pool that she could barely stay awake to eat, let alone go out and attempt to sustain a coherent conversation. It wasn't that she wanted to break off with him, but she wondered what was the point. She didn't see how their relationship could possibly survive the summer—it seemed as good as gone, with another Uji anniversary approaching and her vague plans for a Kyoto trip. Any past relationships that had endured the warmth of spring had always become parched and lifeless by June, as if the heat were solely responsible. Even Lyle, with whom she'd lived most of her junior year, hadn't lasted to July, despite their making it all the way across country cramped in a rusted Honda Civic en route to summer jobs in Alaskan canneries. Caitlin had bailed out in Seattle, and though she'd wanted to be east, nearer her father for that time of year, she hadn't wanted to appear fragile, and so remained west, moved into a dank rooming house not far from a Y, and waitressed and swam until mid-August. By the time she'd returned to college that fall, she was in perfect shape for swim team, enabling her to acquire more trophies and set a new record during her last competitive season. Though her speed had lessened since then—she wasn't competing at all in Japan—she could tell her endurance was close to what it had been that summer in Seattle.

Now in the pool Caitlin began to alternate laps of crawl and backstroke. She loved back flip-turns into the crawl—relished that upside-down rush, the push against the stubbly pool wall, the glide. Every so often she glanced up at the clock. When only five minutes of free swim remained, she picked up the pace and forced herself to race freestyle, shoulders straining, back rising with every draw, legs pumping, until the lifeguard blew the whistle and ordered everyone out. She often clocked herself this way—she could count on his punctuality to the second.

Caitlin clung to the edge of the pool to catch her breath, then hauled herself out and stretched. She could feel the solid strength in her back and shoulders as she did arm rotations and touched her hands to the cool tiles between her feet. Even her thighs were taut and lean again. As she rinsed her heated face in the shower, she thought wryly that she'd be a great asset to someone's swim team . . . in mid-July.

▲ ▲ ▲

Caitlin caught a bus home, and dragged herself up the outside stairs of her apartment building. Her shoulders were already tight—she hadn't stretched enough before the swim. Fumbling for the key, she leaned back against the railing, dizzy. She'd left at 5:30 that morning for her first swim, and here it was after seven in the evening. The sun had long since set behind Shiroyama, but for once Caitlin wasn't annoyed with the mountain shadow and lack of daylight savings; all she wanted now was to eat some instant ramen and collapse on her futon, and tonight she was actually grateful for the premature softness of dusk.

She lifted the tin cover of her mailbox and drew out a single letter. In the kitchen, she pulled the cord of the overhead light and recognized the handwriting of her sister Lee. She dropped her bag, put on some water for the noodles, tossed in a handful of bean sprouts, hastily chopped some spinach, carrots, and pink-edged *kamaboko* and threw them in the pot with the noodles, then sat down and tore at the flap of the envelope; it had been six months since she'd heard a word from Lee, and even then, just a short note to accompany a Christmas gift.

Lee was again in Pittsburgh for the summer with their mother and grandmother, Ma Ruth—their father having remained in Boston as usual. Caitlin hadn't spent a full summer in Pittsburgh since high school, but as she withdrew the letter from the envelope she realized that though she'd chosen to distance herself from Pennsylvania and the politics of her mother's annual summer separations from her father, she was jealous of Lee. She envied those three women together in that big old house with lemon-oiled woodwork, lion's paw tubs, family silhouettes in tiny walnut frames, and on the second-story screened-in porch, high among the tree limbs and rustling leaves, that wooden swing.

The letter was in Lee's writing, but by the second sentence Caitlin understood that it wasn't from Lee but had been dictated to Lee by her grandmother. Caitlin turned the paper over, searching for any words straight from Lee; but all she found scrawled at the bottom under "Love, Ma Ruth" was "P.S. Hi Caity!" She threw it onto the table. Not that she didn't welcome a letter from her grandmother, but she couldn't believe that her sister wouldn't bring herself to add something more substantial. She felt humiliated to have hoped, to have actually believed the envelope might contain some form of reconciliation between Lee and her. Already a year in Japan, and her sister still refused to accept the fact. Even her mother and Ma Ruth had come around enough to write. But not Lee. Sometimes Caitlin felt as though she'd been exiled to Japan, rather than come back of her own free will.

She waited until she'd finished her noodles, changed into a large T-shirt, and crawled into her futon before she took up the letter again and read Ma Ruth's words:

Dear Caitlin,

I'm sorry not to be able to pick up a pen and write to you with my own hand, but I'm simply too exhausted these days to try. Your sister Lee does a fine job of caring for me though, and offered to pen this for me.

Already cynical, Caitlin wondered if those were truly Ma Ruth's words or if Lee had inserted them, a barb, as if to say to Caitlin, "See how good I am? Why aren't you here helping?" She forced herself to continue reading.

I've hardly been out of bed at all this summer. I didn't mind the confinement during the colder months, but it's so hard now with the lawn furniture set up and perennials in bloom and me unable to tend them. I miss my trowel and weed basket. I do sit on the porch every day though, and your mother takes me out for drives—the other day we even went up Mount Washington. And we have all sorts of flowers blooming indoors and on the porch—hanging baskets of fuchsia and impatiens, potted lilies, and even some peonies—so at least I can appreciate some of the summer. What sorts of flowers bloom where you are? Tropical varieties? According to the map, you're quite far south.

Your mother planted some beans, tomatoes, cucumbers, and squash for me this spring, but we won't have many other vegetables this year. I missed the peas so much, we bought them fresh from Burden's farm stand every night for a week. Lee did plant several rows of lettuce and even some broccoli, so we'll see what happens.

Here, Caitlin assumed that Lee had deleted a sentence, a typical Ma Ruth comment like, "We do wish she'd eat something besides vegetables, though, like some of our roasts and pot pies." Ma Ruth had never learned what the rest of them had—that Lee only ate less when urged to eat more.

How is the teaching progressing? Or are you on summer
vacation by now? I understand the school year is longer
there. How unfortunate for the teachers! I remember how
wonderful the summers were all those years I was teaching,
and how refreshed I felt by autumn. Pa Chess always
threatened to go into teaching himself. I hope you have
some motivated students. Those are the gems.

Keep sending your letters. I love reading about your
escapades. I'm glad to know you have a boyfriend. Life is
richer when you share it, isn't it, although I have to say I
was surprised to hear he's Japanese. When are you coming
back? You say you renewed your teaching contract for
another year. Your mother was quite teary the week we got
that letter, but she seems to have adapted now. We all miss
you and anxiously await your return to the Occident. Take
good care of yourself over there.

Love,

Ma Ruth

Caitlin groaned. How could she be surprised her boyfriend was
Japanese? Where did she think Caitlin was living? And her mother
teary! They still didn't get it, Caitlin thought—not her mother, not
Ma Ruth, not Lee. They just kept urging her to come back, never
applauding her for being there. They should all be there themselves,
Caitlin thought. Even Ma Ruth, despite the fact that she'd never
been in Japan to begin with; Caitlin's family had returned to Pittsburgh just before Ma Ruth's planned autumn visit to Kyoto. Yet Ma
Ruth setting foot in Japan might exonerate Caitlin's father, make
her see that the family move to Japan in January of 1969 had been
something worthwhile and enriching, far more than just another
example of Jack's poor judgment, the phrase Ma Ruth had used to
explain away just about any misfortune—nasty weather on a family
outing, a flat tire, sour milk, and larger events that had become family lore: their arrival in Tokyo during the height of the police seige
on student-occupied Yasuda Hall; no phone in their Kyoto house

for months and no TV from which to watch the moon landing from home; and worst, the dearth of available teaching positions for Japanese religion scholars the year they returned to the States. Caitlin had wanted to set the record straight and felt cheated by Ma Ruth's illness. A fantasy she'd begun to cultivate within days after moving to Kagoshima was to outdo her mother by having her grandmother visit her there, and her early days settling in had been consumed by planning that imagined visit.

Perhaps deep down, Ma Ruth understood Caitlin—she'd always been careful to inquire about Caitlin's Japanese studies, even had Caitlin teach her some basics of Japanese grammar and elements of the writing system, and had urged Caitlin to study what interested her, to "follow her fires" as she often put it—but Ma Ruth had never been able to approve of a move that took family any distance from her. Caitlin knew that Ma Ruth was the source of much of the friction between her father and mother, and Ma Ruth was so blindly partial to her mother's point of view that anything that might be construed as hurtful to Caitlin's mother, hurt Ma Ruth. The reverse was also true, and Caitlin had long ago learned that her mother's temper was most explosive when someone had done something to offend Ma Ruth.

During Caitlin's final Pittsburgh visit before moving to Japan, Ma Ruth had been cold and remote, barely speaking to Caitlin, always clamming up it seemed, biting her tongue. Caitlin was fuming; she could understand her mother's sullenness, could accept Lee's feeling betrayed, but she couldn't believe she was getting the Ma Ruth chill as well—after all, she was "following her fires." The day before her departure, washing breakfast dishes after Lee and her mother had both gone off to jobs, Ma Ruth had suddenly blurted, "How can you even think of going over there when you know it hurts your mother so?" Caitlin had just blinked back at her and waited for the storm. "I mean, halfway around the world, and you know the painful memories. How can you do this to her? And Lee. You want to dredge all that up for her too? She's a sick child as it is."

"Oh, for God's sake," Caitlin had said. She'd had a juice tumbler in her hand, and it was all she could do to keep from hurling it at the floor. "Why is everyone so intent on making me feel guilty about this?"

"You could have gone anywhere. Your mother tells me you also applied to programs in Europe."

"But I speak Japanese," Caitlin had said. "I majored in East Asian studies. Why on earth should I go to Europe?"

"But what about the German you learned? Why not go back to your roots? You still have cousins in Bavaria."

"I hardly remember my German, and besides I don't want to go to Bavaria," Caitlin had said gritting her teeth. "I have Irish roots, too, but I'm not going there." Then she was shouting. "You all just want me to go anywhere but Japan! You're the same with my father. You wish his work were about anything but Japan."

"Now Caity." Ma Ruth wiped a towel round and round a saucer. "You needn't bring your father into this. I mean, you must admit you're going a long way away. And it just might not be the best thing for your mother or Lee."

"Oh, great," Caitlin had said. "Now I'm responsible for their problems. I suppose you're going to blame *me* if Lee's weight drops again."

Ma Ruth had squinted. "Possibly."

Caitlin nodded once, then snapped, "I thought you'd be a little more understanding. I guess I was wrong." She shook the glass at Ma Ruth. "You know, Dad was the only one in this whole family who congratulated me for getting into that program. All anyone else could do was think about themselves. Including you." And she had left the room shouting, "Why do you always shelter Mom and Lee? Why hover over them? Maybe without you they'd face their problems!" Caitlin hadn't meant that last remark quite how it had sounded, and she'd paused in the hallway about to return to the kitchen to apologize, but at the slam of the screen door she'd understood that Ma Ruth had escaped to do vigorous battle with weeds in her garden, so Caitlin had continued marching up the stairs to the room she shared with Lee. When she sat down on the edge of the bed that she hadn't yet made, she discovered the tumbler still in her shaking hand.

Lying in her futon, Caitlin now twitched with guilt over those words she'd shouted more than a year before. She dropped the letter to the tatami. It was hard to imagine Lee having to care for Ma Ruth, Ma Ruth bedridden, without her sure, indomitable stride.

She'd always risen long before the rest of them were awake, to begin sweeping, dusting, ironing, disinfecting, polishing, bleaching, weeding, pruning, canning, hardly stopping all day. And every afternoon since she'd retired from teaching high school math until the month last summer when the cancer was detected, Ma Ruth had tutored students. Even when she sat still she was always working on something—the garden log, a quilt, a letter, a calculus proof. Caitlin couldn't imagine Ma Ruth exhausted, unable to hold a pen long enough to write a letter.

She began to wonder if she shouldn't be making plans to go back to the States this summer. To see that cornerstone of her family, Ma Ruth. It would be the first year in ages that she hadn't done that Boston to Pittsburgh drive, that endless undulating stretch of Route 80 with the hills blue-gray, russet and purple in winter, and all shades of green with patches of deep brown and wales of rising corn during summer. She'd made that drive in every type of weather—through sheets of drumming rain and cracking lightning; summer haze with whorls of starlings; thick snow; and crisp November with hunters and dead deer so numerous she'd wished her car were painted orange.

Pushing west across Pennsylvania, she always rushed to reach the pass near Williamsport, then slowed through the steep cuts of striated rock and tufted hillocks, and took her time the rest of the way to Ma Ruth's, savoring the drive, relieved to follow the contours of farmland with shiny barn roofs, huge billboards, and networks of power lines stitching the rolling countryside together. Finally in that western half of the state, it was as if she'd arrived in an older, deeper part of the world and of herself, a simpler, more soothing part, regardless of the tensions in the household she was headed for. Once during an all-night drive for Thanksgiving break, she'd found herself near dawn driving straight toward a creamy, setting moon. The intensity of the moonlight before her followed by bleeding colors of sunrise in the rearview mirror and then to the sides of the car had so invigorated her that she'd arrived at Ma Ruth's positively radiant.

In Japan, she ached for corn tassels, huge maples, and silos. And most of all, lawns. She missed that cool moistness underfoot and the scent of fresh cut grass so much it made her thirsty.

Caitlin went into the kitchen for a glass of water, then returned to her futon, but before climbing in she pulled another pillow from the futon closet. Then she yanked on the cord of the overhead light and lay down with her head on one pillow and her arms clutching tight the second one. She listened to the footsteps of her upstairs neighbor, the rush of water as a toilet flushed, the scrape of a chair on the kitchen floor. Why was her building so noisy, so revealing with sound? She longed for that house in Pittsburgh, with its gently creaking floors, whispering drapes, and the ping of moths careening into the screens. Here she couldn't open her windows to the summer breeze because of the ash. She lived entombed in an air-conditioned chamber.

Caitlin closed her eyes and tried to pretend she was back lying on that second bed in Lee's room, or on that big mattress they used to haul out to the porch, with the breeze blowing over her face and shoulders, the crickets singing her to sleep. But Caitlin knew too well that if she were there in that house, she would no doubt wake to hear Lee sniffling in her bed or to find her bolt upright, a rigid, bony silhouette on the porch swing. Caitlin knew that her presence would only destroy whatever pretense of peace the three women had created, and she just couldn't don their blinders.

▲ ▲ ▲

The phone was ringing, and Caitlin waited for her mother or Ma Ruth to pick up. Where were they? Wasn't it Saturday morning? Weren't they all downstairs? She opened her eyes expecting to see Lee stirring in the bed across the room, or the creeping floral pattern of Ma Ruth's wallpaper, but in the dark she could only make out some chinks of streetlight coming through cracks in her rain shutters, and with a start she realized she wasn't in Pittsburgh. She stood in a rush but stumbled just as she was pulling on the light, and the cord broke in her hand. She reached the phone on its sixth ring, out of breath, heart pounding, sure that someone from the States was calling with bad news.

"Hello, *moshi-moshi,*" she tried to say clearly. She had no idea what time it was.

"Hi, this is me," a voice said. It was Hiroshi, and Caitlin said hello with a sigh of annoyance. He switched to Japanese. *"Are you okay?"*

"Yes," she said wearily.

"What's wrong?"

"Nothing, I was sleeping. What time is it?"

"Eight-thirty, no, eight-forty-five. Sorry, I didn't think you'd be sleeping yet."

She'd only been in bed a half hour. She shook her heavy head to try to clear it, then gave up, dropped down to the kitchen floor, and sat there leaning back against a cupboard talking to him with her eyes shut. *"Are you at home now?"* She thought she could hear the murmur of pub noise in the background.

"Not yet—on my way. I just was checking to see if you wanted to come out first. I guess not."

"No, not tonight."

"Well, how about tomorrow? Without you my English go to hell," he enunciated carefully.

Caitlin smiled; they almost never spoke English together—her Japanese was that much stronger than his English. *"Let's make it Thursday. I have to work late at the education center tomorrow."*

"Okay, Thursday. 6:30?"

"6:45. I get out of the pool at 6:30."

"I thought you were doing morning swims."

"I am."

"And evening?"

"Yes."

"Keito-chan, why? You're already faster than me."

She chuckled for his benefit. *"So where should we meet?"*

"In front of Yamagataya. Carry a red rose."

"Hah," Caitlin said—with her light hair she could be spotted in seconds even in a crowd. She was about to say good night, but lingered instead, toying with the idea of asking if he wanted to come over right then. It would be nice to fall asleep with his body curled around hers—one of his legs across hers, the inside of his wrist pulsing against her breast—as they did at the hotels. In the few seconds of silence as she paused and he waited for her to speak, she could feel the charge between them, his desire and her need to nuzzle up to another body, and she almost invited him, but then she heard the rush of flushing water, footsteps, and voices overhead. She imagined the neighbors listening with paper cups to their parquet kitchen floors, waiting along with Hiroshi to see what she would do. She lowered her voice and said good night, wondering just how disappointed Hiroshi was, and whether he really meant what he said when he agreed with her, that as a foreign female teacher, a public servant in Japan, she couldn't risk being seen with a man in her apartment.

Three

CAITLIN STOOD before the department store searching the crowds for Hiroshi. He often startled her with some gag or another—a squirt gun, a ghoulish mask—so she was trying to remain vigilant, scrutinizing the shoppers and office workers for a glimpse of his face as she combed her fingers through her still damp hair. But her eyes kept returning to a group of children before her playing "rock, scissors, paper" with lightning speed. Caitlin always lost when students at her schools coaxed her into a round—she could never quite remember the rules when four were playing, and she confused the gestures in the second rounds, which puzzled her, because she could recall vividly the speed at which she'd played with clusters of classmates in the Iwakura school yard in Kyoto. As she watched the children before her, attempting to anticipate their moves, a translucent pink rubber octopus dropped before her eyes. She turned to find Hiroshi grinning at her.

He nodded and she put a hand lightly on his shoulder. He was wearing the deep green T-shirt she'd seen in a store on a drizzly afternoon during an impulsive overnight trip they'd taken to Kumamoto—Hiroshi had told his parents he'd be off fishing with friends. In the shop's bright light Caitlin had held the fabric up to his sun-darkened skin, bought it immediately despite its high price and Hiroshi's polite protests, and back in their inn room made him put it on. She'd told him the green reminded her of a cedar grove, or of the dwarfed spruces high in the New Hampshire mountains when she'd joined her father hiking. It made her think of wind, she'd told Hiroshi, and he'd laughed. *"My wind shirt,"* he'd promptly named it. The shirt had been washed plenty since then, the cotton now soft and dulled, but the color was still striking on him, still made her think of trees at cool heights.

"Let's go," he said, jutting an elbow for her. She hooked her wrist through and followed his quick lead down the sidewalk, averting her gaze from the stares of passersby, for it seemed that no matter how well she adjusted to life in Japan, the Japanese never quite adjusted to the sight of her. At least when she was with Hiroshi, people ogled less. Alone, she was often pointed to and spoken of out loud, like a zoo critter.

"Are we walking or biking?" Caitlin asked.

"Walking," he answered firmly. He led her down a wing of the Tenmonkan pedestrian mall then through a maze of lanes and back alleys. She had to skip a step now and then to keep up with him. He'd slow his gait and apologize, but seconds later resume the faster pace. She could never match his energy. He was always moving, restless and impetuous, too, and though Caitlin liked that quality in him—the way he'd suddenly veer off onto a side road to show her an ancient ginkgo tree at some shrine, or drop in on a friend unannounced, or on their way somewhere haul her into a movie theater featuring an animated film from his childhood, or without a word, jump up and run out to the store for *okonomiyaki* ingredients because Caitlin had said that was her favorite dish from when she'd lived in Kyoto—she was sometimes exhausted by his boundless energy and had learned to be cautious when expressing wishes.

They ended up at a tiny basement restaurant where Hiroshi knew the owner. Heads turned when Caitlin entered behind Hiroshi, but she felt the place relax with the owner's warm greeting to them. They sat down at one of four small tables. Hiroshi ordered a bottle of beer from the waiter and directed him to pour the owner a glass of *shochu* from a bottle marked with Hiroshi's name. The owner raised his glass from across the room, and shortly thereafter a plate of broiled scallops and two small bowls of vinegared *wakame* appeared before them.

Hiroshi surveyed the wooden plaques nailed to the wall listing the menu items, ordered half a dozen dishes, and pushed the scallops toward her. She took one, then with decorum moved the plate between them, though she knew it was Hiroshi's style to barely nibble, sometimes not touch the food at all, until Caitlin had sampled nearly everything. She was starved, and it was all she could do to exercise the appropriate restraint. Eating with Hiroshi, and many of the teachers she worked with, she was often reminded of cycling races where, for the longest time, riders hardly pedaled, bikes unsteady, until, with a sudden burst of speed and frenzy, they headed for the finish.

"How was your swim?" he asked as she was swallowing her first scallop and trying not to eye the others.

She sipped her beer. "Fine."

"So, what are you training for? A Kinko Bay crossing?" he asked. She looked up from her glass. He wasn't smiling.

"No, nothing really," she said, "just keeping in shape," and left it at that. He eyed her a moment longer, then let it go. She knew he wouldn't press her, and she felt a twinge of guilt for not opening up to him.

"Right. Well, you doing anything on Sunday? I have to test drive a couple vans. Want to come? Then after that we'll go catch an octopus."

"Octopus?"

"Like Ya-chan here." He set the rubber octopus on the table between them. "I know a great place we can go spearfishing. Have you ever tried it?"

"No."

"Are you interested?"

"Sure," she said, amused. "I don't have any plans." A bowl of edamame arrived and Caitlin picked up a fistful of pods and began popping the tender, salty soybeans into her mouth. The beer on a nearly empty stomach was beginning to make her light-headed.

"How about O-Bon? Do you have any plans for that yet?"

Caitlin frowned, thrown off by his shift of topics. The O-Bon holiday was still a month away.

"O-Bon? I don't know. I'm thinking of going up to Kyoto. Why?"

"Well, I have that whole week off. I thought we could go somewhere, take a trip. Misawa's organizing a camping trip, but we could do something by ourselves like you're always suggesting. Then you could travel to Kyoto the week after, if you're still planning on going."

Caitlin aligned some bean pods on the tabletop. *"Actually . . ."* she began.

"You have four weeks, right? We could take a ferry to Yakushima or Oshima or one of the other islands. Or go up to Aso to hike." Hiroshi had been leaning in close to her, but when the waiter arrived with skewers of chicken, cakes of tofu, oysters, and vegetables, he was forced to sit back, and Caitlin had a moment to collect her thoughts.

"Well, what do you think?" Hiroshi asked when the waiter left.

"Well, first off, I've only really got three weeks. That last week of August I have to teach a seminar Monday through Wednesday," Caitlin said. Then she thought of a ploy. *"Hey, could you get that Thursday and Friday off, the 29th and 30th? We could do a short trip then. Or that week before O-Bon. I'm free then."*

Hiroshi frowned. *"That'd be difficult. The company closes for O-Bon, that's why I get the week off. What's wrong with O-Bon, do you have other plans?"*

"I told you, I might be going to Kyoto."

"For the whole O-Bon week?"

"Two weeks. The O-Bon week and the week after. I'd do some side trips, too."

"I see." He took a chug of beer, then brightened. *"What if I joined you for a few days? We could do a couple day trips together. Then I'd come back to Kagoshima, leave you alone. I wouldn't interfere with your meeting old friends or anything."*

Caitlin wasn't sure how to explain. Hiroshi knew nothing of the Oides, just the fact that she'd lived in Kyoto for a year and a half as a child. She wasn't sure how much she wanted to tell him, and she still wasn't sure herself just what she was planning to do—whether she'd go to the Oides for the entire time, whether they would even be home at that time of year, and if they were, whether they'd welcome her, or if she'd want to stay with them or with some American from the teaching program, or in a cheap inn by herself. She hadn't yet summoned the nerve to write to the Oides.

"Look," she said, *"Let's quit this talk for now. I just don't know what I'm doing yet. It all depends on other people's schedules. But Hiroshi . . ."* She dropped her head into her hands. She wanted to say, Please,

don't you try to stop me too; if I can get up the courage, urge me to go, but she caught herself, knowing full well that if she mentioned needing to get up the courage, he'd want to know for what, and she didn't think she was ready to go into it all with him.

She raised her head. *"I'm sorry,"* she said, *"I'm just tired and hungry."*

"Then here, here," he said, dribbling soy sauce on her chilled tofu and taking skewers of chicken and vegetables from the assortment plate and placing them on her dish. He called the waiter over and ordered more skewers and a deep bowl of rice in tea that was so nicely flavored and hearty with salmon and nori that Caitlin nearly wept she was so grateful. Hiroshi joined her in eating, and for a while they said nothing, just grunted, nodded approval, and raised eyebrows over the various morsels.

Hiroshi pushed the dishes away when he was done, and finally Caitlin was sated too.

"Don't you think you're overdoing it?" he asked.

"I was hungry."

Hiroshi laughed. *"No, no, eat as much as you want. I mean, don't you think you're swimming too hard?"*

Caitlin looked straight at him. *"I don't know."* He waited for her to continue, and she looked down at her hands fiddling with a chopsticks wrapper. *"Sometimes, even now, when I'm swimming twice a day, it doesn't feel like enough. It's never enough."* She wanted to go on, to tell him she felt as though she'd implode if she let up, that it was a form of atonement. She groped for a way to explain without having to go in too deep. *"I just have to,"* she finally said lamely. She wished he'd touch her, take her hand, slide his stool closer, anything, but she knew that wasn't the sort of thing he did in public. She could feel tears welling, and Hiroshi, eyeing her, cleared his throat and rose abruptly to pay the bill.

Caitlin recovered enough to bid the owner the requisite cheerful farewell, then they stepped out into the narrow alley bathed in red light from paper restaurant lanterns. After they'd walked a short ways, she hooked arms with Hiroshi, and she was grateful for this simple comfort, to have this body into which she could lean. Now out of the public eye he pulled her close.

"You want to take the tram or walk?" he asked.

"Walk," she said, and he led her into a side street. They took a zig-zag route past karaoke bars, the rear entrances of restaurants, and locked and shuttered offices, back toward the station where her bike was parked. The walk and the quiet night air felt good, and Caitlin soon felt a semblance of inner peace.

She described her visit to the gardens the day before and the girl she'd met there, the will, and the dinner she'd agreed to attend the following evening.

"So you didn't sign it," Hiroshi said of the will. *"What if she'd jumped because you refused?"*

"I thought of that, but even so, I couldn't sign it. That would have been like helping her, or conspiring with her. What would you have done?"

"Sign it, but tell her I had to do it over by the ropeway station or something, trick her to get away from the edge." Caitlin smiled. She doubted if Naomi would have fallen for that. *"Or grab her and hold her and yell for help,"* Hiroshi added. Caitlin frowned at this one. Sometimes he could be patronizing. But she swung his hand. The darkness between streetlights was soothing, and for once Hiroshi was maintaining a leisurely pace.

"Did you tell her parents?" he asked.

"No, I promised her I wouldn't."

"You'll tell them tomorrow, won't you? You have to." He'd halted in the middle of the street.

Caitlin studied him. It was clear he believed that that was her duty, and he seemed alarmed that she might even entertain the thought of remaining silent. *"I guess so,"* she said, *"I'll need to see how it goes, though, and consider the situation carefully. I don't want to make it worse, make her run away or anything."* Hiroshi nodded, mulling this over, and they continued walking.

"Strange, isn't it," Caitlin said, and he nodded again. She wanted to ask what *his* darkest moments had been, whether he'd ever contemplated jumping from a ledge, whether at train crossings he'd ever felt the impulse to dart in front of an express, but she sensed he'd brush off the question, accuse her of thinking too darkly, and what's more, she didn't feel ready to answer if he asked her the same. She squeezed his hand instead, and gazed at him with the same wonder that sometimes struck her in the middle of making love, that she knew so incredibly little of this man with whom she sometimes

shared her body. They'd exchanged mere shorthand accounts of their pasts, and she knew that in her accounts, the gaps and spaces and the puzzling vague allusions had nothing to do with language or cultural barriers.

When they reached a stretch of unlit road, Hiroshi stopped, pushed her hair back gently, and gave her a long, teasing kiss. She returned the tease, and thought by the kiss that he was suggesting they detour to one of the love hotels, and she was in the midst of calculating whether if they did, she could then stay awake long enough afterward to prepare for classes the next day and still get up in time to swim, when Hiroshi pulled away, nudging her forward toward the next streetlight, guiding her with a firm hand on her shoulder, saying they both should get home and sleep, they had long days ahead. Caitlin recognized this as an attempt to hide his concern for her, for she knew he didn't feel compelled to go home and sleep. He was a night owl—despite his early work hours at the family shipping company, he often urged her to join him carousing deep into the night, pub hopping, lounging in a ridiculous heart-shaped bath at a hotel, ascending some hilltop for a moonlight view of the ash plume, or, if conditions were right according to his geologist friend, trying to catch sight of volcanic lightning.

But they parted early. When they reached her bike they said good night with mere nods, both of them acutely aware of a nearby group of drunken businessmen grown suddenly silent, watching. Caitlin didn't like the display that she and Hiroshi inadvertently became sometimes, the sexual curiosity they seemed to arouse, and the lewd comments they inspired. More than once, right in front of Caitlin, Hiroshi had been complimented for the nice catch he'd made. *"Ja, ne,"* he said softly, apologetic, and Caitlin rushed off into the night, the pitch of her front-light generator rising to a whine as she stood to pedal harder, to get home to her apartment, her private cordoned-off space.

Four

CAITLIN'S LAST CLASS ended at two on Fridays, and unlike her Japanese colleagues at her base school—the only school she taught at on a weekly basis—she was free to leave before the last period. She slouched at her desk in the teachers' room and sipped the bitter remains of instant coffee from her mug—she did not want to fall asleep on the bus and miss her transfer as she had the week before.

Exams were over, summer homework had not yet been assigned, and the students knew they were being danced through a nationwide holding pattern until vacation could officially begin. Caitlin felt harassed. The kids had been less cooperative than usual that afternoon; her ears still rang from their shouting, and her throat was dry and raspy from trying to snare their attention with Pronunciation Bingo.

When the bell rang, and most of the teachers and students had disappeared for their last period classes, Caitlin rinsed her mug and slipped out of the teachers' room with a bow and *"O-saki-ni shitsurei shimasu,"*—excuse me for leaving before you. Downstairs she tossed her slippers into her shoe locker then shuffled out the front door with her feet only halfway into her sandals. When she'd rounded the corner and passed the school and several raucous students leaning out the high open windows shouting, *"Obah-sensei!* Good-bye, *Obah-za-rainbow-sensei!"* she slackened her pace and stooped to adjust her sandal straps.

She took the bus that brought her to another bus that went direct to the West Station, where she extracted her bicycle from the tightly packed lot, donned her baseball cap, and rode toward the river. Her legs had been stiff all day from the morning's overexertion in the pool—an effort to make up in advance for missing her

evening swim—but now she could feel the muscles relax. She pedaled hard up the rise of bridge then let her feet dangle freely as she
coasted down the other side. On her simple three-speed bike, as in
the water, she felt at ease, zipping past gawking pedestrians with
only the hum of fat tires and the hot breeze in her ears.

The ash seemed suspended above the still air today, and she
could ride with her head up. On thick and windy days, even with
sunglasses on and a scarf over her nose and mouth, bandit style, the
tiny particles stung her face, and hours later, she'd still be coughing
and sneezing black. She was increasingly grateful for teaching
assignments that took her far beyond the city, to rural schools amid
rice fields and cedar forests, where the ash collected in quaint wispy
eddies, mere shadows, rather than the thick accumulating mounds
in Kagoshima. During weeks she was assigned to all Kagoshima
schools, sometimes after classes she'd flee to the station and board
the first train to arrive, adjusting her fare and finding her bearings
only after she'd disembarked, somewhere, anywhere down or up
the line, into clean air. In late June, she'd gone as far south as the
spa town of Ibusuki, and for a time she'd wandered the streets envy-
ing the tourists milling about in their cotton robes. Finally she'd
paid the fee to bathe in one of the big hotels, and after she'd
scrubbed, and the last gray swirls had vanished down the drain,
she'd hopped from tub to tub—scalding to tepid to icy to hot—for
nearly an hour before emerging pink and sleepy to catch a train
back to Kagoshima.

Today Caitlin rode lazily through the maze of side streets that
skirted and eventually entered her neighborhood tucked up tight
against the steep rise of Shiroyama. When she reached her building,
she shouldered her bike up the stairs to the landing by her door, fit
the bike cover on, slapped her cap on her thigh, ran her fingers
through her hair, and shook the deposits of ash from folds in her
clothing. Inside she turned on the air conditioner and went directly
to the bathroom to draw water into the deep tub, and while it filled
she pulled the curtains, stripped to her underwear, and lay down flat
on the cool straw of the tatami.

The chilled air spread through the room, and she shivered feeling the sweat bead around to her backside and drip to the mats. Her
forehead pinched with salt, and the skin on her arms and legs

pricked with goose bumps. By her side she absently stroked the grain of the tatami, then she sat up to eye the familiar film on her fingertips; no matter how tightly she sealed the windows, how many towels she placed in strategic draft locations, the fine ash penetrated. During her bath she worked again at her calculations and conversions—her daily, haphazard attempt to determine just how much the newspaper's figure of 2.5 kilograms of ash per square meter per day really was.

Later, in a sleeveless blouse and linen shorts, Caitlin decided she felt too clean for a muggy walk to the bus stop with ash kicking up underfoot and a slow ride across town. She called a taxi instead, and when it arrived handed the driver the piece of paper with Naomi's address, then leaned her head back to watch the afternoon light flicker and jog through the tops of the trees above the rear window. She was pleased to be going to a family gathering, relieved for an evening of the strains in her relationship with Hiroshi, and far from the drunken unwinding of overworked teachers. What's more, she was curious about this family—none of the handful of children of mixed marriages she'd met through teaching were fully bilingual. Few seemed to keep up their English into adolescence. The prospect of an evening of fluid talk and unstilted discussion had immense appeal to her, for in Kagoshima she knew only a handful of foreigners by name—Scott, the other fellow assigned to Kagoshima whom she saw every few weeks at the education center, several language school teachers, a Chinese couple studying engineering at the university, and a Canadian who hadn't shown up at the local yakitori restaurant for a month now. And Caitlin seldom met the other Americans from her teaching program, stationed in the various cities of Kyushu. When she joined their gatherings, she was surprised and alarmed to hear herself grow as effusive and judgmental as the loudest of them, and she often bowed out of weekend retreats or conferences early, eager to shake the clublike talk and regain her usual, more cautious interpretations of the life around her.

Caitlin stepped out of the taxi at Naomi's house, and a nearby group of children suspended their play to watch. She said a few words in Japanese, and they scattered, giggling. She unlatched the gate and knocked on the door. When no one answered she knocked louder, called out *"Gomen kudasai,"* and looked about; she hated this custom of shouting at closed doors. Still no response, so she tried the knob, pushed the door open a crack, and repeated, softer, to the interior, *"Gomen kudasai."*

The upstairs creaked, and Naomi's father bellowed, "Naomi!" Silence followed. "Naomi, the door!" he hollered louder.

"It's me, Caitlin Ober."

"Oh, come on in!" Carl shouted down the stairs. "God, it's five already? I don't know where the hell Naomi's gone off to, she was here a minute ago. Make yourself at home. I've got a trifle more to do up here. Open a beer—there're glasses over the sink."

Caitlin paired her shoes and pointed them outward in the entryway, crossed the kitchen floor, and took a beer from the refrigerator. She held the wet bottle to her forehead, already hot again, pulled a small glass from the cupboard, and looked about for an opener. "Where's the opener?" she shouted.

"In the drawer by the sink," Carl called down.

Caitlin poured a half glass quickly and gulped it down without a breath. Then she slowly poured a full glass and set the bottle down on the table. She stepped from the kitchen into the next room and surveyed the clutter: bookshelves sagging with books stuffed horizontal and upright; a sideboard laden with stereo, records, and scattered cassettes; two dressers covered with assorted pieces of pottery; an upright piano; and in the center a low wooden table. In a smaller room adjacent she could see a sofa, more bookshelves, and near the window a table covered with what looked to be ink-spattered white felt, paint brushes, an inkstone, and rags; Naomi's *shodo,* she thought.

Caitlin grabbed a cushion from a stack beside the piano and sat down, but she felt uncomfortable so low on the floor amid the clutter of high furniture. The sliding doors opposite, frosted and opaque in their lower halves, obscured her view to the outdoors, so she stood again to have a look through the clear upper glass. She peered out onto a trim garden of shrubs enclosed by a concrete wall and was startled to see below her, between the plantings and deep ceramic pots, flat on her back with her eyes closed, Naomi.

She lay there perfectly still in baggy slacks and a salmon-colored T-shirt, so close to the door Caitlin could see drops of moisture and gray flecks on her forehead. Her hands were working at her sides, raising fistfuls of ash then letting it sift lazily back down through her fingers. Caitlin was inclined to drop to her knees just below the frosted glass, but she was afraid the movement would draw the girl's attention.

Naomi's hands lay by her sides again, palms down flat by her hips, and for a moment Caitlin wondered if she were dozing. Then slowly she began to sweep with outstretched arms and legs, out and in. Her head rested snug against the hairy base of a palmetto, one hand brushed a squat azalea, and when her pointed toes came together they just touched the cement strip of patio. Caitlin had the urge to open the door and pull her upright, but she remained riveted behind the glass. Finally, blinking, Naomi opened her eyes, carefully stood, and turned to survey behind her the clear impression of an angel in the ash.

Caitlin slid open the door; "Naomi!" she whispered. She detected a flinch in Naomi's shoulders, but the girl turned her head and met Caitlin's eyes with aplomb.

"What are you *doing?*"

"You like it?" Naomi pointed to the angel.

"Look at you. You're covered."

"Don't say anything. My father's forgotten to sweep again— look at it all! Brush my back off, will you?"

Caitlin stepped down from the living room into a pair of plastic garden sandals and swatted at the grit stuck to Naomi's damp shirt. "It's too fine. It doesn't come off."

"Try harder."

She slapped her hands vigorously across Naomi's back, then brushed with a soft broom that Naomi handed her. "You must be forever dusting out here. How on earth do you garden in this? Are those your father's?" She nodded toward a row of bonsai withering in shallow pots on a sill.

"Yeah, but he still doesn't know how to prune. Or maybe he's just confused about it, you know, sort of feels it's cruel. And he always forgets to water. Even though he's studied bonsai and everything. And he thinks it's my fault if I don't remind him to clean the ash—he knows I like it."

"Don't you ever help with the sweeping and bagging?"

"Not unless he makes me. Why should I? It's nice—smooths everything over and rounds all the sharp edges. I don't care if it buries us all," she said and smiled. "In February he caught me out here measuring the depth with a ruler. He'd been correcting exams all week and forgotten about it. He went crazy—all the neighbors heard him. He made me get an extension cord and vacuum every single leaf. Can you believe it? The plants looked worse when I'd finished." Naomi laughed. "Am I all right now?" She peered over her shoulder at her back.

"Not really. God, how can you even think of lying out here . . . between the heat and the ash . . . " Caitlin's clean blouse now adhered to her spine, and fine particles of ash clung to the hairs on her forearms. "Let's go inside."

"Is my father still working?"

"He said he'd be down in a bit."

"Don't say anything, okay?"

"Again?" Caitlin said, but Naomi looked away.

Caitlin shook off the sandals and returned to the kitchen and rinsed her hands and arms under the faucet. Naomi hurriedly washed up in the bathing area—Caitlin could hear buckets of water sloshing—and reappeared in a clean blouse and skirt. Then Caitlin watched, perplexed, as she began to bustle about apologetically. "Sit down, sit down," Naomi entreated, sending her back to the other room, setting out more cushions, turning up the air conditioner, pouring rice snacks into dishes, and finally bringing a clutch of beer and soda bottles to the table. Caitlin wondered what had become of the will and was tempted to ask Naomi if she'd been to the gardens again since Tuesday. But through the girl's posturing as hostess it was clear that Caitlin was expected to play the role of ordinary guest, no more conscious of her inner thoughts than any friend of her parents.

Naomi disappeared into the kitchen again and Caitlin sat staring at the spines of books, most in Japanese, until she recognized the repetition of a few particular characters; there were volumes on pottery. She pulled a thick tome to the table and flipped through the pages—close-up photos of tea bowls. Many looked rough, almost unfinished and raw with pocked glazes, misshapen sides, and colors slopped on in what seemed to be random design, others were more delicate, reminding her of the soft tastes her tongue had missed when she'd left Japan as a child.

"Who's the pottery fan?" she asked when Naomi set down a plate of cubed watermelon beside the books.

"Fan? Oh, my father's a potter. When he feels like it." They could hear his steps on the stairs, and they held their conversation until Carl appeared in the doorway, taller, it seemed, than Caitlin had remembered.

"Happy heat wave," he said, and they shook hands. As Carl settled on a cushion, Caitlin held up a bottle of beer. He nodded in thanks, offered his glass, and Caitlin poured him a beer and Naomi a soda.

"He made this one," Naomi said, handing a bowl of rice crackers to Caitlin. Caitlin took the full bowl, held it level with her eyes and turned it slowly in the light from the windows—the dark glaze seemed to drizzle down the bowl and swirled with deep rusty hues.

"I love it. It's like bronze," Caitlin said. "Really striking."

"Actually," Carl proclaimed, throwing his arm over Naomi's shoulders, "if it hadn't been for pottery, I might never have come to Kagoshima and had this daughter who brought us together today. *Kanpai.* Cheers." They raised glasses and Naomi blushed. She sipped her soda, set it back on the table with two hands, teacup style, and with a bow of her head slipped out of the room.

"So, you taught today?" Carl asked.

"Well, I wouldn't exactly call it teaching," Caitlin said wryly. "Entertainment, putting myself up for display maybe . . . I'm one of those teaching fellows they send around the prefecture. You're at the university, right? How's that?"

"Good, actually; easier than what you're doing. Unfortunately you're really just a figurehead in that program, you know, the foreign face to make the government look good." He sipped his beer and sprawled out lengthwise on his side with a cushion under his elbow. "It's not bad at the university, keeps me challenged. I teach a mix: expository writing, special topics in contemporary American culture, and my baby, Art in America. I might be able to set you up in composition, or in some of the conversation classes for business students. If you're interested."

Caitlin nodded, grateful. "Thanks, I'll keep it in mind. I'd love to really *teach*," she said. "You know, smaller classes, work with the same kids for several months straight. But I'm bounced around the prefecture doing 'one-shots'—in and out in a day or two—and only at my base school do I stand a chance of learning names. And even there, I see ten groups of twenty or so first-year students, teaching each lesson ten times in a row, before I see the same group again." Caitlin gulped her beer. "Sorry, I don't mean to whine."

"Oh, don't be ridiculous," Carl said. "Gripe away. Believe me I understand. I get the college students who after six or seven years of English have never written a paragraph. They've been taught English as if it were Latin, dead and only useful for entrance exams. But seriously, you should consider applying at the university—I might be able to introduce you to some people."

"Thanks. I'm not sure how long I'll stay here though."

"Why? What's next?"

"I don't know," Caitlin said. "Maybe grad school." It was her stock answer. In fact, she couldn't envision anything in her future beyond her August trip to Kyoto. And even that she couldn't really fathom. But instead of mentioning Kyoto, she blurted, "Kagoshima is getting to me."

Carl laughed. "Kagoshima or the ash?"

Caitlin smiled. "The ash, I suppose."

"You know Sakurajima may be quiet again next year; it's been decades since it was as active as this. You just picked a bad time to come."

"Thanks," Caitlin said.

"Hey, don't get me wrong, it may mellow soon. It cycles. But, you know. . ." Carl sat up and leaned toward her slightly. "Even if it did go quiet, went into repose, it'd start up again sooner or later. It's bound to erupt again like it did in 1914, you know, when it was joined to the Osumi Peninsula. Have you seen photographs of that? Fish were cooked alive, the bay got so hot from the lava flows. And there were huge rafts of pumice—boats couldn't navigate. And the entire bay became shallower."

"You really think it will erupt like that again?"

"Sure. With volcanoes, repose is just a temporary state, however long that calm lasts. Who knows, maybe it will erupt with a vengeance, send forth some good pyroclastic flows next week, ooze more lava across the bay, and we can do away with the ferries."

"Oh please." Caitlin tried to picture a frothing hot bay, and twisted, solid lava reaching to Iso Beach. Immediately she thought of Hiroshi and wondered what he'd do with his weekends if he couldn't windsurf.

"But at least the wind shifts in winter," Carl said. "I tell you, I've never felt so damned emotional about wind currents."

Naomi knelt down by her soda again. Caitlin took a slow draw on her beer and watched the girl look long at her father then turn away as he continued with words she seemed to have predicted. "Maybe we should get advice from Naomi on how to cope—she clearly enjoys it." He gave her a playful punch but she scowled. "Oh, come on," he added, "I'm not making fun of you, it *is* unique, I just don't like living in it. Hey, bring some of your bottles to show Caitlin."

Naomi brightened, left the room, and returned with an armload of small glass jars and bottles all labeled with a date—each containing a different grade of ash. Caitlin examined them closely; some were darker than others, some fine as dust, and one was coarse pebbles—she checked the date. "Yes! I remember that one—it hurt!"

"Five millimeters, the largest pieces in that jar measure," Naomi said proudly.

Carl rose. "Tell me kid, should we be doing anything for dinner?"

Naomi delegated jobs in the kitchen—Caitlin peeling cucumbers, Carl rinsing and slicing pickled daikon, while Naomi assembled watercress and grated wasabi. While they worked, Caitlin asked Carl if he'd been a potter in the States.

"Aspiring. I wasn't serious until I came to Japan to apprentice, up in Mashiko, north of Tokyo."

"How'd you end up in Kyushu?"

"Well, I wasn't wild about the Mashiko style, or the town of Mashiko for that matter, and then one weekend in Tokyo I saw an exhibit of works by a potter doing amazing new variations of Satsuma-ware—not the flowery white stuff, but not the standard heavy dark stuff either—and that decided it. I packed my bags, hitched all the way down to Kagoshima, then spent several weeks checking out potteries in the area. The potter whose exhibit I'd seen finally, grudgingly, agreed to take me on. I apprenticed there for two years."

"But then you quit?" Caitlin asked.

Carl turned from the sink and stood holding the dripping daikon over the floor. "Well, yes, as a full-time potter, I quit. I still go to that pottery on weekends, and one day I hope to build a little studio and kiln of my own outside the city. But just for myself, as a hobby, not a profession. You see, when I first met Akiko, she paints *sumi-e,* and I thought hey, this is great, two artists, what a match, and I had ideas of her painting on my pottery and building our own workshop, but once we decided to get married, we needed steady income, and I just couldn't see us both struggling to make a living that way. I was tired of the world of an apprentice already, tired of the rigid restrictions of being in someone else's workshop, practicing the same traditional forms over and over, and I knew I didn't want to devote my life to my *sensei*'s glazing techniques and style. And it's mighty tough to go it on your own here, especially as a foreigner. I don't know, I guess I don't have the tunnel vision of the artists here. My wife says it's just a matter of discipline."

"She's right," Naomi interrupted as she cut sheets of nori with large shears.

"You think so?" Carl asked with a smile. Caitlin looked from one to the other—Carl leaning back against the sink with his arms crossed, the wrinkled yellow daikon dangling obscenely from one hand, and his daughter arranging the green sheets on a rectangular plate. Naomi brushed her hands off slowly, took the daikon, and placed it on a cutting board.

"Yes," she said. "Japanese pottery wouldn't be where it is now if it weren't for that 'tunnel vision' or whatever you want to call it. You have to have that kind of focus if you want to accomplish anything in one short lifetime." Carl laughed at her solemn proclamation, but Caitlin found the allusion to a short life disconcerting, coming from Naomi.

"Okay," he said, "so it's not a long time to accomplish much. But I don't think wedging someone else's clay or churning out the same old teacups with the workshop stamp has anything to do with focus. That's just the old hierarchical system at work."

Naomi halted her food preparations and sat down in a kitchen chair calmly looking up at her father. Caitlin found herself startled by this frank discussion. After a year in Japan she'd grown so accustomed to the practice of nonconfrontation, that this candid argument threw her, and she bent over the platter and arranged the hand-roll fixings into a neat, color-symmetrical circle. "It's more than that though," Naomi said. "It's training, so that by the time you take over you know everything about the clay, the wheels, tools, glazes, the kiln—everything, it's second nature by then. And the *sensei* knows you're committed, which they have to know if they're going to teach you their life's knowledge."

Carl chuckled. "Oh, I know, and some of that is good, I agree, but come on, stop being so profound and be honest Naomi, how would you feel about *shodo* if for months all you did was grind your teacher's ink?"

A shadow of alarm flickered across Naomi's face, but then she smiled as Carl pressed, "Huh? Huh?"

Caitlin looked from one to the other, and Naomi turned to explain, "I get lazy grinding the ink. Sometimes I cheat and use that instant stuff." She stood. "All right, you win, it's *not* just a lack of discipline. It's more complicated. But you *do* lack it."

"You'd think she was my mother, not my daughter," Carl said to Caitlin. *"Oi,"* he called out gutturally to Naomi, holding up the empty beer bottle.

She sneered at him playfully: "Get your own."

▲ ▲ ▲

When Naomi's mother arrived, introductions were made in Japanese and English. Naomi took the bundles from her mother's arms, peeked inside the paper, and squealed about the freshness and color of the wrapped fish, shrimp, and squid with what seemed to be an excess of enthusiasm. Her mother appeared to Caitlin like an older Naomi but refined, poised, and somehow, balanced. A flurry of apologies ensued—for Caitlin having to bring Naomi home on Tuesday, for their small house and its mess, for being late, for her poor English, and for not preparing a more elaborate dinner. Conversation slipped almost entirely into Japanese and like a shift in wind, produced a cool air of decorum among the group. Caitlin stood up straight and when she spoke, tagged cumbersome polite endings to her verbs. Naomi's voice rose to the appropriate high pitch for young girls' Japanese, and even Carl suddenly seemed less casual. Akiko donned a long apron and by taking their beers into the other room, ushered the two English teachers, as she put it, out of the kitchen.

When all the dishes and ingredients had been set on the low table, they clinked glasses and set about assembling their sushi cones. For Caitlin's sake they elaborated on their own styles—Carl insisting on gobs of wasabi; Akiko emphasizing the placement of the rice and the taste and color combination of ingredients; and Naomi, amused, claiming that the idea was to go around the plate, take exactly one of everything, and roll it up into an enormous sausage.

In addition to the fresh fish, Akiko had prepared tiny clams in sake and butter, and skewers of chicken and vegetables, and she rose midway through the meal to prepare a second set of fresh moist towels for their hands. Later, when conversation had slipped back into English, Caitlin asked where Akiko had come from earlier, if she were an English teacher too, and to this Carl and Naomi giggled conspiratorially. Akiko shook her head and answered in English. "No, no, I'm teacher of *sumi-e,* Japanese ink painting." She gestured toward the felt-covered table, rolls of paper, and jars of brushes in the next room.

"Oh, that's right. So you're all artists then," Caitlin said. "I feel intimidated."

"I'm not an artist yet," Naomi protested.

"But you do *shodo.*"

Caitlin felt Carl's glance dart from her to Naomi, who rolled a stray grain of rice over the table then mashed it under her thumb. "Doesn't matter," she quipped.

Carl and Akiko looked at each other. Caitlin fished for another subject, and too quickly perhaps—she never could judge these silences—changed the conversation. She asked them how they'd managed to raise Naomi bilingually.

"Managed?" Carl said. "Easy. Akiko beat her when she didn't

speak perfect Japanese and I beat her when she didn't speak perfect English."

"Carl!" Akiko said.

"And slang?" Caitlin asked.

"Well, Naomi's spent many summers in Cleveland, Cleveland Heights to be exact—that's where my family is. We go back almost every year. Naomi usually goes to summer camp. And she spent a couple years in preschool there when I was doing my graduate work."

"Slang's the first thing you remember," Naomi said, apparently recovered, and Caitlin could feel everyone relax.

"Well, you'll have to teach me more Japanese slang. I need to be better armed against my students."

"Oh!" Carl said and jumped up from the floor, jostling the low table with his knees, causing the dishes to slide and clink against one another. "I almost forgot!" he shouted. He tripped into the kitchen and returned with four small glasses in one hand and a smoking cold bottle of champagne in the other. "Drum roll," he called. Naomi flipped her chopsticks around and began to tap on the table. He motioned with his hand for Akiko and Caitlin to join in, and when Akiko, giggling, had reluctantly consented he announced, "One week from today we shall enter the sweet realm of summer vacation. Naomi." She stood and Carl handed her the bottle. "Open that window. A thousand yen if you can hit the Ishidas' bathroom window," he said, pointing to a second-story window on the house beside theirs.

"Carl!" Akiko exclaimed with her hands on her cheeks, but Naomi was beside her father at the window, dislodging the cork with her thumbs. Akiko shook her head and turned to Caitlin, who was now resting with one elbow down on the tatami to get a better view. "Please, I'm sorry," she said. "You see, my husband is crazy, very crazy." She covered her ears as if Naomi were prodding a balloon. The cork flew too soon, shot straight up and ricocheted off the eaves with a pong.

"No cigar," Carl said. "Now pour around. Happy summer everyone."

▲ ▲ ▲

At the end of the meal, as Caitlin rose to help Akiko clear the plates, Carl suggested they all go out for a walk. Caitlin voiced her enthusiasm in unison with Naomi, but Akiko demurred.

"You should come too," Caitlin pleaded. "We'll clean up later."

"No, you and Carl go is better. Naomi helps me to prepare dessert."

"But I'm going for a walk," Naomi whined.

"Come on, Akiko, let's all go," Carl said, but Akiko replied in terse Japanese that Caitlin and Carl were to go; Naomi would stay and help. Carl opened his mouth to protest, but Akiko's gaze stayed him, and Naomi glared from one parent to the other, their mouths drawn up into tight little knots. For a moment the three of them stood there silently conversing in another language more foreign, it seemed to Caitlin, than Japanese. As Caitlin slipped into her sandals, Naomi shot her a dark look that Caitlin pretended not to see. She had no intention of entering family squabbles; she'd left hers far behind in the States.

At the first whiff of soft air outside Caitlin didn't care who was where. Summer evenings in Kagoshima were a comfort; the heat eased, the dark masked her light hair, and Sakurajima's plume, she knew from moonlit nights, often smoked straight up, hardly wavering or straying into the city. Caitlin liked to walk alone on steamy nights, meandering through her neighborhood, peeking through open or beaded doorways to the inner lives, sealed off and invisible other times of the year. The sounds calmed her, and she often found herself far from her apartment meandering along the river, the empty playground, and gate-ball court with only the shrill cry of a kite or the crack of fireworks sounding in the blackness overhead.

That evening they wandered through the streets below the Nan-shu Shrine. They could see the flickering blue of television sets, and the tense voices of Friday night dramas and banter of variety shows wafted through the air with the spatters of deep-frying and sloshing of bathwater. Neither of them spoke for some time, and Caitlin began to feel awkward out strolling with this man she hardly knew while his wife and daughter stood at the sink with their dishes.

"Akiko wants me to ask your advice," Carl finally said. "She thinks Naomi confided in you." He looked at Caitlin and gave an embarrassed laugh, then immediately frowned. Staring at the ground in front of him, he continued, "She's a troubled girl lately. We're not sure what to do."

"Well, I doubt that I can offer much advice. I hardly know her," Caitlin said.

"I know, I know. But she seems to like you. You ran into her up at the Iso Gardens, right?"

"Right."

"And she told you about her *shodo?*"

"Well, I know she's done *shodo,* that's all." Naomi had never actually mentioned calligraphy; there was only that brief reference in the will.

"Oh. You see, she's stopped going to *shodo* club after school. Which is odd because she's always loved it, excelled in it in fact. She used to spend hours practicing it with her grandfather on weekends. Sometimes she'd pester her mother to paint something just so she could inscribe it with a poem. And now, boom, she says the *shodo* club is boring. But it's not like she's picked up another hobby or a boyfriend or anything. And she's a *senpai,* you know, a bigwig in the club this year, but what does she do? She bails out and takes off for gardens and temples and long solitary walks. She doesn't see any of her friends. And she's obsessed with the ash. Did she say anything to you at the gardens? Was she alone?"

"Alone? Yes. She sort of followed me."

"And talked to you?"

"Well, eventually. She wanted to show me something she'd written."

"Shodo?"

"No, not *shodo."*

"What?"

Caitlin hesitated. "She asked me not to tell you about it."

"I'll be damned," Carl said. "Akiko was right."

"Well, I don't know if I'd call what she did confiding in me. We just talked a little, and I had her take a taxi home with me. I was a bit worried."

"Why? What did she write?"

"Well. . ." Caitlin folded her arms and saw the paper flapping before her again—Hiroshi was right, she couldn't very well keep its contents from this man. "A will," she finally said.

Carl stopped in the middle of the street and stared. "A will?" he said, incredulous. "What in hell would she want with a will?" Then he hunched over as though she'd landed a blow in his gut. "Jesus," he whispered. His arms hung limp at his sides, and afraid he might sit down right there on the pavement, where a taxi might mow him down as it careened around the bend, Caitlin ushered him over to the edge of the road beside the trickling gutter. He stood still for a while then began walking again, slowly. He opened and closed his mouth, periodically turning as though he were about to speak, then shaking his head and taking another deliberate step forward. They looped back around the block, and in a thin voice, he finally asked, "You think she's that low?"

"I don't know." Caitlin thrust her hands into her pockets and shrugged her shoulders. "I mean, I don't know her very well. I suppose she did have a pretty low opinion of herself that day, but she wouldn't tell me why she wrote it."

"A will, for Christ's sake. Do you have it?"

"No, she took it back, I wouldn't sign it."

"My God, I'd like to peer inside that head of hers. Just crawl around in between all those cerebral folds for a while and find out what the hell's going on."

Caitlin didn't know what to say. "This is sudden then?" she asked.

"Sudden, Christ. News flash." Not far from the house, he stopped again in the middle of the empty street. "And this hang-up with the ash. It's perverse. I try pretending it's not, but it is. I could handle curiosity, but this is bizarre." He seemed angered now, and Caitlin wondered what he might say tomorrow if the impression of Naomi's angel were still clearly defined beneath his shelf of withering bonsai. But then his body collapsed inward again. His skin was sallow and ochred by the street lamp, and the bones in his face jutted gauntly. "You know, if we were in the States, I'd march her straight to a child psychiatrist or go into family therapy. But here, Christ, it's just not done as much. Akiko won't hear of it—she says Naomi would be branded. And true, she's had a hard enough time with bullying as it is, for being of mixed blood, and at times, for just being herself. Anyone different in Japan has a rough time, as you well know, but *kids* who stick out, they're tormented. I'm sure what she's told us is only a fraction of what she's really endured over the years: her milk cartons spit into, shoes pissed on, things she's touched shunned, her words ignored, and the hitting—clapped on the head for the slightest misstep. And incredibly, the teachers, for the most part, condone it. There are never consequences for the kids dishing it out, there's never any concerted effort to make it stop, just a bit of hand-wringing about *ijime* and talk of more studies that ought to be done to shed light on the problem. Look, can I ask you a favor?" he asked, putting his hand on Caitlin's shoulder.

"Sure."

"I know it's not fair pulling you into this, but you being a female and nearer her age than me or Akiko, and being outside the family and all, should she confide in you further, would you keep us advised?"

"Of course. I would have said something the other day, but then you invited me over, so I decided to wait." Caitlin knew this wasn't quite true.

"I guess we'll have to talk to her."

"Well, maybe I should try first," Caitlin said, regretting her words almost immediately. She didn't need any more complications in her life. Especially in July. But she'd already spoken, so she added, "I promised I wouldn't say anything to you. I suppose I should tell her why I did."

"Hey, by all means. Just give me the word, the all clear. Maybe you two could take an outing together or something, a day trip, if you have the time, that is. You could use our car. Do you drive?" Caitlin nodded. "Well, you're welcome to it. Anytime."

"That'd be nice. I could have her give me a tour or something."

"Great. If you don't mind. I mean it, consider it yours, we'll pay for gas and all. Maybe I'll bring this up later on and see how she takes to the idea. But now," he took a deep breath—they'd arrived back at the front gate—"for Naomi's sake, I suppose we ought to put up some kind of a front while we have dessert. As if we were just discussing transitive verbs or gerunds or something."

"Right. Or compound subjects," Caitlin said.

Carl exploded with laughter and slapped his thigh. "Compound subjects, compound subjects, that's a good one," he said over and over, eyes tearing from jarring spasms of relief that echoed off the houses and skitted into the air. Caitlin stared up into the dark patches of sky between peaked tile roofs, wondering how she'd come to be standing with this man on the cracked concrete walkway of his front garden, in a city shadowed by an active volcano, thousands of miles from the murky confluence of rivers where she'd been born. She found a faint star and held it in her gaze as she waited for him to finish laughing and open the gate.

Five

SATURDAY MORNING Caitlin lugged two kitchen chairs out to her balcony and with a dictionary as a lap desk and one chair as a footrest, sat down to write her father a letter. Penning the date on the aerogram, July 13, 1985, her breath caught. The day before. She thought to turn the three into an eight and mail it after the 18th, but shook her head and wrote on:

Dear Dad,

Long time since I've written, I know, I know. Your letters pile up, you're too diligent. Rainy season blues is my excuse. And this ash. To think I could have landed any- where along this archipelago and I'm dropped in the one city that sits opposite a volcano that decides to start hack- ing this year. First thing I do every morning is check the ash report for the direction of the plume. Mounds of ash are everywhere, trains affected, street sweepers can't keep up, people dress covered head to foot and drive with wind- shield wipers and headlights on and skid all over the roads. Neighbors greet each other with ash small talk. During the rainy season here it rained sludge—my windows were stained and filthy. Underfoot it was a silty mess, every- where ash mud. Now the rains have ended and here it is only July and already everyone is waiting for fall when the wind tends to drive the ash the other way—clear to Hawaii I hope.

So, Mom and Lee are down in Pittsburgh again. Happy for

you, happy for them. We all seem to get along better apart.

Teaching hasn't changed. I'm giving up trying to encour-
age students who don't want to use English—I'd rather
practice my Japanese. I'm little more than a curiosity at
most schools, every hair and freckle scrutinized. And I hate
fitting their stereotype of Americans. Often wish I had
brown skin, brown eyes, and dark hair, just to make a
point.

Every letter you ask about my Japanese. No, haven't re-
enrolled in a class, but Hiroshi keeps me challenged with
vocabulary. It's just my reading and writing that suffer. I
work from my texts every other day or so and buy Japanese
newspapers now and then, and I met a young Japanese-
American, no, a mix—Japanese and American—who does
shodo. I'm thinking of having her give me lessons. Actually
I met her whole family—American father, Japanese mother, both artists. More interesting than most of the people I
know here. I guess that's a comment on how dull I find
this teaching life. Practically all that the teachers talk about
is school. But why shouldn't they, I suppose, with six- and
seven-day work weeks.

Vacation's not far off. Hope to do some traveling with
friends. Might go up to Hagi, maybe as far as Hiroshima. I
want to see some new territory. What are you working on
this summer? Have you switched into sabbatical mode?
When are you planning to come over? I hope your
research can wait till after summer, my plans are all firmed
up for August. Best of luck with whatever.

Love, Caitlin

She addressed the aerogram and sealed it. Evasive correspondence, considering the date, she admitted to herself as she brought
the chair back into the kitchen; certainly nothing to match her
father's long ruminations, but a letter nonetheless. She slid it into

her back pocket, then headed out of the apartment, took her bike down the steps, and on the way into town, dropped the aerogram into a mailbox.

Just that morning, she and Naomi had finalized plans to visit the volcanic highlands north of the bay on Sunday. Caitlin hadn't driven, herself in full control minus Hiroshi or any other presumptive male, since her winter vacation, so from the mailbox she biked to a bookstore and bought a hefty all-Japan road atlas as if they'd be heading for some of Honshu's distant peaks instead of a national forest featured on road signs throughout the city. If the excursion went well, she was thinking, there might be other trips.

She'd been hasty in making plans, she admitted to herself on her ride back home, but then as she sat on the floor of her room and scrutinized the detailed inserts of Kirishima and Ebino Kogen, trying to envision the different routes snaking up to the crater lakes, she told herself she'd had no choice after her talk with Carl, that Naomi needed her, and that postponement of an outing could wring disaster. Yet throughout the discussion late Friday evening over Akiko's sweet potato tarts and coffee, Caitlin had repeatedly ignored Hiroshi's voice in her ear, reminding her of their Sunday plans to try spearfishing. Carl and Naomi had even proposed other dates and destinations—a trip the following Saturday south to Mt. Kaimon or an after-school ferry ride to Sakurajima—but Caitlin herself had suggested and finally insisted on Sunday and Ebino Kogen.

A teacher from her base school had once driven her up to the volcanic peaks, to the shrine and alongside one of the crater ponds, but a fine, cold fog had sucked in close to the car and relented not a single expansive view until they'd descended back into the red pines. She remembered the prawn-shaped plumes of pampas grass hissing over the highlands when they stepped out of the car, and now, sprawled on the tatami mats in her apartment, she repeated the Japanese name, *susuki, susuki, susuki,* trying to evoke pictures of the wind-flustered slopes. She'd always aimed to return to the area for hiking but never had, and Carl's offer of the family car had reawakened her intent.

Caitlin picked up the phone and dialed Hiroshi's house to explain the change in plans. His mother answered. *"He's already at the beach, Keito-san*—*left, let's see, about an hour ago. But come visit us anyhow,*" she invited. "*Unless you're on your way to the beach, too, of course. It's been so long since we've seen you.*"

"*Well, actually, I am on my way,*" Caitlin said, deciding at that very moment. "*But I promise to come over soon.*" As she replaced the receiver, she made a note to remember Hiroshi's mother the following day with a Kirishima souvenir.

Caitlin stepped out of her clothes and slipped into her saltwater bathing suit. But as she pulled the straps over her shoulders and felt the taut fabric pressing against her stomach and breasts, the paralyzing dread of crowds, of any sort of company, that afflicted her so often this time of year returned. She stood vacillating, tempted to tear off the tank suit and change back, but the idea of waiting to tell Hiroshi until evening, when Misawa, Mina, and the others would more likely be within earshot, seemed worse. Resolved, she pulled a T-shirt and shorts over her suit and left the apartment.

On the bus she rehearsed her explanation in Japanese, running phrases through her mind, until, bored with the repetition, she let her thoughts wander. When the bus passed under a bridge, and in a moment of darkness she caught her reflection smiling in the window, she realized that for the first time in weeks she was truly looking forward to meeting up with Hiroshi's circle of friends: Misawa, Uma-chan, Naoko, Kosuke, Mina, and sometimes others.

Caitlin had always been grateful to spot them in a crowd; they called out to her and claimed her, shielded her from oglers, and established her before other beachgoers as one who knew her way around. They released her from her roles as teacher and foreigner and except for Kosuke, hardly slowed their Japanese on her account. These friends that gathered on the narrow stretch of city beach to windsurf, or to cluster around those who did, were a constant for Caitlin—always jesting and easy, brushing aside hints of more serious topics. Political issues were rarely debated, and if biting sarcasm or serious talk leaked into the conversation someone was sure to say *kurai*—dark, or *tsumaranai*—boring, deftly changing the subject.

And Caitlin had usually welcomed the levity. She'd been introduced to Misawa, and hence his friends and Hiroshi, through a teacher from Caitlin's school, and since February she'd been included in their activities. Whether perched on stools along a pub bar or sprawled on the dark sand facing the hulking mass of Sakurajima, with them Caitlin had the soothing sense of hydroplaning over time instead of her usual wading and plodding through it.

Since June though, she'd succumbed to what they'd call dark thoughts. None of them outwardly suffered from malaise, which seemed to have no place in a society where people chimed *"Be patient,"* and *"Persevere,"* to even minor complaints. The saying "When in pain, it's best to be alone," seemed to dictate the behavior expected of her. She often wondered how many months or years she needed to know someone before even slightly personal thoughts or complaints could be shared without that predictable stiffening, awkward silence, and blinking of eyes, that said she'd revealed more of herself than she should have. Not that she wanted to pour her heart out, but aware that unless she and Hiroshi were alone she was expected to keep her somber thoughts to herself, and that jabs of cynicism or fragments of discontent too often surfaced in her conversations in summer, she'd resorted to avoiding their company altogether.

As she stepped onto the swath of parched sand, she searched the bay for Hiroshi's sail. When Mina jumped up to greet her she waved her arm and trudged along toward the usual cluster of boards and mats.

"Keito-san!" Mina squeezed Caitlin's arm and leaned back to look her up and down. *"Are you well? You look thin . . . it's been a while."*

"I'm fine, thanks. Sorry, I've been busy. How's your family?" Mina's father and mother ran a small restaurant where Mina worked and where Hiroshi, Misawa, and everyone often gathered.

"Oh, fine. My father still wants you to teach him English. I told him you're busy and anyway that you're forgetting English just like you said to say, but he said he'll cook you a whole hirame *for every new word you teach him."* Caitlin smiled at this new tactic; she loved Mina's father's crisp fried flounder.

But the ash plume suddenly caught her attention. *"Just look at it,"* she muttered. A mere four kilometers away, the nearest lava fields rose out of the bay, climbing gradually, then more abruptly to the clustered peaks of the volcano where the voluminous column of ash boiled up angrily, as high again as the highest peak.

"*Incredible, isn't it,*" Mina said. "*I think I'm glad there's so little wind today.*"

The others stood to greet her and shifted to make space on the straw mats, and Caitlin beamed, pleased to be welcomed so warmly after being evasive for weeks. They pointed out Hiroshi creeping along on his board. When he slowly came about she stood and waved to him, and with one hand he gallantly blew her a kiss. Misawa shouted back in English, "I love you too, Hiroshi," and Mina clapped him on the forehead.

Kosuke offered Caitlin some beer from a plastic jug, but she declined: "*I'm swimming today.*" He looked surprised and Caitlin blushed.

Uma-chan, or "horse-boy"—so nicknamed, it'd been explained to Caitlin, because of his long face—leaned back beside Kosuke against a small cooler that was half-buried in the sand, and they resumed a discussion that Caitlin quickly realized concerned the August camping trip. Caitlin turned, still facing the group but away from the turbulent plume, a maneuver she frequently executed to enable herself to pretend that ash wasn't really spewing forth by the ton, that Sakurajima wasn't really looming there across the bay. When she'd settled herself, Uma-chan asked her preference of destinations—the island Kikaijima or the park around Mt. Kaimon. She said she thought Kikaijima, for the snorkeling.

"*You are coming aren't you? Hiroshi told you, didn't he?*" Kosuke enunciated each syllable more clearly than necessary. Caitlin asked when the trip was.

"*August 9 to 11. Right before O-Bon.*"

"*Oh, I'll be traveling,*" Caitlin said. Mina asked where, and Caitlin explained, "*Kyoto. Maybe Nara and Osaka too, but mostly Kyoto.*"

"*Are you crazy?!!*" Uma-chan exclaimed. "*Don't you know how hot Kyoto is in August?*"

"*As if it isn't hot here!*" Mina said.

"*Well, hot, but we don't have so much humidity, or the pollution.*"

"*No, no pollution, just ash,*" Mina said sarcastically. Then she asked Caitlin, "*Why Kyoto?*"

"*Well, sightseeing. And I need to buy shoes and English books.*"

"*You go all the way to Kyoto to buy books? Don't you know about the post?*" Uma-chan chided.

"*Do you have friends up there?*" Mina asked.

Caitlin nodded but didn't offer to explain. Mina waited, but when Caitlin looked away, so did she. Caitlin was closer to Mina than to any of the others; she was the only one in the group besides Hiroshi with whom she'd interacted on an individual basis. They'd met at a coffee shop several times, Mina had introduced her at her favorite hair salon and helped Caitlin purchase a gas hot-water heater for her apartment, and they'd gone to a concert and once visited Mina's favorite public bath together. But Caitlin had never yet confided in Mina anything of weight, had not yet felt it appropriate; even when they'd been alone, group demeanor had seemed to prevail. It seemed to Caitlin that relationships in Japan seemed to hover on the surface much longer than in the States, and she doubted that even if the rest of the group weren't surrounding them now, she'd explain further to Mina.

Uma-chan was still rambling. "*Kyoto's big and dirty, you know. It's not charming—just the sights are. And you can't swim there. There's no ocean, no bay.*"

"*She's not going there to swim,*" Naoko said.

"*Shouldn't swim during O-Bon anyway,*" Misawa warned. "*The spirits come from the water.*"

Naoko rolled her eyes and turned to Caitlin. "*Keito, go to Gion. And Pontocho. You might see a geisha.*"

"*And go to a club for me,*" Mina said. She began to bounce to an imaginary beat.

"*We have clubs here,*" Kosuke argued.

"*Not like there.*"

"*Who needs them,*" Uma-chan said. "*Stay here, Keito-san. Kyoto's a bore—just temples and noise. And heat. I went in August once and I thought I'd die.*"

"*But the stores are better. And in Osaka you can buy anything,*" Naoko said, "*even large shoes.*" Caitlin tucked her feet under her bottom, and they all laughed; Misawa called them surfboards.

When Hiroshi dropped the sail and dragged the board onto the sand, Caitlin left the others to greet him. She was surprised to find him glistening so dark and sleek, his slight ring of winter beer fat now completely vanished, a sharp reminder of how many weeks she'd been away from the beach, and how many weeks since they'd been to a hotel. Wet, his hair seemed longer than just two days before, especially with his bangs draped over one eye. She leaned forward and pecked him on the cheek. Hiroshi sat down on the board and squinting up at her, described the lousy wind conditions and the heavy ash today, yesterday, every day since the rains had ended. *"But you're here. So I'm satisfied."* He put out his hand and when she tried to pull him up he tugged her down beside him. *"Are you swimming today?"* he asked.

"If you go out again. I haven't been to the pool yet."

"You'll be faster than me in this wind. I'm hungry though. After I eat, okay?" He rose and turned to trudge toward the group up on dry sand. She stood too but remained by the board. *"Come on up with me,"* he said, walking away, his hand outstretched, expecting her to follow.

"Hiroshi . . ." He pivoted. She waited until he'd returned and squared himself in front of her. *"Hiroshi, I'm sorry, but tomorrow I have to cancel."*

"Cancel?" The undraped eyebrow rose.

"I have to go to Kirishima."

"Kirishima? Why? A school outing?" Hiroshi always assumed Caitlin's teaching obligations to be greater than they were. He knew well the time demanded of his friends who'd become teachers, and Caitlin had allowed him to remain slightly deceived, even though as a foreigner she was exempt from countless hours and all sorts of duties. She liked to keep some time to herself, and things did come up; when teachers asked her to join them she wasn't supposed to refuse.

"No, not for school," she said. *"For that girl I met last week. I had dinner at her house last night. When I told her father about the will, he asked for my help."*

"By going to Kirishima?" Hiroshi looked skeptical.

"It's a day trip. Just the two of us. Maybe she'll talk to me more there. And maybe she'll tell me things she wouldn't tell her parents, or her friends."

Hiroshi stood silent before her. Then he flicked his hair back and shrugged as if to say "so be it," and looked up toward the group.

"But I'm still free tonight," Caitlin said. *"If you want to* kyukei," she whispered, using the euphemism "rest" for stopping at a hotel.

He laughed. "Okay," he said. *"But now I want to eat. Then you can swim."*

▲ ▲ ▲

Late that evening Caitlin and Hiroshi stepped from the car in the concealed parking lot of a garish neon-faced hotel and hastened toward the lobby. Hiroshi always kept his head down and ushered her along with a sense of urgency until they were safe inside whatever hotel they were visiting. Sometimes he made her hide her blond hair in a big hat and covered her with an overcoat, and never did they visit the same place twice. Caitlin had asked him once if he were worried about being seen with her, but he'd laughed in surprise: *"No, not me being seen with you. It's you with me. You're a teacher, remember. A blond, foreign, female teacher. And you're known all over this city."*

In the tiny lobby, they glanced at the photos of vacant rooms, chose one, then spoke through a microphone to an attendant behind a Plexiglas partition and asked for two hours. They paid, took the keys, and rode the elevator up.

Inside the room, Hiroshi sat down on the bed, sighed, and relaxed into his old self again. Caitlin turned in circles on the carpet. *"Now I understand. No windows—that's why I always feel . . .,"* she resorted to English, "claustrophobic. You know?" she gestured to the concrete walls around them.

"You want windows, in this kind of hotel?"

"Why not? You could close the curtains."

Hiroshi dismissed this with a snort through his nose; he was already undressing. Caitlin placed her bag on the TV, withdrew her diaphragm, and stepped into the bathroom. The first time they'd made love, Hiroshi, having never seen one before, clowned with it—put it on his head for a hat and listened to it like one end of a telephone receiver. Caitlin had had to have another American from the program send her spermicide from a pharmacy in Tokyo—there was none to be had, as far as she could tell, in all of Kagoshima.

When Hiroshi pulled her down onto the bed, they laughed at its bounce. She nuzzled his neck—if nothing else in this relationship, the fit was certainly right; they were the same height, and the curves and contours of their lean bodies dovetailed perfectly. Hiroshi undressed her and kissed her lightly behind her knees, under her ears, on her eyelids, and she shivered from his touch, from the roaring AC chill, and from wondering, as she had when they'd last made love, if this would be their last time. The further into July they got, with every day of the calendar's relentless progress, the likelier it seemed their relationship's end was near. She'd never made it through a summer with anyone, she kept thinking, and the sudden, pervading sense of doom nearly marooned her right there on the hotel sheets.

She forced herself to follow Hiroshi's moves, rolling about and kissing in a feign of desire, all the while wondering whether she should just stop him right then and spare them both the pain of extracting themselves later from a more complicated, prolonged relationship. But then, as the cloud seemed to descend upon her and nearly suffocate her, a will to do battle returned, and in desperation she urged Hiroshi inside her. With their heads toward the footboard, and their feet on the pillows, they pumped on top of the covers, the fluorescent ceiling light flickering and humming directly above them.

Afterward Hiroshi dozed off, mouth agape, and Caitlin stole into the bathroom. From the toilet she heard him call out to her. He liked her to stay languid beside him as long as possible. She wrapped her arms about her; the air conditioner was on high, and the stainless, porcelain, and tile bathroom was cold even to look at.

When she wriggled back under the covers where Hiroshi was waiting, he turned on his side to face her. She pressed against him for warmth, and they lay there studying each other's eyes above the top of the sheet until Hiroshi abruptly rose. He climbed over her and swung open the door of the small refrigerator. *"Want anything?"*

"Is there whiskey?" she asked. He nodded. *"With water,"* she said.

He climbed back into bed with two full glasses, and Caitlin adjusted the pillows behind them. They sipped at their drinks, and Hiroshi told Caitlin the latest news of the family trucking company, then Caitlin described her dinner with Naomi's family. When they'd both paused, Hiroshi cleared his throat. *"Keito, Misawa says you're going to Kyoto that week of O-Bon."*

Caitlin shut her eyes. *"Yes, I decided."*

"*Alone?*"

"*Alone.*"

Hiroshi turned his glass around and around in his hands. "*Why?*"

"*Oh, Hiroshi, I've explained already. Because I need to travel. By myself. That's not okay?*"

"*But you're always by yourself now. You almost never come to the beach anymore. And I have that whole week off.*"

Caitlin pressed her eyes closed. "*Please Hiroshi, we can go together another time. This time I need to go alone.*"

He eyed her suspiciously. "*Why?*"

Caitlin laughed. "*Don't worry. I might look up some old friends. And maybe some of the other Americans in the teaching program. That's all. I have to keep it open though. And I need to go by myself.*"

"*I see.*" Hiroshi lay still for a moment, then threw back the covers on his side, leapt over her, and disappeared into the bathroom. Caitlin set her glass down on a plastic bedside table and sank under the covers. She listened to him urinate and flush and waited for his return, trying to decide how much more she ought to explain. But when the water thundered on the glass door of the shower, she started. They always showered together after making love. She glanced at her watch; they'd been there less than an hour.

Naked and shivering she stood and rifled through her bag for a hundred-yen coin and popped it into the slot for the television; she'd make the most of their two hours. She wriggled back into bed, patted the covers down close along her legs, and only half-listened to the variety show host pressing contestants with lewd questions and laughing outrageously while Hiroshi washed himself clean of their lovemaking.

Six

THEY HARDLY spoke the rest of the evening and managed only a perfunctory kiss when Hiroshi dropped Caitlin off at her apartment. Inside, she changed into a nightshirt and crawled into her futon, then lay in the dark reviewing her vacation plans and her exclusion of Hiroshi. She was reluctant to enlarge the rift between them, but even if the Oides never answered the letter she planned to write, she would still go to Kyoto, she might visit Iwakura, her old neighborhood, and she wanted to be free to venture there alone, without having to fabricate excuses. He could join her for a Nara side trip, but to limit him to that would entail explaining why she didn't want him in Kyoto. And she just didn't want to delve into the past with him; their foothold in the present was shaky enough.

She ran her justifications around and around, long after midnight, until she finally threw back the damp sheets, sat down at the kitchen table, and began a letter to her sister to clear Hiroshi, Kyoto, and the Oide family from her mind. "How's Pittsburgh?" she wrote. "Want some ash to make it like the sooty old days? How's waitressing? Or is it bartending? You never write, Lee-beans, except when it's for Ma Ruth. Does Mom censor *all* your thoughts? Just because she refuses to accept the fact that I'm back here doesn't mean you . . ." It was no use; she couldn't restrain the venom. She put her head down on her arms and finally dozed off. Later she awoke under the glare of the overhead light with a stiff neck and a loose puddle of drool blurring the few scrawled sentences of the letter.

She settled back on her futon but again could only doze. She kept seeing Naomi—on a sailboard, on the high wall of Caitlin's balcony, at the edge of a train platform—and just as Caitlin drifted off Naomi would topple, and Caitlin would convulse on the futon, lurching to grab the girl. Caitlin shook her head, covered her face with her pillow, but no matter how hard she willed Naomi out of her mind, she reappeared—perched on the high dive, leaning out a gym window, or worse, through Caitlin's fogged goggles at the bottom of the pool.

She awoke shortly after dawn with a pulsing forehead and sat up to read from a Chekhov collection she'd borrowed from one of the Americans in Fukuoka at the last meeting of Kyushu teaching fellows. Sunlight soon outlined her rain shutters, and she could hear her neighbors beginning their laundry and hanging futons, but Caitlin remained holed up in her apartment instead of appearing on her balcony to chat over the partition as she sometimes did on weekends. She gulped aspirin with her orange juice, then shortly before eight, squinting into a brightness that made her eyes ache, she caught a bus for Naomi's neighborhood.

Outside the Johnsons' gate a cat was tormenting a grass lizard; one paw held down the body while the other batted at the separated, writhing tail. She grimaced as she walked past—she'd watched cats do the same in the Kyoto shrine compound. She'd even played with the detached tails herself.

Inside, at the Johnsons' kitchen table, Caitlin stirred creamer into her coffee, while Akiko flitted about the kitchen with a frenzy that made Caitlin wonder if there'd been a change in plans, if all four of them were now going to the highlands. The shopping bag that Akiko dashed to and from brimmed with the ties of bright silken squares holding containers of food, and Akiko only paused in the chair opposite Caitlin long enough to begin a sentence before jumping up for some forgotten condiment—salt, pickled eggplant, soy sauce. Caitlin couldn't shake her dreams, and she wanted to blurt that a high altitude destination would be a mistake. The will had begun to seem trifling to Caitlin when Naomi had agreed to an outing, but now she wondered.

Naomi and Carl descended the stairs one after the other, and Caitlin roused herself. Carl snatched up the car keys and tossed them to Caitlin. "C'mon out. I'll show you its quirks." Surrounded by all the vinyl and Carl's gratitude in the little sedan, Caitlin calmed and even pulled out her map to show Carl the proposed route. When he nodded with approval, she asked, "How's she been?" then added tentatively, "Am I a fool to take her into the mountains?"

"A fool? God no. She'll love it. She seemed better this weekend, quiet now and then, but nowhere near as tense. You're a saint; she really likes you."

Naomi and Akiko came out and set the bag of provisions and assorted other paraphernalia on the backseat, and after the parents had been assured that Naomi had a jacket, umbrella, hat, handkerchief, tissues, extra film, and lip balm, they waved the girls off. Caitlin backed the car out and tooted the horn.

When Naomi had guided them out to the main road, Caitlin said, "Wheels," and grinned.

"I brought tapes," Naomi said, grabbing a duffel from the backseat and withdrawing a handful of cassettes. "You like Checkers?"

"Sure, not too loud."

Naomi slid the cassette in, adjusted the volume, and rolled the window down. She sputtered, then frantically rolled it back up. Caitlin smiled. "I thought you liked it."

"Sometimes." Naomi batted at the ash filtering down onto their legs.

"Wait till we're north of it. The wind's already up."

Naomi nodded. When they were stopped at a light near the edge of town, she asked, "What's the plan?"

"I thought we'd go straight up to Ebino Kogen before the clouds move in. That okay?"

"Fine."

"You've been there, right?"

"A few times, when I was little. We used to stay at one of the big hotels. But Dad hates crowds. So now we go to these dull places way out in the boon . . . what do you say?"

"Boondocks?"

"Right, in the boondocks, and sit and look at each other and eat these long meals and read. I do homework. It's a real thrill. I'm glad he didn't come—he'd already be moaning about bites on the landscape . . . "

"You mean blights."

"Whatever. Blights on the landscape and cursing the traffic."

When the long climb into the foothills began, they drove with their windows open to the sweet hot air. From their first scenic vista they could distinguish fields of taro and sweet potatoes, dots of orange and yellow in the citrus groves, and the clear combed rows of rice paddies at the foot of cedar slopes. Then, as the car droned higher and more lowland wooded hills emerged, Kagoshima's gray sprawl and smoking Sakurajima came into view on the bay. They could make out the humps of the three islands near Kajiki, and Naomi taught Caitlin the names: Okikojima, Hetakojima, and the smallest, Bentenjima, nicknamed Warship Island after being mistaken for a ship and bombed during the war.

In the high plains and craters, thin clouds were already collecting, wisps that slipped by and only momentarily obstructed their views. The grasses undulated above the lot where they parked, the landscape below was a mosaic of textured browns and greens, and fat dragonflies sailed in the gusts as Caitlin and Naomi matched near and distant peaks to features on a bronze relief map. Caitlin felt amused and superior using her index finger on the world below.

They hiked up from the parking lot through thickets of bamboo grass and hardwoods, where even a nonchalant deer grazed, to a lookout amid the *susuki* grass above a pair of gaping crater ponds. But standing with Naomi on the high wind-blown rim gazing down at water far below disquieted Caitlin. Subtly, she thought, she took the girl's arm. Naomi, peeling a mandarin orange, just as subtly turned to shake her off and said, "I think they skate here in winter. I've always wanted to try it. Can you imagine?" Caitlin tilted her head and accepted the crescent of orange Naomi offered her. "Suppose there are fish?"

"Don't know," Caitlin said.

"How would they have gotten here, though," Naomi asked herself.

They returned to the car and drove on to an area of steaming, spurting miniature geysers, where Naomi hid behind yellow-green sulfur spouts and dared Caitlin to go near the hottest, yellowest rocks. They composed photos of themselves before spitting steam, dropped pebbles into boiling springs, and laid their hands over warm rivulets before deciding they were hungry. They fetched the mats and shopping bag from the car and, with a handle each, trudged upward alongside towers of stone cairns to find a quiet protected spot.

"Picnic on the moon," Caitlin said. They had reached a wide elevated depression hidden from the tourists below and from which they could see no green at all, nothing but the now clouded sky above and the black, gray, and white of the torqued and mottled rocks. There was an energy to the depression, which seemed fluid with rocks so oddly placed and fused to one another that they made Caitlin uneasy, as if at any moment they, too, might be flung up from the earth.

They kicked a few stones aside, spread two straw mats, and unpacked their banquet. "My God," Caitlin said, "your mother must have been up since five. Soup, fried chicken, *chirashi-zushi,* daikon salad . . . look, even towels." Naomi shrugged, then for some time the conversation remained centered on food. Caitlin had to eat facing into the wind to keep from chewing on her hair; she'd forgotten her cap and an elastic.

After a while, Naomi lay back on the mat and nibbled at a black sesame rice ball, glimpsing between bites to see what the filling would be. When she bit into pickled plum she smiled, then, surveying their moon depression and the vaporous clouds skitting over them, said, "Perfect. This is good, isn't it?"

"It's wonderful. Thanks to your father for the car."

Naomi smirked. She finished her rice ball and flicked a few black seeds from her palm. Then she tilted her head and eyed Caitlin. "My father asked you to bring me here, didn't he? When you were out walking."

Caitlin held a fried chicken morsel aloft. She swallowed. "No, he didn't ask," she said tentatively. "We just both thought something like this might be a good idea."

"He never lets anyone else drive the car, you know, not even my uncle next door."

"Doesn't your mother drive?"

"Not if she can help it. Dad frets too much, it's easier just to put him behind the wheel. She takes the bus to the culture center when she teaches."

Caitlin finished her chicken and unsheathed a knife to cut slices of white peach. "Well, he didn't ask me directly, if that's what you mean, I just suggested a day trip and he offered the car." She felt transparent.

Naomi reached over for a peach crescent and popped it into her mouth. "You know, I bet I can guess every single question you plan to ask me today. Why I don't go to *shodo* club, why I go to gardens, why everything." Her voice had soured, and Caitlin straightened. "Why does everybody focus on me?" Naomi continued. "Other people change and nobody minds. Big deal, I quit the club." She flipped over onto her stomach.

Caitlin spoke to the back of Naomi's head. "You wrote a will, too. Don't forget that."

"Yeah, one you *said* you wouldn't mention."

Caitlin glanced about the depression. She wiped her sticky hands and the knife, resheathed it, and set it down. Then she stood to toss pebbles, aiming for the top rock of a distant cairn. "Look, I'm sorry about that, but I have an idea," she said between tosses. "If you let me ask questions for a while, then we can switch and you can ask me whatever you want. You can give *me* the third degree."

To her surprise, Naomi sat up. "Okay. Shoot."

Caitlin laughed nervously and settled on the mat again. "All right then, first, tell me why you don't go to *shodo* anymore."

Naomi heaved a great sigh. "Can I have some more tea?" Caitlin filled their cups and waited. Naomi sipped and finally said, "I'll have to give it up sooner or later, so I may as well do it now."

"What do you mean, give it up?"

"Just what I said. Give it up. Stop the club. Oh, forget it, you won't understand." Naomi put down her tea and hugged her knees. Caitlin waited but Naomi just narrowed her eyes. Finally she heaved a sigh and said, *"Shodo* doesn't change anything, there's no point, that's all."

"But what's quitting going to change?"

"I won't be trying to prove myself at least."

"Prove yourself at what?"

"I'm a 'half,' an *ainoko,* get it? You're not. You think it's cool to have mixed heritage, but here it's a curse. So just forget it. I had to quit the club." Naomi lay on her back and settled her forearms over her eyes. "I'm just a schizo," she said.

Caitlin chucked a handful of stones at the cairn. "Look, why not stick with the club. Do whatever else you want to do alongside it. It sounds like you're really good at *shodo*. And you're lucky to have something you're good at. All I can do is swim. You should teach me *shodo*—it might help me learn my *kanji*." Naomi's lips remained sealed in a thin line. Caitlin dropped her voice to a near whisper. "Look, you don't have to tell me why you're doing what you're doing, but you can't just write wills every time things aren't the way you want them to be."

"Oh, forget about that. I never should have shown it to you. I didn't think you'd make such a big deal about it."

"A big deal? How can it not be a big deal?"

"It just isn't. Everybody thinks about suicide."

In that high rocky depression Caitlin suddenly caught a sickening whiff of river water and heard a roaring current in her ears. She shivered on the mat and ran a hand up and down her left leg. Slapping at her calf, in a voice unnecessarily loud, she said, "But not everyone thinks about it enough to write a will."

"Well, forget about it. I'm not going to commit suicide. I'll just stew."

Caitlin smiled at this word. "Well, stew all you want," she said. "Rant and rave. Go nuts. Just don't think about suicide."

"Okay, okay. I said forget it." Naomi sat up. "Is it my turn to ask questions yet?"

Caitlin flapped her hair away from the back of her neck. "You never answered mine." She hadn't noticed the heat at this altitude before, but suddenly she was perspiring in drips she could feel tracking down her ribs. She swung her arms. "Look, why don't we pack all this up and go back to the car. Let's just think for a while." They closed up the boxes of food and stacked them inside the bag. Naomi tossed the silk squares loose over those and looped both bag handles over her arm. Caitlin took the mats.

They came to the crest of the depression and descended back into the tourists and bus groups and the conversations clipped and muted in gusts of wind. Naomi stopped halfway down and looked at Caitlin. "When I was little, at school you know, I'd tell people I only knew Japanese. If my father came for a sports festival or something I never spoke English with him, and sometimes I pretended I didn't know him. Because if I said even a word of English, all the kids started saying, *'Gaijin! Gaijin!'* and 'Dis is a pen.'" Caitlin gently nudged her along as they made their way down the rocky path. "I always planned to go to the very best Japanese high school so I could take the top university entrance exams, you know, prove myself."

"So what happened?"

Naomi stopped and gestured to a cluster of Japanese tourists gathered about a guide with a bullhorn and yellow flag: "I finally got it through my thick head that I'll never be Japanese in *their* eyes."

"But Naomi, you are Japanese."

"Half-Japanese. And officially not even that until recently. Did you know that? They just changed the laws. Before I was only American. Citizenship went by the father's nationality. It didn't matter that I was born here of a Japanese mother. But now I'm both. Till I'm twenty. Then I have to choose—Jap or ugly American." Caitlin glared at her. "You don't get it, do you?" Naomi said.

"I get *it*," Caitlin said, "but not you," and she walked ahead. She paused just before they'd reached the car. "Just forget about everyone else, Naomi. It's okay to be different." Then Caitlin remembered something. "Listen to this," she said: "When it's cold the bird perches on the tree, the duck takes to the water. Each repairs to its own refuge. The truth is the truth in each. Neither is better—there is no better or worse because there is no inequality. Where there is no inequality, the heart is tranquil and the world radiates the light of peace.'" Caitlin spoke this half to herself, surprised she could recall the words.

"What was that?" Naomi asked.

"Something my father used to tell me, words of a Zen master he admired." Caitlin smiled, amused to think that she used to roll her eyes whenever he launched into one of his lofty discourses, and here she was, quoting him verbatim.

They stepped to the side of the path for a family to pass, then Naomi said sarcastically, "Well, does the master account for crossbreeds, you know, of birds and ducks?"

"Oh, come on Naomi." Caitlin threw her free arm up in irritation. "Just be yourself, for God's sake, do what you want."

Naomi laughed, hard, as if this were the most ludicrous thing she'd ever heard. "Be yourself? Hah! You haven't been in Japan very long, have you?"

They loaded the car in silence and drove on to another scenic vista, where Caitlin consulted the map, then turned around and headed back in the direction from which they'd come. "Let's pick up our gifts," she said. The words had come out icily and she could feel Naomi eyeing her.

They stopped at a cavernous souvenir store and restaurant, where they selected boxes of local Kirishima sweets—Naomi for her mother and father and her uncle's family next door, and Caitlin for the teachers' tea table at school and Hiroshi's mother. On the way out Caitlin bought a cold can of coffee from a vending machine. She sipped it in the front seat of the car and leaned her head back on the rest. It was nearly three o'clock, and she was tired of this girl's company. "What do you think? The shrine?" she asked, trying not to sound too cold.

"If you want."

"Well, are you interested? I've been there before."

"So have I."

"Skip it?"

Naomi nodded.

"Okay. What should we do?" Naomi just shrugged. Caitlin decided to be selfish. "There are *onsen* all over. Want to have a bath?"

"Yes!" Naomi clapped her hands. Caitlin was surprised by the enthusiasm. *"Junguru buro!"*

"What?"

"Jungle baths! Let me see the map. I think I remember the name of a good one. Yes! Take a right."

They descended from the high peaks, and Naomi craned her neck searching each bend for the hotel. Finally she pointed to an enormous complex of connected buildings. "That's it!"

"It's okay just to take a bath?" Caitlin asked as she parked the car. "This looks too fancy."

But Naomi laughed, nodding emphatically, and Caitlin followed her into the hot-spring hotel. Naomi had no recollection of the interior though, and they soon found themselves wandering about long corridors, lost. "I was little when I came here," Naomi explained. Eventually they found their way through shops, game arcades, and kitchens, to the baths.

They bought shampoo and small towels from a vending machine, paid the bathing fee, and stepped behind the curtain to the women's side. There were rows of changing lockers and baskets. A school club group was just straggling out from the baths, wet and giggling, a teacher herding them along. Spotting Caitlin, they squealed, made peace signs, and giggled the same inane bits of English Caitlin heard countless times every day—"I am a girl," "Do you know me?" "What time is it?" "Dis is a pen!"—until Naomi growled, *"Baka!"*—Idiot!—to one of them.

"Hey," Caitlin said. "Ease up. If I don't mind, why should you?"

"Because I do." Naomi pulled a basket out and began undressing, tearing at the buttons on her shirt. "You'd think they lived in bubbles."

Caitlin undressed and sat down in a massage chair to wait for Naomi. "God, this place is huge," she said, and popped a coin into a slot in the chair's arm. Naomi smiled when she saw Caitlin stark naked, undulating against the vibrating seat.

With their towels and shampoos they waded through a trough of cool water and entered a terraced spa of shallow pools, waterfalls, and tropical plants. "See? *Junguru,*" Naomi said, pointing to the palm trees perched on the high wall dividing the men's and women's sides. Caitlin followed her to the washing area, a row of spigots with stools and basins running the entire length of the highest tier. Below, beyond the lowest tier, a wall of glass stretched from floor to ceiling, overlooking outdoor greenery and a view Caitlin couldn't quite make out through the steam.

Caitlin stooped and washed hurriedly at a spigot, then ran to the pool with the high slide. She swooshed down after small children into soft warm water. Other children were coming down after her so she moved aside, then sank low in the bath and cupped her hands to pour water over her head. It felt good dribbling down her face.

Naomi was still washing. Caitlin hoisted herself out for another run, and she waved at Naomi from the top of the slide, then pushed off and went careening down. She swam underwater, her thighs and breasts skimming the tiles of the shallow bath, then she sidled over to the edge. With only her head above water she watched Naomi demurely climb the ladder, pause above the waiting children, then, holding her nose with one hand, give herself a little push with the other. Caitlin clapped when Naomi sputtered over.

Caitlin didn't bother covering with her small towel as she dipped in one pool after another, testing the different temperatures, discreetly attempting a few strokes of crawl in the deepest, counting as high as she could in the hottest, and always calling for Naomi to follow. "Try that one," she said once, pointing to a bath empty of people. Naomi stuck her toe in and screeched. Caitlin laughed, and Naomi threw a bucketful of cold water at her. "You knew it was electric!" Naomi said. Caitlin nodded.

Caitlin immersed herself in all the other baths and soaked in the pool on the lowest tier that had the best view through the partially fogged glass before them, over a garden, to hills and distant villages and the vague blue tint of Kagoshima Bay with the three small islands near Kajiki and a hump that had to be Sakurajima. When her fingers and toes had become deeply wrinkled, she stepped out, pulled at a heavy wooden door, and plunked herself down on a bench inside the sauna. She spoke a word of greeting to the woman who sat baking beside her, then closed her eyes. Naomi entered and tucked herself into a corner behind Caitlin, and the other woman actually jumped when Naomi spoke to Caitlin in English. After the woman excused herself, Naomi dropped down to sit beside Caitlin, wiped a mustache of perspiration from her upper lip, and said, "Why are you here?"

"It's nice and hot."

Naomi giggled. "No, here in Japan."

"Oh, I don't know. It's good to live in another country. It clears your mind."

"Why'd you come to Japan, though? Why not Europe? Everyone goes to Europe."

"I lived in Kyoto for a year and a half when I was little, and I studied Japanese in college." This was as much as she'd told Hiroshi, more than she had told Mina.

"Oh." Naomi seemed to mull this over. "How old were you when you lived in Kyoto?" she asked after a while.

"Seven, eight."

"So that's why your accent is good. Most Americans have terrible accents. *'Kohneecheewah, oh genkee desoo kah?'"* She aped them in wide-mouthed form. "But yours is good. You purse your lips. You have Japanese friends?"

"Yes."

"A boyfriend?"

"That has nothing to do with pursing my lips."

"I didn't mean that. I meant does he speak Kagoshima dialect?"

"Sometimes."

"Have you learned any?"

"A few words. He only uses it when he doesn't want me to understand." Caitlin abruptly stood. "I'm hot, let's go." She toweled off the bench, opened the door and Naomi quickly wiped her seat and followed her out into one of the cooler baths on the upper levels.

When they had positioned themselves against pulsating jets, Naomi asked, "Well, why didn't you go back to Kyoto?"

"You can't choose where you go in my teaching program."

"Oh. You still have friends there?"

"Not really, I was little."

"None, no friends at all?"

"Well, just one family my father keeps in touch with."

"Have you visited them?"

"No."

"Are you going to?"

"Maybe. I don't know them very well. My father is the only one who still writes to them. Look, enough of the interrogation, okay?" The water felt tepid to Caitlin now, and she rose, dripping, and said, "I'll be over there." Naomi stayed put and sank down low in the pool.

Caitlin immersed herself in the hottest of the baths. She placed her towel on her head and let it drape over her face as she breathed in the steam slowly. She was grinding her teeth. She counted out what she thought to be two minutes then emerged pink and dizzy, rinsed off at the spigot, and gestured to Naomi that she was going to the changing room. She hoped Naomi wouldn't follow just yet. She'd had enough questions.

▲ ▲ ▲

Late in the afternoon, toward the base of the mountain, they stopped for ramen and mourned their return to the stifling air of the lowlands. They arrived in Kagoshima just after the sun had dropped behind the hills though, and the evening air had already begun to settle upon the city; they had missed the worst of the heat. Naomi had slept most of the way from the ramen shop, but as soon as the engine's hum quit outside her house, she perked up and began effusively thanking Caitlin. She was speaking English, but with the gestures it felt like Japanese, and Caitlin began to answer in Japanese, saying it was nothing, she'd enjoyed the day too. And she had, parts of it at least.

Akiko and Carl appeared beside the car, and Naomi extended a hand for them to smell. "Guess where we went."

"Ah," Carl said. He scratched his armpits and made monkey noises. *"Junguru buro!"*

"Yes!" Naomi shrieked. "The same one, I remembered it!"

Inside Akiko poured tea, and Caitlin took a few sips then said she had to get home to prepare for classes. "I'll drive you," Carl said, and although Caitlin at first refused, looking forward to a bus ride by herself, he insisted. It was his car she'd driven all day, she conceded; the least she could do was let him drop her off. She bade goodbye to Akiko and Naomi, and as soon as they'd pulled out of the driveway, Carl said, "So. How'd it go?"

Caitlin wasn't sure what the answer was, but she fabricated some optimism, saying that she thought Naomi would return to *shodo* soon, and in any case it seemed that she'd just been flirting with the idea of suicide, not suicide itself. She knew this was what he wanted to hear, and she was relieved to find that the rhetoric pleased him; he didn't press her for any more details. Caitlin looked out the side window, ran her fingers through her hair, and caught the faint aroma of sulfur from the baths. She didn't want to talk.

When they reached her apartment she told Carl to keep her posted on Naomi's well-being and thanked him for the use of the car.

"Nonsense," Carl said. "You're a veritable saint. You're welcome to it anytime." She pushed the car door shut, waved, and trudged up the stairs.

At her kitchen table she sank into a chair, squeezed her eyes shut, then slowly began to weep, breathy and silent. You're over-tired, she told herself, but her chest continued to snag. She poured a glass of water, sat back down, and began to curse Naomi for making her miserable. She cursed Carl, her job, her splintered family, and the whole damned ash-ridden town. Eventually she allowed herself to glance at the wall calendar above the telephone and read the date. July 14th, the anniversary. She'd been evading the thought, almost physically dodging it, all day.

She wiped her face with her palms, ran her palms over her shorts, and spread her fingers on the table. The tears stopped. She told herself to breathe evenly. It was swim or sleep, but lap-swim-ming hours at the club were over. She heated a cupful of milk in a saucepan, poured it into a mug, and drank it in a series of short, even sips.

The futon was still out, and she undressed and dropped herself onto it. If she could fall asleep right away she would be all right, she wouldn't have to talk the thoughts away, she wouldn't see that river. Just sleep, she told herself, direct to sleep. Feel the warm milk. Don't turn your head, don't look for that seven-year-old face, don't think of water, just go, straight ahead with blinders.

Seven

CAITLIN PLUNGED headlong into the Oides' letter the next day. She hauled out her Japanese language texts and placed them by the dictionaries on the kitchen table, kept at hand erasers and replacement lead for her mechanical pencil, and every evening that week labored over *kanji* and nebulous grammar choices. She gave up morning swims in favor of sleep, but each afternoon after teaching or putting in the required time at the education center, she propelled herself through an hour of laps. A couple evenings she ate at the yakitori shop, but her conscience ushered her out early and sent her home to hunch once more over the miniscule characters she tried to squeeze and coerce into logical, ordered sentences. Hiroshi called once to attempt to patch things up, but she declined to go out with him.

She'd hoped to complete a draft in two nights but discovered she hardly knew the proper format for a letter. In postcards to Hiroshi she'd always opened with "Hi," even when she followed entirely in Japanese, and she'd never had reason to write a more elaborate opening than *"How are you? I'm fine."* She retrieved all her correspondence from the shoe box in the futon closet and discovered a standard opening in several notes she'd received from Japanese teachers, but still she remained uncertain as to what was warranted in her case. After struggling for hours on an opening paragraph, her scrap paper was smudged dark with erasures.

She skipped ahead to the middle, more straightforward parts of her letter, but even after selecting *kanji,* she found herself floundering with formal endings and polite passives, and her long convoluted sentences had verbs tacked so far from their subjects that even she couldn't distill any meaning from the results. On the third day she started over and tackled the core of the letter—the dates, arrangements, the basic may-I-come-and-visit-you part. She wrote a full paragraph, then tried joining it to an opening line, scratching out sentence after sentence, then came to a complete halt, recognizing what it was that obstructed her progress: after fifteen years of silence she had no idea how much of an apology was necessary.

Caitlin turned up the air conditioner and paced the kitchen over this—the family apology, the associational apology, what she'd been excused from saying because she was only eight at the time, and what her father had said for her and for the entire family when he'd given up his fellowship and they'd returned hangdog to Pittsburgh that summer of 1970, but what, perhaps, she still needed to say. The stubborn side of her said she didn't need to apologize, accidents were accidents, but the side of her well versed in Japanese customs and the protocol her father had drilled into her told her otherwise.

She dug through the shoe box for his long letter—six pages, both sides. She'd memorized his opening:

> I'm writing about what your mother has kept us from talking about for so many years and what has probably driven you back there whether you're willing to admit it or not. Don't put this down like your mother would, Caity, please, keep reading.

She'd read those words over and over last summer, sitting bolt upright at the kitchen table—there in the same chair—before she'd had the nerve to read further.

He could tell her what to say now; he'd offer to write the Oides himself. She fingered the folded paper and felt the raised lines of his penmanship through the last page, his angular, acutely slanted letters, running one into the other, shoving the letters forward it seemed—but she refused to reread his words. She could picture that handwriting so tiny and tight in the opening lines but bold and loose by the final, "Go see them Caity, they'd love to have you." She sneered and said out loud, "I'm here because I'm here, that's all."

She'd written as much in her reply last summer, ranting through her jagged scrawl that it was no business of his to analyze her

motives and tell her what to do; she could live in Japan like any other expatriate, just because she wanted to. "I swim. Isn't that enough
for you?" she'd written.

She winced and stuffed the fat letter back into the bottom of
the shoe box, covering it with other correspondence. She'd hurt
him, she knew, but it was true, she'd wanted a better grasp on the
language, and wanted to teach, away from the States, far from family. Uji'd had little to do with her return, she reassured herself, and
she would visit the Oides simply because she happened to be in
Japan. She wanted to see the old Kyoto neighborhood that she
could picture with as much clarity as the street where Ma Ruth still
lived, or as the Brookline neighborhood where her father was probably just at this moment rising. But now she glanced uneasily about
the kitchen, chagrined. She eyed her clock and the phone, enter-
tained the thought of calling him, then shook her head. Wasn't the
incident and all the subsequent fallout his fault, too? She knew she
wouldn't be able to refrain from hurling accusations if she phoned.
She put the box of letters away, turned on the radio, and got ready
for bed.

Finally on Thursday evening, after an hour of hard crawl at the
pool, Caitlin crafted a general apology that to anyone she asked to
proofread might be interpreted as a reference to her prolonged lack
of communication, but to the Oides could be taken as a direct reference to Mie. She incorporated the sentence into a clear draft that
included all the specifics: the date she planned to catch the ferry
from Shibushi, the hour of its arrival in Osaka, the length of her
vacation, and her alternate travel plans should there be any inconvenience in her visiting at that time. She stood in the kitchen facing
the twin gas burners and read the results aloud; the words sounded
crisp, polite, and confident.

Exhilarated, she called Hiroshi, but he answered groggy with
sleep. Caitlin glanced at her watch; it was just ten o'clock. She asked
if he were okay. *"Yeah, fine. It's just, I was out till three last night,"* he
explained. Caitlin felt jealousy charge up her spine. But who was
she to complain; she'd staked out her week alone. She told him
she'd like to come over tomorrow, if he was up to it; she had sou-
venirs from Kirishima for his family. She didn't mention the letter.
Hoarsely he suggested late afternoon and Caitlin agreed.

▲ ▲ ▲

In the Naniwas' living room the following day, Caitlin sank deep into the sofa and extended her feet far out in front of her; she missed such soft pieces of furniture. All she had in her apartment were some thin *zabuton* cushions, a futon, and hard kitchen chairs.

Hiroshi had finished work and was bathing downstairs. His mother thanked Caitlin for the sweets, poured some iced tea, and joined Caitlin on the sofa. She pulled a grocery receipt from her apron pocket and squinted to decipher notes jotted on the reverse. Mrs. Naniwa always had a store of questions for Caitlin that embarrassed Hiroshi, so his mother produced pencil-marked receipts and bits of newspaper whenever he left the room, and Caitlin had occasionally even come with her own reserve of questions. Today his mother reached down into her second apron pocket and said, *"Ah yes. Today I have two pages."*

She began with short questions, jotting down Caitlin's answers. She asked if there were mosquitoes in America. Bees. Cockroaches. Geckoes. Then she asked what foreign language Caitlin had studied in high school. *"German,"* Caitlin said.

"Not Japanese?"

"They didn't offer it in my school, not then. Are you still studying English on NHK?"

"Oh yes, but I'm still at the first level. I'm so rusty," she enunciated in English and blushed. *"Now, before, you said you sometimes eat carrots, broccoli, and spinach raw. How about eggplant?"*

"No," Caitlin said with a grimace.

"Good. Now, this one is difficult. You said there are different wedding ceremonies, church weddings and weddings in Jewish temples, weddings not in churches, and so on. Now, if the bride and groom have different religions, whose religion do they use—the man's I would think. Or do they mix the ceremonies? . . ." She stuffed the papers into her apron pockets and abruptly rose; Hiroshi was standing in the doorway.

When his mother had disappeared into the kitchen, he dropped hard onto the sofa beside Caitlin. Mrs. Naniwa returned moments later with a glass of iced tea for her son, then promptly excused herself with mumbled words about tending to bills in the office. Caitlin smiled and Hiroshi shook his head. *"You're making her crazy, you know."*

Caitlin shrugged and leaned toward him to touch the wet hair falling over one eye. *"Your hair is so long."*

He flipped it back out of his eyes and asked her about Kirishima. She told him about the jungle baths. *"How is the girl?"* he asked.

"Better I guess. We talked a long time. But I'm not her teacher or anything. I don't think she cares what I say." She paused, then added quickly, *"Hiroshi, are you busy Sunday? We could try spearfishing, like we were going to before."*

He studied her. *"I've made some plans already. With Misawa,"* he said. *"What about tomorrow? Are you coming to the beach?"*

"The beach? Oh, I don't know. I have to finish this letter." She pulled the paper out of her bag. *"I need to send it tomorrow. Would you proofread it for me?"*

"Who's it to?"

"Friends of my father's, from when we lived in Kyoto. I want to visit them next month."

Hiroshi skimmed the letter. *"How well do you know them?"* he asked.

Caitlin hesitated, not sure how much to say. *"They were neighbors when we lived there, good friends. I haven't seen them since then."* He began to read, and his mouth turned up into a smirk. *"I know, I know,"* Caitlin said, *"it's a mess, but it took me all week."*

"No, not that," he laughed. *"It's just so polite—strange, coming from you."* Caitlin lightly jabbed her elbow in his side, then turned away and sat still beside him. Hiroshi had used the intimate "you" as he often did, but today Caitlin found herself tearing and blinking at the sweet sound of *kimi*. She wanted to be as close as the word—to hold him, let the truth seep from her lips to his, without her having to tell it. She put her hands up to her throat and rubbed her neck; she felt as if she were choking. She hated July.

Caitlin stared at the rows of book sets lining the living-room wall, Mr. Naniwa's collection of detective novels. She pulled one of the small paperbacks from the shelf and wiped her eyes at the same time. "Trucking books?" she'd once asked Mrs. Naniwa, who'd erupted in laughter. *"No, no, you know, like cagey Columbo,"* she'd replied. *"He's American, I'm sure. On television,"* and Caitlin had finally caught on—*keiji*, detective. Caitlin took a deep breath, absently flipped through the pages, then replaced the book on the shelf. She dropped down beside Hiroshi once more. She felt brittle. She curled up on the couch with her toes touching Hiroshi's hard hips and watched him. He sat huddled over her letter, making marks with a pencil, inches from her words, her history, her first direct acknowledgement of the Oides since she'd bowed good-bye to Mie's father and followed her own father onto the train at Kyoto Station, her mother and Lee already boarded, bound for Tokyo and life back in Pittsburgh.

Hiroshi scratched away. Her father would never believe it. *"I thought swimming was enough,"* she could hear him teasing.

▲ ▲ ▲

That evening when they arrived at Caitlin's apartment building after a two-hour stop at Happy Fantasy Hotel, Hiroshi pulled up on the emergency brake and left the car running as usual. He turned in his seat, and Caitlin was sharply aware of the routine embedded in their relationship—both of them expecting her to lean across for a furtive good-bye kiss, then step out of the car before neighbors had time to wonder why they lingered. But she felt soft and groggy from their hotel shower, and when she leaned her head back on the seat and closed her eyes, she began immediately to sway into sleep. She let herself begin the spiraling descent, then raised her eyebrows and forced herself awake again. She put her hand on Hiroshi's thigh and said louder than intended, *"You want to come up?"*

Hiroshi frowned. She tried to look him in the eyes but her lids began to droop and she had to jiggle in the seat to keep from slipping back into the haze of sleep. It was illogical, they'd just spent the money on a hotel, but she was too tired to rationalize. *"I mean it,"* she said.

He folded his arms over the top of the steering wheel and squinted into the night, surveying the lot of cars nudged up against the apartment buildings hovering over them. He waved his hand. *"What about the neighbors?"*

Caitlin shrugged.

"But what if someone tells the principal? This isn't America you know."

Caitlin tried to look somber, but she couldn't hold the expression through her fatigue. *"If they fire me I'll look for another job. They can't deport me just for sleeping with you."*

"No, but they can blacklist you—keep you from working in public schools ever again."

"That might not be such a bad thing. Are you coming or going?" she asked. She gripped the door handle.

Hiroshi sucked in his breath and smiled. *"Where do I park?"*

Caitlin directed him to her spot in the lot, vacant and waiting. For a long while she'd forgotten that it went with her apartment, until, one evening, returning from a gathering at Mina's restaurant, she'd found a note tacked on her door, an apology for using her space, someone had guests with a car, here was the apartment and telephone number should she need them to move. She'd stood under the outside light with the shadows of moths flitting over the paper, wondering to what space they could possibly be referring. After that, she'd parked her bike there now and then, airing it, she joked to the neighbors' kids, and reminding herself of her claim to a few more square meters of this country.

When Hiroshi had stepped out of his shoes, it suddenly seemed preposterous that he'd never been past the concrete entryway, that not once had she invited him in, not even for tea midday. He seemed physically larger now in her two rooms, and she could feel the neighbors on all sides sensing his presence, listening through the thin walls and ceiling, noting the number of footsteps and voices—a conversation! She closed the rain shutters, turned on the air conditioner, and put on a cassette. For a change she wished Hiroshi spoke fluent English so the neighbors couldn't eavesdrop on her like she did on them. She knew their voices and moods, their schedules, their coughs, the songs they hummed while shaving or sweeping, the orders they doled out over breakfast, and she found herself alert, tense, and suddenly wide awake—aware that they would not only hear, but picture a man in her apartment. Then she scoffed; *she'd* invited him in. Even so, she whispered when she asked Hiroshi, *"Beer? Shochu? Calpis?"*

He pantomimed his answer, mocking her, and Caitlin brought a bottle of beer and two glasses to the table and poured. *"To all my principals,"* she toasted in a whisper.

"To the American way," Hiroshi said in English. He gulped, and when he took a breath, he looked about her two rooms and nod-ded. *"You're lucky."* Caitlin laughed. Her entire apartment was smaller than some of the college dorm rooms she'd had. *"No, I'm serious,"* he added, *"it's small, but it's yours."* Caitlin was struck by the note of envy. Hiroshi was the only son, and it was tacitly understood that he would always remain in Kagoshima to take over the family business. And care for his parents. But Caitlin had never heard him speak of his situation with any regret except for once admitting that if it weren't for the family shipping company, he'd probably study to be a chef, Kyoto style, like his good friend Tomoki up in Aira Town. Outwardly at least, he always seemed happily resigned to his work and living at home.

"You could live in an apartment as long as it were near your parents, couldn't you?"

"Yeah, but it'd be a waste of money. I have my own room. I get enough privacy."

"But what will your parents say when you don't come home tonight?"

"Nothing." Hiroshi kissed her forehead. *"We Japanese don't notice certain things."*

Hiroshi sat back with his beer, and Caitlin watched his eyes scanning her belongings—her stacks of books on the tatami, the tape deck and scattered cassettes; a sheet of hand-dyed paper tacked to one wall; an enlargement of Hiroshi, Misawa, and Uma-chan hamming it up at the beach on another, and beneath that a photo of Lee and her father eating breakfast under the Brookline arbor; her swimsuits hanging from nails; hefty earthenware sake jugs she'd be-gun collecting after finding one at a temple fair her first orientation week in Tokyo; a dark Satsuma vase with a withered arrangement of flowers that some students had given her; her sack of dirty clothes; the cardboard box of letters in the open futon closet. She felt uncomfortably exposed and stepped into the kitchen to hunt for something to eat.

She blinked into the light of the refrigerator, dizzy; they'd spent nearly two hours on the letter that afternoon—Hiroshi correcting and rereading until he was completely satisfied with the phrasing, then explaining each change. For the first time they'd talked about her travel plans without arguing, and Hiroshi seemed accepting of her solo trip now. Caitlin, in a moment of weakness, had mentioned the possibility of meeting in Nara or Osaka, but he'd inter-rupted— *"Isn't it better that you go alone?"*—and returned to his cross-outs. *"This is good but this,"* he would say, inserting a line, *"is much politer,"* or *"How about this?"* and once, *"If you say this, they'll definite-ly ask you to come."*

In the privacy of her own apartment she could now tell him more, but from the kitchen she watched him pouring another glass of beer, his head cocked and his slant of hair fallen forward, and she felt it was good where they were. They were close and warm for a change, he seemed content to let her go to Kyoto alone, and she didn't see the point in meandering back through time. Her past had nothing to do with their present, she reminded herself; Uji should remain lodged where it belonged—in the past.

She set a plate of toast and the last packet of some rice crackers and peanuts on the low table, sat down beside Hiroshi, and chugged her beer. He had pulled a map of Japan from a pile of her textbooks and papers. *"Where do you want to go?"* he said, and for a moment she wondered if she had misunderstood after all. He caught her puzzled look and added, *"After your trip, I mean, at the end of August, or in the fall sometime, when it's convenient."*

Again, she loved that familiar "you," but it made her uneasy tonight; no one else addressed her that way—*kimi, kimi, kimi,* and it only seemed to underscore a degree of closeness she wasn't sure they had. They were intimate and they were good friends, but she drew lines in their sharing, and she knew that he did, too.

He was fingering the islands below Okinawa now, the amoe-boid blobs of green on blue, and she stared at the dotted ferry lines connecting them.

"South?" Hiroshi asked, his finger nearly on Taiwan. *"I've never been this far."*

"It depends when we go," Caitlin said. *"August and September are typhoon season."*

"Right. Well, we could go later, whenever. Anywhere's fine by me, but just us." He leaned back against her folded futon—she was embar-rassed not to have put it in the closet—and he said in an exaggerat-ed whisper: *"Someplace we don't have to whisper."*

"South would be good," Caitlin agreed. *"We could go snorkeling. Or spearfishing."*

But Hiroshi had stopped listening. He'd raised himself up to get a better look at the photo on the wall. *"Is this your father?"*

Caitlin nodded.

"You look like him," he said. *"May I?"*

Caitlin ducked, and he reached over her head, removed a tack, and placed the photo on the low table before them. *"This is your younger sister? Lee? She looks like you, too."* He bent close. *"Do you have a picture of your mother?"*

"Somewhere," she said, without making any move to search.

"May I see?" Hiroshi said. *"Please?"* His voice was a soft murmur, and he shook his head in wonder. *"Strange—I've never seen pictures of your family. Sometimes I forget you have one."* Caitlin reached for the box of letters and rummaged at the bottom for a packet of photos she'd brought from home. She flipped through to a picture of the whole family standing on the front lawn of her dorm the afternoon of her college graduation. Caitlin liked the picture. The wind had been blowing wildly, and they were all caught bent against it, dresses blown between the women's legs, her father's sports coat ballooning, hair whipping their faces—Caitlin could feel it and blinked her eyes.

Hiroshi held the photo gingerly by the corner points and shook his head again. *"I forget you even come from there sometimes."* He set the photo on the table beside the other.

Caitlin said, *"Me too,"* scooped them up, and dropped them into the box. She shoved the whole thing aside, sliding it across the tatami, with the grain; she loved that sound.

Hiroshi looked surprised. *"Why don't you put them on the wall?"* he asked. *"Don't you get homesick?"*

"Sometimes," she said; the question irked her. Then she attempted to explain. *"I haven't lived with them for a long time. I was at college. And my parents spend a lot of time apart—when I see them it's often only one of them, my father or my mother. We're almost never like that,"* she pointed to the box, *"a whole family."*

Hiroshi seemed to mull this over. Caitlin was about to explain her parents' Boston-Pittsburgh arrangement in more detail, but Hiroshi said, *"What would they say if they could see you now? With me in your apartment."* Caitlin shrugged this off. *"With a man who takes you to hotels with no windows?"* She smiled, but now, not only did she feel her neighbors' presence but her family's, too, as if they had been flown over and joined them in the tiny room.

"*Get up,*" she abruptly said. "*Fold the table and set it in the kitchen.*" And she began to arrange the bedding, unfolding her futon, setting out the extra one, spreading sheets and tossing pillows, the cases embroidered across one end with Ma Ruth's simple floral designs.

When they were both settled on the futon under the cover sheet with the lights out, Caitlin felt childlike beside him in her own apartment, hiding from the neighbors. "*We should tell stories,*" she whispered. "*Did you do that when you were a kid?*"

"*Of course, ghost stories.*"

"*You know any good ones?*" Caitlin asked into the dark.

Hiroshi was silent a minute. "*Is a* kappa *story okay?*"

Caitlin giggled. *Kappa* were legendary froglike creatures; a teacher at her base school had been made to dress up as one at a sports festival last fall. She recalled the flippers, the green tights, the yellow plate tied to his head, the large plastic nose—and the cheers from the bleachers as one of the third-year students led the teacher by a noose around the cinder track.

Hiroshi cleared his throat, rolled onto his side, and draped one leg over hers. Caitlin could feel his breath soft and damp on her face, and she inhaled the faint odor of alcohol. "*Well. A few years ago, on a hot day in July, some students from the university cut their classes and took a car out into the country,*" he began. "*They wanted to find some fresh water for a swim. Not salt water; they wanted a river or pond or mineral spring. So they drove out of Kagoshima without any place in mind, just drove out into the country.*

"*Finally they found a beautiful pond where the water was a lovely aqua from the minerals. They stopped the car and went in swimming. It was a perfect temperature, clean and refreshing, and there was no current at all— the water entered in a trickle on one side and flowed out in a small stream on another. It was beautifully isolated—there was a cedar forest on one side, a mixed hardwood grove on another, and in the distance, taro fields and a farmhouse.*"

"*Where is it?*" Caitlin whispered. "*Let's go!*"

"*Wait, listen,*" he said. "*All of them were good swimmers and they were out in the middle, and suddenly one girl started screaming. The others swam toward her, thinking she had a cramp, but she started floating away. They swam harder and she reached out for them, but it seemed she was being dragged off by something, and she started going under. One of them finally got hold of her hand and he held on as tight as he could, but whatever was pulling her was stronger than he was, and she was torn from his grasp. They tried diving down for her, but they couldn't see or feel anything."*

Hiroshi paused and Caitlin said, *"Is that all? The kappa did it?"* She didn't like the story; it made her restless, and the thought flashed through her mind that Hiroshi knew about Mie, that he was testing her. She stood and flicked on the faintest of the fluorescent lights.

"No, no, there's more. Turn it off. It's better in the dark." Caitlin hesitated, then obeyed and climbed back under the sheet. *"Ready?"* Hiroshi whispered, pulling her toward him. She nodded into his neck. *"Okay, the students were all frightened and got out of the water and went for help. Finally, several hours later, some divers brought up the body. The girl was completely naked and dead. They took her to a hospital, and the other students returned to the university.*

"The next day a doctor from the hospital telephoned one of the students and asked if he'd bring the others out to answer some questions about the incident. So they went, and the doctor took them into a room and said, 'I wouldn't normally ask you to do this, but there's something unusual about this case. Would you mind viewing the body?' The students agreed, and the doctor wheeled out the corpse and said, 'You see, her liver is missing. And then this . . .' The students looked, and they saw that her anus was all torn up."

"Her what?" Caitlin had missed the Japanese word.

"Her anus was torn," Hiroshi said, then added in English, "Her asshole."

"Hiroshi! I thought this was a kappa story."

"It is. Listen. The doctor said to them, 'Now what exactly did you see? You must help us to understand this.' So the students told the doctor what had happened, how the girl was pulled under by some strong force.

"The next week the farmer who owned the pond had it drained by diverting the stream, but they never found anything. The farmer was so scared he decided to leave the pond dry, but gradually vegetables began to disappear from his garden. Soon he had no melons or cucumbers left to sell, the taro plants withered, and while there was still a small sweet potato patch

left in his garden, he decided to fill the pond again. Now it's filled, and his vegetables are healthier than ever, though he puts out offerings by the pond every day—a little of anything he harvests. Each summer the pond looks just as clean and aqua and inviting, and anyone who knows the story would never go swimming there, but someday, some tourists, or some students from Tokyo, or some foreigner like you, will see it and want to dive in."

"So the kappa lived in the pond and got the girl?" Caitlin asked. Hiroshi nodded. *"But why was her anus torn?"*

"Kappa do that. They take out the liver through the anus."

"Why?"

"It's just what they do—with horses, too. They eat the livers."

"I thought they were harmless."

Hiroshi laughed. *"Okay, now you tell a story."*

"I can't, that was too depressing."

"You have to, or the kappa will get you." Hiroshi squeezed her rump and Caitlin jumped. She thought for a while. Ma Ruth used to tell good stories. In fact Ma Ruth believed firmly in ghosts, swearing a ghost in her house made ginger cookies in the middle of the night and rearranged boxes in the attic. *"Okay,"* Caitlin said. *"My grandmother used to tell it to me when my sister and I slept outside with her on the porch in the summer."*

"Your grandmother lived with you?"

"No, we lived with my grandmother. For a few years. And in summers. Ma Ruth is her name." Caitlin was amused to hear that Ruth sounded no different from "loose." She stared up into the dark and tried to hear the story in Japanese.

"Does your family still live with her?" Hiroshi asked.

"Some of the time. She's in Pittsburgh. My father teaches in Boston. My mother and my sister live in Pittsburgh parts of the year. Now listen. When my great-grandparents were first married, they lived on the farm south of Pittsburgh where my great-grandfather had grown up—his father had died and his mother lived with a sister in the city, so they were the only ones left on the Chester family farm." Caitlin smiled to hear the family name with Japanese pronunciation—Che-su-tah. *"It's the farm where my grandfather spent his childhood. But this was before he was born. The farm was a long way from any town, and people came around to the farms selling different things like pots and pans, but every now and then my great-grandparents had to drive a horse and wagon into town for supplies. My*

great-grandmother, Gertrude, would get whatever food, cooking supplies, and sewing things they needed, and my great-grandfather, Karl, would get whatever tools or building supplies he needed." Caitlin stopped. The story had no ring to it with her limited Japanese vocabulary. She could hear Ma Ruth's melodic voice listing off the things Pa Chess's parents would pick up—lard, molasses, flour, bolts of cloth, buttons, soap, canning jars, hinges, nails—Caitlin couldn't possibly translate all the goods, and that was half the story. She could hear Lee asking Ma Ruth to recite more of the list, to name the fabrics and the sweets, to describe the scent of the candles, and what you could buy with a penny—until lying on the mattress on the screened-in porch, listening to the sounds of the city settling below, their mouths began to water. Sometimes they never even got to the tale itself.

"Are you still awake?" Hiroshi asked. *"Keep going."*

"Sorry. They went to get supplies together. Except when Gertrude was pregnant, then she stayed home and Karl went alone. He'd leave early in the morning and come home in the afternoon. One time in the winter when Gertrude was pregnant with my great-aunt, it started to snow while Karl was in town. The snow came down hard and accumulated fast, and by nightfall he still hadn't returned. There was nothing Gertrude could do except wait.

"So she built up the fire in the stove and sat down with some mending. When she finished the mending she made a wool blanket for the baby. When she finished that she started a pair of socks. By the time Karl returned shortly after dawn, she was beginning a scarf for herself.

"He told Gertrude that he'd decided to stop and sleep in a barn rather than continue in the dark in a storm. Gertrude made him breakfast and he told her more." Caitlin trailed off. She could hear Ma Ruth mimicking this great-grandfather Caitlin had never known—"Yah, you know the Lesser place, just before Steuben's fields? I saw light in one window and smoke from the chimney, so I pulled in and went up to the door. They were friendly folk, but said they hadn't any room inside, the children had taken all the beds, so would I mind sleeping in the barn. I said I didn't care a hoot where I slept so long's I was out of the snow, but it did seem odd, that's a big house they have, and I never did see or hear a child there." Caitlin began a translation of this dialogue, then gave up and simply said he slept in the barn. *"This is too difficult Hiroshi. I'm tired."*

"*You can't just stop in the middle. Go on.*"

Caitlin sat up for better concentration. "*Well, Karl began to eat his breakfast, and Gertrude just stood there staring at him. 'You slept in their barn?' she asked him. 'Of course I did, in the hay. It was perfectly clean.' Gertrude turned white, and Karl stopped eating. 'It was clean I tell you. What's the matter?' She began trembling, and he jumped up thinking she was going to give birth right then. But she shouted at him, 'Sit down, fool. I'm not having a child. What did that house and barn look like?'*

"*Karl told her that the house was big and white, but it was dark, he couldn't see much. The woman had taken up a lantern and led him out to the barn and he put the horse in an empty stall, gave it some grain, and then moved around some hay and went right to sleep. He awoke early, when the sky was just graying, went across to the house, opened the door, and left a nickel on the table in the hallway. The house was quiet, and he left without seeing the man or the woman again.*

"*Gertrude asked him if he were sure about this. Karl said of course he was sure, why was she being so strange. Then Gertrude told him to hitch up the other horse to the wagon. Karl argued—he'd just come back after all— but Gertrude was stubborn, and he followed her orders.*

"*So they went back toward town in the wagon. Karl kept saying, 'You're going soft in the brain, woman,' and Gertrude kept saying, 'Show me exactly where you stayed. Show me this Lesser place.' They reached Steuben's fields and drove to the driveway my grandfather had pulled into the night before, but as soon as he turned in he stopped the horse, and they both just stared.*

"*You see, the house had burned down the year before. The couple that had lived there had died in the fire; they were young, they didn't have any children yet. Karl just sat there and said, 'You're right, I'd forgot.' They climbed down from the wagon and walked through the snow toward the abandoned barn. 'This is where I slept,' Karl told my great-grandmother. They felt the loose piled hay and could see the depression from his body, and in a stall they found a recent pat of manure from his horse.*

"*They walked over to what was left of the house. It had burned to the ground except for the front where part of the wall still stood with the door and frame intact. They opened the door and saw a blackened oak table sitting in the hallway, and beyond that all the charred and fallen beams open to the fields and sky. Karl picked up his nickel from the table and they left the house. In the wagon he turned to Gertrude and whispered, 'I spoke with them, Mother. Do you believe me?' and my grandmother, Ma Ruth, would tell us what Gertrude told Karl that day: 'Yes Pa, you spoke with their ghosts. And they probably saved your life.'*

Caitlin lay back on the futon. Hiroshi applauded softly under the sheet. *"Do you think it really happened?"* he asked.

"I don't know. There were more details when my grandmother told it."

"I don't have a grandmother," Hiroshi murmured. *"I never did."*

"I think you had grandmothers, you just never knew them."

"No, never had them at all, my parents just happened." They lay quiet and Caitlin could feel his breathing deepen, then slow as he dropped off to sleep.

Ma Ruth's voice was lodged in her head now, purring those rolling storytelling tones, and she could feel the damp night breeze blowing through the porch above the street in Pittsburgh—she wondered if Lee had slept out there this summer. Ma Ruth wouldn't have, she was too ill; her mother wouldn't have, she never did; but did Lee? Caitlin turned away from Hiroshi. She missed that breeze and that porch, that haven behind the screens, up level with the tree limbs and leaves bandied by the wind. And she wondered with an ache if she'd ever sleep in the same room with her sister again.

Eight

CAITLIN AWOKE to a harsh clanging. She rolled over, blankly noted Hiroshi's absence, and stumbled to the phone in the kitchen. *"Moshi-moshi.* It's Naomi," the voice said.

Caitlin sank to the floor and leaned back against the cabinets. Through the opaque kitchen window she could see that the sun was already high in the sky. "What time is it?"

"Nine-thirty. You still sleeping? Lazy American," Naomi joked, but when Caitlin didn't laugh, she apologized and said she was just hoping they might be able to meet later—for ice cream or coffee or something. Caitlin thought this over, and Naomi added, "I could come out to your neighborhood if you don't want to go downtown."

"No, no, I have to go out anyway," Caitlin said. "Just give me an hour or so. I have to shower and finish up a few things here. Where should we meet?" Caitlin jotted down the name of the shop, took down the directions, and said good-bye.

Then she leaned over the kitchen sink and splashed water from the faucet onto her face. Dripping over the basin she slid the window open, but immediately squinted as her eyes were lanced by the glare from cars in the parking lot below. Through her blind spots and the window bars, she could barely make out a woman on a terrace across the way batting her futons and pulling them indoors; once again, with the ash fallout light and the sky clear, Caitlin had missed another good laundry morning.

Hiroshi must have left before dawn, in time to get home before work; she hadn't heard him go she'd been sleeping so thickly. And dreaming. She still felt ensnared in the dream—she and Lee swimming, then just Lee swimming and Caitlin watching, then Lee here in Japan, leading Caitlin about by a noose, around a track while people cheered. Caitlin kept telling her to stop, she wasn't in costume, she didn't have the *kappa* flippers or the plate, but Lee kept tugging her, and the people kept laughing, then it wasn't Lee at all, and Caitlin slammed the window shut and steadied herself by the drain board as the image zoomed in from her dream: Mie leading her about by a noose. Caitlin hadn't seen the face, but she was sure it was her, posture jubilant as she bowed to the crowds on either side; adult Mie, leading Caitlin around while everyone jeered.

In the bathroom, Caitlin dropped her T-shirt and underwear to the floor, stepped onto the cool tiles and filled a plastic basin from the spigot. She squatted on the low stool and dribbled cold water over her head, down her back, and between her legs, and shivering took up a cloth and scrubbed herself, slowly at first, then vigorously until the skin on her arms and legs stung.

After she'd dressed, she pulled out her Japan atlas, poured a cup of yesterday's coffee from a jar in the refrigerator, and sat down to write the decoy letter to her father:

July 20, 1985

Dear Dad,

Thought I'd let you know I've firmed up my plans to go to Hagi during August break. I want to be somewhere cool and see a different coast shaped by different waters. Ever been there? I'll start in Hagi then go hiking through Yamaguchi where Hiroshi may join me. Hagi sounds perfect— facing the sea, surrounded by hills (without ash), and steeped in pottery.

Last day of classes yesterday. No champagne, no confetti, I'll celebrate after the last teacher seminar on August 2nd, then again on August 9th when I take that train north. But it's a relief at least to know that I'll be working with adults for the next two weeks, that I don't have to face adolescents and the old sea of uniforms on Monday. The other day I asked students what they'd eaten for breakfast, part of a past tense exercise, and one kid answered in slang he thought I wouldn't know—"pussy." I've grown adolescently paranoid again; when they ask me simple questions like, "Do you iron your clothes?" or "Do you like dogs or cats?" I search for hidden insults and traps.

Went up to Kirishima last weekend with Naomi, that girl I mentioned in my earlier letter—her parents let me take their car. I'd been in those tablelands once before—crater lakes, sulfur "hells," and high plateaus from where Sakurajima seems benign. Hope to get back there to camp and hike from hot spring to hot spring.

Not much else new here. Sakurajima is having daily volcanic explosions. Air shocks rattle my windows. The ashfall is intense. I bathe constantly—the ash seems to get under my pores. I don't understand why the towns on Sakurajima are still populated at all—here in Kagoshima is rough enough.

Do you hear from Mom and Lee? Haven't had word from either of them in a long time. How's Ma Ruth holding out? Stay well.

Love, Caitlin

Caitlin tossed the atlas aside, folded the letter, and wrote her father's address on the envelope. Brookline seemed a mythical place now; she saw only tall trees and immense historic homes with wrought-iron lawn furniture in her selective collage of memory, and the weather was always perfect, a firm blanket of snow in winter, and cool, dappling shade in summer. She missed the stature of New England maples, she craved that complete and saturating shade.

As she wrote her return address on the back of the envelope, she wondered how careful a reader her father would be, if he'd ever clue in. Someday she'd tell him the truth, but for now she wanted him to believe this ruse.

She poured herself the last half cup of cold coffee, emptied yesterday's things from her shoulder bag, and sat down to reread the letter to the Oides. She stumbled over some of the new *kanji* in Hiroshi's changes and had to use a dictionary to verify stroke order. Then she put her glass by the sink, wiped the tabletop once more, and with painstaking slowness, copied the letter onto a clean piece of stationery. She proofread each sentence aloud, took a deep breath, and held the letter at arm's length before tucking it inside a matching envelope. She told herself it was the coffee making her hands shake as she licked the flap.

From the shoe box in the other room she retrieved her father's long letter, and without glancing at the text, at any of the six pages of his account, she turned to the postscript after his signature and copied the Oides' address onto the envelope. As she wrote, the sequence of strokes she'd practiced when she was seven and eight came back to her, and led her, through her pen. She could shut her eyes and write that address still.

She returned his letter to the shoe box, stamped both envelopes, twisted her hair up under her baseball cap, and set off toward town, stopping on her way to drop the letters into a mailbox.

Naomi was waiting for her in a booth at the cafe. Caitlin said hello then ran off to the bathroom to dab at her face and arms with a moistened handkerchief and to blow the gray out of her nose; riding her bike had been a mistake.

"So," she said when she sat down opposite Naomi. A waiter brought ice water and menus, and Caitlin chose sweet potato ice cream and Naomi ordered chocolate with chocolate syrup. As they sat back to wait, Caitlin fished an ice cube from her glass and held it to the back of her neck. A family from the next table looked askance at her. "They're going to think all Americans do this," she said to Naomi as she ran the pebble of melting ice over her forehead. "An ancient bathing ritual, to cleanse the soul before eating."

Naomi fished one of her cubes out and did the same. "I'll confuse them." When the cubes had melted, they wiped their hands and faces with napkins. "You must remember you're a little ambassador," Naomi mocked. "That's what my parents tell me every time we go to the States."

"Well, that's not bad advice."

"Maybe. But adults don't get asked as many dumb questions as kids. 'Were you born with slanty eyes?' 'Does your family live in one room?' 'Are you a war baby?' 'Do you eat raw fish for breakfast?'"

Their ice creams had come and Caitlin dipped into a small twist of whipped cream with the tip of her spoon. "I get asked dumb questions, too, you know. How many guns do I own, do I miss my beef and bread every meal, and am I pleased to be in Japan because it has four seasons."

"Morons. Why can't people ask more interesting questions?"

"Such as?"

"Such as what you do or don't like about your own country and theirs. What you *think*. Everyone acts like their country is the best. If they ask for your impressions, when you tell them, people act so know-it-all; you say something positive and it's like they could have told you so, you say something negative and it's like they expected it, you're just a foreigner, you can't appreciate things."

"So, what don't you like about Japan?" Caitlin asked.

"Well, lots. The school exams, the pressure to be the same, small houses and yards, girls aren't allowed to do as much as they can in the States, people don't always say what they mean . . . you know, different things." She paused, then added with a sly grin, "In the States sometimes I lie, do you?"

Caitlin glanced up from her ice cream, wary, having just mailed that letter to her father. "What do you mean?"

"When they ask idiotic questions. Like once I told a girl in Ohio that we eat shark's lips for snacks. She asked the dumbest things, like do we take Sunday drives to China. And her parents were worse. Her mother wanted to know if my feet had been bound."

"When was the last time you were in the States?"

"Last summer. We go every year. Except this summer. I'm too old for the camp I used to go to, and anyway I'm supposed to be preparing for high school entrance exams."

Caitlin chewed on a soft chunk of sweet potato that she'd saved for her last bite, then sat back. "Well, aren't you?"

"Sort of."

"I thought you were going to an international school."

"Maybe." Naomi shrugged, averted her eyes, then said with sudden brightness, "Look, I brought you something." She reached into her bag and handed Caitlin a small wrapped box. "Open it."

"What's the occasion?"

"You'll see." Caitlin undid the wrappings, opened the interior box, and pulled out a small plastic bottle. "Take the cap off." When Caitlin did, the dense odor of hot-spring sulfur assaulted her nostrils, and they laughed. "It's for your bath; you pour a little in and it's just like being at an *onsen*. It turns the water yellow. It's from the Alps—Nagano, I think."

Caitlin thanked her; she was surprised to be so kindly thought of, and for the second time in the presence of this peculiar girl, she felt a shot of guilt, this time for having been irked with her in Kirishima. After all, she reminded herself, Naomi was only fourteen, going through the ups and downs of adolescence; she couldn't be expected to provide the sort of adult female friendship Caitlin was just beginning to realize she missed.

They left the ice cream shop and went window-shopping along an interior strip of mall, stopping to leaf through magazines at a bookstore and burrow through bargain racks of clothing. When they'd reached the end of the covered section, instead of exiting to the street, they turned and walked back the same way, browsing deeper in the shops, talking both in English and Japanese, meandering, taking their time. Here and there Naomi shrieked and dragged Caitlin over to stuffed animals, barrettes, handkerchiefs, pencil cases, erasers, or T-shirts, cooing, *"Kawaii, kawaii,"*—cute, cute; Caitlin admired the objects politely, startled to see Naomi, who could be so sarcastic and sophisticated in English, now so convincing as a silly schoolgirl.

When they'd reached the mall entrance again, Caitlin said she had to get going; she wanted to swim before the pool closed for classes. "Tell your parents hello for me," she said.

"Oh, I almost forgot!" Naomi exclaimed. "They want you to come to the barbecue next Sunday. Bring your boyfriend. It'll be just us, my grandfather, and my uncle's family. Hamburgers and hotdogs. Even marshmallows. We do it every summer. But usually a couple weeks earlier, with more people."

"You'll barbecue outside? What about the ash?"

"Wear a gray shirt, I guess. And hope it's not windy."

Caitlin accepted the invitation as they parted, but she felt that she was being deliberately reeled in by Naomi and her parents. She doubted she could influence this girl, or if her influence would be positive. They had no idea of her background. Carl and Akiko seemed to be reaching out for Caitlin, and she felt uneasy as she mounted her bike, wondering if they sensed her past. People hungered for companionship, she knew, but this felt more manipulative, more urgent, like her mother with Lee, like her mother with her before she'd left for college, sitting at an outdoor café, repeatedly clutching Caitlin's wrist through the meal, leaving her to tackle her sandwich one-handed.

▲ ▲ ▲

The pool was crowded. Caitlin began in the fast lap lane but kept colliding with the feet of the swimmer in front of her, and when she paused to let him get ahead, swimmers from behind bowled into her. When she finally established a rhythm, the pace was so slow that she had to change her breathing pattern, and she couldn't even work up a flush of exertion. Finally she grabbed a kickboard and flutter kicked along in a slow lane, and as her breathing grew regular, it struck her that she'd actually mailed a letter to Mie's family. She calculated the number of days for her letter to reach them and wondered when she'd have a reply. She could always change her mind, she told herself, even go to Hagi, and this made her laugh and take in water through her nose. She sputtered along and swam a few more laps, then gave up the workout altogether.

Caitlin made some instant curry that evening, then, feeling restless, went out to a neighborhood shop for a red-bean ice pop just after dusk. She called Hiroshi when she returned, but Mrs. Naniwa said that he'd just gone out. Caitlin chatted for a while, explaining about justices of the peace, and wedding reception customs. Then, though she didn't feel like drinking, she opened a bottle of beer and leaned back against her rolled up futon to watch TV. The variety show talk took concentration to follow, and even though she hadn't swum hard, she felt physically drained; the patter of jokes and even

ASH / 111

the spasmodic laughing, shrieking, and backslapping soon became a mesmerizing drone. She changed channels and tried to keep herself from drifting off by following a drama, but halfway through her beer she lay down on the tatami and fell asleep.

Moments later, it seemed, she awoke to a dull tapping and someone calling her name. She flicked off the TV, turned out the light, and crouched in a corner. A hand reached through the outer bars and slid open her kitchen window; she'd left it unlocked. *"Keito, it's me,"* Hiroshi whispered, and she turned the light back on and told him to be quiet as she opened the door.

"I fell asleep."

"I know, look at you." He ran his hand through her mussed up hair, then kissed her on the forehead. *"My mother said you called,"* he said stepping out of his sneakers in her entryway. *"Why'd you turn the light out?"*

"So you couldn't see me—I didn't know who you were. You're drunk, Hiroshi, you shouldn't have driven."

"Who's drunk?" He pointed to her opened beer on the floor. *"Who fell asleep?"* She retrieved the bottle, and they sat down at the table.

"Two nights in a row," Caitlin said. *"What will they think?"* She rolled her eyes to the walls and ceiling indicating the neighbors beyond.

"Do you mind?"

"Not if you're quiet, but you should call before you come. And don't come by next week."

"Why?"

"I have that overnight seminar, remember? I won't be here. But you should always call anyway."

"But you called me."

"That doesn't mean I was inviting you over."

"You're mad, aren't you?"

"It's just my neighbors. What time did you leave this morning?"

"About three. Early enough to still pass as night."

"Clever," she said. She wasn't sure why he felt like such an intrusion, but his spontaneous visit struck her as presumptuous.

Hiroshi set down his glass. *"Should I leave? You don't seem to want me here."*

"No, no, stay." She closed her eyes and took several deep breaths, then smiled at him. *"I'm just* bitchy *when I wake up."*

He took a slow draw on his beer. *"Then I'll always leave while you're sleeping, okay?"*

▲ ▲ ▲

He was gone when Caitlin started out of bed at 5:20 from an air shock that thwacked her windows so hard she covered her head to protect herself from the rain of glass she expected but never came. She cautiously stood, saw that nothing had broken, then hurriedly did a load of wash and hung it before the wind brought the ash. After eating cornflakes with raisins, and an iced glass of green tea, she vacuumed the apartment, washed the tiles of the bathroom, swept and bagged the ash on her landing and veranda, placed new moisture absorbers in her closets and dresser to help with the humidity while she was away, then set about planning for the teachers' seminar.

In the afternoon she bussed up to the beach and found Hiroshi and Misawa already carrying their boards to the storage building. She walked alongside them and once the boards were stowed, sat with them briefly on the sand. Across the bay the ash plume rode high in the sky—they guessed over two kilometers—but the wind was shifting, driving it toward the beach. They went back to town in Hiroshi's car, and Caitlin waited while Hiroshi and Misawa showered at the Naniwas', then they taxied, a slow ride with wipers on for the ash, to Tsuketomi, Mina's family's restaurant, for dinner.

Hiroshi was burnished after his day in the sun, and Caitlin kept staring at him, once even making him duck in embarrassment. Their old comfort with each other had returned, and she found herself gravitating back toward him after kneeling at the low table beside Uma-chan or catching up with Mina or joking with her father. Conversation at the table drifted manically from Sakurajima's activity, which that morning had caused windowpanes in Kago-shima to break; to whether women's eye shapes indicated their breast shapes; to when they should make their next jaunt up to Aira Town for baths and dinner at Akinai; to whether Nakasone should cut the strands of hair that crossed his baldness; to whether copyright fees should be paid by every customer who sang karaoke. Only half-listening, Caitlin leaned against Hiroshi and discreetly asked if he'd meet her at her apartment the following Friday when she got back from the seminar. He nodded but gave her a silencing look. She mentioned the barbecue on Sunday, and he said he thought he could make it, but turned back to the others, and she did the same; she'd irritated him by making personal arrangements in public.

She pulled herself away from him, and relocated to a position between Kosuke and Mina and tried to join the conversation. But she couldn't care less about karaoke, the songs all sounded the same to her. She folded a chopstick wrapper into an airplane and sent it Hiroshi's way, and it fittingly nosedived into a dish of dipping sauce for the *jidori,* a raw chicken specialty she couldn't abide. She was tired of group banter and wanted to head out with just Hiroshi. Their relationship had taken a sharp turn, and the ease with which she had adjusted to having him in her apartment startled her. She even felt she'd live with him—or almost; what they had now, two separate places to live in, one of them to be alone in, was really better. She watched him across the table or over the bar when he went behind the counter to help mix the *shochu* drinks with Mina's father, and she had the urge to haul him out of there and tell him everything about the letters, the Oide family and Mie. The struggle to silence herself made her gulp her drinks, and she listed to one side and trailed her hand along the wall for support when she went to the bathroom.

Later she and Hiroshi taxied west to the river, then walked along its east bank, the two of them weaving in the dark, the ash velvety underfoot. He'd decided to sleep at home that night since one of his sisters was visiting from Tokyo. When they reached Caitlin's neighborhood and stopped at an intersection to say good-bye, Caitlin slurred, *"Do you want to know why I swim so well?"*

"Why?" Hiroshi asked.

But Caitlin caught herself, shook her head, and told him to forget it. He shrugged, and she lingered, gripping his hands, letting him think that the tears she wiped away on his shoulder were the product of alcohol and a sentimental reluctance to part.

Nine

THAT SEMINAR week, Caitlin led role plays, demonstrated conversation exercises, mouthed exaggerated l's, r's, b's, and v's to the point of chapping her lips, and repeatedly exhorted reluctant teachers to mingle and talk in English during breaks. Another American from the program, Mandy, had been sent down from Nagasaki—Scott, the other fellow in Kagoshima, had returned to the States for his sister's wedding—and she and Caitlin shared a room at the education center. They conferred after lights-out and before breakfast, then were on stage morning to night leading the teachers, conducting activities, answering questions, and making painfully jovial conversation. They became hams, but Mandy was by far the more natural entertainer. One evening she taught the head of the education center the rules for Jeopardy, made him MC, then led sides in a three-hour game. On another she taught them how to dance the Hustle. And on the evening of the sing-along, though Caitlin handed out song sheets with a whaling song, the "Erie Canal," and "Rock Island Line," and diligently delved into the history of each folk song before leading the singing, Mandy feigned a huge yawn after the second song, winked at Caitlin, tossed her hair back, and woke everyone up with a strutting version of "My Girl is Red Hot, Your Girl Ain't Doodily Squat," followed by "The Girl from Ipanema," making them call out "Ahhhhs" and teaching them to sing with seductive softness.

By Thursday, fatigue had begun to take its toll. Caitlin and Mandy sat together at lunch instead of separating themselves, and several teachers at their table begged for English names, so over dessert the two studied each face, then dubbed them Ben, Myrtle, Harold, Louise, Ernie, Chuck . . . trying not to laugh. Word got around to other tables and soon all the teachers had lined up for names. Mandy and Caitlin racked their brains for new ones, and the afternoon pronunciation drills started twenty minutes late.

When Caitlin and Mandy had a brief respite that evening while the teachers worked on skits to be performed in the closing cere- monies, they sat in a lounge sipping at whiskeys, reviewing the names, and marveling at how quickly they'd been adopted—"Hi Leroy. Oh, hello Hortense. Bertha, on whose skit team are you?"

"You were ruthless," Caitlin said to Mandy.

"Me? You dished out Clarence and Aretha."

"L and R practice."

"Hah." Mandy poured them each fresh doubles then flopped down onto the sofa beside Caitlin. "God, I can't wait till this is over."

"You going straight back to Nagasaki?"

"No way. Guam. I'm psyched. A whole week, every day on the beach, every minute—I'll move at night, hit the clubs, but that's it. Pure R and R, and no one will speak to me in Japanese. Beth, you know, from Fukuoka, she's going too—it's a man hunt, want to come?"

"I'm going to Kyoto."

"Kyoto! In August? From what I hear the heat'll kill you. Why?"

"To visit friends."

"Must be damned special friends. Boyfriend?"

"No, my boyfriend's here. You know Guam's not exactly cool and shady mid-August."

"No, but the beaches . . . he Japanese?"

Caitlin nodded.

"You're lucky," Mandy said, "really."

Caitlin laughed.

"No, I'm serious. I don't speak much Japanese. And I hate studying. Oh, sure, all these teachers are eager to fix me up with their brothers or cousins, even uncles, but talk about strings attached. You've got it easy—don't have to go to Guam for your men."

"There are foreign men in Kyoto or Tokyo if that's what you're after."

"Sure. Urban, pasty men. I want 'em tan. God, you must know some good words—cock, erection, semen—teach me?"

Caitlin choked on her whiskey, and Mandy had to slap her on the back and bring her a glass of water.

▲ ▲ ▲

On Friday afternoon, like camp counselors, Caitlin and Mandy bade the English teachers farewell, calling them by their new names as they departed the center. When the last straggler had left, Caitlin gathered up her things and told Mandy she'd see her Monday for the second half of the seminar. Then, without offering to get together over the weekend or show her around Kagoshima, Caitlin sheepishly took off at a trot to catch a bus.

From the bus stop to her apartment she paced herself with slow and even steps, thinking of iced tea and concentrating on the few parts of her body—toenails, kneecaps, earlobes—that weren't sweating profusely. The heat-bleached sky pressed down, and though she veered and zigzagged to catch every patch of shade she could, the sun was unrelenting. The street trees had been shorn, cut back to below the power lines, and offered only pitiful puddles of shade. She took her pack off her soaking back, carried it to the side, and trod on, dabbing at her face and neck with a handkerchief, and she only flinched slightly when Hiroshi jumped out from between cars in her parking lot. "Welcome back," he said in English and slung her pack onto his back. He looked her over. "*You just swim?*"

Caitlin glared.

"*Sorry. Hey, I brought beer but it's warm—I left it by your door.*"

Caitlin didn't care, so limp and drenched with sweat, water was all she had in mind. "*Have you been waiting long?*" she finally asked. He was blinking the salt out of his eyes and his face shone.

He grinned: "*Five days.*"

Not until they were halfway up her stairs, finally under the overhang's shade, and she saw the mail protruding from her box, did she remember the Oides. She paused, letting Hiroshi go ahead, suddenly wishing that he weren't there with her, then telling herself in the next moment not to worry, the reply probably hadn't arrived. She followed him up to the landing where he'd dropped the pack and stood waiting against the railing. She reached into her mailbox, grabbing all the letters in one greasy hand, and unlocked the door.

She clutched the mail while Hiroshi pressed her for a wet hug. Then she turned on the air conditioner, opened the rain shutters for light, stuffed Hiroshi's beer into her tiny freezer, and guzzled two glasses of water, before leafing through the pile. There it was, after the water bill, an envelope with that familiar return address. She thumbed beyond it, to a letter from her mother, and one from her father that she eyed nervously until she realized it was too early to be in response to her false Hagi plans. She set all the mail on the table and excused herself to use the toilet, then sat on the seat holding her clammy forehead in her hands.

When she emerged, Hiroshi was in the other room leaning against her futon. He'd put a cassette in the tape deck and sat sipping a Calpis drink. *"I made a glass for you,"* he said pointing, and she took the iced drink and sat down at the kitchen table with her back to him, telling him she just wanted to read her mail. She took up the envelope, slipped her thumb under the flap, extracted the letter, and sat up straight as she unfolded it. Sucking in her cheeks, she read, and for the first time in fifteen years, Mie's father spoke to her in the same fatherly voice from her childhood, reassuring her, telling her they still thought of her as a daughter. She'd barely scanned the first paragraph of politenesses and moved on into the yes, yes, please come, they could meet the ferry in Osaka, before the tears were dropping from her cheeks onto her hands, onto the paper and table, her whole body convulsing.

Hiroshi's hands appeared on her shoulders. *"Bad news?"* he asked. She shook her head. *"Homesick?"* She tilted her head, then nodded, for she was in a way, though he wouldn't know what home it was she was sick for, that home of fifteen years ago—her family close and the Oides next door. He wrapped his arms around her, then stood her up and enveloped her, until she pulled away to blow her nose and wipe her face with a washcloth, then with more cold water on the cloth, her back, neck, and stomach.

Hiroshi caught a glimpse of the letter. *"From the family in Kyoto?"* Caitlin nodded. *"May I?"* She nodded again, sat down at the table, and gazed at the opaque window over the kitchen sink, wishing it were clear so she could look through to something—a patch of sky, the wall of a building, a tree branch.

"But they say to come," Hiroshi said when he'd finished reading. *"You're like a daughter to them, they're waiting for you. That's good, isn't it?"* Caitlin remained silent. *"Is it your father? You're thinking of your father? It makes you homesick to hear him mention your father?"* That wasn't it at all, but the excuse sounded right so Caitlin nodded, accepting Hiroshi's comforting words and his solemn vow to make her feel at home here, to be a family for her in Kagoshima. She took some deep recovering breaths and finally smiled, although she felt sick and rotten inside and wanted to drop her head onto her arms, close her eyes and be gone, disappear from her apartment, from Kagoshima, from Japan, from anywhere.

While Hiroshi ran out to the market for groceries, Caitlin sat still with her dripping glass of Calpis, wondering what it would be like to see the Oides minus Mie. When they'd first moved back to Pittsburgh, Caitlin had had a recurring nightmare in which she, her family, the Oides, all the children, families and shopkeepers from the Iwakura neighborhood had boarded a train to leave the city. Everyone was calm, as if the exodus were routine, but as the train began to roll, Caitlin would look around to find Lee and Nobuko, their parents and other schoolmates boarded, but no Mie. Frantic, she'd lean out the window, and there was Mie, stranded on the platform, terror in her eyes, running to catch the accelerating train. Caitlin would lurch awake as the train turned a bend, as she called out, or as she jumped from the train window. They'd been so symmetrical, Lee and Nobuko, Caitlin and Mie, points on a square now missing one corner. And Caitlin supposed that Nobuko would associate her solely with that missing point and that grim July 14th.

When Hiroshi returned, he went about preparing dinner, and Caitlin read her other mail. Her mother's letter was a detailed account of Ma Ruth's recent chemotherapy bout, including the names of her new nurses and the brand of bed they'd bought for home use, then an update of her health since leaving the hospital. "She's in good spirits now, so glad to be home," her mother wrote, "but Caitlin, if this doesn't help, there's little we can do. We are hopeful. I am no longer working at all now, gave up those evening shifts—there's too much to do here at the house." Caitlin wondered how much that was true, and how much was guilt induced by Ma Ruth; Ma Ruth had always felt at liberty to claim an inordinate amount of her daughter's time. Her mother went on to report the weather and a neighbor's tag sale at which she'd found six unchipped dinner plates in her favorite Lenox. There wasn't a word about Lee except after a final line on Ma Ruth—"Lee is a gem, Caity, staying with her many hours reading Willa Cather."

Her father's letter from Boston recounted Ma Ruth's condition in stark, clinical terms, then discussed the progress of his research and his plans to be in Tokyo and Kyoto for several months during his upcoming sabbatical. Caitlin was relieved to see that he wouldn't arrive until mid-fall, although he didn't say whether he'd arranged this in deference to her wishes or to his own work; at least, she thought, there would be no overlap at the Oides'.

Hiroshi was dipping vegetables in batter and dropping them into a deep pan of rushing oil, so Caitlin put aside her letters, cleared the table, and set out rice bowls, chopsticks, and pickled vegetables. He handed her fresh daikon and ginger to grate for the dipping sauce and *shiso* leaves to towel dry, asked for ice cubes for the batter, but otherwise would let her do nothing, so she poured two glasses of beer, doled out some rice, and Hiroshi fed her tempura, patiently frying one or two morsels at a time. Caitlin was grateful, but she ate reluctantly, feeling each bite, no matter how much she chewed, travel the length of her esophagus like a stone.

▲ ▲ ▲

She spent the night alone, and at her request Hiroshi stayed away all Saturday. She woke early, soon after dawn when the newspaper arrived, read it in bed, then put on her lightest cotton shirt and shorts, donned her cap and sunglasses, and took off on her bicycle.

She'd thought of riding south and going out to a pier, or taking an inland mountain road to a local temple, but she found herself instead working her way north through the thickest band of ash. She paused to tie her bandana tight over her nose and mouth, then continued directly east, straight to the terminal for Sakurajima-bound ferries. After boarding with her bike, she rested on an indoor bench, but as the boat jostled its way out of the docks and into the bay, she moved out to the foredeck to watch the volcano slide closer, tactile green and black.

She felt a strange elation, almost relishing the sticky grit for a change, as they approached the island and that gaping upturned mouth, the south peak, the source of the gray ribbon that draped across the bay and fanned over Kagoshima. The volcanic dust felt fine assaulting her skin as they chugged over the bay, and it was even a soft comfort running through her sandals and between her toes when she disembarked and walked her bike over the parking lot to the route that circled the island.

The road cut right through solidified rivulets and hardened gushes of lava that dropped down into the bay. Several times last fall she'd biked the entire circumference of the island, but she hadn't returned since the ash had intensified and roads and hiking trails to the peaks had been closed; her tires skidded easily now on the turns. She began by following the main route, but soon turned back toward the ferry terminal, then ventured onto a side road that went inland and up the lower skirt of the northern peak. She walked her bike up the steep grade and eventually came to an open, level playground, desolate save for eleven enormous model dinosaurs. Caitlin laughed aloud at the sight. With the head of the fuming volcano as a backdrop, the dusty beasts looked surreal grazing and roaring above the bay. This was better than a pier or temple.

She plunked herself down at the heel of an orange tyrannosaurus. Consciously, she straightened her posture and crossed her legs in a half lotus, then relaxed them out in front of her; she didn't need to conform to any particular position in order to meditate.

She stared up at the billowing ash. Though she viewed it daily, the volcano still awed her. She was an easterner, from the Appalachians, used to ancient, worn, fold mountains whose rock rarely shifted, and whose summits never steamed or festered. This mountain with a plume that tumbled in whorls two kilometers high threw hot cinders far from its mouth, rocked with explosions that shook her windows across the bay, this mountain was worthy of reverence. She could see how people might come to believe in a volcano god. Perhaps that's what she needed, she thought wryly. Then she could fashion offerings—a basket of loquats, rice from the first harvest, local *shochu,* products of the seasons—to set out by an altar high up this hillside. Perhaps such ritual would bring comfort.

Her father had often said that life was suffering, but Caitlin had always scoffed; for her life hadn't always been that way. Had he forgotten? Sometimes Buddhist philosophy seemed to negate Mie's suffering in death, and their good times before her death. She acknowledged that if she hadn't felt the attachment to Mie, there wouldn't have been the feeling of loss. But how could she avoid attachment? And what was the point? To know that life is temporal, that all who are born must die, that all that exists must one day be extinguished, had never been any consolation.

The firefly haiku by Basho's disciple Kyorai that her father had taught her as the first anniversary approached had always reeked of adult euphemism, but as she mused beneath the tyrannosaurus she called it up from wherever it had been stored for so many years, turned it over on her tongue, and like a koan contemplated it: *Te no ue ni kanashiku kiyuru hotaru kana*—Alas, the light of the firefly goes out in the hand.

She spent the remainder of the morning hearing that poem, trying to "sweep" away thoughts as she had two years before when she'd joined classmates for a Zen retreat in Vermont. In the shade of the tyrannosaurus it was easier than at the monastery; she didn't have to strive for the painful full lotus or worry about the whack of a monk's stick on her back. Here she relaxed, and with ash particles settling darkly on her hot, damp skin she tried to abandon thoughts as they arose. Was this Zen or basic denial, she wondered. She hoped it was Zen, as she attempted to gaze into the abyss of being on which her professor had lectured.

Ten

SUNDAY AFTERNOON Caitlin and Hiroshi had knocked on Nao-mi's front door, called out several times, and were about to open the door, when Naomi poked her head over a bamboo fence, startling them. "Barbecue's here, at my uncle's." They walked around to the uncle's front door, and Caitlin introduced Hiroshi to Naomi. *"There are garden sandals out back or you can take your shoes with you,"* Naomi explained in the entryway. They followed her through the house and out the back sliding doors, where they stepped into their shoes again. Naomi presented them to her aunt and grandfather, who sat on a bench with glasses of barley tea under the laundry overhang, then to her uncle and cousins Izumi and Hideaki, who lounged with Akiko in lawn chairs under two large garden umbrellas. Carl was the only one out in the open—poking and fanning coals in a small barbecue grill.

"Hot enough for you?" he greeted them. He wiped his drip-ping face with a towel hung about his neck, then returned to his coals. Naomi brought them beer and cocktail napkins, and they sat down in chairs that Hideaki and Izumi had vacated near Akiko and her brother—Naomi's uncle—beneath the umbrellas.

Akiko, by way of introduction, explained to the uncle that Caitlin and Naomi had become friends at the Iso Gardens, and Caitlin was soon asked to explain how she and Hiroshi had met. She elaborated on their mutual friend Misawa and the windsurfing group. *"Windsurfing?"* Akiko asked. *"You do it too?"*

"Sometimes. If it's not too rough."

"But don't you need muscle? Aren't you afraid?"

Caitlin tried to explain that feeling out on the bay, the quiet, whether windsurfing or swimming, and Akiko listened intently until the uncle, with a smirk on his face, suddenly leaned toward Hiroshi and spoke in words she didn't recognize; he'd switched to Kagoshima dialect. Caitlin watched perplexed as he pressed Hiroshi with questions. To one of the questions Akiko gave her brother an admonishing slap on the arm. Hiroshi blushed and ducked, and Caitlin could tell he was trying to delicately talk his way around something. When the uncle laughed bawdily, Hiroshi fidgeted, turned to Akiko, and said in ordinary polite Japanese: *"Caitlin tells me you teach* sumi-e. *I think my sister's friend may have studied with you,"* and Akiko decorously followed his lead. No translations of the uncle's talk were offered, and Caitlin sat awkwardly while Hiroshi and Akiko made conversation clearly and solely for her sake. The uncle poured more beer for Hiroshi and himself, ignoring Caitlin's empty glass. She poured her own and some more iced tea for Akiko.

To Caitlin's relief, Carl joined them and sat down on her right. He asked about her upcoming vacation, and she described her plans to take the ferry from Shibushi to Osaka and then spend time in Kyoto. Everyone looked up aghast. *"Kyoto?"*

"There's no ash," she said. *"They can barbecue in the open any day of the year there."* Carl was the only one who laughed.

"In the open smog," the uncle corrected. *"Our sister lives in Kyoto. Actually, you should go visit her. They live in an old house, true Kyoto style."*

"Oh, that's right!" Akiko said excitedly. *"Sachiko would love to meet you. But take light-weight clothing, Caitlin. Kyoto's a* bonchi." She demonstrated with cupped hands: *"The mountains trap all that city heat."*

Caitlin told them about her arrangements to stay with some old friends of her father's, catching Hiroshi's glance of concern as she did. She continued calmly though, telling them she might also visit other Americans on the program, and that she wanted to buy books. She found it odd that she had to keep justifying her plans; she'd assumed that ash-weary residents of Kagoshima would envy any form of escape. She leaned back in the lounge chair and gradually let the others take over the conversation.

At the hibachi, Hideaki dropped leaves and sticks into the coals to watch them burn. Naomi and Izumi swept in and out of the group beneath the umbrellas offering bowls of chips and dip, scallops and okra wrapped in bacon, and grilled squid legs, and between small talk, the uncle fired questions at Caitlin and Hiroshi. Predictably, he listened more attentively to whatever Hiroshi had to say, but Caitlin was just as glad to be ignored; the man was cloying and condescending. He smiled too much as he listened to her Japanese, and when he asked about her work he seemed only to be testing her understanding of the Japanese educational system.

Akiko was clearly charmed by Hiroshi, hanging on his every word as he spoke with the uncle, so Caitlin turned to talk with Carl, but he'd risen again and was joking with Naomi and Izumi as he set out condiments with the aunt and turned meats in a marinade. Caitlin excused herself, wandered over to the grill to stare at the red coals with Hideaki, and Naomi, with Izumi trailing behind, came up and hooked her arm in Caitlin's. *"We usually have more people than this—it's a little boring this year."*

"Who else usually comes?"

"Some other teachers from the university and their families. But one family moved this year, and the others couldn't make it. Next year we'll do it earlier." Caitlin eyed the two girl cousins. Except for Naomi's freckled nose and the light sheen to her hair, they could have been sisters—same height, same build—and they were even dressed alike in pastel blouses, short skirts, ankle socks, and tennis shoes. *"Are you the same age?"* Caitlin asked them.

Izumi shook her head. *"Naomi's older."*

"Same junior high?" The girls nodded. *"Same clubs?"* Caitlin asked, then realized she'd erred. *"I do badminton,"* Izumi said. *"Naomi does* shodo." Naomi pulled away from Izumi and raised her head pretending to scan the backyard. "Really a boring group this year," she said out loud in English, then lowered her voice to a whisper and turned Caitlin aside, excluding Izumi. "But I like Hiroshi. I bet he *is* the reason you can keep your lips tuckered."

"I think you mean puckered," Caitlin said, then threatened playfully to stuff her head in the coals. But when Izumi and Hideaki joined in with Caitlin's joke by pulling Naomi away to safety, Naomi grumbled at her cousins, shook them off roughly, and walked away by herself.

Hiroshi was still talking with the uncle, so Caitlin wandered over to the terrace and pulled up a chair beside the grandfather. She respected his good sense, keeping to the shade, away from the talk, and after she'd thanked him for having them all there for this meal, they sat quietly side by side for a time, watching the small clusters of the party. Then the grandfather touched Caitlin's arm and raised his chin to point out Naomi squatting by herself in a corner of the garden flicking drops of barley tea from her glass onto a small mound of ash. No one else paid her any attention. Caitlin nodded. *"She's so sad lately,"* he said. *"I'm glad you are kind to her."*

"I haven't done anything, really."

"But she likes you. That helps."

They watched Naomi empty her glass drop by drop. *"You've taught her shodo, isn't that right?"* Caitlin asked. He mumbled something, stood, and with a flap of his hand, motioned for her to follow him inside. As he shuffled through the living room he gestured to some paintings high on the walls with an utterance Caitlin couldn't quite catch, then led her into a smaller tatami room, bare except for a low polished wood table and, toward one corner, a recessed alcove before which he knelt. It was cool and quiet in the room. Caitlin knelt down beside him, noted the white lily in its narrow vase of dark pottery—she wondered if Carl had made the vase—then looked up the alcove wall to the scroll with writing that seemed to drip down the paper. She could only discern a couple of the stylized characters, so asked him to read it for her and tried to follow along as he spoke. His voice was liquid and wavering, and although she couldn't catch many words and couldn't always understand those that she did, she was content just to listen to him there on the cool mat, the party barely audible on the faint breeze and the whine of a cicada just outside the window.

When he reached the end she wanted to ask him to repeat it just to have that voice continue, but he was sitting straight with his face so calm that she didn't dare disturb him. Perhaps it was a poem, tanka maybe, she thought, but she didn't want to insult his reading by asking such an elementary question. So with her eyes she followed the path of the characters again, hearing them in her head as she watched them dance down into one another—the wisps and bleeds, weights and points.

"Is it one of yours?" she finally asked, and he put his hand up in

protest and shook his head. She concentrated on his words, here and there peppered with Kagoshima dialect, as he explained that it had been done by his teacher, and she felt foolish for implying that he'd be so immodest as to hang his own work in the most honored place in the house. She praised the scroll and the lily, which probably complemented the piece of writing, and she continued to kneel by his side, until he rose and led her back to the living room, where he pulled a portfolio from out of a corner, untied the three strings, and opened it to stacks of *shodo* works on thin, nearly translucent paper. *"Now* these I *did,"* he said, leafing through and pulling examples for Caitlin to see. She admired them, but felt frustratingly handicapped; there were many *kanji* she didn't know or were so stylized she couldn't read, and the meanings of the poems often eluded her. Still, she loved the sense of movement, that dance—a dimensional side of writing that English lacked.

"Aah, is he showing off to you?" The aunt, whose name escaped Caitlin, stood over them, chiding. *"The food is all ready if you two care to join us."* She flounced out again. The grandfather hardly seemed to have heard her. He held one sheet of four characters up, and said, *"Naomi is good. This is hers. See? She has the sense of timing; she understands the brush, like her mother. Izumi is no good; she has no patience, just like her father. But Naomi, Naomi and her mother, they feel it. It comes from here,"*—he placed his palms on his belly—*"from the soul, and it moves up through the body into the arm and into the brush. They write with their hearts, with their whole bodies, not their hands."* He pulled out a few more pieces, and Caitlin couldn't discern whose were whose anymore unless they were extremely complicated, in which case she assumed they were the grandfather's.

She helped him tie the strings of the portfolio and replace it in the corner. The grandfather sighed and shook his head: *"She'll come back to it someday, I know. She's too good not to, and she derives too much joy from it. As a little girl, whenever she grew irritable or pained by difficulties with schoolmates, she learned that she could calm herself by getting out her inkstone, rubbing the ink, and turning her mind completely to* shodo. *She draws life from* shodo. *And I worry she'll stay away from it for too long. I might be gone when she finally takes it up again,"* he said. Caitlin nodded, gravely, and they both stood. Then they stepped outside, uttering the requisite phrases as they joined the others—that everything smelled good, they sure were hungry, they were lucky the wind was from the west today.

▲ ▲ ▲

After burgers, barbecued chicken, green salad, corn on the cob, and Caitlin's first German potato salad in more than a year, Carl disappeared. He could be heard next door as he went through his own house, then he returned with a plastic ball and bat and several odd sacks; Hideaki cheered, Naomi and Izumi clapped, and the aunt and Akiko groaned. "It's a tradition," Naomi said to Caitlin, "Every barbecue."

Caitlin and Hiroshi helped gather folding chairs, tote the bases, and distribute the painters' caps that Carl pulled out of a duffle: on the visors, dates, initials, and messages had been scrawled—the earliest on Caitlin's was 1978. Even the grandfather put on his cap, then he too disappeared into the house and returned with a Cleveland Indians shirt. Caitlin laughed as he pointed a finger at Carl and said in heavily accented English so that Cleveland ended up with five syllables, "Ku-ree-bu-ran-do: Besto rocation een za nation."

They walked to a local playground with a fenced-in dirt lot, and Carl assigned teams: Hideaki, Akiko, Naomi, Caitlin, and the uncle against Hiroshi, the aunt, Carl, the grandfather, and Izumi. Caitlin's team started in the outfield; when the uncle took first, Caitlin positioned herself at third. Except for having to be on his side, she was pleased. She hadn't played a team sport since moving to Japan; all her exercise—swimming, windsurfing, biking, walking—was solitary.

After the third inning the grandfather bowed out, unfurled a parasol, and sat down to watch and occasionally cheer from a folding chair. Then as Caitlin's team began to lose, the uncle began to bark orders—how Naomi should stand, where Caitlin should throw, how Akiko should pitch, how Hideaki should cover for the women better. They all nodded, but seemed to be in consensus, ignoring him in favor of having a good time. "My uncle is a traditional Kagoshima man," Naomi whispered to Caitlin as they walked in to bat.

Caitlin lost track of the score, everyone did except the uncle, and she had to restrain herself from making fun of him by faking that she'd miss a catch or pretending to be daydreaming. She and Naomi shouted chants in unison, and the uncle grumbled that there were too many women this year.

At one point, a long fly was headed straight for Naomi, and the uncle charged over and caught it, knocking down his niece in his zeal, but it was Naomi who apologized. Naomi then fumbled several easy plays and the other team scored five runs, so in the fourth inning Caitlin suggested Naomi play third and Caitlin second. When the uncle muscled in on a grounder that Caitlin was well positioned for, she asked him bluntly if he'd prefer to play second instead of first. When he didn't answer she asked again. He acted as if he hadn't heard her, but then it struck Caitlin that of course he had; he just wasn't about to answer to a confrontation. It was his party anyway. She felt as naive as some of the new Americans on the teaching program she'd met at the Tokyo conference in June—so certain they could and should reform Japanese opinions, manners, and customs, so offensively direct, and so impatient and loud in their efforts.

Carl announced the seventh inning stretch and made them sing along with him, before doling out iced tea, juice, and water. He and Hiroshi then played gently to try to even up the score. When Caitlin's team went to bat, Carl murmured something to the uncle, who laughed, promptly bunted, and got to first. Caitlin then hit to right field just out of Carl's reach, and the uncle actually smiled when she crossed the plate after him.

It grew harder to see the ball in the dusk, and Carl's team won easily in the end. Drenched with sweat and streaked with ash and dirt, they could barely see to sign their names to their hats. Caitlin gulped her iced tea. Carl and Hiroshi poured water over their heads. They ambled back to the house, and Caitlin and Hiroshi rinsed under a garden hose while the others washed up indoors. Carl revived the untended coals for marshmallows, and Akiko presented her strawberry shortcake, making everyone whip the cream with a whisk first, passing the bowl from lap to lap.

After dessert, Caitlin and Hiroshi announced they'd be going, but Naomi insisted they wait, ran indoors, and returned with a large package of sparklers. She lit a candle and everyone lit their sparklers off it and waved them about, describing circles and scribbling waves furiously with the light, until the sticks sputtered and went dark, fizzing as they were dropped into a bucket of water. They ignited new ones and tried new patterns, English words and *kanji,* until they'd exhausted the supply and Naomi said, "Okay, now *senko hanabi.*" Caitlin couldn't recall what *senko* fireworks were, though she knew *senko* meant incense, and she gingerly took the threadlike sparkler from Naomi, who lit it, then said, "Just hold it still like that, upside down." She did, and as everyone stood by and watched, a small molten bulb grew, then sprayed delicately—aborning tiny, fragile drops of light.

Naomi handed the *senko* sparklers around, and everyone stood watching their miniature showers. Caitlin took another, and went to a dark corner of the garden by the grandfather. When his went out they both watched the last drops of Caitlin's, and once again the firefly haiku surfaced in Caitlin's mind. She recited it just loud enough for the grandfather to hear, and he made a guttural sound of appreciation in his throat and nodded. The sprays extinguished and the backyard went dark again, and in the moment of quiet before everyone regrouped, Caitlin wondered if there'd been *senko hanabi* among the many kinds of sparklers that she, Mie, Lee, and Nobuko had waved against the darkness of the rice paddies in front of the Kyoto house. Those rice paddies . . . she suddenly recalled. They'd helped plant seedlings both springs, their feet deep in the black, squelching mud, tiny tadpoles wriggling about their legs, crayfish backing away. The memory darted before her, a meteoric flash in the deep night shadows of the uncle's garden, the spent *senko hanabi* still in her hand.

Eleven

LATER, IN THE passenger seat of Hiroshi's car, Caitlin nibbled at the wet biscuit of some strawberry shortcake that Akiko had packed up for them to take home. She was glad not to be driving, to be able to sit back and close her eyes as she chewed on the coolness of a strawberry. They were nearly to Caitlin's apartment before either of them spoke.

"Nice people," Hiroshi said.

"Mmm," Caitlin agreed. Then she straightened. *"Except for that uncle."* Hiroshi shrugged. *"What was he saying about me anyway, soon after we arrived, when he was talking to you in Kagoshima dialect?"*

"Oh that. Keito-san, men like him, they have a different way of thinking. Don't worry about him."

"I'm not worrying. What'd he say? It was about me, wasn't it?"

Hiroshi shifted in his seat. *"He simply said I was lucky to have found you."*

"And what else?"

"Look, it's better if I say nothing."

Caitlin closed her container of shortcake and placed it on the floor mat. *"No, it's not. Be straight with me. I have a right to know what men say to you about me, don't I?"*

Hiroshi sighed. *"He just thought you were a prize, and that if I wasn't careful he might steal you from me."*

"Oh, how nice. And what else? There must be more."

"That's all," he said firmly, indicating the end of the conversation.

But she persisted, despite his glare; she didn't care that he resented this sort of stubborn incompliance. *"Come on. He asked you lots of questions. Why did Akiko hit him?"* They had pulled up in front of her apartment, and Hiroshi left the engine running. *"Why?"* Caitlin pressed. *"I'm not getting out until you tell me."*

Hiroshi exhaled loudly. "Okay." He fingered the keys hanging from the ignition then wiped his palms on his thighs and answered without looking at her: *"He wanted to know if you're blond all over."*

Caitlin sucked in her breath. *"Right in front of me he asked that?"* she whispered. Hiroshi nodded. "Jesus." She leaned her head back on the rest.

"He knew you couldn't understand."

"As if that mattered!" She crossed her arms; she felt invaded.

"I didn't want to tell you."

"What was your answer?" she asked quietly.

"I said I don't know that sort of thing. Keito, don't be mad. Some men are like that. Foreign girls have a reputation. Even you told me that."

"Well, Japanese men are getting a reputation."

"Hey, don't include me. Some *men are like that. Americans too. Anyhow, it's late, you should get out, your neighbors are probably watching us."*

"I hate them all anyway," she said, but she opened her door and swung one leg out.

"Here." He handed her the container of shortcake. *"The seminar ends Friday?"* he asked. She nodded and stepped out of the car. *"I'm not like him, Keito. You know that,"* he said. Again she nodded but closed the door with more force than necessary.

When he'd driven off and the sound of his motor had dwindled and merged with the other night sounds, she hurled the plastic container of shortcake down the street and listened to it bounce and roll on the asphalt. Her eyes were stinging. She walked up the stairs to her landing, but stopped before she'd turned the key and pressed her forehead to the door. Then she trudged back down and out to the road to retrieve the container, still sealed, but oozing its sticky red liquid. She dropped it into the empty garbage can outside her door, the thud echoing off the apartment building opposite, and she was glad—she could feel the neighborhood ears and eyes following her.

▲ ▲ ▲

After the first round of classes Monday morning, Caitlin found Mandy by the hot water thermoses and told her what the uncle had said to Hiroshi. "Figures," Mandy said. "Men here assume you can't wait to climb into their pants. I get approached all the time, don't you?" Caitlin shook her head, no—she didn't. Mandy poured more instant coffee crystals into her mug and added creamer. She took a sip and grimaced. "I wish I liked tea. Anyway, consider yourself lucky you don't get propositioned. Beware the ones who want to practice their English on you."

"I answer them in Japanese. That usually works."

"But not with the uncle?"

"I don't know much Kagoshima dialect—just a few words and some verb endings. If he'd said it in regular Japanese I'd have slugged him. Or at least said something."

"It wouldn't have mattered, Caitlin. Men like him don't care what you think."

Throughout the day of workshops, as she guided the teachers through role plays, Caitlin couldn't help but wonder whether any of them had burning questions about her hair color too. Stop obsessing, she told herself, but she couldn't seem to let it lie, and when she saw that she had a group of all women for the lifeboat exercise, she couldn't resist. In a bored monotone, she explained the planned exercise—a role play to determine which six of ten people aboard a lifeboat should be allowed to live—then offered the alternative of discussing a current topic of particular interest to women. Of course they deferred. She felt devious, then let go with a barrage of questions: How did they feel about late-night pornography on television? Graphic *manga* comics men read on the trains? Had any of them ever been rubbed against by a man in a crowded bus or train? And how did they feel about sex tours to other Asian countries? Finally she shared with them the uncle's words. She was shocked at the torrent that broke from her mouth, the issues she'd buried by reminding herself over and over that it wasn't her society, it wasn't her place to be angry.

She'd embarrassed the women, but she waited, and eventually, timidly, they began to speak on the issues. Bit by bit they addressed each other, not only her, and lo, a bona fide discussion was born. Caitlin listened and encouraged, but it was as if she'd simply needed to air the questions; detached, she watched the discussion progress, unable to focus on their words. She eyed the clock and shortly before the end of the session interrupted an animated argument about offensive men on crowded trains to ask about the uncle. "So, what if a man doesn't touch you, but just says things. Then what?" Caitlin asked.

"Ignore him."

"Tell him it is rude."

"Tell him to bug off," one woman enunciated carefully, and they all laughed; Caitlin had taught them the expression as a joke during skit practice that morning.

"But what if it's at a party, like my situation?" Caitlin asked, and they all stopped talking.

Finally one ventured, "That is very difficult problem."

"Probably you should be quiet. It is his house, is it not?" said another.

"And it was man to man, right? He was not talking to you?" Caitlin nodded. "Then you cannot do nothing."

They all sighed apologetically except for one. "Yes, she can," this woman said. "She is foreigner. She is not Japanese. And she is not married. So she can say something. We cannot. If we are married, our husband will be angry. Or our friend at party. Or our family."

Another woman drew in her breath. "I don't know, but at the party you should be quiet I think. If you don't like something, you tell the people you must leave. You are sick maybe."

"Yes, you should just leave," another said, and again they began to argue and discuss. When the session ended, the women thanked her and dispersed except for one young teacher who lingered by the door. "In America what would you do?" she asked.

Caitlin knit her brow. "I'd say something, even if it made my boyfriend or husband or family or friends angry."

"Yes," the woman said. "I think so. You don't need to worry. Japanese women are strong too, but we cannot be so independent. We must hide our feeling. So in some way we are stronger maybe. Because we must endure in silence. But it is a shame, don't you think so?"

Caitlin smiled weakly and nodded. The woman thanked her, then Caitlin hurried back to her room for the few minutes of solitude before dinner. She had a single this time, on a different floor from Mandy's, and she waved to the teachers gathered in the lounge, but rather than sit down with them, disappeared into her room and closed the door. Her head hurt, and she threw herself on her bed with her arms over her eyes, wishing she could be back in her apartment. Her bladder was ready to burst, but she found the idea of using the shared bathroom repugnant, with all those women flushing over and over so no one could hear the sound of them urinating.

Already she was regretting the discussion with the women; the subject had made her resort to "us" and "they" thinking. She'd been criticizing Japanese men in general despite her disclaimers; in fact, it had been all she could do to refrain from launching into greater criticisms of Japanese society. This bitter resentment had welled up before, and it always alarmed her how her dissatisfactions could so quickly be aligned and pointed in one accusing direction. It was so easy, this criticizing as an outsider; so shallow. She felt guilty toward Hiroshi. He *was* different from men like the uncle.

Yet with the passing of each day lately, she'd felt her self-control diminishing. She'd found herself resenting everyone and everything around her. She turned over on the bed, and a knock sounded on her door. One of the teachers announced they were on their way to dinner. She told them to go ahead, she'd be a couple minutes, and when their footsteps had faded, she emerged from her room and went in the opposite direction from the dining room, down a hall to a pay phone. Hiroshi answered on the third ring.

"I just wanted to say hello," she said.

"Hello," he said, amused. She asked him about his day, told him she missed him, and invited him to her apartment on Friday—*she'd* make dinner this time. *"Should I call first?"* he asked, and she smiled at his taunt. He told her he'd be there, and she hung up feeling better, but fragile. She wasn't hungry, and the idea of a communal dinner with all those teachers eager for her company turned her off. She was in no frame of mind to be the conversationalist that enhanced international understanding, but after lingering a few minutes more in a bathroom stall, she proceeded toward the dining hall. She could hear Naomi mimicking her parents: "Now remember, you're like a little ambassador."

▲ ▲ ▲

For the next four days, Caitlin tried to act the part of enthusiastic instructor, but as she went through the motions of leading discussion exercises, she found herself sorting out what needed to be done the following week—buy her ferry tickets, find gifts for the Oides, read through guidebooks to plan day trips from Kyoto—and she tended to drift into her own thoughts during meals, wondering if she were making a mistake going to the Oides' instead of taking off for a leisurely few days with Hiroshi camping, snorkeling, and windsurfing. She kept telling herself she'd have other opportunities to travel with him, but then the reverse perplexed her; why did she feel so driven to see the Oides now when it would be so miserably hot? Why not wait until a cooler season? And why in the middle of O-Bon, when who knew what ceremonies she might have to perform? Simply to be one up on her father? As Friday inched closer and she realized she departed in just one week, she considered phoning the Oides to tell them she'd changed plans. But in all her daydreams, she never went so far as to imagine what she might say in such a call.

She badly needed to swim—she hadn't been able to use the education center's pool much with her full schedule of workshops, and whenever she was free, it was open to the public, full of noisy swarms of kids. She felt irritable and jumpy with excess tension that finally vented on Thursday evening before the final skit productions, when she told Mandy that she'd have nothing to do with an improvised dance party afterward, and no, she wouldn't teach them American drinking games instead. She would sit at the back of the room and clap politely after each of the plays, then she planned to go to bed and not see another soul until the breakfast bell—she had a headache and couldn't stop grinding her teeth.

She calmed down later, and revised her plans after the skits to sit for more than an hour drinking *shochu* and oolong tea with the teachers in her suite. Some of the teachers began singing, and on the floor, cross-legged, leaning back against the sofa and sipping at her cool drink in the air-conditioned room, Caitlin felt her forehead ease and even joined in when they sang "My Way." It was near eleven when she finally excused herself, but before going to bed, she ran down the hall and phoned Hiroshi to revise their meeting time the following day; she planned to go to the sports club pool first thing when she was done with the seminar.

▲ ▲ ▲

Just the sight of a free swimmer's lane seemed to ease the tension in her neck and shoulders. As she shook her arms and legs before diving in, she cast off that false teacher's facade, finally feeling herself again. She concentrated before the dive as if she were about to race, then reached into the water. She allowed herself a few laps of warm up, then tore into race speed, not bothering to time herself, just pulling, driving herself beyond a week's worth of teaching, her impending trip, the uncle's words, the lie to her father, Ma Ruth's illness, her sister's silence. When she swam hard enough, she left her problems trailing behind her like competitors that she could just see out of the corners of her goggles.

She swam crawl until her legs dragged and her arms felt heavy, then she turned onto her back and squinted into the bright overhead lights, floating, barely drifting. The adrenalin was pumping again. Her body felt aflame, a fire just stoked.

▲ ▲ ▲

She had her hair pulled back into a loose braid, a dinner of salad and pasta with squid sauce nearly ready, and was singing along with a Pretenders cassette by the time Hiroshi knocked. She opened the door, took the large plastic jug of beer from where it had been tucked in the crook of his arm, set it on the kitchen floor, and tugged Hiroshi, shoes on, up the entryway step and into her arms. The embrace was as soothing, as much of a release, as her swim. He laughed and kicked his shoes off, then poured glasses of beer and toasted to Caitlin's vacation. Caitlin set out rice snacks and even some cheese and crackers she'd splurged on, and plunked herself down on his lap.

"So, how was the week?" Hiroshi asked.

Caitlin groaned and leaned into his neck. "Okay. *It's over at least."*

"You're tired. I can tell by your eyes."

Caitlin nodded. *"And you?"*

"All right. It's been kind of crazy. We had to fire two drivers. They were caught transporting illegal cargo in our trucks."

"Like what?"

"Mostly artwork smuggled out of China. Paintings. Some antiques. So I ended up driving a lot to cover." He mimed boredom at the wheel of a bouncing cab. *"But other than that, nothing's new. I missed your futon,"* he said with a wink.

Caitlin smiled. *"Me too. But let's eat first."* She returned to the stove, dished out the pasta, and was about to ladle the squid sauce over when the phone rang. She set down the ladle, picked up the receiver, and Carl's voice erupted on the other end of the line. Quickly she thanked him for the cookout the week before.

"Don't mench," he said. "Especially since I'm calling to ask a favor."

Caitlin slumped down into a chair. "What is it?" she asked.

"Well, Akiko and I were wondering. You're going to Kyoto for your break, right? By ferry to Osaka?"

Caitlin winced. "Right."

"You see, we were wondering if you'd mind if Naomi accompanied you on the ride up. Akiko's sister lives in Kyoto, you know, and we thought it might be good for Naomi to have a change of scenery, be away from us, and maybe check out an international school up there. See, she could live with her aunt that way. Anyway, it's so expensive to fly, and the train takes so long, and we wouldn't send her on the ferry alone, but if you were with her we wouldn't mind. And we'd drive you to Shibushi, of course. She wouldn't be with you at all in Kyoto, we don't want to interfere with your vacation plans whatsoever, but if you wouldn't mind accompanying her just on the ferry . . ."

Caitlin was shaking her head, but when he stopped and waited for her answer she couldn't think of any good reason to refuse. "She doesn't mind going economy and sleeping on the carpet?" she asked feebly.

"Oh, not at all, that's fine by her."

"Well, I'm leaving next Friday. And I'll probably return the Saturday two weeks later."

"Anytime before school starts is fine. But if you plan to stay longer, don't worry, she *could* take the bullet train to Hakata and I'd pick her up there. I mean, she could go *up* to Kyoto that way too, but we just thought, if you're going anyway, and if it's not too much of an inconvenience . . ."

"No, no, it would have been a long ride alone," Caitlin forced herself to say. She rolled her eyes toward Hiroshi, who was watching, puzzled, trying to follow the conversation. "But look, could I call you back tomorrow? It's my first day of vacation, and I'm about to sit down to a celebration dinner."

"Oh, sorry. Congrats!" Carl bellowed. "But Caitlin, look, sleep on this. If it's an imposition, be honest, let us know."

When she hung up she let out a long groan and put both hands to her head. "Why can't I ever say no? Why do I always end up with company?"

"Company?" Hiroshi asked, glancing toward the door, and Caitlin explained in Japanese. He laughed, pulled her to her feet, and handed her her glass of beer. *"To your trip alone,"* he said lifting his glass.

"You think it's funny?"

He nodded. *"Next time maybe you'll let me go with you."*

"Damn," she whispered when she saw the pasta cooling on their plates; she put it back in the pan with a bit of water and turned the burner on. "I won't have anything to do with her in Kyoto," she said, stirring madly. She reached for a jar of olives. "They can't sneak that one in. I'm not going to babysit," she muttered, as she tried to loosen the cover. She knocked a plate down when it finally came open, and when she bent to pick up the shards, she jabbed her thumb and a drop of blood oozed out. Hiroshi squatted beside her, encircled her wrist with his hand, sat her forcefully at the table, and handed her a tissue for her thumb. When he'd swept up the pieces, she inhaled deeply, stood, and served the reheated meal. They ate for a time in silence and Caitlin thanked him inwardly for letting her be, for not pressing her with any more questions about why it was so important for her to go to Kyoto alone.

After the meal, they lingered at the table, talking over their weekend plans for seeing a movie and maybe driving up to Aira Town on Sunday. Then they cleared the dishes, moving around each other with the ease of a long-familiar couple. As Caitlin washed, Hiroshi dried, putting the utensils and pots away in their appropriate niches in Caitlin's drawers and cupboards, and she realized with a snag in her chest that she would miss him terribly while she was in Kyoto. A month before, she wouldn't have believed she'd have become so deeply involved; it was summer after all. But she was growing to depend on him more by the hour, to look forward to talking over the minutiae of each day with him and to feeling the press of his lean body on hers in the dark. What's more, increasingly she'd had the urge to tell him things—about rivers, about playmates in summer, about blue-tailed lizards, about hoarding pills; she felt the need to purge herself before him and be absolved by the very tips of his sienna fingers.

She pulled the plug in the sink, wiped her hands, told Hiroshi to leave the rest to drip-dry, and without another word, drew him into the other room and down to the futon they'd both missed.

Twelve

MERCHANTS IN the Tenmonkan mall had only just raised their shutters and arranged their goods to spill out onto the concourse, but already shoppers and browsers were hovering, pausing, and striding with purpose. Caitlin sat spying on them from a second-story coffee shop, close to the activity but not on display, her pen poised, on the table before her a postcard begun to the Oides. She watched a clerk adjust price cards on lacquerware trays and bowls, and a mother strolling after children darting among pottery displays and hiding amid racks of aprons and bargain dresses; the mother paid them little attention, and as she stopped to inspect shop goods, the two ventured far out of sight, only now and then careening back to her side.

Caitlin nibbled a large piece of toast, spread some jam, then turned back to the postcard, adding the next sentence in the instant the idea occurred to her: she would visit a friend in Osaka the first night, then get herself from Osaka to Kyoto to join them on the 11th. Perfect, she thought—that would give her time to see Osaka and most of a day to reorient herself to Kyoto on her own, away from Naomi, before reuniting with the Oides. Most of a day to gather her nerve.

She completed the card with some polite closings and addressed it; again her pen formed those particular *kanji*—mountain over stone to make *iwa,* boulder; followed by *kura,* storehouse or granary—Iwakura, the strokes themselves resonated with her childhood. She chewed on a thick crust of toast and finished the sharp coffee. Down in the mall she would meander through the crowds to select the last few gifts for Nobuko and Yusuke. She would shop for them, purchase Kagoshima goods for them, yet she couldn't imagine them grown. She couldn't imagine Yusuke born.

▲ ▲ ▲

On Sunday she and Hiroshi drove north to Aira Town, snaking around the mountains edging the bay. The land rose nearly straight up; Ryu-ga-mizu, Dragon's Water, the slopes were called, and within the creases, waterfalls replenished by recent rains plunged down toward them. Caitlin often took the train along this route to her northern schools, and was always uneasy if there'd been much precipitation, fearful the swollen slopes would wash down right over them. They drove inland, past mountains that jutted up so steeply they looked as though they'd sprouted there, over back roads through orchards and rice paddies, then parked, took a short, steamy hike, and followed that with a soak in the outdoor hot-spring bath they sometimes frequented as a group. It felt strange to Caitlin to be there alone, soaking on the women's side, in one of the tepid baths, old women's prattle all around her but no friends. She leaned her head back on a polished rock and closed her eyes, but quickly opened them and started up a conversation with the woman soaking next to her; solitude, recently, had become increasingly unsettling. After the bath, they capped the day at Akinai, the *kaiseki* restaurant of Hiroshi's best friend Tomoki. They ate there once a month or so as a group, and Hiroshi often helped out there on his days off. But this was their first time without the entourage, and again, as she dipped slices of fresh yellowtail into soy sauce, it felt strange, devious even, to sit at the counter, just the two of them.

▲ ▲ ▲

Hiroshi slept over every night that week. Sometimes he came for dinner and stayed on. Other nights he didn't arrive until ten, and Caitlin suspected he'd waited until his mother and father had gone to bed. For them to know that he slept with her was not an embarrassment, but for them to see him brazenly walk out the door to spend the night with her was not only awkward, but wrong. Or so he'd tried to explain to Caitlin. She didn't mind his presence night after night, so constant; once she'd grown to expect him, if he didn't arrive until late she found herself agitated and unable to concentrate on books, letters, TV, anything.

She had the days off and spent them swimming, walking through different parts of town beneath branches of *sasa* tied with paper Tanabata decorations, wandering exhibits in the new culture museum and the art museum, and sitting uneasily in her apartment. She was anxious for Friday to come, and yet each morning that she awoke one day closer to her departure, the dread in her stomach grew more ulcer-sharp.

She could have done anything with this vacation, she thought on Thursday afternoon as she made neat stacks of the clothing she would take on her trip. Gone back to the States, to Pittsburgh and Ma Ruth, though she couldn't picture her as ill as her mother or father described. Or to Guam with Mandy. Anywhere. Yet here she was with ferry tickets for Osaka and plans to spend two weeks in Kyoto during O-Bon of all times. She longed to back out. To tell Hiroshi she'd be ferrying with him to Kikaijima instead. To join Mina and Naoko and Kosuke and Uma-chan, and banter and drink and hydroplane just inches above the complex world.

But she continued to pack. She eliminated several T-shirts and shoved the rest deep into her knapsack. She refolded her shorts so the pleats lay flat. Her hands worked independent of her mind— tucking plastic bags in with towels, rolling dresses together, stuffing socks into sneakers, enclosing shampoo and lotion in plastic bags— as she cursed herself for having to go backward instead of forward in time, for the guilt that propelled her back to Kyoto. She groaned to think how she might have been packing instead for days snorkeling beside Hiroshi in that underwater silence, poking each other, tugging each others' arms and fins to point out new shapes and patterns in the circus of tropical fish.

She threw in a bathing suit, though she realized she might not swim at all for two weeks. She doubted she'd have access to a pool, and could hardly ask the Oides if they knew of one she could use— it would take gall to explain that her sport was swimming. She considered buying some running shoes and shorts to take with her, but Caitlin had never liked the pounding of running, and Kyoto would be too hot anyway. She'd have to settle for long walks and maybe a bike ride—someone would be certain to have a rickety bike to loan her.

When her bag was full, she walked to one of the local markets and bought food to nibble the next day on the ferry. She meandered home along the river, then at her apartment took a chair out to her balcony, sat down, and on impulse, opened all the bags of rice snacks she'd just purchased. She arranged them in a row on the concrete rail of the balcony, and in the late afternoon light, ash clinging to her sweating skin as she looked down over the streets of Hirano-cho, she ate compulsively, only stopping once to fetch a glass of water, while she waited for that familiar white flash of Hiroshi's car in her lot.

MAGMA

Thirteen

IN THE EAST CHINA Sea, typhoon number four fisted and swirled, bearing down with menace on the Ryukyu Islands and gaining speed over open water. Still estimated to be a day away, wind and dense clouds preceded the storm like emissaries, darkening the sky above Shibushi, on the opposite side of Sakurajima, in the eastern-most reaches of the prefecture. For two days Caitlin had followed the progress of the storm, leaning in close to her television set whenever satellite images revealed the tight knot of clouds creeping up the bottom of her screen. One moment she was relieved, the next sickly panicked, that after all these years to summon the nerve, her return to Kyoto might be postponed because of a summer typhoon. Ash had dashed against the car as Carl drove them white-knuckled toward Shibushi Bay, now whipped and frothing in the wind. Just offshore, the tiny island of Birojima had almost complete-ly disappeared in cloud.

But late Friday afternoon, on schedule to the minute, the cap-tain of the *Sunflower* passenger ferry blasted the whistles and began to pull away from the Shibushi piers, anxious, Caitlin guessed, to slip around Cape Toi and head northeast well before the storm began its first lashings of Kyushu. She and Naomi jostled through the passengers leaning into gusts on the upper decks, and at the rails they joined in near-futile attempts to toss rolls of crepe paper through the wind to waving crowds on the pier below. Their first, second, third, and fourth rolls fell short and dropped into the churning waters by the ferry's hull. But when Caitlin heaved the fifth, a man lunged and caught it, and they motioned wildly for him to hand it down the crowd. He passed the still-coiled end of the red tape over heads and from person to person, and finally Carl and Caitlin each held opposite ends.

Together Caitlin and Naomi gripped their end of the tape, and below, Carl and Akiko slowly uncoiled the roll as the ferry pulled away. Akiko was shouting, then Carl was, but over the wind and the engines neither Caitlin nor Naomi could make out the words. Up and down the length of the hull, tapes draped and stretched, snapped and shimmied wildly in the wind before dropping to the water. Carl and Akiko had their arms around each other, and Caitlin and Naomi waved as the ferry hastened into the bay. People on the pier became smaller, and when the wind grew harsh on Caitlin's and Naomi's faces, tearing their eyes, with a final wave they descended to the lower decks to one of the large open rooms where they'd dropped their bags when they'd clambered on board with the other walk-ons.

They had an entire corner to themselves; the ferry was relatively empty considering the number of people that would normally be traveling for the holiday—cancellations had apparently been rampant. Caitlin lay down on the raised, carpeted floor with her head on her pack and felt beneath her the rocking of the boat and the grinding of the motors—the movement penetrated her back and abdomen. She sat up and unfolded a map, traced the route around Cape Toi, and guessed they'd be in the worst of the weather within an hour, then in calmer waters in the early morning.

Naomi was stacking square foam pillows to make a soft backing against the wall for them to lean on. "Here, claim your spot," she said handing Caitlin a long sleeping pad and blanket. Caitlin laid it out then leaned back on her pack again. She twirled a cord of her pack around her index finger, then off again, over and over, winding and unwinding. Naomi beckoned for Caitlin to join her against the foam pillows, but she shook her head and stood. "I think I'll try to find the bath."

"The bath?" Naomi said rising. "Mind if I come?"

Caitlin shrugged. They extracted their towels from their bags and followed signs down to the lowest level of the ship through long narrow passageways where the motion of the ferry was augmented. Naomi groaned. They found the sign for the women's bath and opened the door to the changing room timidly. Two baskets were filled with clothes.

"It must be open," Naomi whispered. They peaked inside the bathing room and were pleased to discover a long, deep tile tub, larger than the women's tubs—which were nearly always smaller than the men's—in many of the inns and hotels Caitlin had been to. Naomi called out to the mother and young girl soaking off to one side: *"Is it hot?"* Just right, they answered, and by the time Caitlin and Naomi had washed under the spigots, the mother and child had left, and they had the bath to themselves. The water really was hot, perfect, though it listed from one side to the other and often poured out in a great cascade. "Weird," Naomi said watching the waves that sloshed back and forth. "Maybe if you floated in here the whole ride you wouldn't feel seasick."

Caitlin sank down so the water just brushed her lips and the lobes of her ears. Though she sat still, she was sharply and uncomfortably aware of their movement, charging through the sea, fast-forwarding in time. She imagined a push on her back, a shove, hurtling her toward Kyoto, and she was unsettled by the fact that she would have no control over her precise geographical location until she disembarked the next day in Osaka. She wished she could swim, even on board the ferry; at least then she'd feel like *she* were cutting through the brine, displacing the seas herself.

Caitlin sat up so the bath water reached just below her shoulders.

"What time do we get in tomorrow?" Naomi asked.

"I forget exactly. Late morning."

"Oh. What are your plans?" Naomi had her head back on the tub rim and her legs stretched far out in front of her, toes just breaking the surface now and then.

"What do you mean?"

"You said you won't be going to Kyoto until the next day."

"Oh, right." Caitlin had forgotten she'd shared this with Naomi. "I don't know, I thought I'd just see what Osaka's like."

"Well, you can have a ride all the way to Kyoto if you want, you know—my aunt's driving to the pier to meet us."

"I thought you were taking a train."

"I was, at first, but she offered to come by car."

Caitlin was calculating what it would, in fact, cost to spend a night in Osaka then train to Kyoto. She didn't really have a friend to meet, and at this point couldn't care less about seeing Osaka or the castle; she just wanted a night on her own, to gain a sense of balance, or to opt out if need be, since she wasn't expected at the Oides' until Sunday. She'd assumed she'd want to be free of Naomi by the time the ferry docked, which is why she'd added fuel to the story about wanting to see Osaka, but now she liked the sound of a ride. She could just as easily spend her night alone in Kyoto as in Osaka. "I might take you up on that," she said.

"If you have time, you should come see my aunt's house. It's old Kyoto style, with wooden slats on the windows and down low at the edge of the street. And it has this little teeny-tiny courtyard in the middle. And stairs outside that go up to the roof. That's where they dry the laundry—up on the roof, not out back."

"Wouldn't work in Kagoshima."

"No, but there's a little roof covering up there. You should come see it."

"If I have time."

"You can stay there if you want. My aunt and uncle already offered."

Caitlin took a deep breath. "Thanks, but I'll probably be busy."

Naomi eyed her. "With what exactly?"

"All sorts of things," she replied, stepping out of the tub as several other women arrived. "There are people I haven't seen in a long time. And Kyoto—I don't know if I'll remember much, any of the temples, you know. I want to see what I can while I'm there. But guess what?" Caitlin said, pouring a bucket of cool water over her back.

"What?"

"No more ash for two weeks. It's all down there." She pointed to the drain beside her bathing stool.

▲ ▲ ▲

After their baths, Naomi unpacked the picnic dinner Akiko had sent them off with, sat back, and hardly touched the food. "I don't feel well," she said. She leaned against the vinyl pillows and nibbled on a rice ball. The boat listed and dipped and climbed the swells and now and then a huge slap of spray doused the bow-facing windows of the cabin. Caitlin rummaged in her pack and pulled out some motion sickness tablets she'd picked up at a pharmacy the day before. "Have one," she said, and they washed the tablets down with barley tea. Caitlin was squeamish too, but even more hungry, and had no trouble sampling everything from the foil and plastic containers.

"So you like temples and things?" Naomi asked when she finally leaned forward to pick through the food for something she could stomach.

"Well, sure. Don't you?"

"Some. Quiet ones. I like sitting on those verandas where you can look out onto the gardens. Imagining what it would be like without any other people around, you know, if it were your own house. Oh no." She put her hand to her forehead. "I forgot to bring my *shuincho.*"

"Your what?"

"My stamp book, *goshuincho,* for temple stamps. Every time I come to Kyoto I add to it. And whenever I go to a different temple in Kyushu. I'll have to get a new one."

"So, what else will you do in Kyoto besides collect temple stamps?" Caitlin asked.

"Oh, I don't know. I have to visit that school my parents want me to go to. And my aunt will probably take me shopping. And maybe we'll go to Arashiyama. Oh, and she said we'll see Daimonji. Will you?"

"Is that a temple?"

Naomi laughed. "I thought you used to live in Kyoto. You know, the big *dai* character on the mountain—they light it on fire. You probably saw it when you were little."

"Oh, that. I don't know. Maybe the first summer. The second summer I'd already left; we went back to the States in early August. When is it?"

"The last night of O-Bon. Friday, I think."

Caitlin sat up rigid and set down her tea. "That's right, O-Bon starts this week."

"Yup, time for the dead to come back," Naomi said. "Here deady-deady," she called in a high-pitched coo as if to a cat.

Caitlin could feel the blood draining from her face.

"But doesn't it seem kind of stupid to you?" Naomi went on in her normal voice. "I mean, how can they possibly come back? When you're dead, you're dead. And anyway, how can the spirits be in so many places at once? They're supposed to be in the altar all the time, but then at O-Bon you escort them from the grave to the altar. And when my grandfather sees a dragonfly near the house around O-Bon he says, *"Rei ga haitte-kita"*—the spirits are back. Like the dragonflies are the spirits too. When we were little he wouldn't even let us catch them in our insect nets till after O-Bon. It's ridiculous. When you die, you die; you become bones and rotting guts and flesh, then finally earth or dust, right? And when you're cremated, just bits of bone and ash."

Caitlin nodded, trying to concentrate on Naomi's mouth forming the sounds of the words, so she wouldn't have to think about the words, about O-Bon at the Oides' or Mie's bits of bone and ash. She chewed her lower lip, wishing Naomi would stop, wishing she could say something to make her stop, but she sat frozen and Naomi chattered on. "My grandfather's the only one in our family who really celebrates O-Bon. He always makes sure the little meal is set out for the spirits, every morning, as if my grandmother—who's been dead for ten years by the way—as if she really eats off it. Then he empties the little dishes into the cat's bowl when the new offerings are ready, but sometimes the cat jumps up to the altar and eats right off the offering stands, and then my aunt has to make the food all over again so my grandfather doesn't yell at her. What's wrong?"

Caitlin rose abruptly, cupped her hand over her mouth, and pretended she was about to be sick. She dashed out of the room and down the hall, but instead of turning in at the toilets, she bolted up the stairs and pushed open the door to the upper deck. The wind fought her, and spray or rain or a mixture of both cut into her skin as she staggered toward the stern. She grasped the railing and stared down at the water, gray and turbulent as it left the hull, then she inspected the darkening sky and the vague shadow of land to her right. They'd rounded Cape Toi, she supposed, and were beginning the northward haul, and she looked enviously at the scroll of land against the ominous dusk; had she taken a train, she could have disembarked somewhere along the way.

She strode back and forth across the less exposed quarter of the deck, but the lurching of the ferry made it hard to keep her footing. Now and then she'd hear people exclaim at the weather as they squeaked the door open and poked their heads out, but no one joined her outside there. What would it really mean, visiting them during O-Bon? Would they go to the river? Light fires? Chant sutras? She wished she knew what would be expected of her. With a shudder, she sat down miserably on a wet bin that held life preservers—the water immediately seeped through the seat of her shorts.

She rose and at the port railing leaned into the wind and stared at the last smudge of gray light between the heavy clouds and the horizon in the west. She searched the dark southern skies beyond the boat's stern, trying to see the swirl of typhoon, the neat and compact knot they showed in satellite shots, but she couldn't distinguish any variations in the light down there—just deep blackness of night and storm. She closed her eyes and let the spray pelt her face.

▲ ▲ ▲

When she finally trudged back into the sleeping room, Naomi jumped up from the stack of pillows. "I was looking for you. Where'd you go? What'd you do, take a shower?"

Caitlin felt her hair, salty and wet. "I went up on deck—I needed some air."

"You okay?"

"Fine."

"You sure? You're pale." Caitlin sat down and looked away. Naomi dropped down beside her and spoke so softly that Caitlin felt her throat constricting: "Caitlin, you look terrible. Are you sure you're okay?"

"Yes, I'm sure," she answered coldly then grabbed a square foam pillow and lay down. Determined to fight tears, she curled up against the wall with clenched fists and closed her eyes. Finally, hearing Naomi rise, Caitlin relaxed at having been left alone, but moments later, Naomi knelt down close behind her. She felt her damp strands of hair taken up into Naomi's hands, and she swallowed the rush of a sob as the girl gently patted and toweled her dry.

When Caitlin began to shiver, Naomi handed her another towel and led her down the corridors and back into the bath. They
were alone again, and they soaked in silence until Naomi said, "I'll
rub your back if you'll rub mine." Caitlin nodded and still sitting in
the tub turned her back to Naomi. But Naomi climbed out of the
water, and at her beckoning, Caitlin followed, spread her towel on
the tiles near the edge of the tub, then lay down on top of it and
closed her eyes as Naomi's palms and fingers began to knead her
warmed skin.

At first the startling feel of her hands, the skin to skin contact,
made Caitlin think of Hiroshi, long for Hiroshi, it had been so difficult to see him set out into the early dawn that morning. She'd
hardly slept, clinging to him as though he might absorb her, keep
her from leaving if she held tight enough. They'd had breakfast at
five in the morning, at her insistence, a somber and sleepy affair.
She wished she were back with him now, talking about anything,
cooking dinner together, even arguing, she'd take it, if only the ferry would turn around and deposit her back at the piers near that
ash-ridden town.

"Relax," Naomi said, "you're all tense," and slowly Caitlin let
Hiroshi's image go, let Kyoto and the Oides go, and just followed
the course of Naomi's hands—down her spine at a creep to the
curve and soft of her buttocks, to the top of her crack then out and
over to her hips, up her sides and along her ribs, fingertips grazing
the sides of her breasts, and up to the nape of her neck, under her
ears, down her shoulders and out her arms. Naomi continued with
slow concentration, leaning her body, rocking her body with the
push of her hands, and Caitlin wondered if Naomi, too, was sensing
the possibilities of skin on skin in that steaming room.

They returned to the tub for another soak, then Caitlin said,
"Your turn," and they stepped out, Naomi lay down, and Caitlin
tried to reciprocate that smooth touch. She tried new routes up and
down the back, light fingers segueing to deep palms, rocking with
the rhythm of her hands. Naomi had nearly fallen asleep it seemed,
and several other women and a mother and little boy entered as they
soaked in the tub a final time. Naomi yawned incessantly. They
dried off and dressed without speaking. "Thanks," Caitlin finally
said as they started out down the corridors, and Naomi nodded

drowsily. She'd never persisted with questions to find what was wrong, and Caitlin was so grateful she wanted to hug her as they listed from side to side there deep in the shuddering hull of the *Sunflower*, battered by the pounding swells of the Pacific.

They returned to the open sleeping room, set out their blankets, and draped their pillows with dry towels as covers. Naomi soon dropped off to sleep, but Caitlin, just after the overhead lights were turned off, slipped out to the bathroom, found a Western-style stall, and sat down on the toilet. She waited until the last of the young girls and mothers had brushed their teeth and gargled at the sinks, then she closed her eyes, brought the image of Hiroshi back, brought his burnished skin in close to hers, put his tongue on her nipples, and held herself until the throbbing between her legs subsided.

Fourteen

CAITLIN'S FIRST thought was a fly, and she kicked each time it lit on her foot. Then she thought, Hiroshi's hand, no Naomi's. But as consciousness bloomed, she noted that each kick was followed by a chorus of giggles and more "flies" alighting—scrambling up her shins, even on her shoulders. She turned over and opened her eyes. Naomi glared back. "Remind me never to sleep beside a blond foreigner again."

"Hallo," one child said above Caitlin's head, and Caitlin pulled the blanket over her eyes. But the hands on her legs and head became more persistent, so she sat up and made a face that caused all four children to collapse in hysterics. *"Ohayo-gozaimasu,"*—good morning—she said, and they whooped with delight. *"What time is it?"* she asked the eldest, then groaned to his reply of *"Six-thirty-five."* *"All right, listen carefully,"* she said. *"You, Oniichan, two cups of coffee. And you,"* she said to the others—a younger boy and two girls, *"a warm washcloth, a rose for the sleeping girl, and two glasses of orange juice, please."* The kids ran off, and Caitlin lay down and closed her eyes again.

"Good work," Naomi muttered.

But it seemed that only seconds had passed when Caitlin heard a voice above her saying, *"Hai, hotto kohii."* She and Naomi sat up rubbing their eyes and laughed; the eldest boy held out two cans of hot coffee from a vending machine. *"I was joking!"* Caitlin said, but he shrugged and thrust the cans toward her. *"How much? A hundred yen each?"* He nodded and Caitlin pulled the coins from the pockets of the shorts she'd been wearing the day before.

They opened the coffee and as soon as they'd taken the first sweet sips, one of the girls came running up and dropped what looked like crumpled paper into Caitlin's lap. Caitlin examined it;

155

the girl had folded a tourist brochure into some semblance of a flower. *"Oh, for the sleeping girl, thank you,"* Caitlin said and gave it ceremoniously to Naomi. Seconds later canned juice arrived, then a warm moistened Anpan-man washcloth. Caitlin and Naomi were wide awake now, and others on the floor were stirring, with eyes turned toward them in amusement.

At seven the overhead lights beamed on and the loudspeaker announced the hour, the types of breakfast available in the snack bar and cafeteria, the estimated time of arrival in Osaka, and the weather report saying that yesterday's typhoon was due to hit Kagoshima that afternoon but had weakened and was turning west; in the Kansai region, sun and clear skies were expected. A few cheers were heard, and the bunkroom came alive. Naomi hurried off to the bathroom to wash up ahead of the "crowds," but Caitlin sat idly chatting with two of the children who had wakened her, until a parent called them away.

They passed the morning reading, playing cards, and sipping tea. Every now and then Caitlin ventured a question as to how Naomi's grandfather celebrated O-Bon, what they did at the grave, what they did at home during the three days—Caitlin wanted to be better prepared. But Naomi was vague on details and recalled little other than cleaning the grave and lighting incense some time toward the beginning of the holiday. When Caitlin sounded irritated that Naomi couldn't remember more, Naomi quipped, "How should I know—my uncle's house has the *butsudan,* and that's where the spirits come back to."

By the time they churned into Osaka harbor the sun was pressing down through a thick, smoggy haze. For the final half hour of the trip, Caitlin and Naomi stood on the decks in the open air—hot but breezy—watching the barges and tugs and eyeing the approaching buildings, cranes, and containers that bowed and shimmied in the heat waves. They were fast approaching Honshu and the Kansai area, where Caitlin had once lived with her family, and Caitlin felt moved as when driving through that pass not far from Williamsport on her way to Pittsburgh. Without a drop of Japanese blood in her body, she somehow felt as if she were returning "home."

Naomi spotted her aunt in the waiting crowd as they descended the gangplank. They made their way toward the woman, dressed in a crepe skirt and neat white blouse, and craning her neck with particular grace. By her straight posture and the clean way in which she bowed to them, Caitlin could tell she was an even more refined version of Akiko. Naomi suddenly assumed a demure air as she offered greetings and thank-yous and introduced Caitlin and asked permission for her to accompany them. Caitlin switched into polite mode, too, as the aunt ushered them toward the parking lot and asked about their journey. Sachiko glided with the erect and seamless control of a dancer, and her speech, too, was careful, with words clearly articulated, never rushed, and softened with Kyoto verb endings. Caitlin, moseying along with her usual gait, felt clumsy and ungainly by contrast.

They hefted their bags into the trunk. Naomi and her aunt insisted that Caitlin take the front seat, and Caitlin quickly complied, since Naomi seemed to be stalling, fiddling with her luggage, pretending to search for a hair ribbon, tissues, then a note from her mother to Sachiko. Caitlin gave them the privacy to speak behind the car and waited for the two of them to climb in, wiping her brow and the back of her neck with a handkerchief. Then Sachiko was beside her, the air conditioner turned on, the car switched from park into reverse and then drive, and that was that, they were off, suddenly weaving through the streets of Osaka, suddenly far from Kagoshima, and though still more than an hour away, truly and finally approaching Kyoto.

But in the tight car with the cool air brushing her arms, and Naomi and Sachiko catching up, Caitlin for a change felt comfortably situated. She was growing weary of thinking about the Oides and O-Bon and was relieved to have someone else in charge. The threesome was soothing. Sachiko was formal but warm and welcoming, and Caitlin had the fleeting feeling that, despite a longing for Hiroshi, at that very moment she would rather be there than anywhere else. When Naomi had filled in her aunt on assorted bits of family and Kagoshima news, Sachiko turned to Caitlin, and it even felt good to engage in the light patter of getting acquainted—how effortless it was, even using polite forms. Now and then, she even tentatively added a Kyoto ending. Sachiko asked all about Caitlin's teaching, and when Caitlin mentioned her childhood time in Japan, Sachiko asked if her father had been a teacher in Kyoto.

"*No, my mother taught English some, but my father wasn't teaching much then,*" Caitlin said. "*He was doing research at Kyo-Dai. He's a religion professor.*"

"*Oh, how interesting,*" Sachiko said with genuine admiration. "*A scholar. Do you have any brothers and sisters?*"

"*A younger sister, in college.*"

Sachiko wanted to know if she, too, planned to come to Japan sometime, and Caitlin held back a snort at the thought of Lee defying her mother and catching a plane for Tokyo or Osaka. "*I doubt it. She doesn't like to leave home. And she doesn't remember much of Kyoto. She was only four and five then.*"

"*How about your parents—have they come back?*"

"*Just my father, for his work.*"

"*I see.*" Sachiko was silent for a while, then said, "*Kyo-Dai . . . in the seventies?*"

"*Sixty-nine and seventy.*"

"*It was a bit like war on the campuses then, wasn't it?*"

"*Yes, scary. Or at least to me it was. I remember being frightened by the university—the students with helmets, scarves covering their faces, holding long poles, all shouting out front. They threw rocks sometimes. And I watched TV at my friend's house, so I saw the water cannons. I didn't understand why my father wanted to work at a place like that, and I didn't like to go near there. He told me I was safe, that it was like a family quarrel and that we weren't part of that family so I didn't need to worry, but still . . .*"

"*Yes. Rocks don't always hit their intended targets. Those were very different days. Universities have certainly changed since then.*" Sachiko shook her head and smiled as if reminiscing. After a moment she said, "*Well, Naomi says you'll be staying with a family while you're here. Old friends?*"

Caitlin nodded. "*Neighbors from when we lived here.*"

"*That's nice. Well, you're welcome to stay at our house anytime. It's small, but you and Naomi can have Mayumi's room—that's our daughter. Naomi says you don't have plans for this evening yet.*" So that was the nugget of information Naomi had relayed to her aunt during the few moments Caitlin was out of earshot, climbing into the front seat. "*Really, you're welcome to stay,*" Sachiko added.

"*Thank you,*" Caitlin said grudgingly. "*But I might look up a friend from my teaching program. What part of the city are you in?*"

"*Yoshida. Not far from Kyo-Dai actually—perhaps it will be nostalgic for you. Our daughter is in Nagano on a hiking trip with college friends, and then will be visiting my husband's family in Nagoya until next week; our son, Jun, is home. He's a* ronin—*you know, failed his college entrance exams so he's just studying this year. He spends every day at the library and prep schools . . .*"

Caitlin was only half listening. They'd turned onto a highway, and by the sonorous inhalations coming from the back seat, she could tell that Naomi had fallen asleep. She gazed out the window at the dense suburbs zipping past while Sachiko described Jun's study routine, her husband's work in an insurance company, and her part-time job at a bank. Caitlin added appropriate comments here and there, but all the while she was straining to recognize any of what passed outside. There were so many more housing tracts and apartment buildings, so much less green than in Kagoshima. To her dismay, nothing looked the least bit familiar, but in fact, so little surfaced in her memory that she didn't even know what she was searching for. As they entered the city limits she felt a trill of fear and excitement. She hadn't remembered that it was such a big city, that it could sprawl like this, and she realized that what she could recall of Kyoto didn't really include the city at all.

The Kyoto she remembered was a series of flashing scenes and vignettes—the house with the separate sliding doors, one to the urinal and one to the toilet she'd hated squatting over because it was just a hole and everything just sat under there until the tank was full and a pump truck came to empty it; the futon closet she sometimes hid in and the *kotatsu* heating table she fell asleep under; the deep, square bath where she and Lee, and sometimes she and Mie, bathed together; Mie's house, and cartoons on a hefty wood-encased TV; a small shrine compound with a grove full of insects; streets and fenced dirt yards where they played hide-and-seek; the pink bicycle from which she fell into a deep trickling gutter; the Japanese tutor who came once a week; the counter with square stools at a local restaurant where she sat with her parents to order. And the school—long corridors they had to sweep, rags drying on racks, book bags hung from hooks on the desks, workbooks with *kanji* grids, fat brushes for *shodo,* onion greens poking up from vegetable beds, chicken coops, rabbit coops, and short shorts on the boys even in winter. Those were the scenes of her Kyoto. She tried and tried, but except for a pagoda, some vague motion inside a department store, and the flower-shaped clock face of the university tower, nothing outside the Iwakura neighborhood came back to her. She had mental pictures of major temples and other parts of Kyoto, but she knew they were borrowed, not originally hers—recollections of slides of her father's, scenes from documentaries she'd watched in college, or pictures from guidebooks.

All around her the city was foreign. Not until Sachiko drove them under the massive red torii of Heian Shrine was Caitlin startled by a sight she recognized. As she cast her eyes on the shrine entrance, she wondered if she could possibly be the same person as the eight year old who'd toured its compound. She twisted in her seat to stare longer.

Sachiko turned off the broader avenues onto narrower streets and finally parked in a lot squeezed between several low apartment buildings.

"Our house is over that way," she said pointing, *"but we don't have parking there."* They stepped out of the comfort of the car into a smothering heat that stunned Caitlin and Naomi—humidity higher than in Kagoshima and no breeze. It was midday, and Caitlin choked on the viscous air. By the time they'd walked the short distance to the house with their bags, the wisps of hair Caitlin wiped out of her face were wet, her eyes stinging with salt. *"Don't worry,"* Sachiko said as she opened the door for them, *"we have air-conditioning."*

Caitlin gulped in the coolness of the entryway as she stepped out of her sandals and up into the house. The tatami was new, pungent, and felt soothing on her bare feet—she wanted to lie down on it, to stretch out in front of the fan like she did in her apartment.

Sachiko instructed Naomi to show Caitlin to Mayumi's room— one of two bedrooms in the back of the narrow house. Naomi pointed out the tiny courtyard on the way, really a light shaft, but striking, with several potted plants and a deep ceramic hibachi of water lilies and goldfish. They set their belongings down in Mayumi's room, and Caitlin knew then that she would spend the night; she asked Naomi if it were truly okay—the few minutes of heat and the contrasting coolness had decided her. She hardly felt like wandering about in such drenching humidity in search of a reasonably priced rooming house or some American she'd met only briefly who would no doubt ask more probing questions than Naomi.

Naomi studied her. "Weren't you going to look up some other friends tonight?" she asked.

Caitlin shrugged. "They can wait," she said; she hadn't even brought along the phone numbers, just addresses, of the three fellows from the teaching program who were stationed in Kyoto. She dropped down to kneel on the tatami—she would stop here until tomorrow, then go directly to the Oides'.

"Well, good, I'm glad you'll be here," Naomi said. Then she added in a whisper, "I don't really know my cousins or my aunt and uncle all that well."

They joined Sachiko in the kitchen for some barley tea and Karukan sweets that Naomi had brought, and the small talk continued. Sachiko was full of questions: How much ash had there been lately? What did Naomi want to see while she was in Kyoto? What were the students like in Caitlin's schools? What had they eaten on the ferry? Had they felt seasick? Was Izumi now as tall as Naomi? How about Hideaki? And had Naomi brought along her art portfolio?

To this, Naomi bowed her head and uttered a soft, deferential, *"Yes, I brought it."*

"Because that school will surely want to have a look," Sachiko said extra cheerfully, sensing her mistake in broaching that subject so soon. *"And us too—I haven't seen your work in ages. But let's wait until another day, when everyone is here, after you've settled in more."*

Naomi nodded. She was still kneeling formally, although Sachiko had long since relaxed her legs to the side. Caitlin noticed that the awkwardness extended to both parties, however—Sachiko pursed her lips and nervously raised her eyebrows during silences.

"And how about your father? Is he still a weekend potter?"

Naomi answered somewhat defensively, *"Yes, and during vacations. He makes most of his pottery during the school breaks. He sent along a tea set for you."* Then Naomi turned to Caitlin. "Be right back," she said in English.

She returned with a wooden box, which she presented gingerly to Sachiko. *"He says it's nothing fancy, but I think it's quite good,"* she said, then as she sat down again, she blushed, embarrassed to have gloated. As Sachiko carefully unwrapped each cup, Naomi fidgeted, finally took up her barley tea and drank it down in three gulps. "I really think it's one of his best. Maybe should have kept it," Naomi said sideways to Caitlin in English. Caitlin refused to meet her eyes. Sachiko placed the tea set on the table to admire—earthen striped cups pinched on one side and a teapot, also finely striped, with a flared rim but no handle. "*It's lovely, Naomi. It really is. He does beautiful work.*"

Later, when Sachiko stepped out of the room to get some photos of Mayumi, Caitlin said to her, "Don't ever do that again."

"What?"

"Use me like that to exclude someone else by speaking English."

Naomi looked startled, then offended. "Fine, have it your way. Just don't ask me for help if you can't understand."

"Oh, Naomi," Caitlin said with a sigh.

Sachiko served them cold *somen* noodles with shredded sesame chicken and julienned cucumbers, then later in the day the three of them braved the heat and walked through the university to Yoshida Shrine tucked up into the hill behind the campus. Immediately on seeing the many steps leading up from the torii, Caitlin recalled playing there with Lee, tossing stones, hide-and-seek, waiting there with their mother, on days the student protests were quiet, while their father finished his day's work at the university. How quickly these buried memories had resurfaced. Naomi and Sachiko were hurrying on, but Caitlin stood entranced, thinking that if she stared hard enough at the trees, the offering boxes, the thick drape of straw rope hanging from a smaller torii, she would see and hear Lee gathering sticks and pine cones, shouting at her in Kyoto dialect. Reluctantly she followed Naomi and Sachiko down and out of the compound, but for the rest of the afternoon at the vast art museum, a destination selected for its air conditioning, she kept straining to hear her sister's five-year-old voice. Lee had spoken Japanese almost exclusively by that summer they left, even responding in Japanese when Caitlin asked her something at home in English.

Late in the day back at the house Caitlin readily took up Sachiko's offer for a bath. In the washroom, Caitlin shampooed her hair twice, scrubbed all over, then just sat on the low stool dribbling tepid water over her back, not wanting to get into a hot bath, but not wanting to dry off yet, relishing the few minutes of privacy and marveling at how suddenly her family had cast off their Japan life that summer they resettled in Pittsburgh. How immediately they all, except for her father, had ceased using a language they'd been steeped in—if you included the tutoring time in Pittsburgh pre-Kyoto—for nearly three years.

When Caitlin finally emerged from the bath, Naomi's uncle, Kojima, had returned. He was dressed in a dark suit, but the jacket lay by his side and his tie was slightly loosened as he sat cross-legged at the table with a glass of barley tea. Indeed, at a glance, he seemed Carl's opposite in demeanor, reserved and commanding in presence, and on behalf of Naomi, Caitlin considered the girl's prospect of three years with this family, and suddenly missed Carl and Akiko. The gravity of the school decision facing Naomi was beginning to sink in. Not only was Naomi having to decide on the type of school and future for herself, but also whether she was willing to board with this family hundreds of miles from home for all of her high school years.

But Caitlin soon saw that she had jumped to conclusions, for although he seemed the traditional type, Naomi's uncle was gentle, jesting and warm with his niece and family. He challenged Naomi to his latest toothpick configuration trick, and Naomi struggled, trying to move only two toothpicks to transform the shape. She did finally figure it out after a hint from her uncle, and everyone applauded. He was certainly better than that uncle down in Kagoshima, Caitlin thought.

Jun, the son, returned from the library, and everyone was amused by the startled reactions between him and Naomi when they saw each other and their changed appearances for the first time in two years. They were mutually shy, but Caitlin caught a vaguely flirtatious lilt emerging in Naomi's voice.

Sachiko prepared and served the dinner, enlisting Naomi's help and refusing Caitlin's, and after soup, dumplings, and assorted Chinese dishes, when Sachiko was doling out small bowls of rice, Kojima cleared his throat and asked Naomi what she thought about her plans next year. Everyone watched for Naomi's response. From Sachiko's and Jun's faces, it was clear they too had been anxious to hear the answer to the same question. Naomi shifted her legs beneath her to return to a proper kneel, and she began with formalities to the family, all the while looking down at her rice, about her gratitude for their willingness to consider such an imposition of several years while she attended high school here. This was form and everyone recognized it as such, and Kojima kindly hurried her on. The imposition was not the question whatsoever, he stressed; what they wanted to know was whether she understood what going to an international school would mean for her future in Japanese society.

Naomi looked her uncle straight in the eye. *"Yes, I do. It would mean I'd have a different future in this society. It would mean I wouldn't be quite Japanese to most Japanese. It would mean I couldn't get into the best Japanese universities if I decided to go to a Japanese university, and that fewer Japanese companies would be interested in me if I went to an American university. But I'm bilingual and bicultural. And I might not always live in Japan anyway. I'm not only Japanese, and this may not be the only society I'd like to fit into."*

Everybody except the uncle looked down at their rice bowls then. The uncle spoke softly. *"Naomi-chan, forgive me if I sound harsh, but you realize that in Japan you don't get a second chance; you choose your course when you're young. You cannot really change your mind along the way, like in America. If you end up deciding you made a mistake, that the international school was a mistake, you still might not get into a good Japanese university no matter how diligent you are. The preparation is completely different. You'd be way behind in your* kanji, *among other things. Look at Jun. Even strong students like Jun must be* ronin *sometimes."*

Naomi splayed her hands on the edge of the table and nodded. She glanced at Jun, who had blushed. An assortment of pickles was passed politely around the table as everyone waited for Naomi's reply. *"I know it's very difficult to get into a Japanese university. But right now I really don't think I even want to go to a Japanese university. Or work in a Japanese company."*

"Well then, what are you planning to do?"

"I don't know exactly, but study art. Different types of art. And I don't need to be in a Japanese university for that. An American or European university is probably better."

"But even art requires a commitment. You should be preparing every day. You can't just give up like you did with shodo. *You have to persevere."*

Naomi pursed her lips. *"I didn't give up* shodo. *That was different. I wish my parents wouldn't talk about me behind my back."*

"How was it different?"

Sachiko interjected quietly, *"Otosan, you're asking too many questions. She just arrived. Leave her be."*

"It's okay," Naomi said with a weak smile. Then she said somberly, *"But leaving the shodo club was not lack of commitment or lack of patience. That was different. I have lots of commitment. I'm drowning in commitment. If I go to the international school you don't have to worry about me being committed."*

▲ ▲ ▲

When Caitlin and Naomi were setting out the futons in Mayumi's room before going to sleep that evening, Caitlin ventured, "I didn't realize you were so serious about studying art."

Naomi was tying on pillow covers and threw a finished pillow toward the head of a futon. "Of course. Why not?"

"That's great, is all. I didn't know." Caitlin arranged the coverlets then sat down on a futon and plopped a pillow in her lap. "Naomi, I don't mean to pry, but your grandfather showed me some of your *shodo*. From what I saw and what he says, you're incredibly talented." Naomi shrugged off the compliment. "So why did you quit?"

Naomi rolled her eyes. "You wouldn't understand."

"Try me."

Naomi glared at her, then said, "I quit the club, not *shodo*. I still practice, in the morning before my mother and father are even awake. For about an hour. Other kids are studying for the high school entrance exams at five in the morning. I'm doing *shodo*. And sometimes *sumi-e* or watercolors."

Caitlin stared at Naomi. "Then why did you quit the club?" she finally whispered.

"Because I'm not learning anything from that *sensei* for one thing. I'm already better than he is—even he admits that, I'm not just boasting. But more than that, I want to know if I can do it without the support of a club. Because at the international school there probably won't be a *shodo* club, and I'll have to continue on my own."

"You don't know that for certain, do you?"

"No. But that's not the only reason. This is a test. I want to test how much I really like it, how committed I am. How much I like *shodo* and painting versus how much I just like being in that club, you know, the friends and all. The way it makes me feel more Japanese. The attention I get. Because if that's what it is, then I shouldn't kid myself; I'll never be a real artist. It means I'm just doing it to prove to everyone that I really am Japanese. Which is why I started doing *shodo* in the first place. And if that's the case, I may as well just go to a Japanese school and go on pretending I'm not different, stop trying to be an artist, and save my parents the tuition money for an international school."

Caitlin was overwhelmed by how deliberately Naomi had acted, by how serious, if irrational, this fourteen year old could be—more focused and determined than Caitlin ever recalled being about anything. "Then for God's sake why don't you tell your parents you're still doing *shodo?* That you're doing watercolors? At least tell your grandfather. I mean, find another teacher if that's what you need to do. But tell them. They're all crazy with worry about you."

"My parents wouldn't get it. Then they'd think I was really foolish for not staying in the club. And anyway, it's not permanent. If I keep up the *shodo* on my own for a couple more months, then maybe I'll rejoin. But I don't know. I learn more from my grandfather. I guess I should tell him. But not my parents. My father would just call me a fretter for the way I think."

They were lying on their futons now, both gazing up at the ceiling, softly patterned in a grid from outside light passing through the shoji. "Naomi, even if they don't have *shodo* at the international school, I'm sure there are plenty of places you can study it after school. Culture clubs, *shodo* societies, art institutes, all sorts of places. This is *Kyoto,* for God's sake."

"Oh I know. And I'll probably do that. But I don't want to miss out on western art clubs and art history, or life drawing, or things I haven't tried before. All the things I'd *gain* from being at an international school. So I need to know if I can keep this up on my own."

Caitlin shook her head. "Well that's a strange way of looking at it. You're being awfully strict with yourself. And causing your parents a fair bit of grief along the way."

"See? That's exactly why I don't tell my parents. No one gets it. Not even you." Naomi turned over in a huff.

Caitlin exhaled noisily and rolled over to face the other wall. She was wide awake. For some time she heard Naomi tossing, but neither of them said another word. Caitlin listened to the unfamiliar creaks of the old house and the sounds of the aunt, uncle, and Jun readying themselves for bed. She guessed it was about ten-thirty. She thought of Hiroshi, just heading out to a pub, and wished she could sneak out and find a phone somewhere. Then she turned on her back, wondering if she'd made a mistake by not staying alone somewhere, then closed her eyes, thinking of the day ahead, wondering if she'd want to be alone if she were.

▲ ▲ ▲

Over breakfast, the family asked Caitlin what her plans were for the day. Caitlin stirred her raw egg into her bowl of hot rice to "cook" it before adding soy sauce; she hadn't thought her plans out herself and was caught off guard when they asked her what time she'd be going to the Oides'. She sipped her soup, stalling, then said she'd look in her calendar later to see what time they'd said, but in fact, in her letter, she hadn't given the Oides a time; she hadn't been able to commit the reunion to a particular hour or part of the day. Late afternoon, she decided impulsively, when she finally glanced at the blank in her calendar and answered to Sachiko standing in the doorway of Mayumi's room. *"Between five and six. But I should call them first to make sure."*

"Go ahead, the phone is in the kitchen," Sachiko said.

"No, no, I'll call this afternoon," Caitlin added quickly. *"Afternoon is better."*

After doing the breakfast dishes with Sachiko, Caitlin joined the Kojimas and Naomi for some touring. Again she strained to recognize the city that passed outside the car windows, but other than the red torii of Heian Shrine, nothing overtly announced itself as having been a part of her earlier life. Not until they'd hiked up a narrow lane and stood—hot and dripping and ducking out of people's photographs—atop the stone steps leading to Kiyomizu Temple, was she certain of having been at that very place before. The high wooden stilts supporting the temple, the smooth rails, and even the three trickling spouts of water from which they all drank were just as they had been. So were the hills in folds behind the temple, and the heat. Caitlin breathed it all in, and hearing the crescendo of the *semi*—cicadas—grew giddy at having resurrected just a bit of that eight-year-old self.

She bought a temple stamp book with Naomi, and they had their first entries inked into the accordion pages. They ate lunch in a small *soba* shop, walked along Pottery Lane, where Naomi searched in vain for bargain pieces for Carl, then drove to the Silver Pavilion Temple, and strolled a ways on the Path of Philosophy in meager shade they were all grateful for. Despite the dense heat, everyone was jovial, and Caitlin, Naomi, and Jun even played a game of hopscotch while Naomi's aunt and uncle rested on a bench under a parasol. Naomi had kept to Jun's side throughout the day, oddly possessive, and she seemed to attempt more sophisticated language when talking to him, struggling, Caitlin thought, to be seen as older than she was. And Jun indulged her, clearly intrigued by his younger cousin and amused by her attentions and questions about his friends, interests, and daily study routines. When Jun tried to ask questions of Caitlin, Naomi would sometimes block them, firing a question at Jun before Caitlin had even formed her answer.

By late afternoon, trudging from the family parking space back to the house, they were all foot weary, hungry, silent, and ready for baths. Sachiko, while running about preparing the bathwater and setting out snacks and cool drinks, called to Caitlin lying on the mats before a fan in Mayumi's room, *"Didn't you want to call that family? It's already quarter to five."*

Caitlin sat up abruptly, and before she could think of another excuse to postpone the call, she was standing before the Kojimas' phone dialing the Oides and hoping with a clenched jaw and closed eyes that she'd hear a busy signal on the other end.

On the third ring a woman's voice answered. Caitlin cleared her throat, opened her eyes, and told the voice who she was.

"Keito-san!" the voice said warmly, *"This is Nobuko! We've been waiting for your call."* Caitlin took a deep breath. She could barely hear the questions that followed, barely answer Nobuko—as to her ferry ride, her whereabouts now, and when she'd be coming over. Her eyes were brimming and she swallowed hard—this was Nobuko, grown Nobuko, little sister of the only real best friend

Caitlin had ever had, Lee's other half from that year in Kyoto, and one corner of the foursome that had seemed so solid when she was eight. She rushed through the call, answered Nobuko as best she could, in clipped Japanese, nowhere near as polite as circumstances dictated, but as polite as she could manage in her flustered state. She said she'd be over in an hour or so, she would get herself there, and she looked forward to seeing them. Then she hung up, returned to Mayumi's room to pull together her few things and tell Naomi and the Kojimas her plans.

Naomi's uncle insisted on driving Caitlin to the Oides' as soon as he stepped out of the bath and Sachiko told him of Caitlin's plans, and Naomi insisted on postponing her bath to join them, then Jun asked if he could go too. Caitlin had always pictured herself making the pilgrimage back to her old neighborhood alone, by taxi, or on foot, and she resisted the offer at first, the group didn't fit with her vision of the reunion. But once on their way, she was grateful for the company, relieved to have Naomi by her side, Naomi to banter with and distract her as they inched north through the city, past the fork in the river and the egrets in the low water, and up toward her old home.

From the small train station Caitlin could easily remember the way, the right, the left, the veer right and then a sharp right, although there were new shops, even a supermarket, and houses where rice seedlings had once stretched in neat, corded rows. But the gutters were still deep off the side of the road, the hills still pushed up close to the houses, the triangle of Mount Hiei still hovered, and there were a few rice paddies left, wet and so green they made her thirsty. Yet when she'd directed them to what she thought was her old block, she suddenly became uncertain, had to look about for other landmarks, and tell Kojima to stop a moment. She was on the right road, yes, the huge tile-roofed farmhouse at the corner told her that, but the other houses were missing. Then she looked closer, saw a young woman, it had to be Nobuko, waving at them from an open gate, and Caitlin realized with a gasp that the Oides' old house, and the tiny house where Caitlin used to live, and in fact the whole block, had been replaced by identical two-story homes.

Fifteen

THEY WERE ALL there, the faces aged but so much the same, and the voices, especially Oide's, resonant of her past. They came through the gate to join Nobuko in greeting her as she stepped out of the car, and they were bowing deeply, beaming and offering their hands, so Caitlin dropped her pack on the asphalt and extended hers. She gave awkward handshakes and bows, wordless greetings, to Nobuko—incredible, Nobuko as tall as Caitlin—and to Oide—unchanged save for some graying. And as she gazed into their eyes, as she tried to think of something appropriate to say, as she clasped both of Harumi's hands in hers, the tears were suddenly unstoppable, fifteen years of dammed-up tears, and she flung her arms tightly about Harumi, the mother of her old best friend. They stood there entwined and shaking as one, sniveling into each other's necks, while the others looked on, down or away. Then with simultaneous sobs the two women released and dabbed at their faces with handkerchiefs. When Caitlin had recovered, Oide gestured and said softly, *"Kei-chan, this is Yusuke."*

Caitlin smiled on hearing her old nickname, and a boy appearing to be about Naomi's age stepped forward. She bowed and shook his hand, the grown hand of the baby she'd never met—born two weeks after they'd returned to Pittsburgh. His face was more like Mie's than Nobuko's, and he seemed uncertain as to how to accept this stranger, this woman he must have heard about through his parents or Nobuko. Caitlin studied his eyes and wondered what he knew, what he'd been told, what image he'd composed of his eldest sister, and just how he construed Caitlin's return.

She barely noticed Naomi, Jun, and Kojima introducing themselves to the Oides, Naomi pressing the Kojima phone number into her hand, the three of them saying good-bye. She barely saw them drive off down the street though she felt her head turn and her arm wave. She was in some delirious state—"I'm here, I'm really here," playing over and over in her head—and she felt a sudden exhaustion and elation as if she'd just reached the summit of some immense mountain she hadn't fully realized she'd been climbing, a mountain whose enormity she hadn't grasped until just now when she'd emerged from shadowy woods to a bare peak of soaring height.

Harumi hooked arms with Caitlin and led her up the walk, but before following her inside the new Oide home, Caitlin turned to peer over the garden wall to the mirror-image house standing on the very lot where she had once slept, eaten, and mourned with her family. Yet instead of any bittersweet nostalgia, Caitlin felt her relief double; she'd anticipated with dread walking through rooms where she and Mie had played, somehow had pictured the two houses unchanged, the scant furniture arranged just as it had been, the open-sewer toilets still reeking, the same dusty shrubs out back. And now she saw how silly she'd been, to think that time hadn't affected change here in Kyoto as it had so drastically in Pittsburgh and Brookline.

These really were old friends, Caitlin noted, as they clustered around a low table in a tatami room that overlooked a strip of carefully landscaped back garden and ate summer noodles. For more than a year now she'd been operating in that rootless expatriate world where nothing of her present connected to her past, where no kin existed except through letters, occasional phone calls and memory, where to others her history was like fiction, and community connections were never defined by family. Yet here she sat in Kyoto with a family eager to hear news of her family, of even her reticent mother and Lee, and Caitlin felt her guilt swell for having taken so long to make contact.

"Kei-chan, Kei-chan," they kept saying, *"do you want more beer? How about some corn? More squid? When did you start studying Japanese again? Can you still curse like you used to? How's your Kyoto dialect? What is your father's research now? When will he be coming over next? More dipping sauce? What does Lee look like all grown? Does your mother still study insects? How is Kagoshima? Do you like teaching? Is Naomi one of your students? Try these pickles—from Ohara just this morning."*

Caitlin nibbled between answers and had little chance to ask questions in return, so fast were the inquiries fired at her from all sides. Yusuke seemed shy but studied her intently; she could feel his eyes exploring her face, her movements when she looked toward other members of the family or reached for more noodles from the communal bowl. It struck her that he knew her father already, from his various research trips since that year they'd lived here, and she wondered what talk, if any, had preceded her arrival. She wondered what this boy had expected, and what he thought now. And she couldn't help but wonder how that summer had affected him, what attitudes and emotions had been projected onto him by the other members of the family during those tumultuous days of his infancy.

She watched Oide and Harumi and Nobuko, the three who'd experienced everything directly, and she thought how ironic that they were still cohesive, that it was her family that had been sundered, her family that never dined around the same table, her parents that were separated half the year. If the Oides could function together as a unit, if the Oides could be well, why not her family? She listened to Harumi and Nobuko with envy and thought of her mother and Lee, the isolating nervous patter the two of them kept up, the exclusive club they seemed to maintain, and the protection from outsiders they seemed to offer each other by some tacit agreement. They'd tried to influence Caitlin, tried to keep her from going to school in Massachusetts, tried to persuade her to live in Pittsburgh each summer away from her father, and tried to convince her that Europe would be more suitable than Japan for a teaching experience. Why were they the ones so affected by all this? Perhaps her mother should have had another child, she thought wryly as she felt Yusuke's gaze on the side of her face—perhaps that would have restored the family's equilibrium.

The dinner was slow and protracted, and more and more casual as each bottle of beer was uncapped. Harumi had long ago shed her apron and now sat leaning on the low table with a small beer glass in hand, waving it as she talked, red-faced and animated. Even Yusuke was given a glassful, and Nobuko, who was teased for the ease with which she drank, continued to pour for everyone and refill her own glass on every round. *"Typical college student,"* Oide said sideways to Caitlin.

When Caitlin finally asked if there were anything on the agenda for the next few days, Oide explained that they would all be on vacation that week, for O-Bon. They could do things together, tour the city, go down to Nara, whatever she liked, they had no plans or preferences. Or Caitlin could go off on her own, they said. *"Be like your father,"* Harumi added, *"he comes and goes just like family when he's here."* Caitlin reddened on hearing her father mentioned, on realizing just how familiar his presence was in this household. *"Do you have any plans?"* Oide asked her.

"Nothing special. Just that I'd like to visit that little shrine near here, and definitely the sento," Caitlin said, referring to the public bath she used to frequent with her mother and sister. They'd walk the short distance there with rinse buckets and towels under their arms, pay the attendant the fee, change in a hurry, and step inside the steamy room. She and Lee used to love those huge baths, so hot and deep they could nearly swim, and full of women of all ages and shapes chatting in the warmth.

But Harumi was shaking her head. *"I'm afraid the one we used to go to was torn down some years back. There's another though, over on the other side of the tracks. We could try that if you'd like."*

They devoured a small watermelon, and after wiping their sticky hands on fresh damp cloths, Oide rose up to a kneel and with some closing words suggested they all get some sleep. Immediately dinner was over, everyone rose at once, and Caitlin stood and turned to follow the others clearing dishes. But as she rounded the end of the table her breath caught. Tucked into the wall she'd had her back to throughout the meal sat a small altar—the *butsudan*.

The shutters were swung open, and set before it were assorted items—a bowl of rice, a small cup of water, some incense, and a bell on a small pillow. Caitlin inhaled deeply, then let her eyes travel upward, above the altar, above the strip of wood trim that encircled the room, though she knew what was coming. Close to the ceiling in somber black frames hung three black-and-white photographs. The first was of an elderly man looking like Oide—that would be Ojiichan, Mie's grandfather. Caitlin could vaguely recall helping him string persimmons to dry from the eaves of his old thatched farmhouse. Next to him was a severe picture of Obaachan, Oide's mother, the woman who'd sewn Caitlin and Mie matching summer *yukata* for a local festival; the fabric had been indigo with a pattern of red dragonflies, and they'd both had bright yellow *obi* and zori with yellow straps. Obaachan's Kyoto accent had been so thick that Caitlin had often turned to Mie for translations.

Finally, Caitlin allowed her eyes to continue to the third photograph—the elementary school shot of Mie sitting bolt upright, her chin raised and her thin lips turned up into just the hint of a smile. Caitlin stared. Her friend looked so young, frozen in time, but so alive, still full of challenge, still taunting with those black pupils focused directly on hers. It seemed preposterous that she wasn't there with them now, that seven was as old as she'd ever gotten. Caitlin bit her lips, feeling as if she were on that train of her childhood nightmares with Mie abandoned on the platform, reaching for Caitlin, scrambling to board the moving carriage.

She gripped the stack of plates in her hands, turned from the *butsudan,* and hurried into the kitchen. Placing the dishes on the counter beside Harumi, who was already washing, she took up a towel and with a vigorous wipe plunged into dinner cleanup.

▲ ▲ ▲

A futon was set out for her in Nobuko's room upstairs, and after saying good night she lay motionless in the darkness, listening to the deep adult breathing of Nobuko and considering her current pinpoint location in the universe—in the bedroom of the sister of her childhood friend. She was reluctant to close her eyes, fearful to find herself back in Kagoshima again, fearful to be gone when she was so relieved to have made it. When she did finally allow herself to sleep, she fell into a disquieting dream in which the Oides asked her what sport she played. She pretended not to hear, but they continued intoning the question, so Caitlin lied and said, "Volleyball." They asked her to demonstrate, but when she made a serving error, they pressed her again. This time she said softball, but again they insisted on seeing her play, and when she struck out, they closed in on her, prodding her firm arms, her swimmer's shoulders, and her thighs. Caitlin sat bolt upright pulling at the terry sheet of bedding tangled about her neck.

She was drenched in sweat and breathing hard. Had she cried

out? she wondered. She half expected to see the Oides surrounding her futon. But in the predawn blue light she could see that Nobuko slept soundly on the other side of the room, and except for the steady whir of the fan, the house was quiet.

Caitlin leaned over and turned the fan up a speed. She stretched out her fingers toward the air and tried to loosen the muscles of her shoulders and back and breathe slowly. Why had the dream question so panicked her? No doubt they already knew her sport, her father was always one to boast, and there'd been all those awards from various swim teams in high school and college. Besides, there was nothing wrong with swimming. She was good at it, she was fast, smooth, cutting; shouldn't you pursue what you're skilled at? But she dropped her head into her hands. She knew it wasn't as simple as that.

She turned over in the damp sheets and stared at the bottom drawer of a dresser; the fan stream brushed her neck in a regular rhythm with each oscillating turn. She began to count the turns.

▲ ▲ ▲

She slept fitfully until nearly seven. The house was quiet, and Nobuko was still asleep when Caitlin dressed and left the room, but she found Harumi in the kitchen still in her bathrobe, sipping coffee before a small TV. *"Good morning! Did you sleep well?"*

"Yes," Caitlin lied. Harumi poured another mugful of coffee, pushed plastic creamer packs and sugar toward her, and Caitlin sat down. While the effusive TV reporter asked morning commuters his questions, Harumi crossed one hand over the other on the table and faced Caitlin formally: *"Kei-chan, make yourself at home again. Stay at your leisure. Welcome back. We still are your number-two family."* Caitlin smiled; that was how she and Lee had referred to them when they'd lived next door. Their number-two family, number-two mother, number-two father.

"Thank you," she said.

"Everyone is still sleeping—it's the first day of vacation. Fried egg, toast, and salad okay?" Harumi said, rising.

"Oh, nothing yet thanks," Caitlin said putting her hand up. *"Just coffee. I was thinking of going out for a walk first. But . . . "* She hesitated

before saying softly, *"Is it difficult, for you, for everyone, my coming back?"*

Harumi sat down again, clasped her hands before her and contemplated. *"Difficult? No. We've been waiting for you for such a long time. No, it's not difficult, just, you know, sad and happy. Sad because we wish your good friend were still here, but happy because you are with us again. But it's difficult for you, I think. Isn't it? Are you okay?"*

Caitlin tightened the grip on her mug. *"I'm sorry I didn't come until now."*

"Oh, that's all right. We understand." Harumi touched her hand to Caitlin's wrist and said in a whisper, *"Honestly, we understand,"* then stood blinking, and busied herself at the counter.

Caitlin took a few more sips of coffee, then excused herself and slipped outdoors for a walk. The thought of breakfast had no appeal, oddly enough—often in Kagoshima she rushed out of bed so ravenous she nearly had the shakes as she toasted bread or cut fruit onto her cereal. But she had no appetite just then; what she craved was outside air.

Cicadas were breeping and droning as she sidled around the car in the tight driveway. It was already hot, but not uncomfortable yet. She paused on the concrete bridge that spanned the deep gutter and stared down into the trickle of water that ran over algae and fallen leaves. They used to poke sticks in there, sometimes even climb down to go after a frog; now and then they'd see snakes. She peered down at the feathering stream, recalling the torrents that would flow after a heavy rain.

Then she walked up the street and turned left—at least the neighborhood layout was still roughly the same, though so many of the houses had been rebuilt, and so few of the fields remained. She walked to where the woods began and in through the small red torii where she and Mie had pitched stones to see if they'd land on one of the crosspieces for good luck. Inside the compound she approached the old Noh platform where they'd secretly sung and performed plays, then the main shrine building with its drape of heavy hemp and cut paper at the entrance.

A money box was still there, so she tossed a coin in, shook the rope to ring the bell, clapped her hands, and stood silent a moment. Then she turned and sat down on the steps and looked about. The shrine was just as deserted as it had always been. Trees still dripped with moss, and there was the row of cherries where they'd stalked cicadas with her mother and the grasses beneath where they'd hunted for beetles and hoppers and competed to discover any insect that her mother might not be able to identify, just to be that one special person she'd gloat over for finding something unusual that day. Crows cawed from the high cedars, the steps were still green with mildew, light streamed down in pollen motes. The shrine complex felt smaller, to be sure, but other than that, and her own larger self, she couldn't find a single indication that fifteen years had passed since she'd last sat on those foot-worn stones. And as if the torii had been the gateway to her memories, recollections of her Kyoto childhood now crowded around her. She tilted her head back and succumbed to the reveries, of those hours spent in the shade of the shrine compound, dropping unsuspecting ants into ant lion pits and pouncing on grass lizards, and then beyond those wooded grounds, to the jump-rope routines and ball games in the streets, board games belly down on the tatami of their living room which doubled as her parents' bedroom, pollywogging in the rice paddies, evening games of *oni-gokko,* Sunday outings with the two families to parks or temples, she couldn't recall where exactly, those days with all eight of them together, parents and kids, arguing one moment, giggling the next, singing, completely enlivened. She brought up a full array of memories, anything preceding that July trip to Uji, and by drawing a date line at the end of June 1970 she was able for once to enjoy the nostalgia, revel in it. She remained there on the steps of the small shrine, chuckling and frowning, musing until an older woman tottered into the complex and Caitlin bid her good morning and left her to make her offerings in solitude.

▲ ▲ ▲

She spent the day with the family at home, and late in the afternoon she, Nobuko, and Harumi took a bus downtown to shop in the city's main food arcade. The crowds thronged around particular stalls, rushing to make last minute O-Bon purchases, and the merchants hawking their wares were all the more hyped by the frenzy. Caitlin followed behind the two women as best she could, ducking out of the way of other shoppers and flattening herself against less popular displays whenever Nobuko or Harumi paused to consider some pickled vegetables, pastel sweets, or gray, flecked *konnyaku*. Near the bus stop on the way back, Harumi hesitated at a stall selling bundles of chrysanthemums, Japanese lanterns, and greenery, but Caitlin heard Nobuko prod her forward: *"We can get those tomorrow, Mother, at the cemetery."* So there were plans to go there, Caitlin thought, and a waft of nausea visited her throat.

When they arrived home, Oide said that Naomi had called, so Caitlin located the piece of paper with her number, still in the pocket of the shorts she'd worn the day before. She spoke briefly to Jun before he handed the phone to Naomi.

"Hi lady, would you like to sign my will?" Naomi giggled. "Just joking. How are you?"

"That's not exactly my idea of a joke," Caitlin said.

"Oh, you take things too seriously. So, tell me, how is it being back in your old neighborhood?"

"Well, interesting." Naomi's first words had thrown Caitlin off balance. She paused before adding, "A lot of it's just as it used to be. So it's a little eerie. But nice. What have you been up to? Did you visit that school today?"

"No, no, everything's closed until next week. I have an appointment next Monday for an interview and all that stuff."

"You don't sound too thrilled."

"Well, would you?"

Caitlin wasn't in the mood for Naomi's sullenness. Her English sounded more grating than usual, excessively, nasally American, as if Naomi were trying to emphasize that half of herself. Caitlin answered with a sigh.

"Well look," Naomi said, "the reason I called is to find out if you want to go see Daimonji together. Jun and I are going, and we thought maybe you'd come and the Oide kids too, I can't remember their names."

"Nobuko and Yusuke."

"Right. Well, we thought we might go early, find a good spot by the river, and take a picnic dinner."

"When is it?"

"Friday, last night of O-Bon."

"Sounds good," Caitlin said. "But I need to talk it over with them. Can I call you back tomorrow?" They said good-bye and Caitlin shook her head; she suspected she'd be seeing more of Naomi this vacation than she'd intended.

Caitlin dined with the Oides at a local restaurant, for which she was grateful—the idea of eating below Mie's memorial picture made her uncomfortable, now that she knew where it hung. It was hard enough just eating lately. She ordered shrimp *okonomiyaki,* her old favorite, but after a few bites she began discreetly picking the shrimp out of the cabbage pancake.

Both Yusuke and Nobuko were pleased at the thought of a group Daimonji viewing when she mentioned it, and they immediately entered into an argument as to which section of the riverbank was the best place to station themselves. Yusuke wanted to be upriver, Nobuko down. *"We'll let Kei-chan's friend and her cousin decide,"* Nobuko finally said diplomatically.

▲ ▲ ▲

When Caitlin rose the next morning, she found that both Harumi and Oide were already up, bustling about the kitchen, more industrious than seemed necessary for breakfast. *"Turn that off,"* Oide said in an undertone to Harumi, and she flicked off the TV. Oide sat down at the table with Caitlin and poured coffee for them both. *"O-Bon preparations, for the* butsudan," he explained. *"Haru likes to have everything done the morning of the thirteenth. She's diligent about that, so everything is set up before* o-haka–mairi."

"*Before what?*" Caitlin asked, but immediately the meaning came to her: *o-haka,* grave; *mairi,* visit. *"Oh, right, when is that?"*

"Around dusk, this evening. Will you join us?" When Caitlin hesitated he added softly, *"Mie would be so pleased."*

Caitlin nodded.

"Breakfast?" he asked cheerfully.

"No thanks, just coffee."

"Are you sure?" Harumi added, as she served Oide rice and miso soup and a small broiled fish. The smell of the fish turned Caitlin's stomach, and she gulped her coffee to drown the odor. *"Yes, just coffee's fine."*

Harumi didn't stop to sit down with them, but continued arranging things in a basket on the counter. When she was satisfied, she said to Caitlin, *"Come, I'll show you how we set this up."*

Caitlin followed her out of the kitchen, then with a start realized she was being led directly to the altar.

A small table had been set out before the *butsudan,* and on it already was a large lotus leaf filled with gourds, some fruits, and several vegetables—a cucumber, a pepper, and an eggplant with toothpicks protruding. Harumi knelt down and set the basket beside the huge leaf, and showed Caitlin its contents: *"Dried gourd,* somen *noodles,* kamaboko, *shiitake—you see, no meat or fish even, all vegetarian. It's for the spirits."* Caitlin nodded. *"Later I'll prepare a little meal for them, I'll show you,"* Harumi said, then, after adjusting a small plate of *hagi* sweets, she rose and returned to the kitchen. Caitlin continued to stand there staring dumbly at the offerings. Some of the pastel colored sweets they'd purchased yesterday at the market had been set out as well, and she had to admit, the whole altar even looked festive. She continued to gaze, though she could feel Oide now watching her from the other side of the room.

The *butsudan* both repulsed and attracted her. This was where the family focused on the dead, this was their memorial spot, where they communicated with their ancestors, their past. Her stomach churned.

"Go ahead," Oide said from behind. She could feel the blood pulsing through the veins in her neck and temples. *"Here,"* he said and pointed to the cushion directly before the *butsudan.* She knelt down clumsily—her legs giving out on the way. The sound of Harumi's bustling in the kitchen stopped. Oide dropped down beside her and then, so close she could feel his warm breath, smell the fish he'd been eating, he lit the incense stick and told her to fan it so it smoked, then place it upright in the small pot of ash. She waved her hand, and the smoke ribboned around and up, and Caitlin felt the eyes of this whole family, the eyes of her own family, and of some grown Mie that she didn't know, that might resent her for their very opposite situations in life and death, watching her.

"Then ring the bell," Oide said, stepping back, and Caitlin looked over her shoulder at him. He gave an encouraging nod, so she took up the small mallet, inhaled deeply and sounded the small brass gong.

She put her hands together and closed her eyes as she thought might be appropriate, as she'd done with her father years before at temples, but she didn't know what to think or say to herself. She'd half expected to hear Mie's voice after the thread of bell tone died, and she realized her shoulders were tensely hunched as though braced for a blow from above. The room was silent. Her blood sang. She tried to clear the audience of families from her mind, tried to be sitting there alone, but she suddenly felt embarrassed, and opened her eyes.

The tiny wooden Buddha stared back, reproachful, from the center of the altar. So she shut her eyes tight again and spoke hastily, silently, to herself and to the spirit world: *"Mie, I'm back. Please don't hate me."*

Then she opened her eyes and sat beholding the dark shelves of the altar, avoiding the Buddha in the center, gazing instead at the tablets, and at the deep grain of the wood. Oide was no longer beside her, and the running of water and the ring of dishes sounded again, lightly, from the kitchen. Caitlin couldn't move. She sat tense, her feet tingling under her buttocks. Behind the cluster of offerings she now noticed a small, busty doll clothed in bell-bottoms and a hot-pink blouse, and beside that a red stuffed dog that startled her with its familiarity—Caitlin remembered it from some festival they'd attended together, no, the Osaka Expo she suddenly recalled—Caitlin had begged for a blue one, Mie the red one.

She stood quickly, and stumbling on feet numbed from kneeling, she left the room and went down the narrow hallway to the toilet. She tried not to sound as though she were fleeing, tried not to slam the door, tried not to sound pathetic, as she sat down upon the closed lid of the toilet, dropping her head into her hands and letting the tears and sweat drip through her fingers to the skirt of fuzzy rug below.

▲ ▲ ▲

When she finally rejoined Oide and Harumi, who at least acted as if nothing had happened, she presented a calm self and even forced herself to down a bowl of rice with nori and soy sauce. The salty taste, at least, was soothing.

The TV news was now on and Caitlin was immediately distracted from her own troubles by what was obviously the reason Oide had asked Harumi to turn off the TV—coverage of a plane downed the night before in the mountains of Nagano, only 4 of the 524 on board having survived. Most of the passengers had been bound for family O-Bon visits, and in horror Caitlin followed the somber broadcast and the intrusive reporters ruthlessly struggling to get a quick word or sob from bereaved relatives. *"Horrible, just horrible,"* Harumi said over and over. They sat watching for a long while, numbed.

Eventually Oide went out to the back garden and puttered over the potted plants and shrubs, and Harumi and Caitlin finished cleaning up the kitchen. Afterward, not wanting to see or hear any more about the crash, Caitlin sought refuge in the small living room and began leafing through magazines, not paying attention really, just running her eyes over the glossy photos and reading whatever headlines she could. Yusuke poked a tousled head in to say good morning on the way to the bathroom, and shortly Harumi came in to pull several albums from a high shelf and place them on the table before Caitlin: *"You might want to look at these,"* she said. *"But don't look too closely—you'll see what an old woman I've become!"*

Caitlin lifted the books onto her lap and slipped the top one out of its protective box. *"January 1969 to June 1969"* read the spine. Slowly she turned the pages of age-discolored snaps, and somewhere in February found the first few shots of her family, at a dinner at the old Oide house. Stiff poses with polite smiles—they hadn't known them well yet. In April she found Mie and her heading off to school, and gradually more and more glimpses of her family in between those of outings or events with people she didn't recognize. In July of the next book, there were her parents jubilant, clapping before that wood-framed TV set, and Caitlin read the penned caption—July 21, 11:56. For a moment she was stymied, then got it—the moon landing. She remembered waking at dawn to traipse over to Mie's house to watch the live broadcast. In August, there she was with Mie in the dragonfly *yukata,* and in October with her again at the sports festival—two scrawny girls in gym outfits, both on the red team, squatting with their classes to wait their turns, marching in the opening parade, running races, scarfing down a picnic lunch, and finally, close up to the camera, arm in arm, grinning such self-assured smiles. They looked so at ease together, and Caitlin knew she'd never had another friend like that—one around whom she could fling her arm so casually.

Nobuko came in smelling of soap. She peered over Caitlin's shoulder and said, *"Ahhh,"* on seeing the shot of Caitlin and Mie. They gazed at the photo together in silence. *"Do you have a copy of that?"* she asked, and Caitlin shook her head. *"No? Well let's make you one. Or here, take this one, we'll make another,"* she said pulling the photo from its sleeve and placing it on the coffee table. No tone of sadness, no edgy avoidance of the subject, no blame, Caitlin noted. Nobuko left her alone again, so Caitlin turned the pages and continued to pore over the photos.

She scrutinized her own mother and father, parents she barely recognized for their levity, the warmth they exuded for each other even in groups, and the kick they seemed to get out of even the difficult, ludicrous situations captured on the Oides' film: grimacing in front of Oide's car, sunk low on one side with a flat tire; sarcastic glances at the camera as they wiped up some spilled liquid from tatami; a grin over the fence as her mother hung laundry in the narrow back garden; and exaggerated expressions of exhaustion as they hiked up a wooded path, their faces glistening with sweat. There were snapshots of her mother and all four of the girls returning from insect expeditions, holding up the plastic cages to show the day's finds, and a shot of her father at work at the kitchen table, his hair disheveled, nearly to his shoulders, papers scattered everywhere and not just one, but two large bottles of beer before him. How incredibly staid and reserved they seemed now by comparison.

She moved into the next book, through a makeshift Christmas dinner at their old house, the Oides' New Year's feast, seasonal festivals and gatherings, most of which included her family, and the sun tower and pavilions of Expo '70. Eyeing these records of the Oides, Caitlin wondered where the photos that her parents had taken were now kept. She remembered both her mother and father making Lee and her pose, making them squint up from whatever they were doing, she knew they'd had a camera, yet she'd never seen any of those pictures after they'd returned to Pittsburgh. Had her mother had the audacity to throw them out? Or did her father keep them on some high shelf in Brookline. She wondered how many photos there were.

The last book on Caitlin's lap was labeled "April 1970 to September 1970." She flipped through, barely glimpsing the shots of that spring, cherry blossoms, carp kites, school functions, but as she reached the month of July she slowed, fearful each time she turned the page. She lingered over several photos of the Oide family, all four of them on the small wooden bleachers before some overlook with blue-green undulating mountains in the distance and steep slopes of cedar, some clear-cut, leading down to a valley—the silver river could just be made out to Harumi's left. Then suddenly a single blank page, and next a photo Caitlin had never known to exist, of Mie and her both in yellow dresses and hair ribbons, insect nets poised and insect cages about their necks, her father and Oide flanking them, on a footbridge over a rushing current of water— Uji, she realized, a passerby must have taken the picture for them when they were on their way to the temple, the last photo of Mie. For next was a single shot of the interior of the house set up for the funeral. On the following page were a few guests dressed in black, then another blank page and then a weary looking Harumi standing before their old car with a swaddled infant, Yusuke, in her arms.

The photos continued, but Caitlin put all three books back into their boxes and picked up the picture of Mie and her. Mie stared back at her so utterly self-confident that her current absence seemed that much more absurd. "For God's sake, Mie," Caitlin whispered to the photo.

▲ ▲ ▲

They spent the afternoon in Ohara, visiting a shrine and temple and taking their time along the lane of pickle and souvenir vendors. For a late lunch they stopped at a restaurant where Caitlin ordered a soothing boxful of *chirashi-zushi*—the mixed sushi dish she loved but never bothered to make herself, yet she barely touched the large plate of sashimi that Oide ordered for everyone. She made a lame defensive comment about the heat when they asked if she didn't like raw fish anymore, and then grew angry with herself for sounding like Lee with excuse after excuse. When they returned home in the

late afternoon, Caitlin went out for a walk, with no particular destination in mind. She circled the neighborhood and ended up at the
new supermarket. She was about to step inside when she stopped
herself, and at a quick pace, walked farther down the main road to
the small shop that sold sake, rice, various groceries, and snack food
in metal racks still arranged as they had been when she and Mie
rode bicycles there with their few yen of spending money. She
glanced up and down the aisle of brightly packaged snacks and
zeroed in on a box of chocolate-covered pretzel sticks. She paid the
cashier, who looked at her sideways with recognition. The box
barely fit in her shorts pocket and made a large bulge that she tried
to conceal when she arrived back at the Oides'.

The bathwater was ready she was told when she came downstairs after dropping her things in Nobuko's room, and she understood by the tone of Harumi's voice that she was to bathe at once so
the rest of the family could follow. She climbed back upstairs for
clean clothes, but she wasn't certain just what one wore to a cemetery to greet spirits from the otherworld. She decided against her
skirt and examined her three summer dresses; one badly needed
ironing, another was too casual and baggy, so she opted for a prim
rayon shift and hoped it wouldn't be a hot evening.

The family was indeed dressed up but hardly formal, although
Harumi and Nobuko both wore stockings. Harumi dashed about
pulling items from cupboards and stuffing them into a shopping
bag until Oide finally said, *"Enough, enough,"* and they piled into
the car and drove about fifteen minutes to a cemetery that climbed
the west side of a hill in even terraces. They stepped out of the car
and adjusted their clothing and hair, then Caitlin followed the family to a small shed where an elderly man and woman sat on stools
behind buckets full of chrysanthemums, Japanese lantern plants,
purple and yellow flowers that Caitlin couldn't name, and all sorts
of greens. Harumi and Nobuko deliberated and selected some
flowers and a packet of incense while Oide and Yusuke collected a
bucket and wooden ladle. Caitlin stood to one side and watched,
apprehensive.

They climbed up through the square plots of family tombs in
twilight; the sun had already set over the city behind them. Paper
lanterns were strung along the main walkways, and families were

dispersed here and there pouring water over the graves. The air was sweetly scented with flowers and incense set out to smoke, and the gentle sloshing of water, the murmurs of good evening, and consultations between family members as they arranged the offerings were balm to Caitlin's nerves. Harumi led the way with her shopping bag, Oide was next with the empty bucket and ladle, then Nobuko with the armload of greens and flowers, Yusuke with a small bundle in a plastic bag, and Caitlin behind him.

Finally they turned left into one of the narrow terrace aisles lined with graves on either side, and before one of the rectangular plots Harumi and Oide stopped, and everyone set down what they'd been carrying, caught their breath, and flapped their clothing. Caitlin's dress was sticking the length of her spine.

She stared at the tall central slab of polished stone marker before her and read down the characters: *"Oide Family Grave."* The central marker was flanked by smaller stones, and to the left sat a broad, low, polished slab partially covered with writing—names above dates. Caitlin eyed the entry to the farthest left, the most recent, a name she couldn't read but was probably Ojiichan or Obaachan since the date was some three years before, and the age seventy-six. The next entry presented more unfamiliar characters, a date only seven years before, and the age sixty-eight. Then she saw the name she knew too well, the age seven, and that loathsome month and day in the year Showa 45.

Oide had gone off to find the water spigot, Harumi was doing some general tidying of the family plot, and Nobuko was separating the flowers into two bundles, one for each hole in the narrow stones on either side of the main grave. Caitlin stood back with Yusuke, who shrugged at her and looked about with unease.

When Oide returned with the bucket of water, he gave Caitlin a nod to follow him. *"First we wash the grave,"* he said, and the water fell from his ladle and glanced over the stone. *"Actually Harumi was here last week doing the real cleaning and scrubbing; today it's just symbolic. Here,"* he said, handing the ladle to Caitlin, so she dipped it into the pail, raised it above the stone, and with a tilt, watched the streaks of wetness dribble down the stone and catch in the dark cuts of the characters. She handed the ladle to the others, and they each took turns. Nobuko set the flowers in the holes that served as vases, then pulled them out and ordered Yusuke to go off for more water. When he had filled the holes, the flowers were again set in place, and once Harumi had pinched off particular leaves and tugged at certain blooms to arrange them just so, they set out the various offerings from the bags: a stack of the pink, green, and yellow sugary flowers they'd bought in the market; rice crackers; a can of beer—*"For my father,"* Oide said with a wink; a ripe tomato—*"Tomato?"* Yusuke asked in disbelief, and Harumi answered defensively, *"Obaachan loved them";* and a small packet of children's hard candy. Caitlin reached into her shoulder bag and pulled out the box of chocolate-covered pretzel sticks, concealing the opened top with her hand. *"May I?"* she said to Harumi. Harumi looked from the box to Caitlin and whispered, *"Of course."* Caitlin set the box on the stone beside the hard candies then stepped back.

Oide handed them each an incense stick and lit his from a candle that he set in a holder before the grave. When he'd fanned the incense, and the smoke began drawing its lines in the night air, he put his hands together and stood silent before the grave. Then Harumi took her turn, standing in silence for longer than Oide had, then Nobuko, then Yusuke, who was reprimanded for barely putting his hands together before retreating, then Caitlin stepped forward. She'd dreaded this moment for years, felt as though she'd be standing trial once she stood before the stone that marked Mie's ashes, but she lit her incense from the candle, fanned it gently, and set it in the holder with the other sticks and put her hands together. She thought of the photo of the two of them arm in arm, and she could almost smile to herself as she closed her eyes and barely whispered, *"Mie-chan, konbanwa."*

Then she faltered. She cleared her throat and continued. *"Enjoy the pretzel sticks. I kept half for me. So we could share . . . like we used to . . ."* She wanted to go on, to tell Mie that the shop still sold the same ices she'd liked, that cicadas still sang in the shrine complex, that she still remembered the songs they used to sing there, but Caitlin could no longer keep her voice to a whisper. There was so much she wanted to say, to apologize for all her years of living, all those years she'd been granted, all the years Mie had missed for slipping on a rock.

She crouched down to touch the curves and cuts of Mie's name and young age in the stone. She drew her nails along the grooves and felt the cool wetness of the stone on her fingertips, felt the permanence of the granite, and then she felt the drape of Harumi's arm around her shoulders. Through her own struggle for breath, she could just make out Harumi's words—gentle, barely audible: *"Mie-chan, your good friend Kei-chan has come back."*

Sixteen

THE MOOD WAS subdued when they returned from the cemetery. They made a hasty dinner of chilled tofu, *edamame*, and a salad of cooled steamed vegetables and beef, then sat limply about the table. Harumi seemed worn out, Yusuke bored, and conversation was barely sustained by Oide, Nobuko, and Caitlin. Midway through the meal Harumi flicked on the TV to catch updates of the plane crash. Oide stepped into the kitchen at one point, discreetly wiping his eyes, and then, while pulling another bottle of beer from the refrigerator, the phone rang, and they all caught his burst of surprise and sudden enthusiasm—Yusuke perked up, glad for a less morbid distraction, trying to guess who was on the other end of the line, and his mother turned the TV volume down and motioned for him to be silent. Caitlin only registered fragments of the conversation. But then Oide's figure appeared in the kitchen doorway, and he was saying in Japanese as he looked straight at her, *"Yes, yes, she's here. No, no, no trouble at all, we're enjoying her company after such a long time. Just a moment . . ."* and Caitlin was the only one in the room looking perplexed, everyone else having guessed who it was long before Oide held out the phone to her and said, *"It's your father."*

Caitlin stood slowly. *"My father?"* she said in disbelief, but she took the receiver from Oide and went into the kitchen and sat down at the table. The TV volume was turned back up.

She put the phone to her ear and listened. She could hear her father clearing his throat, then his breathing. "Hello?" she said, tentatively.

"Hello, Caity. How are you?" he said, his voice so clear and close she jumped, expecting to see him across the room.

"I'm fine. How about you?"

"Hot," he said. "Already eighty-eight this morning. But I shouldn't complain—I'm sure it's worse in Kyoto. How are you surviving that heat, the old iron pot, as they say?"

She fingered the phone cord. "Okay." She was completely flustered, embarrassed about her letter outlining the false plans to go to Hagi. "How'd you know I was here?" she finally asked.

"Oide-san wrote to me, Caity," he said softly. "He was so pleased to hear from you."

"Oh." Caitlin closed her eyes and took a deep breath. She should have known. "Are you in Brookline?"

"Till tomorrow. Then I go up to the White Mountains for a few days of hiking."

"And Mom?"

"Still in Pittsburgh. Your grandmother's prognosis seems to be getting worse, Caity. I may go down soon to help out."

"Really? That bad? Is Lee still down there?"

"Yes, but she'll be coming up at the end of the month to spend a few days here before going back to college. Your mother will probably end up staying down there through the fall, we'll just have to see."

"Lee never writes you know." The words came out without warning, sounding more petulant than Caitlin had intended.

"I know she doesn't, sweetheart. But we'll call you when she's up here, how's that? Or if I go down to Pittsburgh."

Caitlin felt her throat constricting. "That'd be nice." They were both silent for a moment.

"Are you okay?" her father asked. "It's tough what you're doing, Caity, I know. But has everything been all right there?"

"Yes, fine." The words came out in a squeak. She took a deep breath and whispered, "They've all been so nice."

"Yes, I knew they would be," he said, and Caitlin could hear the quavering in his voice, too. Then he cleared his throat and added, "What do you think of the old neighborhood?"

"Well, it's really changed in some ways. In others it's just the same. Our house is gone, you know."

"Oh I know, that rickety old thing. Have you been around the city much? Or outside the city? Gone anywhere?"

Caitlin thought she read the real question between the lines,

Have you been to Uji? and arched up, defensive. But she stifled the urge to say, "Don't push me," and instead paused and replied curtly, "Various places. Tomorrow we may go to Nara. And Friday's Daimonji."

"Ahh, you're lucky. O-Bon's a good time to be in Kyoto, other than the heat. When do you go back to Kagoshima?"

"Next Friday."

"By ferry?"

"Yes, barring a typhoon." Caitlin said coolly. She could almost smell the tension that had suddenly sprung up between them. She wished he hadn't alluded to Uji. Or had he? Perhaps she'd read too much into the question. She tried to add warmth to her voice. "So when are you coming over?"

"Looks like November now. For about two months, maybe three, in Tokyo and Kyoto. Maybe you can come up for a visit or two. And I'd love to get down to Kagoshima to see all this ash I've been hearing about."

"Great. I'll show you around." She suspected she ought to add something about Hiroshi, but didn't. There was another silence, then Caitlin suddenly said, "Dad, give Ma Ruth a hug for me when you're in Pittsburgh, will you?"

"Of course. But try not to worry. She's determined to tough it out. She's getting lots of attention, and she's still as stubborn as ever. She makes Lee read her the same chapter of *My Antonía* every day now, insisting she hasn't heard it yet. If I go down later this month we'll all call you, okay?"

"Okay."

"Listen, you take good care of yourself. Remember, as they say, it's the hardest of the hardest things to be born a human being. Be gentle on yourself. You know what I mean."

She could barely utter a response. "I will." She wanted to make the conversation continue, wanted to keep his presence there in that kitchen, next door to the place they once called home, but all too quickly he was saying good-bye, and she couldn't think of a stall with her throat all in a knot.

She placed the receiver in its cradle. The TV droned from the next room, and Harumi and Nobuko were exclaiming aghast as a newscaster described in the words of a surviving flight attendant how the plane went into "Dutch rolls," and that it seemed that at least one passenger had had the presence of mind to write a will. Caitlin rose and, looking down at the tatami as she passed the Oides still seated at the table, excused herself and went upstairs.

▲ ▲ ▲

She pulled a cushion over to the single window in Nobuko's room, and resting her crossed forearms on the sill, looked out into the night. She hadn't turned the light on when she'd come upstairs, so her eyes were well adjusted and she could make out dark lumps of hills to the north and east, and faint stars where the halos of street lamps didn't intrude. She could hear drums and bamboo flutes in the distance practicing for a festival, the revs and stops of a motor scooter navigating the back streets, the tinkle of wind chimes, and periodically, the crossing gates at the local train station. She closed her eyes.

So many of the sounds and smells were just the same. Then what if they were all there again, living next door to the Oides? She wished she could see her family in Kyoto; she ached for them to be all together once again, without the tiresome defenses, the mindless bickering and antagonizing. To have her mother there at their old kitchen table with her again, carefully reviewing Caitlin's Japanese textbooks, and in a neat hand, writing the English translations beside the words Caitlin didn't know so she could follow the classroom exercises the next day. Every evening after Lee had been put to bed, before reading from an English chapter book, she and her mother worked on Japanese: reviewing, studying, preparing. This had been her mother's role, Caitlin recalled, taken on with zeal, this assisting with the language, conferring with Caitlin's teachers, struggling to translate the memos that came home in her hard leather backpack. Incredible, now, to think that her mother had studied the language herself so intensively, that her mother must have undertaken to learn at least 400 *kanji* herself, just to keep abreast of what Caitlin was doing in school. How she longed to have that mother here again, with that same infectious energy, their heads bent close over the page, sharing sighs of frustration and exhalations of triumph.

But it was as if that mother had vanished with Uji. The only vestige of Japan was her packed lunches. The nurses she worked with had always raved about them—full of colorful morsels, bits of sweet potato, marinated eggplant, sliced chicken with sesame seeds sprinkled on top, spinach dressed with miso sauce, a tiny cup of fruit, some rice or pasta, all tucked in neatly, suspiciously reminiscent of a Japanese *bento*. She'd had to pack compact *bento* boxes for Lee to take to preschool and for Caitlin's special events, and the technique Caitlin had watched her strive so hard to master had never left her.

But aside from food, and except as it pertained to her husband's work at the university and his travel schedule, Arlene no longer discussed Japan—and it was clear that she never intended to revisit Kyoto or any other Japanese destination. That much she'd actually verbalized when Caitlin had defended her plans to apply to the teaching program—"Well, don't expect *me* to come visit you. You're on your own there"—and Lee had even accused Caitlin of aggravating her mother, intentionally tormenting her by going back. "I guess I shouldn't expect a visit from you either," Caitlin had said sarcastically, and Lee had stormed out of the room shouting, "At least I care about my mother." Caitlin had rejoined, "That's not caring, that's clutching!" Lee never even sent letters to Japan, as though she thought some part of her would actually enter the country with her handwriting and thereby betray her mother and grandmother. It was all too obvious; Caitlin and her father were the only ones who would ever return to Kyoto.

And though Caitlin was looking forward to seeing her father in the fall, she bristled again at the thought of his phone call. When she'd first picked up the receiver to his breathing, she'd felt pursued once again, pushed and nudged toward counselors and psychiatrists, and she still felt a twinge of annoyance that he'd asked such a leading question about where she'd been. Nonetheless, she was glad to have heard his voice; she had to admit she longed to see him, it'd been over a year. Even if he did meddle. Even if she had been found out.

She turned and rested her back against the windowsill and eyed the top of her knapsack. She suddenly felt like reading that letter. The idea of it up to now was enough to make her head throb. But she'd been stifling her curiosity about her father's words of a year ago ever since she'd arrived at the Oides', and now she leaned forward, drew her pack toward her, and pulled the thick letter from the rear of the top compartment. She was glad she'd brought it with her. She flicked the overhead light on to its lowest setting, then sat back against the sill again, and before she could stop herself, she reread for the first time the letter she'd received the previous September.

August 28, 1984

Dear Caity,

I'm writing about what your mother has kept us from talking about for so many years and what has probably driven you back there whether you're willing to admit it or not. Don't put this down like your mother would, Caity; please, keep reading.

But Caitlin disobeyed even on this second reading to turn and look out the window, recalling the day his letter had arrived in Kagoshima; the light blue packet jutting from the tin mailbox by her door as she mounted the stairs with her bike after a day of teaching. She'd turned it over and over in her hands, feeling for photos or forwarded mail—how strange, a letter so thick from her father—and she'd brought it inside to the kitchen table, pausing to pour a glass of ice water between tearing the envelope open and reading the first lines. But after the opening paragraph, hours before sundown, she'd risen to close the rain shutters. She'd turned a single fluorescent ring light on and squinting in the whiteness, had sat back down to finish reading. She'd kept the shutters closed straight through to Monday morning and left her apartment only once that whole weekend, for a brisk and solitary walk along the river late Sunday evening.

Now, by the window in Nobuko's room, Caitlin continued reading:

Silence is your mother's way, but I think you're willing to remember. I'm pleased that you've gone back, and I hope your return is a sign that you're able to accept what happened. It doesn't go away by not thinking about it, Caity.

Lee is due in from Pittsburgh this weekend though your
mother will remain until the end of the month while Ma
Ruth recovers from the surgery. I'll drive Lee out to get
her settled in her dorm, something about which your
mother is making a big deal, with weekly memos so I don't
forget a single item that might increase Lee's comfort.
Classes start for me again next week so I'm savoring these
last quiet moments under the arbor. I'd send you a cluster
of these grapes if I could, and this pungent heady scent
with the portentous chill in the air. Autumn in Massachusetts, Caity, I wonder if you'll miss it.

It will be nice to have Lee back. Your mother is reluctant to
send her by herself though and even worked out some
intricate plans for Lee to do her first semester in Pittsburgh
until she could leave Ma Ruth alone again, but Lee seems
to have cultivated some sense of late; she made her own
plane reservation for Saturday afternoon. She feels that one
year off was more than enough. Maybe someday your
mother will learn to loosen those strings—but her clinging
makes me sad more than angry. Arlene still can't forgive
herself for being absent that day, for trusting you and Mie
to me, for allowing herself to relent and stay home; she
seems to think that accidents can't happen under the
watchful eyes of mothers, that little and even not so little
girls are always safer with her.

She'd wanted to join us at that temple in Uji you know, to
be out of doors with a change of scenery, but Harumi, Mie's
mother, was almost nine months pregnant, uncomfortable
and reluctant to go anywhere. Your mother offered to take
all the children off her hands, but Harumi said no, leave the
young ones, Nobu-chan and Lee, she could manage them,
but at five and four those two were a handful, so in the end
the two women stayed home with them together, your
mother's sacrifice to allow us some quiet at the temple
where Oide-san had arranged for me to meet the priest.
You and Mie would be fine with us we all knew; you were

older, you could sit still, and more important, you were self-absorbed and content so long as you were together.

Do you remember that priest, Caity? Do you remember sitting on the veranda with him, swinging your legs and mimicking his imitations of the sounds of the various *semi* in the garden before I ran my questions by him? You always refused the word cicada, even after we returned to the States, and I understand your insistence; *semi* seems more apt for that incessant whine in such damp heat. Your Japanese was so good then, Caity, you always astonished me with vocabulary that appeared from nowhere. If you were stuck for a word you turned to Mie, and in whispered conference the two of you puzzled out your needs. I'm sure the language has come back to you easily, I'm sure you feel her influence even now.

I can see you both then, side by side, clasping your teacups with two hands and looking at each other, smiling, such secrets between you, then laughing suddenly, at what? your swinging legs? tea with a priest? us adults? We never knew. You held hands when you walked, interpreted for each other, and sang songs in your own nonsense language with your lithe arms around each other's shoulders, Mie on tiptoe to reach your eight-year-old height.

You were charmed by each other. If you liked something Mie liked it too, and if Mie liked something you made yourself like it. I remember watching you, one of those Saturday nights when we ate together. Harumi had planned some dish with octopus and set a bowlful of the boiled red arms on the table to cool. I was in the doorway and when Harumi turned away I watched you follow Mie's example, tentative at first, then eager, stealing the arms and furtively biting off the hard round suckers as if they were kernels of corn. I laughed, and you jumped, startled to have been discovered, but then continued, reaching for new arms and dropping the used and pocked ones back into the same bowl.

After dinner those nights you two would pull at the torn *fusuma* doors and shut yourselves in the next room. We'd hear you practicing and hear Mie ordering you and Lee and Nobu-chan about, making you imitate exactly those pop singer gestures. Occasionally you argued. Lee and Nobu-chan often emerged in tears, and once you flounced into the room and screeched back at Mie, "I hate you," then let go with a tirade you must have learned on the school yard because Harumi and Oide's eyes widened and they burst out laughing. Those performances were the only times you two seemed to be in conflict, but you never stayed mad long because we always had a show before returning to our house, the four of you standing on the sofa for a stage, clasping air microphones and singing and moving your arms and legs like Mie's favorite idols.

I miss her for you Caity, I miss the friend she could have been to you now. You might never have achieved that same confiding closeness again, but you'd still have that best-friend history to share. I think hard about why she isn't there for you, I try to fit her death into the idea that we're all just bubbles on the sea, precious and tenuous, likely to pop at any moment and return to the effluvium, but I'm still saddened, Caity; I wouldn't make a good Buddhist.

When I'd finished my questions that day and we'd left the priest, I remember that Oide and I paused in the car park after we left the temple. We'd planned to return directly to Arlene and Harumi; their hands were full with the younger girls, and it was Sunday, father's day to help with the children. The rainy season had just ended. It was hot and steamy still, but there was a thin blue sky above the trees and no threat of drizzle for a change. So on impulse we left the car at the lot and walked down along the river. There were cherry trees lining a walkway, there might be *semi,* why not, we thought, you girls would like it, and we wouldn't stay long.

We could have bought ice cream instead, Caity, gone in and out of a few shops, toured Byodo-in or just plain gone back, but we didn't. Do you see what complicitors we all are? Do you see the power of chance, the haphazard way our fate is made, the myriad choices involved in the final outcome of any single event?

You and Mie had your insect cages hung around your necks, and as we walked along that lower path sometimes you took them off and swung them like purses unmindful of the poor critters inside. The heat was stifling. We must have been there about noon, and it felt like a steam bath where Oide and I hunched down to catch our breath while you two hopped along the rocks. You shrieked beside the rushing water, thrilled by all that commotion, and we warned you both to keep back, and you did. You really did. That's what I don't understand.

Your mother never believed we kept our eyes on you, our ears out for you. But you weren't the daring sorts, you were too content with yourselves to need to try things you knew you weren't supposed to, and when we stood and started walking just ahead of you, we turned periodically, walked half backward so you weren't much out of our sight. When you got too close to the edge we called to you and you came scurrying up, just like that. You never challenged us or the world, you didn't need to, we were incidental; you were two girls, Caitlin and Mie, outside after the rainy season, giggling in your cotton dresses and the open air busy with flying insects.

You never could tell us how she got into the water; for a week you couldn't even speak. We soothed you, cradled you, salved the leg you kept rubbing, treated you with all the tenderness we could summon, but you wouldn't answer our pleas to speak, mumble, utter anything. Finally, impatient and frightened, worried I was losing you too, washing the dishes one evening not long before we left for the States again, I hummed the beginning of Mie's favorite Four Leaves song and behind me at the kitchen table you cried out, "Don't," but I acted dumb. "Don't what?" I said. "Don't sing that song," you said, and carefully, tentatively, I reeled you back into the speaking world with a bald-faced lie: "I didn't know I was singing."

My guess has always been that she suddenly ran recklessly after a dragonfly or butterfly, leaping to follow the erratic flight, but didn't stop at the bank. Perhaps she thought the rushing water was firm, and stepped off the rocks like a cartoon character to the mad current beneath. She wouldn't have simply jumped in, or leaned too far over the edge; she couldn't really swim—we'd seen her fear at the beach in Shikoku a month before. Or maybe she'd dropped her net, reached for it on impulse, and fallen. But it was quick, however it happened, because just a few paces ahead of you, Oide and I never saw nor heard a splash.

I cannot understand why we didn't see the movement; the slightest change in our peripheral vision would have had us turned and running—we were fathers, after all, we would have jumped at a wet toe. But there were students helping us later, lined up along the bank, and maybe we'd been watching them, in the distance. Maybe I'd tripped, or sneezed at the very moment, I don't know. I cannot recall those seconds just before your face when it had already happened; I cannot recall what I was thinking or what I was saying in those seconds while it did. I wonder what those seconds are for you, Caity, if they exist at all, or if that time is a blank erasure from your memory.

There, at Uji, you ran toward me, and I can still feel the velvet algae in my hands from when I picked you up, gathered you up in my arms after I turned and saw you coming toward me, your teeth bared, arms outstretched stiffly before you. Your bright yellow dress was damp and green-brown where you must have sat yourself down, and your knee was bloody, you must have fallen.

I scooped you up when you came running, and you arched your back and made to scream but only a bubble of noise came out. I bent close to catch any words as I ran, but you shook your head so hard it knocked against mine and I had to hold you down by my waist as I ran, we ran, Oide ran, down the bank following your pointing arm, following that expression on your face, your lips peeled back and quivering around that bubble of noise that told us that Mie had fallen into the foamy water, that you had tried to reach out—your bottom on the wet rocks—but that she had drifted too fast, that she was swirling downriver or was caught by then, snagged somewhere on the bottom.

I know I shook you and screamed at you, "Where? Where?" and bless you, at least you could point accurately. We couldn't have been running long, with the others who must have seen, before we waded in, combing the rocks and muck on the bottom with our feet, our knees, our hands, falling over in the pounding current. I can taste that water still, smell the muck that I wore to the hospital and later in the taxi back to you—waiting, shivering and silent, curled up beside the winter hearth in the priest's house where I'd brought you before following the route of Oide and the ambulance to the hospital.

Oide touched her first. He yanked her up and started banging her on the back, squeezing her chest, shaking her upside down, telling her to breathe, breathe; I had to pry her from his hands to get her onto the shore and try mouth-to-mouth properly, he didn't know the right procedure.

But I lose you then baby, I can't see your face, all I see is

Mie's under mine, in mine, and I wonder what it was like
for you to watch your father crying over your best friend,
forcing his breath into her nostrils, into her little mouth,
and into those bloated lungs you'd laughed with for more
than a year. I felt you there, I felt your eyes watching, but I
can't imagine your face. I felt Oide watching his daughter
slip away, I felt Harumi and Nobuko and even the unborn
baby, now Yusuke, watching and telling me not to give up,
to try harder, breathe! I tried pumping Mie with my own
life but she had already gone, and you, I'm sure, by then,
you knew.

I'm sorry for you, Caity, I'm sorry for all of us, we never
bargained for any of this when we set out in Oide's car to
interview a priest for my research.

The wake was small. I didn't take you. I couldn't bear the
thought of you seeing your best friend's photo framed and
draped with black ribbon, the incense, the hush. Your
mother and I took turns going, took turns staying with
you and Lee.

We couldn't have continued living in that neighborhood;
even if Arlene had been willing to stay in Japan, we needed
to leave the Oides in peace, without us next door as daily
reminders. And we needed to apologize with some gesture,
which ended up being my forfeiting the fellowship and
returning to Pittsburgh. We didn't even stay as long as the
forty-ninth-day ceremony; once we'd decided to go, we
wanted to go, to get you girls settled in again back home
before the school year started. And it was tormenting you
to stay there—I could see that. You needed help, and I
knew that that help needed to come from English-speaking
professionals—so we thought we had to return, do you
see? But now I wonder if I erred, if I should have stayed
in Kyoto, just moved away from the Oides, let you heal
over there, instead of shuttling you off to Pittsburgh where

no one but us shared any of your life, the good or the bad, of the eighteen months before.

We can all find plenty to feel guilty about, you, me, your mother, Oide, Harumi, Nobuko and Lee, and even Yusuke. But don't suffocate yourself Caity; either none of us is guilty or we all are.

Go see them, Caity, talk to them, visit Nobuko, you'll hardly recognize her. She's asked about you every time I've been back, she's seen your pictures, seen those glimpses of your growth, and she'd love to know you. Their address and phone number are below. Go see them, Caity. I know they'd love to have you.

Caitlin dropped her chin onto her arms, swallowed painfully, and stared out at the rooftop tiles and the tops of cedars brushed yellow-white from the rising three-quarter moon. Her longing for her father, her sharp resentment of him and his meddling, her sympathy for him and anger at her mother, and her acute feelings of guilt became one swirling, pulsing miasma.

She rubbed her forehead and refolded the letter, then sat staring outside with her head resting on her forearms. Even when Nobuko entered the room behind her and flicked the light setting one higher she didn't rise, although she turned to acknowledge her. *"I brought you some cake,"* Nobuko said, setting down beside Caitlin a small tray with a cup of tea and a plate holding a fancy pastry. Caitlin thanked her.

"Is your father well?" Nobuko asked from a formal kneel, her brow knit with concern. Caitlin mustered a smile—*"Yes, yes, thank you. I'm just a little homesick is all."*

Seventeen

THE NARA DAY TRIP was postponed because of drizzle that was predicted to last throughout the day, so Caitlin set out by herself on Wednesday, armed with an umbrella and a city map. She took a train and bus downtown and walked in and out of what shops were open despite the holiday, toured Nijo Castle and its expansive rooms of tatami, sat under the dripping eaves at Nishi Honganji, roamed back streets until her shoes were soaked through, then bought an English language magazine and newspaper and sat in a coffee shop reading.

She perused a few articles, lingered over travel advertisements and events calendars, but could not seem to concentrate. Her eyes continually darted about the shop, and her father's voice sounded in her ears. Over and over she heard snatches of his letter and fragments of the phone conversation, and she had the unsettling feeling that she had replaced the receiver just as a dialogue was beginning. She squirmed on her seat, resentful of the rain because what she really felt like doing was walking, miles and miles of pumping her legs, from one end of the city to the other. Under the coffee-shop table she had her shoes off, and her shriveled feet made her wish for a pool, wish she could be prunelike from the end of a long swim rather than rain.

But at least she was out of the Oide house; that alone brought measurable relief. Mie's spirit was supposed to be visiting the home until Friday, and although Caitlin agreed with the glib Naomi—once you're dead, you're dead—she felt increasingly uneasy in the house, around the altar and among the offerings of food that she half expected to disappear as Mie and the other spirits devoured them.

In the back alleys and side streets, Caitlin had encountered monks on bicycles and motor scooters, making rounds and hurrying in and out of homes—this was their busiest time of year as they were called upon to recite the sutras before household altars. Caitlin had earlier asked if the Oides would have a monk to their house, and Harumi had said no, although they had invited one each year that there was a death in the family. *"Not this year,"* she'd said. *"Now O-Bon is a happy time, a celebration. We're together again, in a way."* Caitlin wished that instead of a persistent dread, she too could feel that warmth of reunion.

The worst part was that everywhere she went, and now directly behind her, the television was tuned into the airline crash, and a pall seemed to have settled over the city while the horror sank in as to what the passengers had suffered in the interminable minutes before the plane slammed into the mountain. Caitlin couldn't stomach the news reports—the charred and scattered rubble on the steep mountainside; repeated footage of the young girl, one of four survivors, being hoisted to a helicopter; relatives struggling to scale the slopes to lay flowers; technical discussions of "Dutch rolls." To Caitlin the crash seemed a cruel but fitting addition to O-Bon, a catastrophe designed intentionally to depress her further.

Unable to swallow the rest of the coffee, her stomach queasy, Caitlin paid her bill and left the shop. In a department store she purchased a cheap pair of slip-on tennis shoes, then she wandered other floors, aimlessly strolling between aisles of kitchen appliances, pausing to examine pottery and glassware, trying on a skirt and more shoes. By late afternoon, the drizzle had let up, so to reach the train, she hiked across town rather than take a series of buses. Her legs were aching, her heels blistered by the time she finally boarded the train, and she slumped in her seat as it sped toward Iwakura.

But when she debarked in her old neighborhood and crossed the tracks to begin her walk toward the Oide house, she noticed activity in the local school yard. She observed men from afar, puttering and conversing in the dirt playground where she had once run relay races and lined up for class pictures. The concrete block school looked the same, albeit smaller and in need of paint and patching, the surrounding trees nearly hiding it from view now. Funny, she hadn't even thought of trying to visit. Then she wondered, though it seemed impossible, as if she were thinking back to another century, if any of her teachers still taught there.

She stared at the building she'd entered six days a week for the better part of eighteen months, then wandered over by the gate for a closer look. Four men were struggling to set up a dais in the center of the yard as a man on a ladder adjusted the height and drape of a string of lanterns. Caitlin finally called out to ask what was going on, and descending the ladder, one man explained that the neighborhood O-Bon festival would be held there that night—they were fortunate the rain had stopped.

Caitlin mulled this over as she stopped at a small market to pick up orange juice, beer, and dessert cakes for the Oides. Had she been to this festival their first summer in Iwakura? Perhaps—she couldn't recall—but Obaachan had sewn her that *yukata*. The following summer, fifteen years ago, she would have missed it, coming as it did a month after Mie's death and a mere week or so after Caitlin and her family had flown out of Japan, up through icy polar airs to a stop in Anchorage, where she had refused to budge from a waiting-lounge chair and had had to be carried stiff-limbed and wailing by her father back onto the plane headed ultimately for Pittsburgh and her grandparents' house—far, too far from Mie, whom she felt she was deserting, whom she couldn't believe would not wake up. She handed the grocer the correct change, saddened for her young self, herded back to the States before she'd grasped what had happened here in Kyoto.

When she reached the house, she set down her bags in the kitchen, collapsed into a chair with a glass of water, and recounted her day to Nobuko and Harumi, busy at the sink counter slicing vegetables and preparing cuts of *maguro*. Caitlin mentioned the festival, and to her enthusiasm they raised amused eyebrows. They relayed the information to Oide when he came into the kitchen, and everyone agreed, why didn't they all go after dinner?

Caitlin bathed, soaking long in the tub until her face was flushed and her legs felt light once more. Then she changed into clean shorts and a sleeveless shirt and joined the family downstairs. The simple dinner, rosebuds of *maguro* slices on rice and grilled eggplant and okra, tasted good to her, and she was grateful for Harumi planning a meal that was easy on her ever-churning stomach. When they'd finished eating, Oide suggested they leave the dishes on the table, and everyone hustled out to the driveway. Yusuke had declined to go at first, claiming to want to stay home and follow reports on the plane crash. But when they had all piled into the car he came ambling out of the house and climbed into the backseat grinning sheepishly. They drove the short distance to the school, and Oide found a parking space not far from the entrance to the school yard, which was clogged with men distributing paper fans and children urging their parents to move faster. Caitlin walked beside Nobuko, accepted a paper fan, and entered the school yard.

She felt the moist dirt under her sandals and had to suppress the urge to kneel down and scoop some up in her hands. She could still feel it on her knees, the sting when she'd tripped and rubbed the skin raw. And she could feel it dusty on her face and gritty in her teeth when it billowed up in the wind. She was thinking of the sports festival, and that photograph of Mie and her, arm in arm. That was here, Caitlin thought, right here, and she stared hard at the dirt as though there might still be some lingering evidence of her Iwakura childhood preserved between the tiny soil particles.

Nobuko and Harumi walked on either side of her, and Caitlin could hear Harumi take a deep breath and clear her throat. Yusuke had separated himself from the family, but joined up with them repeatedly, hanging behind Caitlin with a friend or two, as if to show her off. Caitlin was catapulted into the public eye once more, strolling about with the Oides, who greeted neighbors and led Caitlin from food stands to stalls selling masks and a large basin of goldfish surrounded by children attempting their catches with tiny paper nets. She was stared at as intensely as in the small rural schools she sometimes visited outside Kagoshima—unabashed, giggly stares—but now and then, she was eyed in a different way, by friends of the Oides' who clearly knew who she was, and moreover, remembered her. Although they smiled, and she smiled warmly and bowed back, she felt uneasy with the recognition, wondering if they thought ill of her for returning, for resuscitating that ugly past.

When the dances started up, one of Harumi's friends introduced her daughter and her two friends, dressed in floral summer *yukata*, their hair drawn up in buns. The daughter looked vaguely familiar. *"I'm Mami. You were in my class at school, with Nakano-sensei, remember?"* Caitlin searched her face and saw the hint of a young girl she couldn't quite recall. Then Mami added, *"You were in my han when we took care of the rabbit together, and you sometimes ate the carrots yourself,"* and Caitlin laughed, recalling their amazement at her munching the raw sticks.

"And you gave me silkworms, right?" Mami nodded. *"Now I remember—you showed me where to find really big mulberry leaves!"* Mami nodded and seemed about to say something more when the music started. She took Caitlin by the arm and before Caitlin knew where she was being led, they'd joined a small circle of women that formed loosely, then expanded and spread outward like a water ring as others joined in the slow procession around the dais where several men sang and played on drums and small flutes.

Caitlin concentrated on the simple hand motions of the women, raising and waving her paper fan and dipping with her knees and clapping low and high like Mami and her two friends, who had clearly rehearsed the dances. After a full rotation around the dais, Nobuko and Harumi fell in line behind Caitlin. When the next song started even men began to join in, and finally some younger boys, as a lark at first, but soon in earnest—Caitlin even spotted Yusuke with several of his friends, hysterical and mocking, but trying to follow the various moves nonetheless.

The drums, the flutes, and the nasal voices of the singers, somewhat discordant, were rich and intoxicating, and Caitlin was disappointed each time a song ended, reluctant to stop even for the few moments before another piece started up. She had seen women dancing at a temple complex near her apartment in Kagoshima the summer before on an evening she'd gone out on her bicycle after dark to cool down, but she'd never taken part in the lulling circular procession. Tonight, though she couldn't follow most of the words, and she didn't have much idea as to the meanings of the dances save for references to Mt. Fuji, the moon, and rice fields, the sounds of the voices and the reverberations of the drums seemed to reach through to tingle her very marrow and draw her along. She felt as if she could go around and around the dais at that slow, entrancing pace forever, that with every turn another person from her past would join the circle, that if she continued long enough even her family, the way it used to be, and Mie, might join in too.

But eventually the musicians stopped, and the circle reluctantly dispersed. Dazed and breathless, Caitlin felt as if she'd just been woken from a trance, and she stood half weaving in the quiet. Oide brought them all sodas in pinched glass bottles with a marble that rolled and tumbled with every sip, and Mami gave Caitlin her phone number and said to call her to get together sometime before she went back to Kagoshima. Caitlin agreed—until now, she'd forgotten these other classmates and old friends with whom she'd shared that year and a half of her childhood.

Caitlin meandered with the Oides along the stalls of broiled squid, grilled noodles, and *takoyaki*—the fried batter balls with bits of octopus that had been Mie's favorite. Caitlin bought a plastic trayful and offered them around. Later a lottery was held at which Oide won a bag of rice donated by a local liquor store. They waited until the final items, a bicycle and a small TV, were raffled off and a singing competition had begun before finding Yusuke and heading for home.

Fanning herself in the backseat between Caitlin and Nobuko, Harumi reached over, squeezed Caitlin's hand, and whispered, *"Such a long time since we've done that. Thank you, Kei-chan."* Caitlin nodded, content.

Soon after they arrived home, Caitlin bid everyone good night and set out her futon. She changed into a nightshirt and sprawled on top of the cool sheets. Her legs throbbed as she lay in the dark, but the festival had turned her fatigue into a vague feeling of satiety. Perhaps O-Bon could be a time of happy reunion after all, and after seeing other old classmates like Mami, maybe she'd focus less on the loss of Mie. It wasn't long before she dropped into a deep sleep.

But sometime before dawn she awoke with a start and stood up on her futon, panicked. She checked to see if Nobuko were truly asleep, rushed to the doorway, and peered down the hall, but no one was there. The voice had been perfectly clear. Mie had spoken into her ear so close she'd felt the breath tickling, the warm moisture beading. Caitlin sat down cross-legged and rubbed hard at the cartilage of her ear. She was tempted to wake Nobuko.

She sat rigid in the still night, listening with intense concentration to every creak and tick of noise. The whisper in her ear was never repeated. It was a dream, Caitlin told herself, but a long time passed before she allowed herself to lie down again, stiffly, on her back, and hours before she turned onto her side and fell asleep.

▲ ▲ ▲

The sound and feel of the voice remained with Caitlin the following morning, and she found herself questioning her own logic that it was just a dream, wondering more and more if Mie's spirit could in some way speak to her during O-Bon. Now and then, in the car on the way to Nara, as they walked around the enormous bronze Buddha seated on lotus leaves in the great hall, as they waded through the milling deer begging for handouts, she'd hear the whisper and swat her ear in irritation.

The voice colored the whole day, and it was a struggle to express her appreciation for the temples and shrines. Not until they stopped for a late lunch, and she and Nobuko were seated at a separate table from the rest of the family in a crowded restaurant, was she able to shake the sound of Mie's whisper. Tentatively, she mentioned it to Nobuko as they sipped oolong tea while waiting for their chilled soba, and although Caitlin had expected her to raise eyebrows and dismiss the notion, she smiled and nodded. *"Yes,"* she said, *"it happens sometimes. My mother used to hear her all the time. It doesn't happen to me much, probably because I don't think of her as often."* Caitlin ran her hands through her hair; she didn't know what to say. *"Don't be alarmed,"* Nobuko continued, *"it's good that you heard her, it means you were thinking of her, and that would make her happy.*

Caitlin shook her head with admiration. *"You're so calm about her death. You and your whole family."*

"Oh, well, now we are. Don't be mistaken. We've had our difficult times." Nobuko's voice dropped. *"We wish she were here. We all wish I still had an older sister. Just as you do."* She glanced at her parents several tables over. *"You know, it's my grandparents who are really responsible for us being, well, as you say, calm."*

"Your grandparents? The ones I knew?"

Nobuko nodded. *"I lived with them after the accident. Yusuke too some of the time. For nearly a year, they were like my parents. My father came to visit when he could, but he could never stay long; sometimes he brought Yusuke, and sometimes he left him there. My father was always so sad then, and I was often rude to him. Obaachan often had to scold me.*

"Then on Boys' Day—I remember because we had just set up the carp kite for Yusuke—my grandfather told me we were going to see my parents. I

remember that Obaachan cut my hair carefully and we dressed up and took a bus to our home. My parents weren't expecting us, but my father was so pleased to see us. We went inside, and I said hello to my mother, who didn't seem quite sure who I was, then out of habit I went to the end of the living room where our toys were. It was mostly just as it had been, except right on the little fold-up table we used to use for coloring, there was an altar set up—we hadn't had a butsudan *before that—and a big photo of Mie wrapped in black ribbon and surrounded by her favorite toys. And one of her dresses was laid out. Later I learned that my mother had been selecting clothing each morning for Mie, making three meals a day for her, setting out the futon at night for her, and spending several hours each day at the cemetery."*

The noodles arrived, but neither Caitlin nor Nobuko made any move toward the food. *"Ojiichan called me into the other room and made me kneel formally in front of my mother. And he handed Yusuke to my mother. Then he said to her, 'Look at your son and daughter here. These are your children. These are your living children. They need their mother. You must leave your grieving and become a mother again.' I don't remember much else about that day, but not long afterward my brother and I moved back home. The altar was put in another part of the living room and Mie's clothes were given away. And my mother gradually got better."* Then Nobuko took up her chopsticks, sighed, and shook her head. *"But that began the most difficult time for me. You see, while I had been at my grandparents', I think I still believed Mie was alive somewhere—at home, or someplace. But when I went back home, and she wasn't there, and she didn't sleep next to me at night, and she didn't keep me from playing with her favorite toys, then I knew she was truly gone."*

Nobuko stirred wasabi into her dipping broth and began to slurp at the noodles. Then she leaned toward Caitlin and said, *"You know, I think the time when our family really began to heal, all of us, was the one-year anniversary when your father visited."*

Caitlin started. She hadn't known he'd gone back so soon. Money had been so tight then, they were still living with Ma Ruth, and she couldn't recall him taking a long trip at that time. She wondered if her mother had known he'd gone back, or if he'd used some ruse, a job-hunting trip or a visit to his parents in Wheeling.

"You see," Nobuko went on, stirring her dipping sauce, *"my mother wasn't sure she could receive your father, and there were long discus-*

sions about whether to have him stay at the house or not. In the end, of course, they did invite him to stay, and I remember it as a warm reunion. I don't recall the one-year ceremony, but I remember choosing flowers for Mie. Anyway, that's when I think my family began to get better. My mother started taking me to swimming lessons. And I finally stopped wishing Yusuke would turn into an older sister. So . . ." Nobuko paused to slurp at a long string of noodles. *"Enough about us. What about your family. Tell me what Lee is like now—I wish she would come over here, too."*

"Well," Caitlin began, and she chewed slowly as she tried to focus on Lee, wondering how best to describe her sister without being critical, without pointing to the ever-burning friction between them. *"She's thin, too thin; she has a problem with that. She goes to college in Connecticut, although right now she's living in Pittsburgh with my mother and grandmother—my grandmother's ill—and I think Lee has a job bartending. Or maybe waitressing. I forget. She doesn't like to write letters."*

"Do you think it would be okay if I wrote to her? Do you think she remembers me?"

Caitlin nodded emphatically, but she couldn't envision Lee's reaction to a letter from Nobuko, and she wondered just how much Lee remembered. They'd never talked about Kyoto after they'd moved back to Pittsburgh, only occasionally used Japanese words to describe what they were doing in play, or made oblique references to their old house or bikes, but Caitlin hadn't heard a word about that time in Japan escape Lee's lips in at least ten years, so Caitlin couldn't be sure. But of course Lee remembered Nobuko; of that much Caitlin was certain—they'd spent nearly every day of that year and a half playing together, attending preschool together, and at the Oides', Harumi watching the two of them while Caitlin's mother tutored afternoons around the neighborhood.

"Of course, write to her sometime," Caitlin urged. *"But it would have to be in English, you know. She doesn't understand Japanese at all now. I could help you if you want."*

"Maybe I could convince her to come visit, like you. To be an exchange student or something," Nobuko said. Caitlin nodded, biting her tongue to keep herself from uttering a sarcastic "Good luck!"

When Caitlin finished her lunch, she asked for a cup of hot tea despite the heat of the day. The restaurant was animated and full, and Nobuko's talk had released her from the vortex of the dream in which she'd felt so trapped. Since Nobuko was still slurping her noodles, Caitlin eavesdropped on conversations around her, catching snippets here and there over the general din of voices and restaurant clatter. The tea warmed her insides, and for a time she felt a great comfort sitting there across from Nobuko.

But later, with some red-bean ice cream chilling the length of her esophagus, she found the unease returning, and she began to jiggle a leg under the table.

The Daimonji fires were a day away, and she was nervous, as if Mie would be present, as if Caitlin had to pronounce some formal good-bye to her—it would be the last night of O-Bon after all, and those would be the farewell fires. Caitlin wondered if she'd feel relief once those flames had been extinguished. She was growing tired of this notion of the spirits visiting; she wanted to stop thinking about the dead.

She waited impatiently for Oide to pay the bill, eager to be out of the restaurant in the open air again. For she was beginning to feel that whenever she was indoors, spirits were swirling above her, even in this restaurant, hovering up there with the noodle steam somewhere amid the wooden rafters.

Eighteen

CAITLIN, NOBUKO, and Yusuke set out Friday afternoon for the banks of the Kamo-gawa, laden with stacked picnic containers of food that Harumi had helped them prepare, rush mats to sit on, and thermoses of tea, cans of soda, and a jug of beer for Jun, Nobuko, and Caitlin. The trains and buses were packed with people headed for the river, and when they finally reached the banks and met up with Naomi and Jun at the western end of the agreed-upon bridge, groups were already jockeying for territory. They sidled through the crowds and tossed their mats down to reserve a grassy spot while Naomi and Jun walked ahead to scout out other possibilities. When the two returned shaking their heads, all five of them set about unpacking the picnic. Once everything had been arranged, they popped open sodas and poured beer.

They were all quite formal at first, Naomi and Yusuke awkwardly shy. Yusuke hung close by Nobuko, but when Nobuko and Jun began comparing tales of college entrance exams, Yusuke just watched the crowds shuffling past, and Naomi started telling Caitlin in English about her week and Mayumi's, Jun's sister, expected return to Kyoto the following Monday.

"Naomi, speak in Japanese," Caitlin suggested, but this silenced Naomi altogether. *"What time is it, Yusuke?"* Caitlin finally asked, a lame attempt to draw him in.

"A little before seven."

"And this all begins at eight?" she continued. He nodded. *"Are the other four mountains lit up at the same time?"*

He hedged, and Nobuko piped up, *"They're lit five minutes apart."* Then she joined Caitlin, working to pull the fivesome together, doling out food, and acting like a hostess. *"We should be able to see both the Daimonji and the Myoho fires from here—that's why it's so crowded. Some people run around the city trying to see as many of the five as they can, but you'd have to have a car to do that."*

"Or a plane," Yusuke added.

"When I was little," Naomi added, tentatively, *"my father wanted to see at least three of the fires, so after Daimonji, and I guess Myoho, he made us run to the car, then drove like crazy to get near the one shaped like a boat. By the time we got there it was almost out. It was more like a deflated rubber raft,"* she said, and even Yusuke smiled. The conversation continued with different O-Bon experiences, then shifted inevitably to the recent plane crash. Caitlin guzzled her beer, hefted the jug, and poured around, relieved to hear the conversation rolling on its own, despite the morbid subject matter.

Around them, couples and families scurried to claim what open space remained, and, as if on cue, a squat creamy moon rose over the hills. Down by the playgrounds, on the riverbank's lower level, clusters of people lit off firecrackers and roman candles and swung sparklers in wide arcs. Soon the grassy area of the banks was taken up, and people began to stand directly in front of them, blocking the river, the hills, and even the moon. *"Don't worry,"* Nobuko said. *"We'll stand when it starts,"* but Caitlin was annoyed to have their picnic hemmed in by all those legs and bodies. She wanted space and a clear view of the fires ignited to guide the spirits back to the other world, as though in the flames and smoke she might catch a glimpse or waft of Mie.

At first sight of the twinkling bonfires far off on the slope of Mount Nyoigatake, Caitlin stood with the others and tried to peer over the crowds. Soon all the fires were lit, delineating the three bold strokes of *dai,* the character meaning great. But suspended there beyond the river, the *dai* was small, strangely ornamental. Though she "oohed" in concert with everyone, she was disappointed by how remote it was. Without the heat of burning or the snap of flame, or even a trace scent of smoke, there on the crowded riverbank in the heart of the city, she felt too distant for any sense of farewell. She had somehow expected a grander, more intimate sight without the distraction of the surrounding throngs. All around them cameras flashed. "Wishful thinking," Caitlin muttered. "Too far away."

"Speak Japanese, Caitlin," Naomi said to her sideways.

Minutes after the *dai* was fully lit, the crowds began to mill and shove. *"Just like that everyone goes home? It's still burning!"* Caitlin said in disbelief, thinking of the gatherings of teachers that dispersed just as suddenly when a principal or department head announced the end of the party and everyone put down their chopsticks, midbite, bowed, and left the tables.

But Nobuko was craning her neck for a view upriver. *"We must be on the wrong side of the bridge for the Myoho fire. Do you want to try to see it?"* she asked the group. Naomi and Yusuke nodded vigorously and began packing up the picnic while Jun and Nobuko jostled ahead to determine the best location. When they'd fought their way back, Nobuko said, *"Hold hands, and if anyone gets separated we'll meet at 8:30 right by that streetlight, okay?"* Jun and Nobuko were already holding hands, and Caitlin saw Naomi roll her eyes at this, but everyone held on in a line with Jun leading, then Nobuko, Yusuke, Caitlin, and Naomi. They wove and pushed in tiny steps through the teeming crowds, so thick with everyone headed in the same direction that when they'd crossed the street to inch down the other bank and people began to push and press from behind, Caitlin began to panic, certain they'd be shoved right off the steep concrete embankment to the dark river below. "I don't like this," she said to Naomi, who was clutching tight to her arm.

"We're lemmings," Naomi said.

"That's what I'm afraid of."

Caitlin gave all her concentration to her footing until they were more safely positioned on the level, lower tier. They continued to weave through the tangle of people, until Jun finally stopped. Then they stood perspiring in a huddle, pressed in by bodies all around them, straining, up on tiptoe vying for first sight of the second sending-off fire. *"There it is!"* Nobuko cried, and gradually the bonfires of the two multi-stroke characters of *Myoho,* "the supreme law of Buddha," were lit on a low hillside to the north. Again the flames were distant, twinkling like a constellation. They stood and watched until the fires began to fade and flicker, and the crowds shifted again, this time more slowly, to go off to other festivities, bars, or home. The group stayed put and unfurled their mats again, and as the crowds receded they sat down fanning themselves. Nobuko poured more beer and tea and offered the sweet cakes that Sachiko had sent with Jun and Naomi.

Caitlin gazed a while longer at the darkness where the fires had been, trying to imagine the smoke spiraling up to the clouds and thinning air, guiding Mie's spirit back to the other world. But she couldn't envision any sort of other world, only textbook layers of the atmosphere and its gaseous constituents, and beyond that, space, multicolored planets, moons, asteroids, and stars.

When they'd finished the sweets and Caitlin was brushing sugar off her fingers, Jun reached into his bag and placed several packets of fireworks on the mat. *"Senko hanabi?"* Caitlin asked of a small packet. Jun nodded and Nobuko patted his arm and said, *"Good idea!"* Everyone looked pleased, except Naomi, who, midway through reaching for one of the packets with roman candles and assorted flares, glared at Nobuko and the hand that had patted Jun. "I'm going for a walk," she said abruptly in English and stood up. The others glanced up bemused, and Caitlin had to resist the urge to reach up and yank her back down to the mat. Jun began to rise but Caitlin motioned for him to sit. She let Naomi walk off a ways before excusing herself and following.

For some time Caitlin walked along the riverbank a few paces behind Naomi. Then when Naomi stopped and squatted to watch a man wading out in the river to light off fireworks, Caitlin squatted down beside her. "Naomi, I don't know what's bugging you, but you're being rude."

Naomi snickered softly.

Caitlin added, "Please, just do me a favor and let's go back there."

Naomi turned and looked past Caitlin to where they could make out the dark figures of Jun, Nobuko, and Yusuke waving sparklers through the air. "Nobody cares if I go back there but you, so why should I?"

"Naomi, stop it. Everyone cares. There's no need to act this way. Now come on." Caitlin stood and gave a firm nudge to Naomi's elbow, but Naomi shook her off and walked several steps farther down the bank. Then she stopped, looking out to the middle of the river. "I'm going to help that guy light fireworks," she said, and she began searching for a place to climb down the steep embankment to the water.

"Knock it off!" Caitlin said, grabbing her, but the glint of surprise followed by anger in Naomi's eyes told her she'd been too rough and hasty.

"Leave me alone," Naomi menaced, "I'm going for a swim."

Caitlin tightened the grip on her arm.

"Let me go. You're a hotshot swimmer. Rescue me."

"Cut it out," Caitlin said. "We're going back there together, now," she said.

"Let go," Naomi said again, shaking the arm that Caitlin was squeezing. "I'm going for a swim. Rescue me if you care so much."

"Damn you, Naomi!" Caitlin shoved her back from the bank. "You take everything for granted, like it will always be here for you. Stop feeling sorry for yourself and look at all you've got! Look at your talent, would you!"

"Talent? Ha!" Naomi shouted. "You don't know what you're talking about. All I've got is a little ability and some drive. Big deal. You want me to do a dance?"

"Yes, damn it! Do a dance. For your ability and your drive. For your talent which you seem to be blind to. And for all the people who care about you."

Naomi snorted, but Caitlin continued, her voice high, cracking. "And for this night. For the fact that you can come out and do all this." She waved her arms wildly to include the river, the embankment, the restaurants and teahouses bright behind them, and the shadowy mountains opposite. "Some people don't have this. You just take it for granted, but some people can't drink tea, or light sparklers, or walk along a river, or scream, or anything! Don't you see?" She was holding both of Naomi's arms, shaking her forward and back.

"Don't you?" The anger left Naomi's eyes, and Caitlin saw confusion welling in its place. "They're nothing. They're just . . ." Caitlin felt her face contort but she kept on: ". . . they're just whispers, subjects of offerings . . . like Mie . . . nothing else . . . can't speak, can't grow . . . can't grow . . . and they can't think . . . they can't even be!"

With a whimper, Caitlin released Naomi's arms and crumpled to the ground. There she pulled herself into a ball, held her knees tight, rocked on her haunches, and took gasping breaths of air between sobs. She was aware of Naomi staring at her, and finally dropping down beside her. Caitlin buried her head deep in her arms.

Eventually, her chest quieted. She wiped her face with the front of her T-shirt and noted the river and the roman candles that seemed to shoot directly from the man's torso. She rubbed her eyes, and looking back in the direction from which they'd walked, she could see the silhouettes of Jun, Nobuko, and Yusuke. Jun had a sparkler that illuminated his face. Then Nobuko and Yusuke had sparklers too. She glanced at Naomi, still squatting there beside her. Naomi offered a tissue; Caitlin took it and blew her nose. After a moment, Naomi ventured tentatively, "Who's Mie?"

Caitlin stared out at the man in the river. He didn't even have waders on.

"Who's Mie?" Naomi asked again.

"It doesn't matter," Caitlin said.

"She's dead, isn't she?"

Caitlin gave her face another swipe with her shirt front. "Can we go back now?"

"Was she a friend? From before?"

"It doesn't matter, I said." Caitlin stood, and Naomi, without hesitating, followed her back to the others.

Nobuko glanced from Naomi to Caitlin when they rejoined the group. Caitlin reached out and took a single *senko hanabi* from Jun's outstretched hand and lit it from the cigarette lighter Yusuke held out.

As the small flame flickered, Caitlin caught Naomi's eyes grazing her face, then Nobuko's. Nobuko looked away. No one said a word. But then Jun and Yusuke turned to Naomi, who bowed slightly as she took one of the sparklers and held it to the lighter. Still no one spoke, and soon all five of them stood with *senko hanabi* between their thumbs and forefingers, little spritzes of fire dropping from the tiny molten globes into the darkness.

Nineteen

THE NEXT MORNING Caitlin lay still on her futon and pretended to be sleeping while Nobuko rose and dressed. Her body felt battered, and her head was pounding from all the beer. She wished she could descend back into the nether regions of sleep to obliterate both her hangover and her thoughts: here it was the 17th of August, O-Bon was now over, and Mie's spirit was supposed to have returned to the other world—it all seemed so anticlimactic.

When Nobuko left the room, Caitlin burrowed in the pillow and argued with herself that she hadn't expected anything momentous to occur, hadn't expected actually to commune with Mie or feel the shiver of her spirit against her skin. But she had come to expect something, forgiveness or release, yet here she was feeling just the same, if not worse than before O-Bon. Weighted. With what she wasn't sure, but she felt that suffocating pressure that had made her panic as a child when she was stuck at the bottom of a playground scuffle, dirt and pebbles grinding into her face, all those limbs and bodies bearing down on her.

She lay plastered to her futon. Close to her head she studied the stitching on the pillow cover, the wrinkles of the sheet, the hairs on her wrist. Finally, when the late morning sun began making the air in the room too thick, and sweat trickled even behind her knees, she forced herself to roll over, and with a great heave, sit up.

Her head pulsed. She surveyed the room—Nobuko's dresser and futon, the still curtains covering the open window, her own backpack and pile of clothes. This was not where she belonged anymore, taking up Nobuko's space. She wanted to call Hiroshi that instant and tell him she was returning early.

At the thought of him, longing shot through her body, and she closed her eyes and imagined waking in her apartment with him beside her, still asleep, flat on his back with one arm raised by his head. But he'd be gone this time of the morning, so she shifted images to their first meal back together again, of the deft way he pared vegetables with the chopping knife he'd bought to keep in her kitchen, of the way he could talk with her, look at her while he was slicing away. He'd made delicate Vietnamese spring rolls the night before she'd left, and a spicy Thai soup. She stood and pulled at the coverlet and folded it briskly. Her life was down in Kago- shima, not here, steeped in the grim, unbudging past.

She took a makeshift shower pouring plastic bucketfuls of water over herself in the bathroom, dressed, dragged a comb through her hair, and finally joined the family in the kitchen. Nobuko handed her a cup of coffee with a sympathetic smile, and Caitlin searched her face and demeanor for signs of a hangover, a comrade in suffer- ing, but found none. Perhaps only Caitlin had overindulged; it was always hard to tell how much she'd drunk, hard to gauge when to stop, since glasses were always topped off and kept full. No doubt Nobuko had been working too hard at diplomacy to have drunk as much as Caitlin; for it was Nobuko who'd managed to salvage the Daimonji outing—well after the fireworks, on the way to the bus stop she'd somehow gotten them singing songs, and suddenly with contagious excitement had insisted they all duck into a tiny shop for huge steaming bowls of ramen, after which, with bellies warm and full, it was impossible for any of them to continue to feel badly, even Naomi, who'd rallied and taught them an old Oberlin song she'd learned from her father.

Harumi cleared a space for Caitlin at the table, and although Caitlin was hardly feeling sociable she brought her mug over and sat down while the family had breakfast. By now at least, no one both- ered to press her about eating in the mornings. As the others sipped at soup and poked their chopsticks into the glistening flesh of grilled sardines, Caitlin held her coffee close to her nose to keep the aromas from heightening her nausea.

The family was discussing plans for the rest of the weekend. It was Saturday morning, the following day the last day of the holiday week, so they were trying to come up with an appropriate way to cap their vacation. Oide said he was busy with some colleagues that afternoon, so he suggested a Sunday trip up into the mountains to a river gorge. They could even take a small boat downriver. Yusuke was so excited by this he stood up, and Nobuko set her chopsticks on their rests to clasp her hands and applaud as her father described the route he was thinking of. Harumi was laughing at all the enthusiasm, but when Oide turned to Caitlin and asked, *"What do you think? Can you stand another excursion with these monkeys?"* she held her tongue; with all the talk of a day trip it was suddenly clear to her, as if someone had removed a blindfold so she could read her cues, what she had to do on Sunday. She had one more place to revisit—and not with friends, not with a soul except herself.

"Kei-chan, you'll come with us, won't you?" Yusuke asked.

Caitlin set down her mug. *"I'm sorry, but I'm afraid I have plans,"* she said, now resolute. They all showed their dismay, and Caitlin, embarrassed, feeling devious, tried to cover up. *"I made arrangements to join some friends. I think we're going hiking."*

"But can't you see them another day?" Yusuke asked in a half whine. Caitlin felt her face go hot.

"Yusuke, that's rude. We can do something together afterward," Harumi scolded. Then turning to Caitlin she asked, *"Friends from your teaching program?"*

"Yes. I'm sorry—I made the plans a while ago. But I don't have anything scheduled today," she offered as a way to cheer up Yusuke, to assuage her guilt, and to keep her mind off what she had rashly set herself up for the following day.

"Ah, then," Oide said and immediately stood to phone his colleagues and excuse himself from his obligations so they would indeed have a last free day all together—*"That is, until the next time you come,"* Harumi said to Caitlin with a wink.

The weather was supposed to be clear on Sunday, Caitlin had heard on the kitchen radio, so Uji would be hot, though probably not as steamy as when they'd gone at the end of the rains. One of her guidebooks upstairs could tell her how to get there, and she could stop at an information center for a map . . . *"How about doing that drive into the mountains today?"* Oide asked her, and with that she was snapped back into the family conversation. *"We could walk along some trails, eat somewhere along the river . . ."* Caitlin heard something more about shops, but she was barely listening as she nodded and smiled.

When everyone ran off to change clothes and get ready, Caitlin asked Harumi if she could make a phone call to Kagoshima. *"Of course,"* Harumi said, then trotted upstairs. Caitlin had the kitchen to herself. Though she was resigned now to stay in Kyoto as planned to the end of the week, she needed to hear Hiroshi's voice. She poured another cup of coffee and dialed his number.

"Keito-san! Good morning!" It was Hiroshi's mother. *"He's just back from work, walked in the door just seconds ago!"* Caitlin exhaled with relief; it was on the early side for Hiroshi to be done on a Saturday morning—he started at five and often wasn't finished until eleven, and here it was only ten. She waited, expecting his mother to go get him, but instead Mrs. Naniwa continued to rattle off questions about Caitlin's trip, the food, the weather, and the sights of Kyoto. Finally when Caitlin's answers bordered on rudeness, Hiroshi's mother excused herself to call her son from his room.

"Hi, how's Kyoto?" he said in English. He sounded pleased to hear from her, and once again Caitlin was bowled over by the profound effect of his voice on her emotions. She pressed her fingertips to her forehead as she searched for words.

"Hi," she finally said, but she didn't know where to go from there. Hiroshi waited, then began for her, asking about the ferry, the heat, and her friends. She wanted to spill everything, to tell him that the only friend that really mattered to her was him and that her father had been right all along, that what she would do tomorrow was the real reason she'd majored in East Asian studies and applied to the teaching program. That she was finally about to go where she should have gone months before, years before. That though she was determined, tomorrow was too big for her. That she wanted to leave for Kagoshima right now. Go off on a trip with him. She closed her eyes and held her breath.

But Hiroshi teased her with questions, and somehow she managed to answer, even echoing his light humor. Eventually, their familiar ribbing calmed her, and thoughts that just moments before had been in chaos and about to tumble out, were restored to their former guarded region. She could tell him everything when she returned to Kagoshima.

Hiroshi asked about Naomi. *"Oh,"* Caitlin said with a groan.

"She's okay. Up and down. The more I get to know her though, the less I understand her."

She gave Hiroshi the information for her ferry arrival the following Saturday. "Can you pick me up? In Shibushi?"

"Saturday? Well, I'd planned to go windsurfing," he teased.

"I'll have Naomi with me. I could call her father if you want."

"No, I'll be there. It's no problem. Really. We'll just put her in the trunk."

Caitlin laughed. Then after checking to see that no one was within earshot, she added, "You'll stay?" meaning at her place that night.

"I thought you needed time alone," he taunted.

"I've had enough. How was your trip to Kikaijima?"

"Oh, we didn't go. Another typhoon was predicted after you left. So we went hiking up in Kirishima and camped just for a night."

"How was that?"

He paused. "Well, it was crowded, we hit a two-hour traffic jam on the way up, the campground was overflowing, and there were hundreds of people on each trail . . . but you weren't one of them."

Caitlin held the receiver aloft, squeezed her eyes shut on the tears that were pooling, and tried to swallow. She wanted him to be right there in the kitchen with her. She wanted to be enveloped by him, consumed by him, so that she was she no longer, so that she wouldn't have to bother with Uji. She tried to quiet her too quick breathing, and she could feel herself growing dizzy. His voice far away, Hiroshi was asking if she were still there, hello, hello, and what was wrong, and with deliberation Caitlin brought the receiver back close to her mouth, touching her lips, and said, "It's nothing."

"Kimi . . . what's going on? I wish you'd tell me," Hiroshi said, his voice soft but stern. He asked for the phone number at the Oides' and said he'd call her the next day.

"Actually, call me tomorrow night, Sunday night. I'll be better then, I promise," she assured him. "And maybe I can explain some then."

"Okay, tomorrow night. What time?"

"Anytime in the evening. I'll be better, I think." They said good-bye, and Caitlin sat still for a few minutes rubbing her temples. Then she trudged upstairs to prepare for the family outing. She felt as though gravity were working double on her, and by the time she reached the top step she was leaning hard on the banister.

She virtually sleepwalked through the rest of the day. With great effort, she mustered a modicum of enthusiasm at the various sights—for sweets that Harumi made her try in one tiny village, for pencil-thin waterfalls that dropped to deep gorges, and for tall, broad-trunked cryptomerias within a temple complex—things she'd normally have delighted in. Only when they were on a boat, whisking along downstream, did she fully wake from her daze. Harumi and Oide were suddenly silenced as tour guides, ashen as they held rigid to their seats, and Nobuko seemed to be wincing through her smile as they were borne swiftly along. Caitlin gripped the gunwale and tried not to look at the water curving swiftly away from the hull but to keep her gaze fixed instead on the folds of mountains, trees hugging the precipitous gorge walls, the curve of the route ahead, a two-story teahouse they were passing. She suspected they were all looking with longing at the teahouse, a solid, stable wooden structure with hardwood posts pinning it to the ground. All except Yusuke, of course, who sat beside her on the bench, blithely grinning, positively enjoying the ride downriver.

Twenty

CAITLIN HAD HER knapsack packed with a thermos of chilled barley tea, handkerchiefs, a guidebook, her cap, and three nori-wrapped rice triangles. But after her coffee she stalled, changing out of her shorts into a loose, denim dress, making toast to slowly nibble, braiding and rebraiding her hair, and in the living room discreetly checking a road atlas's tiny map of the town of Uji. She was thinking of postponing, telling herself that it didn't really make sense to go on a Sunday after all, the town would be that much more crowded, the riverbank too peopled, and the heat even more overwhelming. She could wait and go midweek, get an earlier start, and instead spend today by herself somewhere—up on Mount Hiei, maybe in and around Enryakuji; she was thinking of the cedars she'd read about at that temple compound atop the mountain from where you could look down to Lake Biwa, thinking of how the breeze would feel and sound up there, when the phone rang and Harumi called out, *"Kei-chan."*

Caitlin replaced the atlas on the shelf, went out to the kitchen, and picked up the receiver. At the sound of Naomi's voice, Caitlin flinched, but she forced some warmth into her voice as she dismissed the girl's apologies for her behavior during the Daimonji picnic. As she spoke, she sidled out of the kitchen into the neighboring tatami room and plunked herself down on a cushion, then turned so that she faced the sliding glass doors to the garden instead of the *butsudan*.

"I don't know what was wrong. Really. I'm not usually like that," Naomi was saying; Caitlin rolled her eyes but held her tongue. "Anyway, I have something for you. Could I bring it over?"

"I'm on my way out right now," Caitlin was quick to say, still not a hundred percent certain where she was going.

"Well, could I meet you somewhere?"

"Not today, I'm afraid. I'll be out all day."

"But it's important. I really have to see you. You're the only one I can talk to. Please Caitlin." Naomi was beginning to sound panicked, and Caitlin felt an annoying prick of guilt, which she chose to ignore.

"Look, I'm sorry," Caitlin said, "but I'm about to go out the door." Naomi's voice was grating, and Caitlin suddenly stood. "I'll be back this evening," she told Naomi. "You could come over then. Or tomorrow. I don't have any plans tomorrow whatsoever. Okay?" Naomi remained silent, and Caitlin twirled the phone cord. "How about it? Tomorrow?"

"Oh, forget it, just go take a long swim," Naomi blurted.

"A swim?" Caitlin asked, amused by this attempt at an insult. Then Caitlin rotated on the cushion to fix her eyes on the little carved Buddha in the shrine and added with slow deliberation: "Well, I just might."

"Fine. Lay an egg for all I care!" Naomi shouted and hung up.

"Damn," Caitlin muttered as she replaced the receiver. She stood still, her face inches from the phone and the textured wallpaper around it, nostrils flaring, her chest rising and falling with her rapid breathing. Then, sensing eyes on her, she abruptly turned and called out as cheerily as possible *"Jaa, itte-kimasu"*—Well, I'm off— to Harumi and Nobuko at the kitchen sink, picked up her pack, and stepped out the front door into the glare of an August morning. She lifted her braid up off the back of her neck then set off down the driveway at full stride.

The morning was harshly bright, and she had to squint even under the bill of her cap. The hills to the west seemed to be fading into the heat, and the rice paddies had lost their cool sheen. Everything looked white and beaten under the sun that was fast approaching its noon zenith. She hurried down the street toward the bus stop, sticking close to buildings and concrete walls that provided a narrow brim of shade.

The bus took her straight to the Keihan station, and she caught the next train for Uji, finding a window seat all to herself. In the same carriage were several families laden with thermoses and picnic bundles, but no one sat opposite her, so she soon removed her sandals and put her bare feet up on the seat. She leaned her throbbing head back, and as the train rocked and gathered speed, she hardly noticed what scenery slipped by, she was turned so far inward with trepidation.

She remembered they had taken a car that day fifteen years before, the Oides' little white Toyota, and though Caitlin couldn't recall anything specific about the drive southward, she could envision what it must have been like: she and Mie in the back, the entire seat to themselves, room to roll about, share snacks, tell stories—privacy as the fathers talked in front, a space of their own. It was a special outing to go off with just their fathers. They often went places with their mothers and sisters, but to go off with just their fathers was a real excursion. In her father's long letter he'd mentioned that they'd visited a temple to talk with a priest, but try as she might, Caitlin couldn't recall the veranda he'd mentioned, or the priest. She had a picture in her mind of that scene, but she knew that it was based on nothing other than the letter. Why had she blocked out that portion of the day? Why hadn't her memory erased what had happened at the river instead?

When the train pulled into Uji a half hour later, Caitlin stepped onto the platform warily, as though the town itself were a being alive and aware of her return, ready to suck her into its waters. She shuffled toward the exit, and as she handed in her ticket, asked the way to the information center. She was dismayed to hear that it was situated at the opposite end of the bridge, that the first thing she would have to do was cross the Uji River.

Outside the station, she was about to stall by turning left and walking along the bank she was already on—she could explore the shops and the lane that led down this side of the river first—but she caught herself, and told herself aloud, "Cross the bridge."

So she placed one foot before the other, fought the force that weighted her legs, and went up the little rise that led to the old bridge, and there she was, above that hideous current, that horrible green-brown rush. She traversed the walkway, gripping the pale weathered railings, and when she reached the little jut of a landing where a few people had paused for the view of the island upriver, she hurried past and continued to the other bank.

She was visibly shaking when she found the information booth and in an uncharacteristically small and timid voice, asked for a map of the town. The attendant in the booth took her timidity for tourist nerves, and was especially kind, first effusively complimenting her Japanese, then describing in detail the temple-villa, the island, the stone pagoda, the cormorant fishing trips, and the various possible routes for seeing the sights and scenery. Caitlin only half listened to his pitch, waiting for him to hand over the map he was pointing to.

When she finally stepped away from the booth, coveted map and assorted brochures in hand, she continued on the road away from the river, and at the first vending machine, slipped in a hundred-yen coin for a vitamin drink. She downed that in several gulps then bought another to slowly sip. She looked over the material the information man had given her.

Her thought had been to re-create that day, to follow their route through the town, but she had no idea where to start, which temple they'd been to. And according to her father, that was where she'd been taken afterward, while he caught up with and stayed with Oide at the hospital. A hearth, he'd mentioned. And slowly an image appeared—an old *irori* sunk in the floor where someone, probably the priest, had grilled *mochi* over the coals. But she doubted herself; no one lit those hearths midsummer, and grilled *mochi* was a winter treat. Yet after the incident she had shivered for days on end—chilled despite the heat. Perhaps the priest had lit the hearth after all, to soothe her while her father was with Oide. Back home, she recalled, her mother and father had finally pulled out the winter *kotatsu* table for her to sit at and sleep under, in steamy mid-July.

But she had no larger picture of the temple, only the hearth with its brass tongs and wire screen for grilling the *mochi*. She had no idea in which direction to head, whether the temple had been right in town, one of the famous ones, or a lesser one on the outskirts or in the hills. The tourist map was of no help; there were dozens of temples and in every direction. She regretted now that she hadn't been more open with her father—he'd have gladly pointed the way—or that she hadn't asked Oide. Onward, she told herself, she simply couldn't relive that part of the day. Her memory began after her father's interview with the priest, with that walk along the western bank of the river with their insect cages, down from the old pink-railed bridge to the path along the waters. So Caitlin tossed her drink bottle into the bin by the vending machine, and forced herself to retrace her steps to the bridge.

But soon she stopped and turned away from the water once more to roam a narrow lane of shops. She finally found a florist, counted out a dozen yellow chrysanthemums—yellow, bright yellow for Mie—then as she was paying, asked for three more. Outside the shop she headed toward the river, her gait more sure, and just before the bridge she turned off and descended the concrete steps to that treacherous path.

She trod carefully, noting with interest that the current of the river hadn't diminished in the way that the buildings and houses and playgrounds of Iwakura seemed to have shrunk with the years. Rather, the current seemed to be just as menacing, if not more so, and Caitlin wondered how she and Mie could possibly have been allowed to walk alone beside it. What could her father have been thinking? She felt guilty when ideas like this became whole in her mind, hating to side with her mother, who never seemed to want to accept the freakishness of what had happened, but seeing the foaming water so close, so fast, she had to wonder about her father and Oide, and question their judgment in being anywhere but right by their sides. There were children and families on the path today, playing on that lower bank, a few with insect cages like Caitlin's and Mie's, and Caitlin observed that the parents, although vigilant, didn't hover over the children or insist on their walking single file or holding hands. She clenched her jaw, and it was all she could do to keep from shouting at the parents, "Keep them back, for God's sake!"

Caitlin picked her way along the riverbed path, guessing where she and Mie might have held hands, where they'd inverted their insect nets over their heads, and where their fathers might have paused to look back and check on them. She'd thought the exact spot of the accident would have been obvious to her, and she inspected the bank, walking up and back, trying to picture the shape of the rock she'd eventually sat down on. But no rock and no points on the bank emerged as particularly familiar. It occurred to her that rocks situated next to a force such as the Uji current shifted positions, and that although there would have been flowers laid there in the days subsequent to Mie's slipping in, though she'd pictured the bouquets still marking the spot all these years, they were long gone. Nothing was evident. She resigned herself to an approximation.

She found a raised boulder in what she thought was the general vicinity and sat. The water poured downstream, screaming in her ears. She was hot, feverish under the harsh midday sun just back from the edge of the river. She set her day pack down on the ground behind her, unwrapped the chrysanthemums, and dropped them in a loose pile onto her lap. Then she sat rigidly, facing the water she'd detested for fifteen years. Now and then she inadvertently picked up a flower and rolled the stem back and forth between her fingers so hard she nearly crushed it.

The current was indeed stronger than she'd remembered, and she stared at the white water curving around and over the rocks before her, the sinewy coursing, the whole sickening rush toward the bridge and the place where Mie had finally caught in some grasses at a slight bend in the river. The distinctive smell of the water assaulted her—that fishy, cold-water odor that had lingered in her nostrils months after they'd returned to Pittsburgh, causing her to suddenly and violently shake her head in the middle of a test at school, in the backseat of their station wagon, or during Sunday dinners in Ma Ruth's dining room.

Air bubbles rode the surface and hurtled downstream, stretching and popping with the strain of the current—the current that had allowed her to win so many freestyle races in high school and college, the current she'd always conjured up before diving off the block. Always, as she'd watched the line on the pool bottom through her goggles, as she'd kick-turned and pumped ever harder, she'd imagined she was beating that current, pushing ahead of it and reaching Mie just in time. Her father wouldn't get there in time, but she would. How many times had she replayed that fantasy? How many dozens of races had she won?

She rubbed her left leg. The skin of her calf tingled in the exact spot, as if skin cells could have memory, where years before, Mie's hand had grazed—splayed fingers, one nail scratching—as she'd slipped in. Caitlin stood, shook her leg, then sat down again. Her hand chafed hard that side of her calf—she hadn't felt the itch so persistent in ages—as she tried desperately to suppress the irksome thought that was gathering in the fore of her mind. She closed her eyes, but then it was there, formed and complete, taunting her: If she'd reached down with her left hand, she could have grabbed Mie.

In high school, for a while Caitlin had dated the goalkeeper of the soccer team. She'd loved to watch his hands reaching for the ball, loved to watch him dancing before the goal as a wing or inner from the other team dribbled toward him, and especially loved to watch him face down a penalty kick, eyes wide, body alert and ready to pounce in an instant in any direction. If she'd had reflexes like that, she used to think, she could have grabbed Mie.

But even with quicker reflexes, at eight years old, Caitlin wondered, would she have actually reached out? For hadn't she calculated, hadn't she measured, in that split second while Mie's hand ran down her leg, the danger of her being pulled in, too?

The itching intensified, and Caitlin rubbed her calf harder, burning the skin. She hated Mie's hand ever reaching, ever descending, and she slapped at that itch, first with one hand, then with two. Finally, in a teeth-grinding frenzy, she gouged with her nails, digging to make that tingling stop, to make Mie's hand never to have traveled down her leg; scraping her calf with the same helpless fury that had engulfed her in the weeks after the accident. She clawed viciously, until the skin began to break in dark welts and lines.

Finally, at the sight of blood droplets oozing, she stilled her hands, clasped them together to stop them, and watched them shaking there in her lap, the tips of several of her fingers smeared red. Then she held her head and groaned. With the back of one hand she scattered the chrysanthemums to the ground. If she could only have that moment to try again, to see what would happen if she reached out, even with mere eight-year-old strength, to grab Mie's wrist. She despised that image of herself frozen with terror, arms pinned uselessly to her sides—the picture charged at her, loomed close, and she doubled over.

She sat covering her eyes until the picture finally dissolved. When other images began to eclipse it, when the careening flow of the Uji River before her came back into focus, she inhaled deeply.

The sun pressed overhead. Several people were fishing from the opposite bank. Her leg stung sharply, and she ran her fingertips over the swelling, broken skin. She pulled a handkerchief from her pack, wet it with some barley tea and dabbed at the open wounds. With a tissue she wiped her face. Then she sat quietly, and as she listened again to the roar of the water, she covered her mouth. She hadn't realized until now how much she hated rivers. This river. This urging, hurtling flux.

With a heave she stood, then crouched over the rocks to gather the scattered chrysanthemums. She edged closer to the water. With each step and each bloom she retrieved, she scanned the area around her feet. A lizard. Skitting along with the finest blue iridescent tail. That was what they'd seen. Mie had exclaimed, and they'd followed its meandering path as it scurried over slippery rocks and through tufts of moss. Until they'd realized with sudden horror how perilously close to the edge they were. That was how it had happened—for when Mie turned in a panic to step away from the water, she lost her footing and slipped in. Or was sucked in, Caitlin thought. For other than a short gasp of surprise as she slipped, there was no sound. And the one time Mie's head had bobbed up, not even a gurgle. Caitlin had always imagined drowning to be a noisy, violent death, with cries for help and a gradual glug, glug, glug, but Mie had disappeared without a word.

If she'd only been able to swim, Caitlin had often thought afterward, believing that had it been Caitlin she'd have ridden the current, kicked with her feet, and stroked her arms until her head was above water. The river was shallow, it wouldn't take long to reach the surface, she'd always thought, never accounting for rocks in the way, tumbling eddies, or being caught off guard, without a full breath of air before being dragged under. But even in calm water, Caitlin knew that Mie would have panicked; Caitlin had tried to teach her how to float when their two families had gone to the sea several weeks earlier, but whenever her body started to sink, instead of fluttering her hands, kicking, or pushing against the water, Mie would jerk in alarm, her bottom would drop and she'd take in a mouthful of water. So of course, in the Uji River, in white water, Mie swirled, sank, and disappeared.

And Caitlin, eight years old, but already a good swimmer, had stood there. Knees locked, arms rigid, frozen. Hadn't even put out a hand. She'd simply watched her go.

Seconds afterward, Caitlin recalled, she'd sat down, having realized at last that by quickly sitting and putting out a foot she could keep her own balance and possibly reach Mie. But by then Caitlin could tell that Mie was nearly to the bridge—by the antics of a boy pointing and scrambling along the bank—and no sooner than she'd touched her bottom to the wet rocks had she stood and fled to her father, tripping over the rough ground.

Caitlin could remember every yawning second as they'd sprinted down the bank, she in her father's arms, beside and then behind Oide. And as long as they were running, she in her father's firm grasp, she still believed in fathers, in the infallibility of parents, in the sweet myth that children don't die. But seeing Mie plucked out by a fistful of her hair, limp and lifeless, eyes bulged wide in permanent fright, seeing Oide shake his daughter, seeing her father cover Mie's mouth with his, pinch her nose, pound her chest, seeing the hushed crowd, the lights on the ambulance, and the panic in her father's eyes as the medics put her best friend on a stretcher, made Caitlin rigid and cold with the understanding that parents were not, as she had believed, invincible.

Caitlin's foot was now inches from the water; the coolness brushed her toes. She eyed some foam bubbling out in the river where a rock poked through the sinewy surface, and she watched the speed of the water as it traveled around the solid obstacle. She tried to follow a floating stick with her eyes as it was flung toward the bridge. But the water moved too fast; she'd never beat this current no matter how well she swam.

And there it was; she could silence everything by jumping in herself. She mulled this over as she had every year since the accident. She pictured the leap, the slap, the sinking. The rush down river, the smack into a rock.

So, there on the riverbank, she stretched as she would on the swimmer's block before a race. She shook out her shoulders, arms, and legs, and still clutching the chrysanthemums, she stepped forward, bent over, touched her fingertips to the mildew-slippery rocks beside her toes, and crouched, waiting for the imaginary starting gun. Head down by the water, loose strands of hair and the tip of her braid being pulled in the current, body taut, arms now back like wings, she was ready to spring. She rocked forward, on the brink.

But then, just lightly, as a mere breath of vapor on her neck, she felt Hiroshi's *"kimi."* Startled, she crooked her neck. Balance lost, she tried to stand, trailing a foot in the water, but she slipped and landed on her rear on a boulder with a hard slam. Her teeth rang with the impact. Mouth agape, she crept back away from the water rubbing the small of her back and right buttock. Her elbow smarted, but in her fist she still held the flowers.

Humbled, it dawned on her that the moment she'd invested with such import had just passed ignobly. She dropped back onto a rock, then shivered and slowly stood, still rubbing her sore rump. So that wasn't my destiny, she mused to herself. But even if she'd jumped, she knew, she'd never just have submitted.

For it was true, despite the enduring guilt, Caitlin had never felt that she should have drowned instead, or that she shouldn't be alive because Mie was dead. Just that Mie should be alive. And that she should have saved her, that she could have. But if she'd reached down—and it always came to this nagging question—would she have caught that hand? Or would there have been two funerals for two little girls that steamy summer in Kyoto?

Caitlin drew a single chrysanthemum from the bunch and held it out over the water. *"Gomen-ne, Mie-chan,"*—I'm sorry—she whispered, and tossed the flower in. As soon as the stalk hit the water it was borne swiftly downstream. When it became a mere point, a tiny nub of French knot on a Ma Ruth pillow sham, she tossed another. Once again she waited until the speck of yellow had nearly disappeared. She did this with each flower, the pause between tosses long and heavy like the pause between the tolling of funeral bells. And with each toss, Caitlin felt lighter, as if each chrysanthemum for every year since the accident had weighed tons, as if the flowers themselves had been pressing on Caitlin all this time.

▲ ▲ ▲

Caitlin finally pulled on her knapsack and turned back to the path. She noticed a small cluster of people gathered above the river wall and another paused on the riverbed path watching her, and she ducked her head and made her way along the rocks carefully. When she'd climbed the steps up to the road and felt once more the heat of the asphalt under her sandals, she glanced in either direction. She had no idea what to do next and collapsed onto a bench beside a vending machine. She poured out some tea from her thermos and drank gratefully.

When her stomach rumbled she considered briefly the rice triangles in her pack, but instead crossed the street and stepped into a touristy noodle shop to order a bowl of tempura *soba*. While waiting for her order, she found the bathroom. Her leg was raw and stinging. She flushed the toilet, moistened her handkerchief under the wash water that poured from the cane-shaped spigot into the tank, and dabbed at the wounds. At least she'd worn a long dress that would hide them from sight.

When the bowl of *soba* was set before her, Caitlin was so impatient with hunger that she seared her lips on the hot broth. The tempura was dense and soggy, and the noodles machine-cut, but she thought she'd never tasted anything so good, and when she reached the bottom of the bowl she asked the waitress for more of the broth to drink.

Leaving the restaurant sated and calmed, and cooled from the air-conditioning, she decided on a whim to call Oide and ask him directly where that temple had been. She found a pay phone and dropped in some coins and waited. Harumi picked up. Flustered, Caitlin asked if Oide were home.

"He went to the driving range. He should be back in a couple hours. Why? Where are you?" When Caitlin didn't reply, Harumi grew alarmed. *"Kei-chan? Are you okay?"*

"Yes, I'm fine." She paused. *"I'm in Uji,"* she added softly.

Harumi was silent, and Caitlin waited. Finally Harumi said, *"I see."*

Caitlin felt her courage returning. *"I had to come back here. I'm sorry, I didn't really have any plans to meet friends."*

"Yes, I understand."

"Well, I was wondering, I should have asked before I left, but do you know the name of the temple where my father talked to the priest? I'd like to stop in. Do you know how to get there?"

She could hear Harumi wiping her nose and clearing her throat. *"Yoshizato-dera. But the priest passed away some years ago. I believe his son is now in charge."*

"Do you know where it is? I have a map here." Then Caitlin listened while Harumi recalled the route. Finally Caitlin found the temple symbol where she thought it was located. She described the strokes of the characters to Harumi.

"Yes, that's right. Like 'fragrant village.' I think you can walk there. And the family name is Ishii."

The temple was back on the other side of the bridge, set deep in the woods. Caitlin crossed over the river again with a slightly surer stride and headed down a lane of shops that soon gave way to dense forest. The uphill walk felt good and she passed few people. Shrill choruses of cicadas peaked and ebbed, and the road was cool and shaded.

When she reached the roofed temple gate, she quickly stepped through, but as she approached the main hall she hesitated, suddenly intimidated, and veered off to wander through a garden, then in and around tombstones in an adjacent cemetery. O-Bon had been over for two days, and bouquets of flowers now sat wilting in their containers while armies of ants ran pell-mell over oozing, melting sweets. The polished graves stood in the open sun, too bright after the long, cool walk, and Caitlin soon grew uncomfortably hot and thirsty and decided not to linger. She wandered back to the main hall and on the wooden steps removed her sandals, one still soggy from her river slip. Then with a deep breath she went inside.

She could barely see anything at all in the dim light after the glare of the cemetery. Once her eyes had adjusted to make out more than shadows, she knelt down on the tatami and sat still, fanning herself before the gilt Buddha. After several minutes she wandered down a connecting corridor until she ran into a monk. She asked where she might find the priest. The monk led her into a small receiving room, then disappeared, and soon a man who looked to be in his forties entered. Caitlin bowed her deepest and introduced herself, explaining that her father had known his father, and, after a moment's hesitation, that the priest's father had been especially kind to her the day her childhood friend had drowned.

"Ahh," he said and introduced himself as Susumu Ishii. Caitlin gave her full name and explained that she had come back to Japan the year before and was a teacher now in Kagoshima.

The priest nodded over and over. *"Now I remember,"* he said. *"I came home for dinner that evening to find everything hushed and the hearth going. I thought my mother had fallen ill. But then my father pulled me aside and explained. My mother had lit it for you—you were shivering."* He paused, then added, *"I'm so sorry. It must have been very difficult. Would you like to see my mother? I'm sure she remembers you. She cried and cried over you. Of course, she mourned for the girl who drowned and for her family, but she especially cried for you. Your shivering pained her so."*

Caitlin had completely forgotten about the priest's wife. And she couldn't recall her father ever mentioning her—how odd, Caitlin thought. Yet this woman must have been present, pouring the tea, serving the sweets or whatever they'd had on the veranda, and helping to entertain Mie and her, and yes!—some images were coming back—helping them search for insects in some courtyard or garden. No doubt, later, she lit those coals, found the *mochi* and grilled it for Caitlin, and held her while she waited in terror for her father to return from the hospital.

Caitlin followed the young priest back down the corridor and through the main hall, then through other long wood-floored corridors to an area that was closed off to the public. He led her into the private home, and Caitlin couldn't help gasping; they were standing in the room with the square sunken hearth in the center, and beyond some old sliding doors, the *engawa* veranda and garden. The picture in her mind had been correct after all. Barely able to hold herself up anymore, Caitlin eased down onto a square *zabuton* cushion, and the priest excused himself and went off to find his mother.

When the old woman entered she dropped to her knees and bowed deeply over and over, touching her head to the mat, as if Caitlin were the one to be venerated. Caitlin bowed back and blushed as the woman continued to prostrate herself and utter words Caitlin could barely catch. The priest, himself flustered, translated into simpler Japanese for her: *"She's speaking in the local dialect. She's very moved to see you. She's been thinking of you for so many years, wondering how you were, wondering how you had overcome the pain. Your father came back once, but that was when my father was still alive and she had been out and so hadn't been able to ask all about you, and my father had only asked a few simple questions. She's very, very pleased to see you and honored by your visit, and by your long journey back."*

Caitlin nodded, overwhelmed, speechless. The young priest found his mother a cushion, then retreated.

Caitlin finally found her voice, but a feeble *"Thank you, I'm glad to be here again,"* was all that came out. The priest returned with a tray of tea and wrapped sweets, then once more with an oscillating fan, and although he began to prepare the tea, the woman wiped her eyes and nudged him aside, insisting on doing it herself: *"It's my honor after all,"* she said. Caitlin was floored by the attention, and the idea that she might not have had the nerve to ask Harumi for the directions struck her nearly dumb.

Returning to a standard Japanese that Caitlin could more easily follow, the woman asked about Caitlin's life from when she'd last seen her in July of 1970. Caitlin sipped at the local tea and nibbled a sweet, stalling to search for words. She gazed into the wrinkled face waiting patiently opposite and realized that this woman whom she'd met only once before somehow knew her better than anyone— even her father. For how could Caitlin ever really talk to her father, who also shouldered the blame for Mie's death? It wasn't at all like her father had said in his letter—"Either none of us is guilty or we all are." No, exactly three of them were guilty: she, her father, and Oide. And she knew that if she ever spoke at length to her father about Uji, she would not be able to keep folded the accusing finger that wanted to ask why, why, why hadn't he been there beside her, why hadn't he been there to reach down with a sure father's hand, why hadn't *he* saved her best friend Mie?

This woman had seen Caitlin's shivering. And she'd seemed to fathom the depth and dimensions of the horror. So Caitlin took a full breath and hurled herself into the past, telling about herself forthright and open for a change, trying to omit the little white lies she'd grown so used to fabricating, trying to fill the misleading gaps. She told about her swimming, her Japanese studies, her parents' summer separations, her father's long letter the year before, her decision to return to Kyoto, and the warm reunion with the Oides.

The sun shifted, and Mrs. Ishii rose to close the sliding shoji doors part way to block out the brightness and heat. Then she sat right back down, saying, *"Go on."* The woman drank in every word, nodding, intensely interested, and finally, when Caitlin was explaining her teaching job in Kagoshima, her one-shot visits and teacher-training seminars, when Mrs. Ishii was making the third pot of tea, the priest entered with a huge lacquered tray of sushi he'd had delivered. Caitlin was ravenous. Even the fish roe, which she usually avoided, looked tempting.

But before she took a bite, after the priest had disappeared once again, she looked at the old woman and blurted, *"I could have saved her."* Mrs. Ishii seemed only slightly taken aback, and waited for her to continue. Caitlin closed her eyes, and confided. *"If I'd been quicker, reached out, I could have saved her."*

When Caitlin opened her eyes, Mrs. Ishii was gazing back at her. Then the woman looked from Caitlin out to the garden, where yellow light filtering through fronds of waving bamboo was quickly giving way to deep shadows. *"So that is your burden,"* she said, and sighed. *"A heavy one."* But then she knelt forward toward the table and in silence filled three small dishes with soy sauce and handed one to Caitlin. She took one for herself, set the other at a space for her son, then looked at Caitlin. *"But you mustn't be crippled by guilt. Learn to hold onto some thoughts, but let others, like guilt and regret, pass on. Death comes no matter what. We cannot really save anyone, can we? And death's timing is not always fair,"* she said, and Caitlin suddenly felt this woman's loss too, the death of the priest.

Caitlin nodded. Then she surveyed the sushi platter, her chopsticks poised, but before selecting a morsel she stopped herself. She gazed out at the garden before them. While the cicadas were still droning, while the coins of mottled sunlight still danced on the stones, while the breeze still made the bamboo trunks bend and knock against one another, she asked if she could go out to the veranda. *"Of course, of course,"* Mrs. Ishii replied. The old woman stood with effort, pulled the shoji doors wide open, and Caitlin set down her chopsticks and passed through to the *engawa*.

She sat down on the smooth, worn boards and dropped her legs over the edge. They touched the ground, but if she lifted them just a bit she could swing them back and forth without scuffing the pebbles and moss below. She swung them gently at first, then vigorously, legs alternating, then together. And with that rhythm, the nonsense song they used to sing about cicadas, dragonflies, and snakes came back to her. She swung her legs and softly at first, then louder, sang:

Semi, semi, koko-bop, *semi, semi,* bop!
Tonbo, tonbo, lollypop, *tonbo, tonbo,* pop!
Mushi, mushi, soda pop, *mushi, mushi,* pop!
Hebi, hebi, belly flop, *hebi, hebi,* flop!

Mrs. Ishii lowered herself to sit down on the veranda beside her. *"Yes, you sang that. I remember now,"* she murmured. And she, too, dropped her legs over the edge, swung them gently and tried to join in singing the words that Caitlin and Mie had sung fifteen years before while careening through streets on little bicycles, while stalking *semi* in the shrine's grove, while splashing in the tub together, and while sitting there on the temple veranda with their fathers, the priest, and this woman.

Twenty-one

BY THE TIME CAITLIN returned to the old neighborhood, dusk had given way to night. She searched east over a dark rice field for signs of a rising moon, but the night was so black that she could barely discern where the sky ended and the steep ridges began. She had left the temple as the sun was easing down through a haze behind the cedar tops of the Uji hills, having called the Oides again from the Ishiis' private quarters, to tell Harumi she'd be late and that they should go ahead and eat without her. Then, after the priest had said good-bye and gone off to his duties, Mrs. Ishii had walked Caitlin out to the temple gate. Caitlin thanked her for listening, and for remembering her all these years, and promised she'd be back again soon. *"I'll be waiting,"* the woman had said. *"But don't take too long; I might not be here much longer."* She'd tapped her foot on the ground and glanced down, as if to say here, on earth.

"I'll be back before I leave Japan," Caitlin had assured her, then amended her answer: *"I'll be back before a year is up."*

Now, as she trudged along the familiar turns in the road, she reflected on her day in Uji, her initial phone call to the Oides, reaching Harumi instead of Oide, and she heard again the long pause when she'd told Harumi where she was. She wondered when Harumi had first visited Uji after Mie's drowning. If Caitlin's mother had lost a child, she might never have gone back to the site. She couldn't picture her mother setting out offerings, lighting incense; her way of coping with "the incident" had always been to deny its existence. Her mother's words whenever her father pressed for family therapy were "You keep wanting to bring it back. Year after year. All I want to do is put the incident behind us, and I should think for the girls' sake you'd be willing to do that, too."

But Harumi would have ventured to Uji, with flowers to toss into the river and some of Mie's dolls or favorite foods to place on the banks as a means of consoling her daughter's spirit. She'd have been heavy with Yusuke then, and it would have been difficult for her to reach the very spot where Mie had gone in. Then Caitlin stopped in her tracks: How would they have known where to place the offerings? Only Caitlin had seen Mie slip, and in the shock that followed she'd never been able to describe to anyone what had happened, only a feeble, "She fell in!" once she'd started talking again. Mie's parents would have had to guess the spot, just as she'd had to today. And not even Oide could have explained to his wife exactly how their child had been taken. Caitlin released a long sigh; they must have wanted desperately to know. Through all these years, Caitlin had kept those final moments of Mie's life to herself. She'd have to tell Harumi and Oide about the lizard; they would savor such a detail, a final image of their daughter spellbound by some slithering critter.

Caitlin continued down the road, still musing. Mrs. Ishii had said Caitlin's father had been back to Uji, but how soon? He'd have gone alone, or with Oide, to place offerings on the bank. Not with Caitlin's mother, she knew, for Caitlin and Lee hadn't been left in someone else's care until they were back in Pittsburgh, settled once again in Ma Ruth's house. When, though? When he'd returned to Kyoto for the one-year ceremony? Recently? Did he make a point of visiting each time he was in Japan? Maybe someday she'd have the courage to ask him these things—maybe this fall.

By now Caitlin was dragging herself up the street, every step an ache to her stiff buttock and sore legs. She was looking forward to being back with the Oides, soaking in the bath, then doing nothing other than sitting around the kitchen table with them, watching some melodramatic television movie, sipping a beer and munching on salty snacks. She turned abruptly into the liquor shop and purchased several bottles of beer and some packets of rice crackers to ensure the realization of her simple fantasy. Then she quickened her pace over the last stretch of road along the open rice paddies to the Oide house. She crossed the rain gutter bridge, went up the driveway, and opened the door.

She'd anticipated a soft and kind welcoming, even an understanding embrace from Harumi, but when she stepped into the foyer and called out *"Tadaima,"*—I'm back—from the sudden hush she knew something was wrong. Harumi came running and stared at her.

"What happened?" Caitlin asked.

"Is Naomi with you?"

"No, why?"

Oide appeared from the kitchen, and he and Harumi exchanged looks of dismay.

"She's gone," Oide said. *"Her aunt and uncle haven't seen her since the early afternoon."*

Caitlin's fatigue was concentrated in her legs, and her knees began to buckle as if they were bearing the brunt of the news. She handed the beer and rice snacks to Oide and set her pack on the floor, but she didn't know whether to take her sandals off or not, whether to go in the house or out. She leaned on the wall.

Harumi grabbed her hand and gave her a tug. *"Come in, come in. Take a rest. And you must call the Kojimas. They were hoping she'd met up with you."*

Caitlin slipped out of her sandals and followed them into the kitchen. Nobuko and Yusuke greeted her and bathed her with long, concerned looks, which Caitlin took to mean that Harumi had told them where she'd really spent the day. She sat down at the table with them, and Nobuko rose immediately to prepare a cool washcloth while Harumi brought a glass of barley tea. Caitlin wiped her hands and face and drank the tea mechanically while she tried to grasp the situation. She struggled to read Naomi's mind. But what a convoluted mind to read. She could have gone anywhere. Done almost anything.

When Harumi dialed the Kojimas' number, Caitlin wearily took the receiver. Naomi's uncle answered, and Caitlin delivered the disappointing news that Naomi wasn't with her; she hadn't seen her all day.

"Well, she went out around one o'clock. Told Jun she was going for a walk but never came back. We've searched all over the neighborhood. Now the police are looking too. Can you help us? Do you have any ideas?" He sounded panicked.

"Well, a few," Caitlin said to calm him while she racked her brain to come up with places Naomi might have wondered off to.

Temples, she thought, thinking of their conversation on the ferry. Naomi had said she loved to sit on temple verandas. *"Have you tried any temples?"* she asked.

"They'd be closed by now."

He was right. Yet it would be just like Naomi to sneak in after dark, or to enter during the day and hide until everyone was out of sight and the temple locked and shuttered. *"You might have the police check different temples anyway. Those with good verandas. Quiet ones. She told me she likes to sit there sometimes."*

"Well, if you think so." Kojima didn't sound convinced. *"Where else? You seem to know her better than any of us."*

Why did people seem to think that? She'd known her all of a month. *"I'm not sure. A lot of places I'd try would be closed by now. Like gardens. She's probably just gone off somewhere by herself to think. She does that sometimes. You haven't called Carl and Akiko yet, have you?"*

"No, I didn't want to worry them. But I'll have to call soon, it's already after eight."

"Well, don't call just yet, if you don't mind. Why don't I come down and help look for her and if she doesn't show up by ten we'll call. I'm sure she's just being stubborn. She was pretty angry at me this morning."

"She was angry at the world this morning," Kojima added.

Caitlin promised she'd be over soon and hung up in a daze. She told the Oides she was off to the Kojimas'.

"You can take our car, if you'd like" Harumi offered.

"I'm too tired to drive," Caitlin said quickly. She didn't think she could face navigating unfamiliar streets alone in a car just then. *"I'll call a cab."*

"No, no, I'll drive you," Oide said with finality, and Caitlin readily agreed. He seemed especially anxious to help.

In the car, though, Oide seemed ill at ease, clearing his throat every few seconds and almost talking to himself. Caitlin thought she knew what was on his mind and finally offered, *"I went back to Uji today."*

Oide gave her a startled look as if that wasn't at all what he was thinking about, then he said, *"Ah, yes, Harumi told me. Thank you. We used to go there once a year, on the anniversary, but we haven't been since the thirteenth-year ceremony. We just go to the grave now."* He paused. *"I hate seeing that river."*

Caitlin nodded. *"So do I. Sometimes other rivers."* They were down near the university now, where her father had done his research when they lived there. She wondered if her father, too, cringed around white water.

"And I still can't drink Uji tea," Oide added. *"I know it's ridiculous, but I just can't."*

Caitlin nodded sympathetically. *"I went to Yoshizato-dera,"* she said. *"Mrs. Ishii actually remembered me."*

"Yes, of course, she's a kind woman, isn't she? She still sends us chugen and seibo gifts every year. We used to go see her every time we went to Uji. She always asked about you. She was so worried for you, for how you might be suffering. I think she knew you'd come back someday."

"Then she knew more than I did," Caitlin said. Oide nodded, and they were silent the rest of the way, although several times he took a quick breath as if he were about to say something. Each time he shook his head as if checking himself and kept silent.

▲ ▲ ▲

The Kojima house, its very timbers, seemed to reek of tension. The air in the receiving room felt as though it were stretched taut around them, and all eyes were on Caitlin, as if she knew the answers and could instantly lead them to Naomi. Oide had followed her in and asked what he could do to help, if there were any places he might try searching. The Kojimas looked to Caitlin for suggestions.

"Where have you tried so far?" she asked.

Kojima sighed loudly and rattled off the umpteen temples Jun had phoned, the train stations, streets, local playgrounds, and gardens that they and the police had checked, and then he threw his hands up in exasperation. *"She could be anywhere! She could have taken a train to Tokyo for all we know. She could be injured!"*

Caitlin shook her head. *"I don't think so. I'm sure she's just gone off by herself. It's just like Naomi. My guess is she'll be back in an hour or two, hungry and tired. The neighborhood police are still out searching? Well, let's continue to call temples."*

Using a map and looking up the names of temples in the phone book, then taking the numbers and making the calls at a neighbor's house so as not to occupy the Kojimas' phone, they gradually began to cover the eastern side of the city. Oide stayed and helped with this enormous task, making a list of temples that didn't answer for further follow-up. They all knew this approach was far-fetched, but the work kept them occupied and gave everyone a sense of purpose. Caitlin excused herself for a solitary search through the deserted neighborhood, forcing herself through a dimly lit labyrinth of pathways that brought her to a side road she recognized as being right by the university.

Instead of turning toward the campus, she headed uphill to Yoshida Shrine, where she'd so clearly recalled Lee's voice. In the dark the compound lay deserted and she stood wary at the top of the long stairway listening. "Naomi?" she whispered, then started at the rustling of cut paper crisscrosses hanging from the thick rope of the torii. She surveyed the eerie quiet, the ghostly cedars, and suddenly a deer loomed into view. She remained motionless, waiting for it to resume foraging, then took a step forward and laughed—it was a statue! Emboldened, she bellowed "Naomi!" then turned and clopped down the steps.

As she backtracked she called to Naomi every few steps and stopped to listen, head cocked, for the slightest noise. She wasn't convinced Naomi would respond though, and after a time, picked up the pace sensing Kojima's discomposure heightening with every minute she prolonged her absence. Back at the house she could appear more industrious with the temple-calling task.

By 10:15, Kojima was agitated. *"We have to call Carl and Akiko. It's much too late. They really must know."*

For Naomi's sake though, Caitlin protested. She knew Naomi's relationship with her parents was strained enough. And Caitlin felt responsible—Naomi's plea for help couldn't have been much more blatant. *"Can't we wait just a little longer? Maybe we could go search the streets some more,"* she pleaded. *"Fan out in different directions."* But she was beginning to feel panicked herself. She tried hard to believe what she was saying to Kojima: *"She'll be tired by now. Wanting to come home."*

Kojima equivocated, then finally agreed. *"But only until eleven,"* he stressed. *"At eleven we call."*

Then, just as Oide was explaining which area he'd cover for

another neighborhood search, the phone rang. Everyone froze as Kojima ran to answer. *"Hai,"* he said, and not a breath could be heard as they watched his face for some twitch of reaction to the words at the other end. Please be Naomi, Caitlin thought, then she joined in the collective sigh when Kojima said, *"You found her! Where? And she's all right?"* Suddenly he was choked up and couldn't find his voice. He motioned feebly to Caitlin, so she took the receiver from him, not having any notion who was on the other end.

"Kei-chan, it's Harumi. Nobuko went outside to get something from the car just now, and she noticed someone sitting in one of the rice paddy paths across the street. She went to have a closer look, and Naomi called out to her. She's fine but she won't come inside, and she only wants to talk to you." Being singled out intensified Caitlin's sense of guilt. *"But tell everyone not to worry—she's okay. Nobuko just took some dinner out to her."*

"Thank you," Caitlin said. *"We'll be right there. Keep an eye on her for us though."*

"Of course. But Caitlin, I think she only wants to see you."

Caitlin awkwardly explained this when she hung up the phone. Kojima at first protested, insisting that he should go pick her up himself and bring her back immediately so she could apologize to the police and everyone else who'd been combing the streets for her. But his wife and son quickly convinced him that he should simply have a beer instead, that Naomi should come back of her own volition, there was plenty of time to apologize, and that Caitlin should be the one to go to her. Caitlin reassured him that she'd phone as soon as she'd talked to Naomi.

So Oide drove her back to Iwakura. What a day this had become, Caitlin thought. Her head was swimming; a perfect expression for her muddled state, she thought, but then she found herself wishing for a pool, wishing she could feel the water buoying her limbs, bathing her face, and muffling the world around her. She had no idea what she could do for Naomi. Or what she'd say. Other than sorry that she hadn't been kinder that morning.

Oide didn't say a word the whole way, although now and then he glanced sideways at Caitlin then shook his head as if still arguing with himself.

▲ ▲ ▲

Naomi sat on the damp ground hugging her knees. She was perched on a raised earthen path that ran between two fields of tall rice. An empty *ramen* bowl with chopsticks laid across the rim sat before her.

Caitlin said nothing until she was standing directly opposite.

"Don't yell at me. Just don't," Naomi threatened.

"I won't," Caitlin said, and sat down. The rice plants beside them bowed and rustled in the light breeze, and frogs resumed their chirruping. Caitlin waited for her eyes to adjust to the dark—the moon had yet to rise, although the sky was finally brightening above the ridge of near hills. "How did you get here?" she finally asked.

"I walked."

Caitlin raised her brow. "It's a long way from your aunt's house." Naomi looked down and shrugged. "Are you warm enough?" Caitlin asked. It was a strange question to pose on a hot August night in Kyoto. Naomi nodded and slapped at a mosquito.

"I'm sorry I couldn't see you today."

Naomi didn't say anything.

Caitlin tried again: "I had a hard day too."

Naomi scoffed.

Caitlin rose to a squat. Not that she'd expected sympathy, but the earth was damp, the mosquitoes were biting, and her stomach was growling again. "Look," she said, "you've eaten?"

Naomi nodded. "Nobuko brought it out."

"Well, I'm kind of hungry. There's a little yakitori shop down the street. Mind if we talk there instead of here?" Naomi shrugged. Caitlin took the bowl, stood, and offered a hand to Naomi. She refused the hand but followed Caitlin out to the road.

Caitlin started to cross the street toward the house, but Naomi stopped. "I just need to change my clothes and get some money," Caitlin explained. What she really wanted was to rub some ointment onto her leg and switch from her dress to a pair of pants. The scraped skin stung, and she didn't want to have to discuss it with Naomi. At the Kojimas' she'd had to hide it under the skirt of her dress; at least she'd been sitting on the floor most of the time, and everyone had been too preoccupied with Naomi to notice the way she'd constantly shifted her weight to keep her calf out of sight.

"I'll wait outside," Naomi said as if Caitlin were laying a trap.

"You can wait in the *genkan* while I run upstairs." Naomi pondered this. Then Caitlin pointed at Naomi's clothes. "You're damp though. Come upstairs. You don't have to talk to anyone. Just follow me. I'll find you something dry." Naomi shrugged slightly, and the two of them walked up the driveway and into the foyer of the Oides' house. Caitlin made sure the coast was clear, which was easy since the family was gathered in the kitchen, and they went upstairs. Caitlin squeezed some antibiotic ointment onto her leg and pulled on some cotton drawstring pants, careful to keep her left leg toward the wall, then found a pair of her shorts that with the elastic waist, looked as though they might fit Naomi. Naomi changed while Caitlin pulled some bills from her backpack.

On the way out, Caitlin ducked into the kitchen, explained where they were going, and asked Oide to call the Kojimas, to tell them that everything was okay and that Naomi would probably spend the night at the Oides'. They all nodded, and Nobuko whispered that she would set out futons for Caitlin and Naomi in her room, and she'd sleep in Yusuke's room.

When Caitlin reached the foyer Naomi asked if Yusuke were there. Caitlin nodded. "Do you want to speak to him?" she asked, but Naomi shook her head vehemently.

Outside they walked a ways in silence. The moon had just crested the ridge, and the blades of rice plants in the fields had turned silver. Across one of the paddies they could see a couple of drunken men weaving as they urinated into the water. "Poor frogs," Caitlin said, but Naomi didn't smile. They continued without speaking.

Finally Naomi asked spitefully, "So where *did* you go today?"

Caitlin looked directly at her. "Uji. You know where that is?"

"Of course I do," Naomi said sullenly, dropping a pace behind Caitlin. A few steps later she caught up and asked, "Why'd you go there?" then blurted, "I could have gone with you."

Caitlin stopped in the street. "Hey," she said softly. Naomi folded her arms and turned away. "Look at me," Caitlin said. Naomi finally glanced at her. She seemed about to cry. "I'm sorry I couldn't see you. I'm truly sorry. But I had to go. Alone."

"What was so important? Some friend?"

Caitlin exhaled and looked away. "Yes, a friend, I guess you could say. I mean, I should have gone there years ago. And if I had, then I could have spent the day with you. I'm sorry. But that's just the way it worked out. It took me fifteen years to get up the nerve to go back there, and once I'd finally made up my mind, I had to go."

"Why?" Naomi was still peevish.

"Stop being angry with me. Okay? This is just how it is. I'm not yelling at you for worrying everyone, am I? So let up on me." She waited a moment then started again, calmer. "Sorry, I've had a long day too." She took a deep breath and looking straight at Naomi, spoke in monotone. "I went to Uji. I went to the spot where Nobuko's older sister died. She used to have an older sister. And we were best friends when I lived here. But on a trip to Uji one day, when we were walking along the river, Mie fell in. So I went back there. I'd never been back there."

"You mean she drowned?"

"Yes."

"You saw her drown?"

"Yes."

Naomi mulled this over. "How old was she?" she finally asked.

"Seven."

"How old were you?"

"Eight."

"Did Nobuko see, too?"

"She wasn't there."

"Oh," Naomi said, then she nodded and repeated, "Oh," with awe.

Caitlin started walking again and now Naomi kept pace beside her. Neither of them said another word until they were inside the yakitori shop deciding what types of skewers to order. When a small plate of grilled shiitake and another of chicken and scallions arrived, Naomi finally ventured, "Did you jump in after her?"

Caitlin shifted in her seat. "After Mie? No. The river was too fast." Another plate arrived and Caitlin popped two *tsukune* meatballs into her mouth one right after the other.

"Did anyone jump in?" Naomi asked.

Caitlin finished chewing her large mouthful. "No. She just

went . . . ," and Caitlin made a motion with her hand to show the speed with which Mie was borne downriver. "There was nothing we could do." Caitlin fiddled with the menu. That was a lie. She should remedy that, insert the truth about reaching down, but the moment had passed. Naomi continued to press with her questions. "Were your parents with you? I mean, couldn't you have thrown her something? A log maybe?"

"Our fathers were with us," Caitlin said, but instead of laying the blame on them as she easily could have, she grew defensive. "Naomi, you have no idea how fast she went. And she couldn't swim even in calm water. There weren't any logs or life preservers or poles or handy little things like that lying about. It was a white-water river."

"Oh." Naomi was silent. Caitlin tossed aside the menu and impetuously ordered some expensive grilled ginkgo nuts.

When they'd been served, Caitlin turned the questions away from herself.

"So. You wanted to see me. Pretend it's this morning. I'm here."

Naomi scowled and fiddled with some empty wooden skewers. "I didn't bring what I was going to give you."

"You don't need to give me something whenever you want to talk to me. I'm listening. What was up?"

Naomi shifted and stalled, nibbled at some eggplant, then set it down.

"Are you homesick? You miss your parents?" Caitlin asked gently.

Naomi rolled her eyes. "No. I mean, yes, a little, but that's not it." She breathed in deeply, then, looking down at the counter before her, said, "I have that interview tomorrow."

Caitlin put the heel of her hand to her forehead. She should have known. "Oh, God, I'm sorry," she said, "I forgot all about it. You're worried, aren't you?"

Naomi thought for a moment. "No, not about the interview, all I do is talk at that. But then, afterward I'm going to have to make up my mind. About everything."

"What do you mean? You still have time. You don't have to apply right away." Naomi still looked forlorn. "Do you think you want to go there?" Caitlin asked.

Naomi whispered her answer. "Yes. I mean, they really teach

you how to think, and research and everything, not just cram you with numbers and facts so you can pass entrance exams. And I'd be exposed to lots of different ideas and viewpoints of course. I'd be freer, you know, it's not so stifling as in a Japanese school. It'd be the best thing if I want to study art. In the long run, I mean."

"Then that's good, isn't it? You're closer to making your decision, right? So what's the problem?"

"Well," Naomi finally said, her voice high and wavering, "it's going to be the beginning of my becoming less Japanese. Like this year is my peak. After this it's downhill. I'll become less and less Japanese the more English and other stuff I learn." Caitlin waited, but Naomi didn't say anything more and finally looked to Caitlin for her response.

"Naomi. You'll never be less Japanese than you already are. That doesn't change."

"I'm only half as it is," Naomi reminded her.

"And half you'll remain. "Double' is what some people say. And what's wrong with that?" Naomi didn't reply. Caitlin tried to make her enthusiasm contagious. "Naomi, think about it, if you go to that school you'll be staying with the Kojimas right in Kyoto—you can't get much more Japanese than that! Think of that house. Think of your aunt and uncle. You'll probably become more Japanese than you would if you stayed in Kagoshima with your parents and went to a Japanese high school!" Caitlin gave Naomi a friendly pat on the back, but that seemed to be all that was needed to loosen the tears welling in Naomi's eyes and send them streaming down her cheeks.

"Hey," Caitlin said softly. "I'm sorry. I didn't mean to make light of this. But you have a *choice* with your education, Naomi. You're lucky. Most Japanese kids don't have a choice."

"But I want both," Naomi cried. "I want it both ways. What would *you* choose?"

"For school?"

"No," and Caitlin could just barely make out Naomi's next words: "When I'm twenty . . . Japanese or American . . . citizenship?" And she broke down in hiccuping sobs.

Caitlin quickly paid their bill and led Naomi outside. She walked her home hugging her close with one arm around her shoulders. "Your father's right, you know. You are a fretter. Wait and see where you are when you're nearly twenty. I mean, where you are with your life. What your interests are. What your priorities are. Where you think you'll live. What you think you'll do. But stop worrying. Especially about something like citizenship."

Naomi leaned against Caitlin. "But what if I make . . . the wrong choice? What . . . if I make . . . a mistake?"

"It's only citizenship, Naomi, only paperwork. It's not you, it's not your identity you have to choose. You don't have to shift allegiances, beliefs, or languages or anything."

"But I don't even know who I am now," Naomi whimpered. She felt so fragile that Caitlin thought if she picked her up and cradled her in her arms she could carry her home without even altering her gait.

By the time they reached the Oides', Naomi had stopped crying but looked withered and ready to collapse. Caitlin bent down and helped her remove her shoes then led her up the stairs without stopping to say hello to whomever was still up watching television.

Nobuko had indeed made up the futons, turned on the air conditioner, and even set out some pajamas and a robe for Naomi, who now stood in the middle of the room with a dazed look. Caitlin helped tug the girl's shirt and shorts off, then watched as Naomi, already half asleep, pulled Nobuko's pajamas on. Then she laid Naomi on the futon, pulled the light terry cover over her, and turned out the light. "Roll over onto your stomach," Caitlin said. Naomi complied, and Caitlin gently massaged her shoulders and neck; Naomi felt limp under her touch. Then Caitlin sat down on the next futon and was about to say a few words about not worrying, not dwelling on her confusion, but from the sound of her breathing Caitlin could tell Naomi was already asleep.

Caitlin lay back on her futon; she wanted to drift off, her eyelids were already fluttering, but she knew she should go speak to whomever it was that had waited up. She forced herself to stand, go back out to the hall and down the stairs.

▲ ▲ ▲

It was Oide, and he immediately flicked off the TV, stood, and poured her a glass of beer when she entered the living room.

"*Thanks,*" she said, and they sat down at opposite ends of the sofa.

"*It's yours,*" Oide said, pointing at the bottle of beer. "*You never got a chance to drink it earlier.*"

"*Ah,*" Caitlin said nodding.

"*How is she? Everything okay?*" Oide motioned upstairs.

"*She's exhausted. And confused. She thinks too . . . shallowly, no deeply, much too deeply about everything. But she's already asleep. Sleep should help her.*" Caitlin struggled to come up with the right words. "*Thank you for your kindness today. I'm sorry to have troubled you. Her parents would be grateful,*" she said. She sipped at the beer to be polite, thinking she'd get away in just a minute, but Oide seemed to be stalling.

"*Not at all,*" he was saying, "*I know what it's like to lose a daughter.*"

Caitlin nodded, waiting for him to say whatever was on his mind, but when he didn't offer anything she finally blurted, "*I'm sorry, but I'm so tired, I've just got to go to sleep.*" She eased forward on the sofa and was about to stand, but Oide cleared his throat, and in a voice awkward and a bit too loud said, "*You had two phone calls today.*" Caitlin turned to face him. "*One this evening when we were at the Kojimas', from a Naniwa-san.*"

"*Oh, Hiroshi.*" She sat back once more on the sofa and took another draw of beer. She'd forgotten that he'd agreed to call. It seemed like a week ago that she'd spoken with him. The clock on the wall said just after midnight—she'd have to catch him tomorrow.

"*Haru explained that you were helping a young friend of yours; apparently he guessed right away that it was Naomi.*"

Caitlin nodded. "*And the other?*"

Again Oide cleared his throat. He looked down as he spoke. "*From your father. This morning, just after you left. We shouted after you but you had gone. Nobuko even got on her bike and rode down to the bus stop.*"

Caitlin straightened, alarmed. "*Yes, the bus came right away. Did something happen?*"

"*I probably should have told you sooner, and Haru could have explained when you called, but it seemed you were on your way to the temple and she didn't want to keep you from that, and then Naomi disappeared, and I thought that given the confusion and the difficult day you'd already had, that perhaps it would be better if I waited. Forgive me if I made the wrong decision."* He coughed. *"Your father was on his way to Pittsburgh—your grandmother died on Thursday. I'm very sorry."*

Caitlin stood, stunned. *"Thursday!? Today's Sunday!"*

"It seems he was away until Saturday, their time, and your mother was trying to reach you in Kagoshima. I'm terribly sorry." Caitlin sat down slowly. *"Can I get you anything?"* Oide asked. She shook her head. *"Well, feel free to use the phone. It must be a little before noon there now."* Oide stood. *"I'm going upstairs, but make as many phone calls as you like. And please let us know if you need anything."* He bowed deeply.

She nodded and stood there dumbly as he left. She opened her mouth wide and breathed in and out noisily as if she couldn't get enough oxygen through her nose. Why hadn't her father called until today? And what was she doing here in Japan? She tried to collect herself and distill her swelling anger into a more pure form of grief. She'd spoken with her father just last Tuesday when he called from Brookline. Yet for four days Ma Ruth had been dead, and Caitlin had been carrying on as though all were normal.

If they'd told her, she could have gone home. Caitlin winced at the thrust of that idea: she should have been in Pittsburgh this summer. Instantly she ached to be back in that house. She could hear the creaks of the floorboards and the radiator knocks, and feel the grass out back under her bare feet and the coolness of the flagstones that led to the raised beds of the vegetable garden. She'd have returned in a minute, put herself back into that house, strained conversations, unfair accusations and all, if they'd simply conveyed the urgency. She would have liked to have seen Ma Ruth once more, even shriveled and diminished. Regret began to boil.

Caitlin crouched down on the floor. Once more she wanted to pour ginger ale into one of Ma Ruth's tumblers, take it out to the porch, and sit on the swing, listen to the jays and the traffic, and watch her grandmother solve a calculus proof on a tray table, her pencil scratching madly across a scrap piece of paper. But it wouldn't have been like that had Caitlin gone back this summer. She'd have been helping Ma Ruth use the toilet, propping pillows behind her head, pureeing her food, administering medicine—all those mundane tasks her mother had written of, and that Lee had no doubt performed. Somehow the illness had never seemed real to

Caitlin, having experienced it only from afar. The cancer had been discovered the August before, two months after Caitlin had moved to Kagoshima. Granted, she'd been aware Ma Ruth in recent months was bedridden, but she'd always assumed recovery; she hadn't really believed death would come to her grandmother anymore than she'd believed life would come back to Mie.

Her mother had now lost her mother, Caitlin thought, the last of the generation that shielded her from old age. What a dutiful daughter Arlene had always been, careful to say and do the right things. Always considering and deferring to her mother's point of view. Abandoning her own career to care for her. Perhaps, then, Caitlin ventured, Ma Ruth's passing would bring a measure of relief; perhaps her mother would now take charge of her life.

Caitlin could remember when her mother had quit a job she'd coveted in Boston in order to be able to spend more time in Pittsburgh caring for Ma Ruth. Or so went the excuse. Ma Ruth hadn't been ill then, just aging, slowing. Caitlin knew it had been a convenient way to gain distance from her father—rather than work out their differences, she'd chosen to stay at Ma Ruth's, where her actions were nearly always looked upon with favor. Caitlin had been in her first year of college then, and she hadn't known about her mother's move to Pittsburgh until she'd asked to speak to her father once when her mother'd phoned: her mother had simply said after a pause, "He's not here, Caity, I'm in Pittsburgh. Didn't you know?"

So what now? Would her mother move back to Brookline? Plunge into a new nursing job? Or would she stay in Pittsburgh, go back to part-time nursing there, and take over the house? The house—Caitlin couldn't imagine anyone else owning it; she couldn't even imagine the furniture rearranged. Ma Ruth *was* the house, and she shuddered to think of it without her. Caitlin ached to be there—not now, not with cousins and aunts and uncles milling about preparing for a funeral. She wanted to be there the way it used to be, her parents in the second-story front bedroom, crickets sawing away outside, the slap of footsteps in the street below, and Lee and her on the porch on a mattress under the frayed crazy quilt with Ma Ruth.

She swilled the last of her beer, then went into the kitchen, filled the glass with tap water, and gulped. She brought the phone receiver to the table, sat down, and dialed Ma Ruth's number, half expecting her to answer. There had always been only one phone in the house, in the front hall, and Ma Ruth had lorded over it, but Caitlin wondered if that too had changed in the last year. Finally a voice she didn't recognize picked up.

"Hello, this is Caitlin," she said, thinking it was one of her cousins.

"Caity. Hi." It was Lee, her voice muted though the connection was clear.

"Lee, I just got Dad's message. What happened?"

"Well, Ma Ruth had a stroke on Tuesday. She never woke up."

"Didn't they operate? Couldn't they do anything?" Caitlin couldn't help but sound annoyed—it seemed absurd, what with all the life-saving technology they had these days.

"It was a major stroke, Caity. She'd have been almost completely paralyzed, they said. And it was risky to operate anyway since she was so weak and her blood count so low from the chemo. And she'd already decided she didn't want to be on any life-support devices if she didn't stand a chance of recovering. In some ways she's lucky. She's been spared a lot of misery."

Caitlin felt utterly removed hearing Lee's matter-of-fact description. "How's Mom?" she finally asked.

"Okay. They're out now. Mom dragged Dad to Ma Ruth's church."

Caitlin raised her eyebrows. "And how are *they* doing?"

"Okay. Mom's been holding up well, and Dad's been pretty easy-going."

"So what do you think Mom will do now?"

"What do you mean?"

"Well, do you think she'll move back to Brookline?"

"Caity, give her some time, we haven't even had the memorial service."

Leave it to her to be defensive, Caitlin thought. Though she was tempted, she didn't take up the fight. "When's the service?"

"Next Saturday."

"I wish I could be there."

"That'd be nice."

On hearing the word "nice" from Lee, even delivered with a bite, Caitlin felt tears welling. She could hear Lee cough on the other end. "It's been hard on you, Lee, I know." Caitlin paused, but Lee didn't make the effort to fill the gap. "I'm sorry I'm not there," Caitlin went on. "And that I won't be there next weekend to help out." She knew though, that if she asked, someone would gladly pay for her airfare home. Lee seemed to know this too. But Ma Ruth was already gone; what was the point? Besides, by Sunday she could be back in Kagoshima. And it occurred to Caitlin, standing there in Kyoto feeling the old friction with Lee in Pittsburgh, sensing the emptiness of the house without Ma Ruth, and thinking of Hiroshi in Kagoshima, the lure that he was, that Kagoshima was home now. And Kyoto.

"Do you know where I am right now, Lee?"

"Ah, Japan, I think. Isn't that where you live?"

Just like her to be wise, Caitlin thought. She let the comment go. "I'm back in Kyoto, Lee. At the Oides'. Our number-two family." Silence. Caitlin continued: "The house is a new one, and there are lots of other new houses around but the neighborhood is just about the same. You go out the front door to those rice paddies where we caught those tiny pollywogs. And the old farmhouse is still there, the one with the garden where we watched the monkeys stealing the soybeans, remember? And I've been to the shrine where we used to take our insect cages. And the other shrine near Dad's university, near where we used to see those student protesters we thought were soldiers. Remember?" Lee was silent, painfully silent, and Caitlin knew she'd gone too far. She hoped Lee wouldn't hang up. She continued in a softer voice. "Nobuko is wonderful, Lee, she asks all about you." And Caitlin realized then that she was sounding just like her father—trying too hard. And Lee would resist. She struggled for a gentle tone. "Write me a letter, okay?"

"No one's had time for letters. You'd know if you were here."

Caitlin closed her eyes and counted seconds in her head, but the words slipped out anyway. "Why can't you stop blaming me?" she hissed.

There was a pause, then, "I don't know what you're talking about."

Caitlin sucked in her breath and swallowed a barrage of words.

Finally she said in a flat voice, "Right. Well. Sorry. When will Mom and Dad be back?"

"Not for a while. They're having lunch with the minister and then going off to do some planning for the service next week. They should be back around four."

Caitlin calculated. That would be five in the morning for her. "Well, tell them I called. And that I'm at the Oides'. Dad has the number. They can call in the late evening. Your evening, I mean."

Caitlin said good-bye, gritting her teeth as she set down the receiver. Then she turned out the lights and felt her way up the stairs to Nobuko's room and her futon. For all her fatigue though, she couldn't sleep; she lay there sprawled on the coverlet staring at the ceiling, conversations with Mie, her father, Mrs. Ishii, Naomi, and Ma Ruth tumbling over and over in her mind and blending nonsensically with one another.

And clearer than all the others, she could hear Lee, the baiting comments and stony silences that had always provoked Caitlin. Sisters they were, aged twenty-three and twenty. Yet they still couldn't talk, still weren't friends. They'd shared the same family, the same home, the same bedroom, but Uji, it seemed, had blasted them into different orbits.

Twenty-two

NAOMI WAS STILL sleeping soundly when shortly after ten the next morning, Caitlin slipped into a T-shirt and shorts, caught sight of her raw and puffed left leg, changed into the cotton drawstring pants, and tiptoed out of the room. In the kitchen Harumi was hunting through the refrigerator making a grocery list. She straightened when she saw Caitlin.

"Oh, you're up. Your father just called. He said not to wake you." Then she lowered her voice, crossed her hands formally, and bowed. *"I'm terribly sorry about your grandmother. This has been very difficult for you."* She muttered several other phrases Caitlin couldn't quite catch but that sounded like offerings of condolence. *"I'm sure it's hard to be so far away, but perhaps if you think of us as family you won't feel quite so distant from all your relatives. We could light some incense later if you'd like."*

"Thank you," Caitlin said. *"I'd like that."*

Harumi nodded and returned to her list. *"Naomi's still asleep?"* she asked as she jotted something down.

"Yes." Caitlin glanced about. No one else seemed to be home. *"It's so quiet."*

Harumi continued rummaging through cupboards. *"Yes, back to normal,"* she smiled. *"Nobuko is out with college friends, Yusuke is at soccer practice, and Yasu is at work. Can I get you anything while I'm out?"* Caitlin shook her head, poured her usual mug of coffee, and sat down at the table. *"There's rice and soup made, or toast and salad if she prefers that. And she's welcome to borrow any of Nobuko's clothes if she needs anything."* Caitlin thanked her. She suspected that Harumi was heading out now simply to give Naomi and Caitlin time alone together.

But Caitlin wanted some time to herself; she hoped Naomi would sleep long enough for her to call Ma Ruth's. When Harumi had finished her list, called out a farewell, and pedaled down the street on a bicycle, Caitlin reached for the receiver and dialed the Pittsburgh number once again. There was no point in calling Hiroshi this early—he'd be working until late afternoon.

Her father answered on the first ring. "Caity! I was hoping you'd call soon."

"Sorry, I know it's late. Is Mom still up?" Caitlin hadn't heard her mother's voice in months, and she couldn't quite imagine what she must be feeling, that sensation of knowing there was no parent above you, your head suddenly bared, no shade, no more protection between you and the cold, harsh skies above.

"She's on the porch. I'll get her in a moment. Listen, I'm so sorry you got the news secondhand."

Caitlin nodded as if he could see her. She asked him how things were there.

"Well, better, I think. It's just Carol and Lou and us here now." Carol was her mother's younger sister. "So it's quiet at least. Your mother's cousin Iris left this afternoon—but everyone will be back for the service next weekend. You're welcome to join us if you want."

"I know, thanks."

"But at this point I don't know how much sense it makes for you to fly back here, do you?"

"No, I don't think it makes much sense at all." she said. Then she couldn't help but whine, "Dad, why didn't you call me sooner."

"I was in the White Mountains, Caity, hiking. I didn't check in with your mother until Saturday, and then I had to get back to Brookline before I could call you. And of course your mother didn't know where you were until I explained when I got down here." Neither Caitlin nor her father said anything for a minute. She tried to picture her mother's reaction to the news that she was back in Iwakura.

"Well, how are things in Kyoto?" her father finally asked.

Caitlin rubbed her forehead. She didn't know how to answer. Naomi was in crisis. There was Uji. And now Ma Ruth was gone. "Okay," she finally mustered. "I'm ready to go back to Kagoshima though."

"Oh?"

On the tip of her tongue were her reasons—Hiroshi, fatigue, wanting to get Naomi back to her parents, the Kyoto humidity, the desire to be back in her own space—but what slipped out in a quick exhalation was, "I went to Uji yesterday."

There was a brief silence. "Good for you," her father said gravely. "Not an easy trip for you, I'm sure."

"No." She hadn't meant to confess quite so abruptly.

"Are you all right?"

"I think so. I saw Mrs. Ishii, at the temple."

"Did you! Oh, I'm so pleased. I hope you gave her my regards."

"I did." Then they both paused. "How's Mom?" Caitlin asked, and she could hear her father draw a deep breath.

"Well, worn out. This is tough for her. But I think once the service is over, and once Lee's off to school she'll be better. In many ways Ma Ruth's death was a comfort you know. She was deteriorating fast, and it pained your mother terribly. So she's grateful, considering what probably lay ahead, I mean. Of course she's saddened, too. I'll put her on in a second." Then her father dropped his voice. "But right now I'd say your mother's biggest concern is Lee. She's worried sick about her. We all are."

"Lee?"

"She's not well, Caity. She ate decently this evening, but in general she's just barely maintaining. She looks as skeletal as she did back that time when she was a sophomore in high school."

Caitlin leaned her head into the heel of her hand picturing her sister's bones protruding, recalling their conversation the night before, and Caitlin's strong, no doubt antagonizing, words. She grimaced; she'd probably made things worse. She'd had no idea Lee'd regressed. Why didn't anyone ever tell her things? "Do you think I should come home?" she asked. "I mean, she hates the fact that I'm here."

"I know, I know. But Caity, that's not your fault, and truthfully, I don't think any one of us in the family can do a whole lot for her right now. Write to her, even if she doesn't answer, and give her plenty of support, but she's got to pull out of this on her own, and with the help of professionals. Family pressures make it worse; just family attention even. But we'll be going up to Brookline after the service, and she'll be returning to campus the next week. She's agreed to begin seeing a counselor there at least. And a nutritionist. So we'll just have to see how that goes. All the relatives popping in are only making it more difficult."

"She's worse than Mom about Japan you know."

"Well, she has yet to come to terms with all that. We've each had to. She just may be the last. Anyway, I'll go get your mother. She's been anxious to talk with you."

Caitlin heard the thunk as he set the receiver down on the telephone table, then the clop of his footsteps—strange to hear shoes indoors—as he went to the porch to fetch her mother. Then she could hear her mother's heeled footsteps with his, and his voice, "She even went back to Uji." Caitlin nearly dropped the phone; the word had been taboo in their family for so long. She waited to hear a reply from her mother, some indication of shock or condemnation, but then, "Caity?" her mother was saying warmly into the phone.

"Hi, Mom. How are you holding up?"

"Well, I suppose I'm managing. Better now certainly; it's nice and peaceful here again."

"I'm so sorry," Caitlin said, her throat tightening, voice high. "I wish I were there. I should have planned on coming home this summer."

"Thank you." Her mother paused, collecting herself. She never liked to cry in front of people. She would just go silent, close her eyes, and stay that way, until the wave of grief or sadness or anger passed over her. Caitlin felt wretched, so many miles distant, picturing her mother holding her head high and stoic against her tears. She waited, and her mother's return to the conversation came sooner than she expected. "Don't be hard on yourself," her mother was saying. "We had no way of knowing. We were waiting to see what the doctors said in the next month about the cancer, and if the news had gotten any worse we'd have flown you home sometime early this fall. But the stroke came out of nowhere, Caity. No one had a chance to say good-bye. We wish you were here, too, but honestly, there was just no warning." Another silence followed, then her mother cleared her throat and said, "I understand you're at the Oides', Caity. I hope they're all well."

Now Caitlin closed her eyes. She fell forward slightly with the enormity of what she'd just heard, her mother finally making the connecting arc over continents and oceans to this neighborhood where parts of her, whole facets of her personality, had lived and then died with such intensity. "They are. They're all well," she replied softly.

Then she heard her mother suck in her breath. "Is everyone there? Home I mean?"

"No, not now. Harumi just went out shopping, and everyone else is out, too," Caitlin replied. She could hear her mother sigh, with what seemed like relief. "No one's here, except a friend of mine who spent the night. She's still sleeping."

"I just wouldn't know what to say to her," her mother said hoarsely.

"What?" Caitlin asked, perplexed, thinking of Naomi upstairs.

"Haru-san," her mother said, a name Caitlin hadn't heard issue from her lips in fifteen years. Her mother continued, "I wouldn't know what to say, Caity. I mean," she added, her voice now warbling, "I still have both my girls."

A sob hit Caitlin like a thunderclap. She convulsed with it and swallowed hard. When her voice returned, it was little more than a rasp. "It's okay, Mom," she said. "Oide and Harumi think so, Nobuko and Yusuke, too. Really, it's all right you still have us both."

▲ ▲ ▲

A short while later, Caitlin listened again to the footsteps in the hallway and waited for her father's voice. She stretched the phone cord to reach across the room for a tissue and hastily wiped her eyes and face.

"Are you okay?" her father asked when he came back on.

"Yeah," she said.

"Your mother's a wreck."

"I know. Do you need to go?"

"I don't think so, not yet. Carol's holding her. Lou's making some tea."

"Give her a hug for me." Caitlin couldn't remember ever saying this about her mother to her father. To Ma Ruth, maybe, but not her father.

"I will. Caity, listen." His voice had dropped again. "Your mother may join me for part of my sabbatical."

It was a moment before it dawned on Caitlin that he meant in Japan. He'd said it so matter-of-factly. "What?" she said.

"She may come over with me in October. She might not stay long; it depends on how Lee is doing. But your mother figures she may as well travel a bit before she starts working again. I think we'll try to get down to Kagoshima sometime in November."

"You're kidding."

"No, I'm not."

"She actually said she'd come?"

"Pretty much. She said she'd consider it. 'November's a good time of year there,' she said, mulling it over like it's a real possibility. Just this afternoon."

Caitlin was momentarily speechless. "Well then," she finally sputtered. "I'll have to figure out some place for you to stay. I mean, my apartment's tiny. I can't believe it. Don't forget your umbrellas."

"Why, is November wet?"

"No, the ash, Dad, the ash!" Caitlin could have done a cartwheel right there in the Oides' kitchen—her mother talking of Harumi, her mother mentioning Japan! She didn't dare assume she'd come—there was plenty of time to back out—but the fact that her mother was even thinking about setting foot on Japanese soil again, the fact that she was even acknowledging the country's existence was like a long-awaited welcome back from exile for Caitlin. And no doubt for her father, especially her father. They must be getting along then, Caitlin noted.

They talked more, somber as they discussed Ma Ruth's death, the cremation, the two pounds Lee had lost in the last week, and the house—no it wouldn't be sold, her father said, not for some time anyway. They were still deciding what to do, whether to rent it out, whether Jack would try to find a teaching position in Pittsburgh the following year, or whether Carol and Lou might move in.

"Maybe I'll move in," Caitlin said on impulse.

"What, is this your last year in Japan?"

And she pondered the question. What *were* her plans after this year? She was free to do what she wanted. Up until now, she'd been pushed and pulled by the tides of her past in Kyoto. And she'd never been able to think beyond Uji, never having imagined actually getting there. Or getting past a visit there. Her future had always led up to and stopped at Uji. So now what? Would she return to the States? Move up to Kyoto? Stay with Hiroshi?

She shook her head and laughed. "Who knows?"

Her father laughed, too, and told her they'd call her next week before or after the memorial service, so she could speak with everyone. Caitlin explained her travel plans, that by late Saturday she'd be back in Kagoshima, then said good-bye, hung up the phone, and sat back down at the kitchen table.

The house was completely still. And her body felt still. Calm. She hurried into the other room and stood before the *butsudan*.

The altar was no longer as festive. Many of the *chugen* presents that had been received and displayed had been put away, and the fruits, vegetables, noodles, and full set of miniature lacquerware had been replaced with more simple offerings—a bowl of rice, some water, a white peach. Caitlin knelt down and carefully lit some incense, fanned out the flame until the smoke ribboned upward, then rang the bell softly. In a rush, so that she could finish before Naomi woke, she whispered, *"Mie, they might come back—together, my mother, too."* She paused. *"If she does, if she comes to this house, don't be angered if she doesn't sit down here and greet you. But she thinks of you. I know she hasn't forgotten you. I know she misses you, too."* Caitlin bowed her head and squeezed her eyes shut, and while she was at it, silently, she bade Ma Ruth a formal and final farewell.

Then she returned to the kitchen. She sipped at her tepid coffee, glanced at the clock, and looked away. Who cared? She didn't have to go anywhere. There wasn't a thing she had to be doing, and Naomi was asleep. She pushed the mug away and placed her hands flat on the wood of the table. She took a long, satisfying breath; for once she felt at ease. She didn't have the urge to swim. Her fingers sat still without the nervous impulse to drum or tighten to a fist. She didn't even feel obliged to pursue that line of thought about her future plans. For it didn't matter. She was steeped in quiet, in that same calm and serenity she felt after one of Sakurajima's volcanic explosions rattled her windows, that stillness of relief, before wonder set in as to when the next eruption would send her off her chair and seeking cover. Only this time she felt the repose might truly last.

She laid her head on her hands to rest in the old grammar-school fashion; sleep beckoned, and she followed, drifting in its sweet current. But then muffled, as if from a great distance, she heard a door open, and soon after, the sound of feet padding down the stairs.

Twenty-three

CAITLIN WATCHED from across the table as Naomi mopped up egg yolk, dragging a corner of toast in broad sweeping strokes. First her fingers drew the strip of toast along with a twist of her wrist, but soon her elbow rose, her arm swung with the flowing motion, and her posture straightened. Head cocked, Naomi began marking the radical of a *kanji,* as if she were with brush and ink. Caitlin followed the stroke order with intrigue, wondering which component would be added to the radical, but suddenly self-conscious, Naomi glanced up and scribbled over it. She mopped the plate clean and began to nibble at the toast. Her posture returned to defeat, but Caitlin noted that her eyes were brighter at least.

Caitlin tried to recall herself at that age. She could remember jeans she wore, shoes, earrings, but she had no sense of how she'd appeared to someone several feet away, studying her the way she now studied Naomi. She could recall sensations, moods, and places: waiting for her event at swim meets; predawn winter practices when her hair froze afterward on the way to the car; the circles of cliques in the junior high corridors; the inside of her locker. She would linger by her locker, fingering her books, feigning academic decisions, all the while agonizing over which group to join before the bell rang for homeroom—until she discovered one day in study hall that she was actually adept at putting up a joking front to her classmates. How easy it was to dupe them into thinking she was having fun.

From then on, she went through a period of chronic lying, and the circles formed around her. The more she lied, the more friends she had. She pretended to have boyfriends at other Boston schools and made up weekend ventures and pranks. And they bought it.

After a while she forgot what was true and what wasn't, and she began to lose track of who she was and who she wasn't. And once she'd begun acting chipper, her mother eased up on her, stopped the embarrassing calls to classmates' mothers to arrange shopping outings or museum trips. As long as she feigned good cheer, she was left on her own in the afternoons. She could close herself in her room and brood, take off on her bike, ride to the arboretum and just sit, or even hop a bus or the T and head to Back Bay, Cambridge, or the Common and lose herself in the crowds.

But she could remember afternoons when she'd lie on her bed unable to raise a limb. When she couldn't stand even the sound of the clock radio. When she covered her face with a pillow and tried to imagine being smothered. And summers in Pittsburgh, those stultifying summers when Lee was still young enough to go off and play but Caitlin couldn't bear the thought, when she wasn't old enough for jobs other than occasional yard work or babysitting and when, except for swim workouts at a Y, day after day she'd sit on the front porch, not reading, not moving, just wondering why she was there. Sometimes Ma Ruth would discover her, haul her up by her shoulders, and force her outside to weed, prune, paint, or run to the market, just to get her in motion—"You have a life, girl. Live it!" she'd scold, and at the recollection of these words, their tone so clear, Caitlin started.

Naomi looked up from her plate. "What?"

Caitlin touched her hands to her ears. "It was as if I just heard my grandmother's voice."

"Then she must be thinking of you."

Caitlin shook her head. "No, I don't think so. I found out last night that she died. My parents had called yesterday."

Naomi stopped chewing. Then she bowed and muttered something in Japanese—she seemed at a loss for the words in English. Eventually she added, "Were you close to her?"

"Well, yes, she was my grandmother." This sounded more impatient than Caitlin had intended.

"Did she live in Boston?"

"No. Pittsburgh. That's where my parents are from. Where we spent summers."

"Oh." Naomi sat back, then frowned.

"What?" Caitlin asked.

Naomi bit off a corner of toast. "Nothing."

"Come on, tell me."

"Well, I just hope Yamashita Ojiichan doesn't die soon. I doubt he will, not for a while—he walks a lot. And he has a glass of *shochu* every night like that man who's a hundred and four. Did you hear about him?"

Caitlin nodded. "From Miyazaki."

"Think he'll make a hundred five?"

"I don't know."

Naomi seemed to be weighing the odds, then said, "My grandfather and I were talking about going to China next year. There are ferries now, you know. We'd go on a *shodo* and *sumi-e* trip, see places the masters painted and buy supplies."

"Really?" Caitlin said, shocked to hear Naomi volunteering anything about *shodo*.

But Caitlin's enthusiasm seemed to trigger a sudden nonchalance. "Yeah, well, we'll see." Naomi stood and set her plate in the sink.

Caitlin rose. "Naomi, don't take him for granted. If he's made the offer, and he's well enough to travel, do it. Do it while you have him."

"Yeah." Naomi placed both hands on the edge of the stainless drain board, as if to close the conversation.

Caitlin had her mouth open to say more, but held her tongue and sat down again. Naomi remained at the sink, motionless. After a time, with slow deliberation, she began to wash her dishes.

Caitlin glanced at the clock. "So. What time should we leave for the interview?"

Naomi turned to eye her. "We?"

"Yeah, we. I can go with you. Wait in a coffee shop or something while you have the interview and tour. I have letters to write anyway. If you want."

Naomi's eyes widened but conveyed neither pleasure nor displeasure. "The interview's at one o'clock. I should call my aunt though, she was going to take me." Then a deep shadow crossed her face. "I guess I should apologize to her."

Caitlin nodded. "Yes, and to your uncle. He was really panicked. Tell you what. You call them and make sure it's all right if I take you, and I'll go get myself ready." On her way out of the kitchen she gently shook Naomi by the shoulders. "But don't fret about yesterday, okay? Just apologize," she said, and went upstairs.

Caitlin was already roasting in her cotton pants. She changed into a light dress then went into the bathroom. She rubbed some ointment onto her gouged leg, then rifled through the medicine cabinet, and with some gauze and tape, concocted a bandage that covered most of the scrapes. They weren't especially deep, but against her pale skin they looked frightful. She hadn't thought up a story yet, but she wasn't sure she wanted to admit the truth about this one to anyone. She hoped the skin would be mostly healed by the time she saw Hiroshi.

She studied herself closely in the mirror. Her hair was straggly and unkempt. She couldn't remember the last time she'd had it cut, and she didn't know why she hadn't noticed until now, but it was thin at the ends and too long for her face. Which was pale, considering it was summer. She hunted for an elastic in her toilet kit to pull her hair back, thought of wearing her baseball cap, but decided it'd look ridiculous with her floral print dress. She tried to get a glimpse of her body in the mirror, but it was only a medicine cabinet mirror, and even craning her neck she could only see down to her waist. She felt like she'd lost weight, too much maybe, but it was impossible to tell with her loose dress and such a small mirror. Her sides did feel bony. She pictured Lee, those protuberant shoulder blades, ribs, and knobby elbows.

Caitlin put away the bedding in Nobuko's room, and when she heard Naomi hang up the phone, she threw her hairbrush into her day pack and made her way downstairs to join her. But she stopped still in the entrance to the front room when she discovered Naomi kneeling before the *butsudan*.

Caitlin followed her gaze as it traveled from the wooden altar up to the transom and the stark black and white photographs of Mie and her grandparents.

"That's her?" she asked, pointing at Mie.

"Yes."

"Her name was Mie?"

"Mieko."

Naomi nodded. Then she turned to Caitlin. "Will you go home for your grandmother's funeral?"

Caitlin shook her head.

Naomi stood. "You know, we could go to a temple and light incense for her. Your grandmother, I mean. And Mie, if you want. Let's pick out a temple to go to today. After the interview, okay?" Caitlin nodded and pursed her lips together, looking past Naomi. Naomi switched modes for her, turning away from the altar. "My aunt gave me directions to the school. We take the train, then a bus. But Caitlin, I don't have any clothes." Naomi was dressed in the outfit she'd worn the day before—shorts and a sailor-type shirt that made her look much younger than fourteen.

They went upstairs to Nobuko's room, rummaged through her closet, and finally found a simple short-sleeved dress that looked to be small enough. Caitlin wrote a note to Nobuko, thanking her, as Naomi washed up and changed.

On the train, Naomi grew introspective and quiet, and Caitlin thought she was mulling over her future again, the nagging citizen-ship decision that was still six years away. Caitlin let her ruminate alone and sat quietly beside her watching the houses and stations outside and the housewives, mothers with children, and elderly people that boarded the late morning train.

When they transferred to the bus Naomi began to fidget. Caitlin assumed she was growing more nervous about approaching the school; it was a momentous occasion, after all. But Naomi startled her by turning suddenly and whispering, "Caitlin, listen to me. Don't think I'm crazy. But did you ever think maybe I'm her reincarnation?"

Caitlin was taken aback. "What?"

"Maybe I am. Just think about it."

"My grandmother's reincarnation?" Caitlin laughed a loud exaggerated laugh.

"No, no, Mie's," Naomi said. "I wasn't born yet when she died. You see? Maybe I'm her reincarnation. Maybe it's fate, our meet-ing." Her face lit up as she said this.

"Naomi!" Caitlin wanted to howl at the idea. For it really was preposterous, that Mie would have grown into a moody adolescent, that even an atom of her old playmate lay inside this dark and fretful girl who made ash angels and wrote wills and practiced *shodo* in secret. Caitlin would never be able to throw her arm casually about Naomi. And she knew that if Mie were grown and sitting there on the bus with them, she'd have thrown back her head at the idea and laughed that rich, bubbling Mie-chan laugh.

But Naomi persisted: "I mean it, Caitlin," and though she said it with a playful gleam in her eye, Caitlin saw that she did, in a way, mean exactly what she was saying. And Caitlin could see by the look in her eye that this was an offering, that Naomi was holding out her hand saying that she, Naomi Yamashita Johnson, was offering to replace Mieko Oide.

"Oh, come off it," Caitlin said with a scowl; the notion of reincarnation was absurd, and the idea of anyone attempting to actually replace Mie irritated her, like her mother's perpetual attempts to assign Caitlin a best friend each time she advanced a grade in school. There *is* no replacement for the dead.

Naomi continued to gaze on her expectantly, and Caitlin folded her arms. "Stop it, Naomi, get serious. We're almost at the school." The words had come out with venom, and Naomi turned away in a sulk.

They sat quietly for a bit. Caitlin wondered how it was that this girl had become part of her life. The more Caitlin thrashed to be free of her the more entangled in Naomi's world she seemed to become. Just another week, she thought, till they were back in Kagoshima and she could deposit Naomi on her parents' doorstep. She let out a sharp sigh of punctuation, and Naomi, still looking out the window said, "I didn't mean anything by it. It was just a thought. Don't be so sore."

Caitlin nodded. She could see that Naomi was blinking back tears, and now Caitlin began to feel remorse for having once again reacted so emotionally to a fourteen year old's fantasies. This was no time for Naomi to be down. Caitlin forced a smile, and patted Naomi's thigh. "It's okay," she said. "I'm sorry."

They rode in silence for a while, then nearly missed their stop. "This is it!" Naomi shouted. She jumped up and hollered for the driver to reopen the doors. When they'd stepped off the bus, oriented themselves, and started walking in the direction of the school, Caitlin apologized again, adding, "I think I'm still tired from yesterday."

Naomi nodded. They walked through the school's imposing brick and cast iron gate, and Caitlin pointed out different features of the school, trying to cheer Naomi; if she remained sullen, Caitlin knew there was no telling what she'd say in the interview. They had about fifteen minutes to spare, so they strolled about the small campus: down corridors between classrooms bedecked with bright posters, maps, and charts and where some teachers were busy at their desks or up on chairs creating new displays—such a vibrant contrast to the barren classrooms in the Japanese schools Caitlin taught at; to the library where Caitlin ogled row upon row of literature in English, racks of magazines, and not just one but several English language newspapers; and out to the dusty heat of the athletic field and track. A few teams were practicing in preseason workouts—track, soccer, and tennis—and for a while Caitlin and Naomi stood at a chain-link fence, watching and listening. English and some bits of Japanese and occasionally other languages were shouted between players, and only some of the students there looked at all Asian in appearance. "It really is a mix," Naomi noted quietly, as though she'd always doubted the reality of an international school or, more particularly, the existence of other children like herself who spanned two or more cultures.

They retreated to the shady footpaths and finally turned back toward the classrooms and administrative offices. Once they'd found the correct building and finally the room for Naomi's interview, Caitlin told Naomi she'd meet her at the school library in two hours. That would give Naomi time to explore the campus on her own and to talk to some of the students after the interview and tour. Naomi nodded and straightened. But before pushing open the admissions office door, she stalled there in the hallway and eyed Caitlin.

"What?" Caitlin asked.

Naomi shifted her weight on her feet. "You don't think there's any chance of it?"

"Of what?"

"That I'm Mie's reincarnation."

Caitlin rolled her eyes. "Naomi!" she said, but this time she was careful to appear amused. Naomi stood before her, waiting, eyes pleading, chin just perceptibly trembling.

Caitlin weighed her options, contemplating various possible answers. For some strange reason, Naomi's future seemed to lie in her hands, in the very answer she gave. "I don't know," she finally said. "I suppose you do have her forehead. And Mie could draw pretty well."

Naomi grinned. And pulled her shoulders erect. Then she turned the knob and disappeared behind the pebbled glass of the admissions door.

REPOSE

Twenty-four

THE LATE AUGUST sun had smoothed the waters, and as the ferry eased toward Shibushi Bay the air was muffled and still except for the low growl of the engines and the cries of gulls trailing the stern. Boats that passed near the mouth of the bay seemed to do so silently, and everything seemed to list and creep in slow motion. A mountain grew by degrees from a blister to a peak, and small rises of hills and buildings wavered and swayed in the heat.

Caitlin and Naomi stood on deck squinting at the approaching city, so small and contained compared to Kyoto and Osaka. Naomi gazed dreamily along the shore and down into the spray by the hull. She'd spotted several dolphins off the bow somewhere between Shikoku and Kyushu, and she continued to search for them even as the boat slid closer to port, past the crest of Birojima. Caitlin leaned on the rails, now and then tilting her face toward the blazing sun attempting to put some color back into her cheeks.

Only the water now separated her from Hiroshi. She had the impulse to dive overboard and race the laboring ferry, four frustrating hours delayed due to a typhoon that had hit land in Wakayama the morning of their departure. They'd been two hours late leaving Osaka, loaded but docked as the storm raged away from them, pushing north toward the Japan Sea. Caitlin and Naomi had swallowed motion sickness pills before they even boarded, and no one bothered to purchase crepe paper rolls to toss. The Kojimas bade them a hasty farewell then turned into the dark pelting rain to begin their cautious drive back to Kyoto. On board, Caitlin and Naomi had passed time bathing, reading, and writing postcards they'd neglected to write in Kyoto. When finally the ferry heaved off the piers, it strained and lumbered against driving wind and swells for hours into the night. In the morning Caitlin was surprised to awaken to blue sky and a smooth ride but dismayed to hear in the announcements how much they'd been delayed. She knew Hiroshi would have checked with the ferry line for her arrival time before driving to Shibushi—it was typhoon season after all—but the wait was agonizing. At least now, approaching Shibushi, the seas were calm and nothing more stood in their way.

She'd spoken with Hiroshi twice more since the day after visiting Uji and hearing of Ma Ruth's death, and with each conversation her longing for him had grown more acute and physical, with adrenaline rushes in her jaw and that same coursing in her calves she felt when nearing a precipice. Yet when she'd lain aching for him in Nobuko's spare futon at night, her body curled, arms reaching for him in the thick night air, she'd worried that distance might be distorting, that she wanted him more simply because of his absence. She worried, too, that when she finally saw him he might look different, less appealing, less hers—and that first instance of vague distaste had always indicated the end of a relationship for Caitlin. She didn't want this to happen yet with Hiroshi. She wanted to get things out in the open, tell him what the Kyoto trip had really been about, and see where that led them. But she tugged self-consciously at her braid of unkempt hair. She hoped that Hiroshi had missed her as much as she thought she'd missed him, that his longing was fervent enough for him to ignore her gaunt appearance.

When the ferry finally sidled up to the dock, grinding gears and groaning as it slowed and turned against the current, Caitlin and Naomi went below to collect their luggage and join the line of passengers waiting to disembark. Naomi set her suitcase on the floor and sat down on top of it, but Caitlin stood with her heavy pack on her back, refusing even to set down the shopping bag of parting gifts from the Oides she was so anxious to bolt the moment the line moved. The public address system played a muzak version of "Auld Lange Syne" over and over, and Caitlin grew hot and sweaty; her shoulders were aching when the door was finally opened and people began to nudge forward. Naomi struggled to keep up as Caitlin hurried down the gangplank and stairs, searching the faces of the waiting crowd below for Hiroshi. By the time she spotted him, he was already striding toward them across the parking lot, grinning.

She stepped onto the pavement and smiled back. Her calves twitched. He flipped his bangs just slightly and gave her a little nod that she returned. He politely greeted Naomi then turned back to Caitlin. His eyes seemed to gather her in close to him, but he barely made a move toward her. Damn the Japanese reserve, she thought, and she leaned forward to envelop him in a bear hug. But the weight of her backpack threw her against him with unexpected force, and they both tumbled down onto the pavement.

"Oshidashi!" Hiroshi exclaimed from the ground in the voice of a sumo sportscaster, naming the style of push. *"Ober wins the match!"* He brushed himself off, laughing, and helped her to her feet. Naomi stood by and clapped, onlookers smiled, Hiroshi bowed to Caitlin as if she were a high-ranking wrestler, and Caitlin was by then too embarrassed to carry out the hug. Hiroshi took Naomi's bag, and they followed him to his car.

Naomi climbed into the backseat, and Caitlin settled herself up front beside Hiroshi who already had the key in the ignition. Caitlin was reluctant to start just yet. She had the urge to give him a hard and furious embrace, upright this time, or to sit still for a moment, just drinking in each other's presence, but as soon as they'd sat down, he was looking over his shoulder backing the car out, shifting gears, and negotiating the lot. And he was chatting with Naomi in rapid Japanese. Caitlin felt an annoying shot of jealousy, the pang of an outsider, wishing Naomi would vanish if only for a moment. She wanted him to herself. She was bursting with all she had to say.

As they turned onto the main road she told herself to relax. They'd have plenty of time alone together. There was no rush to anything anymore. Naomi would only be with them for another couple hours. After shifting into high gear, Hiroshi reached over for her hand, and she gave his a squeeze, although she could feel Naomi's eyes on them like lasers. She tried to pretend they were alone as she held his fingers and felt his sweat mingle with hers for the first time in two weeks, but his touch felt remote and public. She drew back her hand.

He sensed her irritation and smiled at her. *"Everyone's waiting for you. Misawa, Mina, Uma-chan,"* he said, and Caitlin looked askance, picturing a welcome brigade at her apartment—but she understood he hadn't meant literally waiting, rather they were looking forward to seeing her again. This was his public way of telling her he'd missed her. Caitlin nodded and returned his smile. *"Mind if we go to Tsuketomi tonight?"* he added.

She tried to hide her disappointment. She'd been looking forward to an evening alone with him and would have preferred seeing the whole gang another night. She had so much to say if she was going to start telling the truth, and she was discouraged that he hadn't read her mind accurately. But then again, she thought, he probably had; he simply knew what was appropriate and what wasn't. For, as she'd been reminded over and over since that evening in late February when the crowd she'd gone to a pub with began arm wrestling and Hiroshi, whom Caitlin beat, had offered her windsurfing lessons, as she'd learned through their subsequent meetings with the group on the beach and their attempts at private evenings out and hurried stints at love hotels, her relationship was not only with Hiroshi. Tonight was Saturday night, and group protocol called for Caitlin and Hiroshi to appear at the restaurant for a welcome-back party.

"No, not at all," she told him, reminding herself once again that they would have ample time to themselves, later. As she resigned herself to the plan, she realized she wasn't all that miffed. She could already taste Mina's father's flounder, his ground chicken and scallions broiled in huge clam shells, and the *shochu* sours with the enormous lemon wedges perched on the rims of the glasses; she'd enjoy seeing everyone again, being snug in that cocoon of friendship—she felt as though she'd been away for months.

Hiroshi shifted the conversation to include Naomi. He asked all about Kyoto, the temples, the department stores, Daimonji, the new subway, and Caitlin felt herself and Naomi both sifting through emotionally charged experiences to recall a few simple events and physical places for him.

They asked for Kagoshima news and Hiroshi explained that the Sakurajima rim road was closed due to explosions and flying lapilli, so they would take the inland route and circle the bay, about a two-hour drive. They were all quiet for a while and when Naomi had fallen asleep in the back, Caitlin took the opportunity to rivet her eyes on Hiroshi's profile. She watched him flick his long bangs back out of his eyes, watched his chest lift and fall, watched him blink at the road, slide his hands along the steering wheel, and finally turn to her. She leaned over and kissed him on the cheek and he turned to meet her mouth for a moment.

"Everything okay?" he asked quietly.

She nodded. *"When we get back, we'll talk,"* she said. In answer, he leaned perilously toward her for another kiss. Caitlin tried to keep her eyes on the road for him as they swerved.

After that they hardly spoke—they seemed tacitly agreed to and comforted by the silence. Caitlin gazed out the window at farm plots, rice fields, and sharp hills, and Hiroshi put his hand on her knee. She soon nodded off. Some time later she stirred almost with instinct as the road began approaching Kagoshima Bay.

Caitlin pointed to the signs and whispered, *"Can we take the bay route instead of the highway?"* Hiroshi nodded—it was cheaper anyway. Caitlin was pleased; the afternoon was clear, the water would be sparkling under the low sun, and despite their long ferry trip they weren't in any particular rush. They followed the local road by the three jutting islands whose names she'd forgotten save for the nickname Warship Island. And although Caitlin was enjoying the private time with Hiroshi, she woke Naomi for their first full view of Sakurajima and its ash plume smoking upward.

"Hey, we're back," she said giving Naomi's leg a little shake. "Look." Naomi sat up and slid over to the window. She smiled sleepily.

"They say it will be the highest monthly ashfall since the observations started in '69," Hiroshi said.

"Really? Any new damage?" Caitlin asked.

"Some solar hot water heaters hit by stones, power outages one day from ash and rain, train service disrupted. Explosions, volcanic lightning, nothing unusual." He grinned at them.

Caitlin was on the bay side of the car, and she gazed on the roiling cloud, towering today, as at an old friend. From this distance she couldn't possibly hate those billions of particles of ash—earth spewed upward to float over the lava slopes, the bay, and her city. Instead she was awed by the energy, and she opened her window to lean her head out closer to the upturned mouth across the water, the earth's vent. She was glad to be back in Kagoshima. And calm or active, repose or not, Sakurajima was part of life in Kagoshima. There was no point in trying to will it into silence, in trying to still the menace or pretend it wasn't there. To cope, she could journey back to Kyoto, visit her father in Tokyo during his sabbatical trip, borrow Carl's car, escape to *onsen,* sweep and scour, but she would accept the challenges and rewards of this dusty life in the volcanic zone—for another year at least. As Naomi had said, volcanoes deserve respect; their city was indeed honored to be visited by these particles ejected from the deep, to be daily witness to the ever shifting earth, and to know how close the fire really is.

Farther south, with her fingers tapping the roof of the car, Caitlin felt those first stinging ticks on her skin, and she rolled up the window. Her resolve began to crack, but she patched it by thinking of travel. She recalled Hiroshi's fingers wandering over her atlas, over those green blobs of beckoning islands south of Kyushu, and she looked hard at him and tried to picture what it would be like to spend three, four, five days in a row with him, morning to night. He fidgeted under her steady regard and asked, *"What?"* but she shook her head and said, *"Nothing."* They could plan later.

She fondly noted the tall palms spaced along the shoreline and the steep slopes of Ryu-ga-mizu—Dragon's Water. She released her shoulder strap and leaned forward against the dashboard to glimpse the high falls, white ropes of water twisting downward, but today, a clear day in August, she felt no threat, no sensation that the whole slope might ease down over her. The vegetation was different here, so dense and tangled, and she was pleased to be back in the sub-tropics, ash and all.

At Naomi's house, Carl and Akiko rushed out to greet them before Hiroshi had even turned off the ignition. They glanced expectantly from Caitlin to Naomi and back to Caitlin, but the girls' faces registered little other than fatigue. Carl hefted Naomi's bag from the trunk and motioned for everyone to follow him into the house, so Caitlin took Hiroshi's hand and reluctantly followed Carl and Akiko up the walkway to the door. They were asking about the trip, and Caitlin filled them in on the delays, the rough seas followed by the placid morning on the ferry. Everyone expressed relief that they'd traveled by boat, considering the plane crash, and Caitlin was reminded once more of that girl, the footage she'd seen over and over in Kyoto, of her being lifted into the air on a swinging cable, high above the plane wreckage, rising to her new guilt-soaked life as a survivor. They'd recovered wills passengers had written hurriedly aboard the doomed plane, and television news lately had focused on little other than recovery efforts, the four survivors, the cause of the crash. As she settled onto a cushion in the living room, Caitlin shook her head to clear those grim thoughts, and with a struggle brought her mind back to Naomi's house to make small talk with Carl and Akiko. She felt uncomfortable though, devious—they'd never heard a word about Naomi's disappearance. Caitlin could feel Carl trying to read her face as though a letter grade for Naomi's behavior might be posted somewhere on her forehead, and she tried to appear positive and upbeat.

"Well, your safe return calls for a celebration. Champagne," Carl boomed, and when Caitlin tried politely to decline, he added with an understanding glance toward Hiroshi, "Just a quick toast," and she and Hiroshi assented.

Naomi seemed delighted to be back, basking in her old familiar space, although Caitlin caught her one moment surveying the books, pottery samples, newspaper clippings, jars of paint brushes, dirty coffee cups, scattered cushions—all the incredible clutter— with a mixture of consternation and dismay. Caitlin, too, noted the stark contrast; except for the kitchen, which had been bursting to overflow, the rooms at the Kojima house had been tidy and spare, and everything seemed to have had its designated place.

Carl stood Naomi in the living room with the bottle of sparkling wine and pointed to a pencil holder on a bookshelf in the next room. "A thousand yen if you knock it down." Naomi took aim as she urged the cork out of the bottle with her thumb. For a long while nothing happened, then the cork shot across the room, hitting a wall calendar that immediately dropped out of sight behind the book case. "No dice," Carl said as Akiko mopped up the foam dripping from the bottle.

They all clustered around the low table in the small living room with glasses in hand, and Carl poured around. "Welcome back," he toasted, and everyone drank. Then he set down his glass and jumped up. "I have something for you vagabonds." He opened the sliding door to the back garden, disappeared onto the veranda, then returned with a child's small sand bucket. "I didn't want you to feel you'd missed anything." Naomi peered inside, then Caitlin, and they both groaned at the sight of the fine ash. "5.3 centimeters," he announced to everyone proudly. "Not bad, eh?" He laughed and leaned back against the sofa and looked at Caitlin and Naomi. They smiled at each other under his penetrating gaze. He seemed ill at ease, as if he were awaiting an actual prognosis of his daughter, and he switched into more formal Japanese. *"So, you survived the motion of the boat. What was the weather during the rest of your visit? And Dai-monji—you had a nice evening for that?"*

Though eager to be off alone with Hiroshi, Caitlin obliged with more details, trying to get Carl and Akiko to relax; they were acting as if their daughter were a guest. She and Naomi described the party the Kojimas and Oides had thrown the night before their departure, in a private room of a restaurant, where they'd sung pop songs and karaoke ballads for nearly two hours, solo and in twos and threes, Mayumi, Naomi's older cousin, outperforming them all. And Caitlin told them about the tiny coffee shop they'd crammed into afterward for cake, and finally about the traffic jam in the driving rain en route to the delayed ferry. Naomi went on to describe the arcing flight of the dolphins at the bow of the ferry, and the bath in which they'd bathed twice, then she abruptly stopped with a glance toward Caitlin. "Dad, let these guys go," she said. "They're both tired." Caitlin tried not to look too grateful.

"You're right, you're right. Off with you," he said, and he practically shooed them out of the house.

Caitlin embraced Naomi on the walkway and bowed to Akiko. Carl walked Caitlin and Hiroshi to the car. He thanked Caitlin for being an escort, and she could only smile with decorum at his understatement. "Everything really went okay?" he asked in a low voice as they climbed in.

"Yes," she said.

"She liked the school?"

"I'd say so," Caitlin said, as she climbed into Hiroshi's car. "There's a darkroom, printmaking facilities, and three potter's wheels, which, incidentally, she said she couldn't wait to start using." Carl raised his eyebrows in disbelief. "I'm sure she'll tell you. She was really impressed. And she's been invited to come back for another visit when school's in session so she can meet the art teachers and sit in on classes."

Carl clasped his hands and bowed in gratitude. "Fabulous. Well, thank you again. You're the best, Caitlin. And come over soon. We'd like to hear more. Maybe we'll have an end-of-summer party," he added, and Caitlin and Hiroshi smiled, bowed from their seats, and said good-bye.

They drove in silence for a few minutes, then Caitlin let out a tremendous sigh. Hiroshi looked sideways at her and laughed. "Free at last, right?" he said in English, but with some confusion of the l's and r's that gave Caitlin pause.

"Sort of," she said, then continued in Japanese: *"I made a kind of agreement with her."*

"Agreement?"

"That day I took her on her interview. When we left the school we went to a temple to light incense for my grandmother, and she began talking about her grandfather and shodo. Afterward we went to an okonomiyaki *restaurant, and while we were cooking our pancakes on the grill Naomi came up with this agreement. I couldn't really refuse; I mean, she was so positive."*

"What sort of agreement?" Hiroshi said impatiently.

"Well, I study kanji. *And in return, she studies* shodo *with her grandfather and works on watercolors when she has time. And we meet now and then to check each other's progress."*

"Less windsurfing for you, I guess."

"Not really." She put her hand on his knee and gave a squeeze. *"And who knows, Naomi's not exactly . . ."* She tried to come up with the word for stable, but gave up. *"You know, anything can happen,"* she said.

"Right," was Hiroshi's reply, and Caitlin was amused to detect a hint of jealousy in his voice.

Hiroshi parked in the space outside her apartment and lugged her backpack up to her door. Her mailbox wasn't exactly bursting, but there was a good sheaf of letters and bills that she pulled out and placed on the kitchen table once they'd stepped inside. He turned on some lights, set her pack down by the futon, started the air conditioner, then joined her in the kitchen. They left the rain shutters closed.

He found a bottle of beer in the refrigerator and poured two glasses. They clinked and gulped, wordlessly.

Then Caitlin set down her glass and stood still, just staring about at her space, her "home," and she could feel Hiroshi follow her eyes over the double gas burner, the stainless steel sink and drain board, the squat refrigerator, the tape player in the other room, the rolled up futon, the plastic vacuum and uncoiled hose, the drawn curtains, the nails with her swimsuits, her sake jugs, the map and photos on the wall. She touched her fingers to the top of the refrigerator and felt the light film of ash. For once she resisted the urge to wet a towel and wipe down all the surfaces.

She picked up the mail from the table and thumbed through—a letter from her mother, two from her father, one from a cousin, a postcard from her classmate Mami in Kyoto that Caitlin began to read, but Hiroshi reached his hands around her from behind and whispered so close in her ear—*"Can't you read that later? We're supposed to be at Tsuketomi in about an hour,"*—that she dropped it on the table and turned to face him.

Her heart was racing. He was holding her shoulders and looking straight into her eyes. There was no hiding; he would have to know about Mie, about the hand she'd never offered, about Mrs. Ishii, and about her mother's years of denial and Lee's illness, about everything prior to her arrival in Kagoshima . . . before they went a step further in this relationship, before they drank one more sip of beer from the same bottle, sat down to one more meal at the same table, or lay down on the same futon. She started to tell him how much she was finally willing to share, but he pressed his mouth over hers and the words were lost in his hard kiss.

Hiroshi reached over the vestibule and turned the lock in the door. Then, as he pulled her close in the middle of the kitchen, as she sank against his chest—nearly sank through him, she saw Ma Ruth's house on its sloping street, saw herself and Hiroshi standing in the kitchen there, holding each other by Ma Ruth's porcelain sink, calling to each other through the high-ceilinged rooms, dropping their clothes down the laundry chute she and Lee used to play in, and sitting on the porch long after dark on warm summer evenings. They could go there, next year. They could rent the house. Open a restaurant somewhere where Hiroshi could be chef.

She almost blurted this out loud, but then when she tried to picture Hiroshi in Pittsburgh, away from the family business, surrounded by English speakers and with no beaches for hundreds of miles, she realized she could create no image of him outside of Japan. Could their relationship survive anywhere but Kagoshima? And could it even survive here? For what would happen to them when her past had pulled up alongside their present and sat there idling in full view?

She leaned back to have a better look at him, brush his bangs out of his face, and stare into his dark pupils, and she had the sudden sensation that Sakurajima was about to thunder with one of its explosions. She tensed, waiting for the clap and the rattle of windows, but then he was kissing her again, his tongue running over her teeth that needed brushing, his hand roving through her hair, and she reminded herself that there was no point in bracing for explosions, that she had to accept the volcano's licit might. As she skimmed her fingertips down Hiroshi's vertebrae, she tried to regain that feeling of calm she'd had that morning in Kyoto after talking with her father. She tried not to think about the future but to firm herself in the now. And then—by the thick malt taste of his tongue, by the shifting peak of his shoulder blade under her hand, and by the press of his fingertips in the small of her back—she knew that she would tell him everything, that she would tell him all.

Now he was tugging at her shorts, creeping them down below her knees, and she pulled his T-shirt up over his head as he dropped closer to the floor. His hands wandered down her legs and he was kissing her thighs. Then he stiffened, and Caitlin shivered; his fingers had stopped on the flaking scabs of her left leg, just beginning to scar.

She cringed as he examined her calf closely then straightened. *"What happened?"* he asked.

She faltered, not knowing what to say. She could stop and make him listen to the truth now, but she was hesitant, now that the moment was here, and she could see he was impatient for her, his desire paining him. So she shrugged, led him to the futon, and turned the light down low; later she would tell him everything, she vowed as she batted ash from the sheets she pulled from the closet.

This melding of past with present and moving forward would be harder than she'd thought, and she began to wonder if there really were a repose, or if calm were merely an illusion because the magma was always there, always boiling, always seeking a vein of release. How could she begin to tell him everything from back then, she wondered, as his tongue passed over her molars, her lips, her neck, her breasts, her now. As she pulled him into her, raised her pelvis to him, she wondered, once again, if this would be their last time.

But moments later when they both lay limp and close, sated and sedate, Caitlin drew a terry coverlet over them in the now-cooled room, and she turned Hiroshi to face her. *"I need you to listen. I need to tell you some things,"* she whispered. And he nodded knowingly, as if he'd been expecting these very words. *"Even if it makes us late,"* she said. And again he nodded, as if he'd known all along that they'd make some excuse for arriving tardy to her welcome-back gathering at Tsuketomi.

So Caitlin took a deep and reaching breath, turned onto her back, and alternately speaking up to the ceiling and directly to Hiroshi, she brought forth her past, starting with the news that her family would move to Japan, with their nervous arrival in Kyoto, with the unpacking of the few treasured belongings she'd been allowed to bring to their tiny home in Iwakura, and with her shy and fateful introduction to the girls next door, Mieko and Nobuko Oide.

And Hiroshi lay there listening while Caitlin stopped and started, teared and trembled and sometimes choked, but plodded on with her past, inching it forward, bringing it ever closer to their warm and pulsing bodies under the coverlet, nudging it into full view, advancing it into their present. And Hiroshi stayed beside her quietly—waiting, nodding, absorbing it all, urging her on through Mie's slipping into the water, through Caitlin's dumbly standing on the bank then running for her father, and through her inability to cry, to speak, to utter a sound even when Haru, sobbing, seeing her for the first time after the accident, gathered her into her arms— Caitlin wooden in her embrace, unable to return the hug, unable to lift her arms even or put out a hand, unable to accept, or unwilling to comprehend, the paradoxical deep pain and simultaneous offer of consolation from Mie's mother.

Hiroshi listened intently, rising only once to place a box of tissues on the tatami by their pillows. He insisted she go on even when his stomach rumbled loudly, nudged her gently to continue even when the rectangle of pebbled glass that was the kitchen window turned from orange to rose to blue-black, even when the phone rang and neither of them made a move to answer it though Caitlin knew it might be her father and relatives up early, getting ready for the memorial service in Pittsburgh. She told him the events. And she told him the emotions.

She told him that during that first year back in the States, back in Pittsburgh, in those long empty months when the taste of food didn't matter, when toys didn't interest her, when she hated sleeping, and even more hated waking, that in the interminable period before she'd joined the swim team just after her ninth birthday, she'd read the labels on all the prescription medicines, household cleansers, fertilizers, and pesticides at Ma Ruth's and pondered daily which one or what combination would kill her the fastest. And she told Hiroshi that she, at nine years, had even composed a farewell note to her family and the Oides, but that the fear of physical pain and the fear of botching it, not the fear of dying, had kept her from ever attempting suicide that first year, that worst year, back in the States. She told him that swimming had revived her and kept her alive, had made her stop greedily handling the pills Ma Ruth kept in a drawer in her bedside table, made her stop sneaking into Ma Ruth's room after school to touch the little white-and-cream orbs to her tongue, to steal a few at a time and hoard them in a little film canister she kept hidden in the hollow at the base of a lamp on her own bedside table. She told him that every swim meet was a chance to save Mie, and that the tears shed with each new record she set had had nothing to do with the thrill of victory.

And she told him that she'd shunned and refused to cooperate with the psychiatrists and therapists and the endless parade of counselors her father had steered her toward not because she agreed with her mother that they should forget about Uji, but because she'd believed that these people would somehow try to make her feel better about what had happened to Mie, exonerate her, meliorate the pain, somehow help her to live with Mie's death, and she'd always believed fervently that she should never feel better, never accept the finiteness of what had happened, never truly live, only suffer. And she told him that she'd hated her father for his talk of Uji and hated her mother for her silence, that she'd hated her grandmother's support of that silence, and that she'd resented her sister for never letting her get close and that she'd often wished as a child that it had been Lee instead of Mie who had drowned. And she told him that she'd often fantasized that if she ever went back to Uji, she'd throw herself into the river, join Mie, but that when she really did go back, felt the spray of that fast water in her nostrils again, she'd stood ready but instead of jumping, managed only to land on her bottom and tear at the leg where she'd last felt Mie's touch.

And then her breath caught, and she paused and dropped her voice as she told him that she'd never allowed a relationship to progress this far. She'd never allowed herself to share this much because she'd never felt she had the basic right to love and to be loved, never had the right to reach womanhood—with Mie left behind, the hand that had grazed her never to grow, the whole self of Mie reduced to ash sitting forever beneath a gray, cut and polished stone.

Caitlin lay back on the pillow, and the tears dribbled down the sides of her face and collected in her ears. There wasn't a single recollection remaining that she hadn't exposed. There wasn't a single gap that she hadn't filled, nor a sole white lie left to erase.

When Hiroshi dabbed at her eyes, cheeks, and ears with a tissue, she turned to look at the clock face; they'd been lying there for nearly two hours. She closed her eyes in exhaustion for several minutes, then hoisted herself up onto one elbow and put a hand gingerly to Hiroshi's cheek. His eyes were moist, and she began to tear again herself. *That is my whole past,* she said. *That is me, the me here in Japan and the me who was in the States. All of me.* He nodded. She rubbed her thumb over the soft beneath his cheekbone, then she gathered in her breath and in a whisper barely audible, asked of him, *Well, what do you think? Do you suppose I have the right to love now?*

He studied her face, and she waited tensely, wondering whether he would answer straight away or if he might just rise to dress himself or step briskly into the shower. She would reach for him if he got up to go, that much she knew. But he remained there beside her, breathing evenly if shallowly, staring into her eyes and her now bared self.

Then he turned, and she swallowed a sob as he threw back the coverlet, moved down to the base of the futon, and kneeling, tucked his fingers under her left calf. Ever so slightly, he raised her left leg toward him. And cradling this leg in his hands, he bent low. Then she watched only half believing as, with eyes closed and without a sound, he pressed his lips softly to the side of her calf where Mie's fingers had brushed, and he kissed her scabs, her wounds, her finally healing scars.